EVERYTHING FOR LOVE

Cranberry Hill Books 1–3

NALA HENKEL-AISLINN

AUTHOR'S NOTE

Dear Reader,

Thank for your choosing to read the full Cranberry Hill Clean Series!

These are clean romances. Sexual intimacy takes place, but it is not described.

I hope you enjoy the stories!

Nala

FREE NOVELLA... AND MORE!

The first two books in this box set feature the stories of Katy and Summer. Their enemies to lovers stories will make you laugh, smile, and feel a little misty.

But their stories started back in college...

"Operation Vengeance"
Two roommates join forces when their boyfriends turns out to be the same guy...
How will they get even?
Click and download for free!

Do you like contests, prizes and **FREE READING**? Click to join my Reading Group for all the fun.

COPYRIGHT

All the characters in these books are fictitious, and any resemblance to actual persons living or dead is purely coincidental.

Copyright © 2020 by Nala Henkel-Aislinn

All rights reserved.

No part of this book may be reproduced, or stored in a retrieval system, or transmitted in any form or by any means, electronic, mechanical, photocopying, recording, or otherwise, without express written permission of the publisher.

Published by Nala Henkel-Aislinn

Edited by Hot Tree Editing

A CRANBERRY HILL *Clean* ROMANCE

Blueprint for Love

NALA HENKEL-AISLINN

DEDICATION

To my husband, partner, love of my life, and Alpha Reader (naturally), Eric.

To Taylor, Dara, Keegan, Piper, Al, and Dave.

To my wonderful friend and Alpha Readers, Eric, Regina and Wendy.

1

Katy's hands slid off the steering wheel of Goose, her brave road-weary Subaru. The rain had slacked off to a steady mist that hit her windshield in waves.

Goose's wipers had started chug-chugging somewhere in Montana but continued to sweep the water clear like a hero. She'd expected the Pacific Northwest to be frigid in November, but it had been mild. Wet and mild. The rain added a level of miserable she hadn't prepared for when she left Chicago.

She should call it quits and go back to the motel. The run-down Cozy Motor Inn had been a welcome sight after ten hours of driving. But after checking in and parking in front of her unit, an itch had come over her. Instead of doubts and questions about this cross-country trek, she'd been excited.

My house. I own a freaking house!

But here she sat, a block away from the freaking house in question, and the familiar doubts flooded back.

How am I going to turn an abandoned house into an inn? Was the question that popped up most often. But now came the one she dreaded. The question that only crawled out when it was dark. *Is this the last joke of my mother's bitter sister?*

She looked at her phone. The red marker of her inheritance was eight minutes away from the wavering dot that marked Goose's location. The road ahead of her was black. Since the last streetlight wasn't even a faint glow in her rearview mirror, she wouldn't be able to see much when she got there. And if she could get a glimpse of the seven-year abandoned house in Goose's headlights, what if it was an outright tear down?

The darkness and pulsing waves of rain made her eyes droop even more.

She rolled down the window to let a spray of misty rain dampen her face. She rolled the window back up, wiping the water away with her coat cuff.

"What's eight more minutes of driving?" She asked, patting Goose's dashboard. "It's not like I have to get out. Or even stop."

She turned on her high beams, which only gave her a few extra feet of visibility. The rain picked up its pace and Goose's wipers groaned to keep up.

"Okay, buddy. Just don't break down so I have to sleep on the side of the road and get murdered by the local serial killer."

She shifted Goose into drive and pulled through the intersection.

As her dot on the map drew closer to the red marker, she noticed the faintest light ahead. She frowned.

The longer she drove on the narrow, curving road, the larger the light loomed.

"Huh," she said, pulling off to the side of the road. The lawyer's documents and her map app said hers was the only house for a couple miles.

A tilted post further up caught her eye, and she chanced flicking on her high beams. Two-five-two-five. *Definitely my house.*

She killed her headlights, and even in the warmth of her car, goosebumps broke out.

Bright light poured in a narrow beam from the expanse of windows of the house, bouncing off a tilted porch, and creating eery silhouettes of a spindly hedge.

"What the hell," she muttered. Summer had bullied her into accepting this inheritance. But seeing that light flipped a switch in her brain. This was hers. And someone was in it. The tiredness from moments ago drained away, replaced by a flood of anger.

She climbed out of Goose, careful to close the door quietly. She crouched as she slipped past the driveway to the yard.

Her clothes were dark, but her puffy coat was shiny in the light. She pulled up her hood and crouched beside the bushes, her feet finding their way through the uneven ground until a clump of something caught her toe.

"Oof," she said, falling onto her hands and knees with a solid thud. And then "Crap!" as her hand sank into a cold mush of grassy goo. She crouched tighter against the dead hedge that bordered the yard, worried that her voice alerted the squatter who at any moment could look out the large front windows and see her.

She wiped her hand the best she could on the straw-like grass then kept crawling, keeping tight to the shadows of the bushes until she got to the edge of the porch.

He must feel very secure that he won't be caught if the light from inside was an indication. It was punishingly bright and cast square spotlights to the left of her on the lawn.

Now that she was here, she wasn't sure what to do. It had been instinct that made her park and jump out of her car. Instinct and outrage.

From inside, she heard footsteps that got louder and louder, coming toward the window. She pressed herself farther into the prickly branches, telling herself the pain was worth it. She heard a muffled, low voice from inside and strained to hear what he was saying.

"... is that right? You're naughty, aren't you?" A husky male voice floated out, with the barest hint of a Cajun twang softening the word "that" to "dat". The voice paused and then laughed. Another pause, and then, "You could have stayed here, darlin'. It's rustic, but there's plenty of room. You still can. Bring another bottle of wine back with you...." The voice faded as the footsteps carried it away.

Her jaw clenched as she eased her body away from the poking sticks. Some squatting jerk was not only living in her house; he was trying to hook up in her house! As she thought the words, she punched the damp, weedy ground.

Should I call the police? She wondered. She didn't know what the protocol in this state was, since the house wasn't in her name yet. She walked her feet under her body and slowly stood until she could peer into the window. Even on her tiptoes, she couldn't get that great a look into the house, but she saw a ladder with a paint can on it, a half-painted wall and some kind of tarp-covered thing in the far corner.

She heard the footsteps again and hit the ground flat out, her legs immediately going cold as her jeans soaked up the wet lawn water.

She gnawed at her bottom lip. This was definitely her property, and yet some squatter was... painting the living room? It made no sense.

When she thought it was safe, she pushed up to her knees and crawled closer to the hedge. She needed back up for this one. And only one person could give her the advice she needed—Summer.

Pulling out her phone, she fished in her hoodie's pocket for her earbuds and plugged them in. She opened her Skype app and tapped the name Summer in the contacts list. After two short bleeps, Summer answered.

"Katy, what on earth...." murmured a voice from her dark screen. That's when Katy realized that if it was eleven at night here, it was one in the morning back in Chicago.

"Oooh, sorry, but I've got a situation," she whispered.

"Did Goose break down? Because you should be calling triple A, not me," she moaned. Katy heard a rustling on the other end and a second later her phone lit up and Summer appeared, white-blonde hair mussed, wearing a man's dress shirt and surrounded by the fancy marble walls of her boyfriend's bathroom.

"Goose didn't break down. There's a man in my house! Do you think I should call the police?"

"A man in your...? I thought you weren't going to the house until tomorrow. Why are you there?"

"I thought it made sense to get a look at the place before meeting the lawyer tomorrow."

"Ugh, girl..." Summer complained. "Get a look at the place in the middle of the night? When there's probably no electricity on?"

"You don't have to sound so logical," she muttered.

"You don't even have the keys yet. Were you going to break in?"

"No, see? That's my point! The property is in a Trust until I claim it. So whoever's in it is trespassing!" She hissed the last word, her indignation nudging her voice into a higher pitch.

Summer rubbed her face and pushed her hair behind one ear. "I can barely see you. Turn on your dome light."

"I'm not in my car."

"Where are you?"

"I'm right outside the living room window!" Katy rose enough to hold the phone up to show Summer the living room and then yanked it down again. "Did you see it? He's doing some kind of... something to my house!"

"Get out of there! Right now!" Summer hissed. "You don't know what's going on; you don't know if that guy's crazy or what. Get back to Goose and go to your motel..." she paused, looking up and away from the phone. "Sorry, babe," she called to someone off camera. "I'm just talking to Katy. I'll be done in a minute." Summer looked back at Katy with a frown. "I woke Nick up. No, wait—*you* woke Nick up. And now he'll be cranky."

"Sorry. Okay, you're right. I'll go back to the motel and let the lawyer deal with this."

"Good. I love you. Stay safe." The women waved to each other and signed off.

Katy slid the phone into her pocket and turned to crawl back to Goose, squinting to find the least wet path. Before she could move, a hand yanked her up by the multiple necks of her clothing layers.

"It looks like I've caught myself a prowler," accused the deep voice she'd heard moments ago, except now its tone wasn't sexy or flirty.

The zippers of her coat and hoodie cut into her neck as he held her up, her toes barely touching the ground. A "grrrg" gargled out of her constrained throat.

"There's nothing to steal here, kiddo, but I'll hang on to you until the police get here all the same." He dropped her onto her feet and clamped her upper arm painfully, dragging her through the sharp branches of the hedge and to the dark driveway.

Her instinct was to jerk her arm and dig her heels into the ground so she could break free and run to Goose. But the way he pulled her along didn't let her get proper leverage.

"Hey!" she finally shouted, and his grip loosened. Putting all her weight into it, she jerked her arm free and tumbled backward. The gravel dug into her elbows, her teeth clunked together, and her head snapped back, shaking her hood loose.

The squatter spun around, and in the light from a side window, she watched surprise spread across his face.

"You're a woman," he stated, surprise turning to confusion.

Massive construction boots stomped down on either side of her sprawled legs, and he loomed over her. The light shining from the side window angled through his eyes, making their brown color glow like dark whiskey. Under his raincoat, he wore a white T-shirt and basketball-style shorts. His black, wavy hair, dark-framed glasses, and light beard fit her memories of the New Orleans guys she'd met on spring break. Rich frat boys who thought they owned the world.

His eyebrows lowered in a dark line over his eyes as he glared at her. She had to admit; he didn't look at all like she'd pictured a squatter would look. Realizing her mouth had dropped open, she closed it with a snap and gave him her best glare.

"Wow, you're a genius. You almost strangled me!" she accused, rubbing the sore spot on her neck where the zipper had dug in.

"I thought you were someone else. What are you doing, lurking around out here?" he asked, but it sounded more like an accusation.

Katy scrambled to her feet, bumping against him when he didn't move, and staggering a few steps to keep her balance. A hint of cologne broke another illusion she had about squatters.

She brushed the gravel from the palms of her hands. "Lurking? You're the one who assaulted me on my property! Plus, you're trespassing," she shouted at him.

"You're the one who's trespassing. I could literally throw you off the property if I want to," his voice sounded reasonable and calm, but there was a sneer behind the words that made her hands fist.

"I am not trespassing. You're squatting on my property, and I'm going to call the police." Katy turned to march down the driveway toward her car when she felt his hand clamp down on her upper arm again, although not as tight this time.

"Not so fast. I think we should go inside and sort this out. Don't worry; the police will get here soon enough." He steered her around in a wide arc and then let her go, gesturing for her to go ahead of him down the weed-choked driveway.

"You expect me to believe you called the police?" She refused to budge, folding her arms on her chest.

"You don't look like you believe me, so call them yourself. I'm happy to wait out here with you. I'm keeping you in my sight until I know what you're up to."

"I told you—I own this place."

He just stared at her, but placed himself between her and the road—and the safety of Goose—and mirrored her stance. "Okay. The police will be here in a few minutes. I'd like to wait it out inside if you don't mind." He gestured to the bare legs below his shorts.

Her own legs were two popsicles and her hands were going numb. Something about his calm voice and the respectful distance he kept made her decide that waiting in the house wouldn't be such a bad idea. That and the fact that it started to rain in sheets.

"Okay, let's wait inside," she griped.

He pointed to a rectangle of light ahead, and she walked toward it, seeing a porch and an open-windowed door. "Watch your step," he cautioned as she walked up the stairs, and she looked down to see rubber cords snaking across the threshold and down the porch, out of sight into the dark.

She entered a kitchen that was in the middle of a remodel. There were partially opened boxes all over, a few that revealed cream-colored cabinets. He'd stacked other boxes of flooring near the doorway on the other side of the room. She craned her neck to see the tile on the top box matched what she could see through the doorway. The floor had a gray, wood grain, from what she could see between the cardboard pieces he'd taped to make a safe path.

The walls were a warm shade of light gray, and there was a gorgeous white crown molding that ran the circumference of the room. The colors matched some of the palette swatches she'd put in her "style ideas" folder, and she had to bite back an appreciative "ooh."

This man was her enemy. She couldn't let the least bit of respect creep into her already-formed bad opinion of him. Speaking of the enemy, she glanced over to give him a glare but instead saw a strong jawline and throat that made her mouth dry. She decided it would be better to look away before trying to talk tough.

"You'd better have the documentation to back up all this illegal activity you have going on here." Despite her best attempt, the words came out husky and low instead of high and threatening.

"Oh, I do," he replied, unconcerned. "I'm curious to see why you think this is your property. Where is your documentation?"

"In my car!" She jutted her chin out. "I can go get them...." She turned toward the door, but he stepped in front of it, making her almost walk into him.

"I don't think so, honey," he said with that sliding, New Orleans cadence.

"I'm not your honey." She backed away, jamming her hands in her pockets. His sexy voice probably worked on most women, but not her.

"Let's sit down and wait." He pointed to the brightly lit area straight ahead.

She followed the cardboard path into a large room. To the right was a staircase that led to the second floor, and to the left was the room she'd seen from outside, making a T shape. This middle area looked like it could be a dining room.

He pointed ahead to the front room, and she continued on the cardboard path.

Walking through the wide entrance, she saw the ladder with paint and two unfolded camp chairs. She could look out the front windows to the overgrown grass where she had just been. In the middle of the windows were double-windowed doors.

He stood with his hands on his hips, watching her. He looked her over and gave her a half smirk as if he found her lacking.

"You're going to feel stupid when I show the cop my lawyer's letter." She crossed her own arms for emphasis, refusing to sit down.

He just stared.

"And then you'll have to pack up all your stuff and get out." She looked around the room at the various construction tools and equipment—much more than she'd been able to see when she peeked in from outside. On the far end of the room, under the canvas she'd glimpsed earlier, were piano legs and foot pedals. Under other circumstances, she would have questioned him about it, but to show interest in anything felt like it would reveal a sign of weakness. "I hope you have someplace to go." She looked back at him, her lips a thin, tight line.

He grunted a neutral "Huh." The smirk remained.

They stood in silence for a minute, and then she opted to sit down with a "Hmph." She heard a clank of glass and looked down to see the back chair leg had bumped against one of two empty wine glasses. An empty wine bottle stood farther away.

She crossed her arms and went back to scowling at him. He backed up a few steps to lean against the doorframe. His eyebrows stayed in a thoughtful line over his eyes and his gaze stayed riveted on her, probably analyzing how likely she was to attempt an escape.

"Don't worry. I'm not going anywhere until the cops get here," she sneered.

There was a slight raise of his eyebrows, but otherwise, he was silent. Katy shrugged and ignored him until the police arrived.

Quicker than she expected, perhaps only three minutes from the start of her silent vigil, she saw headlights turn into the driveway and heard the crunch of gravel.

"That was fast," she murmured, leaning on the canvas arm of the chair to glimpse the cruiser.

"Marshall doesn't live very far from here," the man said, stepping into the dining room until he could keep both her and the kitchen door in sight. A knock rapped, and the man called out, "C'mon!"

Katy stood up as the officer walked from the kitchen into the room where Basketball Shorts stood. They gave each other one of those traditional "bro" handshakes—a hand grab and a chest bump with a single shoulder slap.

Great. She rolled her eyes.

"How you doing, Mitch?" the policeman said more than asked, and he followed this Mitch character into the front room.

"Not bad, not bad. How 'bout you?"

"'Bout the same, I guess," he answered.

"So this is your prowler," said the policeman, stepping closer to look her up and down. "Definitely not Cody, Cody being a kid and all." The officer wore a fleece-lined brown jacket that had an Island County Sheriff patch on the front, but underneath he wore a T-shirt and sweatpants. He was shorter than Mitch, with red hair and matching freckles. Even though they both wore bulky jackets, his build was slight, while Mitch's build started with broad shoulders and ended with toned calves. Her face got hot, so she looked down to gain composure, only for her eyes to wander back. *Dammit, get a grip, Katy!*

"I am the owner of this property, and he is trespassing!" Katy raised her arm and pointed an accusatory finger at the brooding Mitch, who stood unaffected with both hands in his coat pockets.

"I'll get to that in a second. I'm Deputy Marshall Sinclair." He held out his hand to Katy, and she reached out to give it a firm but brief shake. "What is your name, ma'am?"

"Katy Williams. Katherine Williams, actually." She didn't think the situation merited the cuteness of Katy.

"And is that your vehicle you've hidden on the side of the road? A green Subaru with Illinois plates?"

"Yes, that's my car. Which is not hidden, it's parked safely to the side of the road as to not obstruct traffic," she corrected with icy politeness. She caught the corner of Mitch's mouth quirk up again, and she narrowed her eyes. "I can go out there right now and get the paperwork that proves I have a legal claim to this house, and that he is trespassing."

"Well, I have my doubts about some of that, but can you tell me if there's a lawyer in town whose name might be on the paperwork?" he asked, rocking back on his heels as he looked at her with one eyebrow raised.

Katy stared at Marshall as her mind tumbled over the paperwork, scanning her memory for names. "Carlisle and Associates!" she said triumphantly as the letterhead popped up in her mind's eye. "I've been dealing with Rally Lawson."

The two men shared a look, swiveled their gaze back to her, and then back to each other.

"So, here's the missing heir," Marshall said to Mitch, scratching his jaw. The man named Mitch pulled off his jacket and threw it on the floor in disgust. After a second, he picked it up and tossed it onto the other camp chair.

"Damn," he muttered, sliding a thumb and forefinger under his glasses to pinch the bridge of his nose.

"That's right—" Katy folded her arms across her chest. "—heir and soon-to-be property owner."

"Here's the thing, Katherine. Can I call you Katy?" Marshall asked with a friendly smile. "You just seem more like a Katy than a Katherine. No offense intended." He held his hands out in assurance.

"Katy is fine," she allowed, wondering what this "thing" might be.

"The thing is unless your paperwork includes a title to this property with your name on it, you're the one who's trespassing. This property is technically owned by Washington State, and Mitch here filed a legal statement of claim and posted a hefty bond for access to it, on the grounds he's contributing to its maintenance and repair. The claim also confirms that he has an intent to purchase the said property once the legal allotment of time has passed to allow the heir," he made a small motion at Katy, "to appear and officially claim the said property. And when I say official, I mean paperwork and such. Not showing up on said property..." He checked his watch. "... in the middle of the night." Marshall made a show of looking around the room at the construction materials. "And from what I can see, he's legally fulfilling his obligations."

"But," Katy started, but Marshall stopped her by holding up one hand.

"As far as I'm concerned, there's no criminal act happening here unless Mitch wants to file trespassing charges. Do you want to do that, Mitch?" Marshall looked at him inquiringly. Katy glowered at Mitch as he swung his eyes from Marshall to her. His eyes narrowed slightly and

15

the corners of his mouth turned up. Katy parked her hands on her hips, daring him to try to press charges.

"Nah, I guess I can let this drop." He paused. "This time."

"There won't be a next time, right, Katy?" Marshall asked. "Tomorrow, you can get hold of Rally and do whatever you came to town to do, and get things between you settled. However." Marshall turned and pointed at Mitch. "If you see Cody poking around here, let me know. I'll put a little pressure on the kid to make sure he's not getting any ideas about your tools again."

"Appreciate it," Mitch said.

The two men shook hands, and Marshall turned to give Katy a little wave. "Nice to meet you, Katy. I hope you enjoy your stay in town." And he left.

She stood there, shaking her head in disbelief. Finally, Mitch cleared his throat.

"If you don't mind," he said, and swept his hand toward the kitchen.

Straightening her spine, she stalked past him and into the kitchen. She pulled on the doorknob, but when Marshall pulled the door shut, it must have jammed on the cords that ran over the threshold. Mitch reached around her and jerked the door open, causing her to jump out of the way or get her head bonked by the door.

"I hope the next time we meet you're not crawling in my front yard in the dark," he said, no emotion in his voice. Katy stepped midway through the door and then turned to face him. She saw him shudder as cold November air blew in.

"Just so you know, and you can tell your friend Marshall this too—I intend to live here, in this town, and in this house." Standing in front of him, she had to tilt her head back to hold his eyes with her own. She'd added a healthy helping of scorn to her words to see if she could prod a reaction from him. She got the opposite.

"Good luck with that, Katherine." His voice was cool and his smile was icy. He swung the door closed, forcing her to hop outside to avoid a door in the face. She heard the click of the lock and watched his back as he walked away without a glance.

She stomped off the porch, down the driveway, and was still

stomping when she got to Goose. Inside, she started the engine and blasted the heat. She took off her down coat and covered her wet legs, rubbing them to get the circulation going and try to get rid of her frustration.

Her throat felt tight and her eyes burned. She wasn't used to being disrespected and... just not liked. Her whole life, everyone liked her. Well, her biological family excepted. She didn't want to think about that though. She'd just made a bad impression on the local law enforcement and the officer's legal squatter friend.

Once she warmed up, she put Goose into gear and headed back to the motel. *That did not go well*, whispered the dark voice inside her. *You knew they wouldn't want you here. Instead of the motel, maybe you should keep driving, back to Chicago.*

"No," she told the voice out loud. She wasn't giving up. She just needed a plan. She was good at making plans.

She braked Goose to a halt at the four-way stop, feeling more certain than the last time she was there. This house wasn't just an inheritance from a long-forgotten aunt. This was her destiny. And you don't walk away from destiny just because an arrogant so-and-so wants you to.

2

"Dammit!" Mitch yelled as he threw the short pieces of two-by-four on the floor in disgust. He'd spent most of the morning so far scouring the house from top floor to basement for his task list, and the last place he thought it could be had just come up empty.

Looking around the dimly lit basement at the various materials he'd stacked in neat piles here and there—aside from the off-cut two-by-fours he'd just thrown—he wracked his brain for other places the list could be. It had every item of work required, right down to supplies, timelines, inspections.... Thinking about it made him nauseous. He should have made a spreadsheet, but that's not how he liked to roll.

He picked up the thrown pieces and stacked them with the other bits and scraps from his work so far. Maybe he should go visit with Suze and have a coffee. He wasn't a guy who threw stuff around; he was the clear-headed kind of guy who thought problems through and didn't just react.

He'd had a lot of practice dealing with trouble, and he was pretty damned good at it. But this thing with *the heiress* showing up, as he thought of her... it spooked him. He could have the whole town on his side, but it wouldn't let him bend any laws. He could have hired Rally himself, if she hadn't already been handling the estate. After this much time, he didn't think he'd needed to. Now he wondered what legal recourse he had, because she looked to be the stubborn type.

He took off his glasses and rubbed his eyes. It was cold down here, and he had a good hour ahead of him if he wanted to rewrite his task list and get back on track for the day. Even though there could be an ugly ownership fight, he felt like he should plow ahead with the work. November through February were his slow months, and he planned to have a soft open near Christmas, maybe a couple bookings for New Year's and keep working one room at a time until he was done.

"Dammit," he said again, softer this time. He'd waited and worked and waited and worked so long to get this place to where it was. He was so close, and now everything was sliding out of his grasp.

Tentative footsteps upstairs snapped his attention to the ceiling. Jamming his glasses back on, he ran the length of the narrow basement and up the stairs. If Cody thought he could sneak back.... He ran up the stairs and spun around the doorway at the top, continuing to the kitchen where the sound had come from.

But it wasn't Cody. It was *her*. The heiress. The newest pain in his butt, dressed all in black like an elitist east coaster. Her sleek, black leather boots over tight black pants disappeared underneath the bottom of her shiny North Face parka. Glossy cocoa-colored, shoulder-length waves topped everything off, making her face and neck look as pale as porcelain. As she turned to look at him, he met massive brown eyes that almost drowned out her face.

When she saw him, she turned to face him, interlacing her fingers and bouncing up and down once on her tiptoes. "Hi," she said, and gave a small half wave with one hand.

"Well, well, well. Couldn't stay away, huh?" he asked, folding his arms over his chest. She was a tiny thing, or maybe the dark clothing just made her look that way. Instead of the anger of last night, she was pouring on the charm. He was curious to see what game she was up to. Fancy chicks like her always had some angle.

"I called out when I saw the door open." She shrugged, sliding her fidgety hands into her coat pockets.

"Not loud enough, it seems. What do you want?"

"I want to apologize. For yesterday." Her shoulders slumped, and she sighed. Her cheeks blushed and she looked at the floor and then at him. She had a little dimple in one cheek. "If I had known about your statement of claim, I wouldn't have overreacted when I saw you in the house. I really thought you were some kind of squatter."

"A squatter who brings his own construction tools?" He smirked. She was buttering him up for something, but he wasn't falling for it.

She stepped toward him and then veered slightly toward the piano. "Yeah, I didn't know what to make of that. But my girlfriend told me I should leave, and that's what I was trying to do when you caught me." She walked over to the canvas-draped piano and put her hand on it.

"Your girlfriend told you? Was she outside too?"

"No, I Skyped her when I saw you. Was this piano here when you started renovating? It doesn't look like there's any other furniture," she prompted, looking around again curiously. Only construction gear and materials lay scattered around the room.

He hesitated, trying to puzzle out why she cared, when it hit him. "Oh, you're wondering if some antique furniture might be part of your inheritance. Sorry to disappoint, but that's my piano. The house has been empty for several years."

"*Your* piano?"

He tried not to be insulted by her look of surprise. She lifted the edge of the canvas cover to peek underneath and then looked back at him with a tiny smile that popped that dimple out again. *Dammit.*

"Yeah, my piano. Look..." He backed up a few steps to give her a clear path to the door she came in, but stumbled on an extension cord. His cheeks warmed and he looked away. "I appreciate the apology, okay? I accept. Now we should probably go our separate ways until this legal mess is all cleared up."

She dropped the canvas cloth and brushed her hands together to shake off drywall dust. Her fingers were long and smooth and he watched as they rose to tuck a strand of hair behind her ear. "Could I just look around a bit? My appointment with the lawyer is in a little while, and I want to just... get a sense of the place." Her eyes got impossibly wider as they took in the room, the unfinished hardwood floor of the living room, paint cans, and lastly the disarray of the kitchen.

"I don't know; it's a real mess. Things lying all over. If you trip and get hurt, the last thing I'd want is you suing me on top of everything." Mitch rubbed his jaw. Actually, he loved showing people the work he'd done. Of all his past projects, this one truly had his personality in it. He looked at her standing there, uncertain. "Plus, there's a lot of work still to do. A *lot*! Every minute not working puts me behind schedule." He ignored the image of Suze and a big cup of coffee that he had been about to let divert him just a few minutes ago.

"Really? How much work?" Uncertainty and nervousness made her words hesitate, and he had an idea.

"Well, the support beams in the basement. And the plumbing. Some of the roof trusses look like they might be rotten." The lies spilled out of him so easily he had to mask his enjoyment. Every word found their mark and her expression changed from uncertain to gloomy.

"Sounds like a lot of work," she said, tucking her hands into her pockets. She sounded upbeat, but he saw her shoulders slump.

"It is. Plus, there's a shortage of contractors so it's just me. Luckily, I do this kind of thing, so...." He let that play out and saw her shoulders slump even more. "You *might* find someone to complete the project before next fall. Seattle's only a couple hours away. Just remember to allow for travel time in your budget. Man, that can really add up." Her eyes rounded even more as she leaned toward him in surprise. *This is too easy.* He tried to hide a smile.

"All the same, I'd still like to see it. If you have a few minutes."

He decided it could only help his new plan "Operation: Overwhelm" to show her around, so he spent the next twenty minutes exaggerating all the work still to be done to the house, throwing additional made-up tasks in, and making sure there was the perfect amount of danger added. He tried to ignore the moments when she'd touch an original fixture or vintage piece of trim to admire it—the same pieces he'd seen and vowed to keep when he'd first walked through the house.

And he clamped down on his emotions when she shared how her distant aunt—the only family member she'd ever loved—had told her childhood stories about the house and her dream of seeing Katy living there. And her own dream of running a business that revolved around nurturing travelers the way an inn does.

"Huh," he grunted at different parts of her story, determined to keep in mind how she was ruining his long-held dream of restoring this beautiful home.

Despite his plan to remain distant and not make eye-to-dimple contact, her subtle floral perfume and soft voice were getting to him. "Well, that's the house. Now, I've got to do a supply run, so I'll have to...."

"Oh, I understand. I'll head out and get ready for my meeting."

They were on the second-floor landing, looking down at the stairs that emptied onto the open space of the main floor. As she turned to step down, she stumbled. He reacted automatically, wrapping both arms around her and pulling her back. Later, he would wonder why he didn't just grab her arm. She likely would have only gone down on one knee, not tumbled down the stairs in a heap. But the heap was the picture that had jumped into his head, and instincts took over.

"Oh!" she said, startled. She sounded dazed and leaned back against his chest, completely still except for her breathing that made her chest rise and fall rapidly. Her head tucked easily under his chin and her hair smelled like... something he couldn't describe. He shoved the thought to the side just as she jerked away and jogged down the stairs.

"Sorry about that. Thanks for the help," she called behind her, stopping only when she was on the main floor below. She looked around and then up when she realized he hadn't followed her down. "Uh, either I or my lawyer will be in touch. Thanks for the tour. I appreciate you taking the time out of your busy day."

Mitch shoved his hands in his pockets and looked down at her. Clearing his voice, he responded cleverly with, "Yeah." He watched her walk into the kitchen and heard her close the door and still he didn't move.

His mind ticked over the surprises he'd had in the last twelve hours. First, that the heir existed at all. Second, that she'd shown up in person instead of dealing with everything through Rally. And last, that she was cute. Cute in a way that he avoided. He preferred practical relationships, not the kind that tangled up a guy's emotions. Those were destructive.

But none of that mattered. He'd hit an obstacle to his plan, and he just had to figure a way around it. This *heiress* was trying to manipulate him into something, and she'd be sorry when she found out perfume and family sob stories couldn't influence him. Or big brown eyes. Or a spunky personality and cute laugh. He shook his head.

Operation: Overwhelm, he thought. It was a plan that had a lot of promise. He just had to stick with it and not get distracted by her counter measures. He rubbed his shirt where her head had pressed. He'd had tougher enemies than some fancy-smelling rich girl from the East Coast.

3

Katy started Goose's engine, but sat staring at the old house for a minute. Her heart raced and her hands were shaky. She'd been a little alarmed at her slight trip on the stairs, but feeling herself hauled against Mitch's chest had been like jumping into Lake Michigan on New Year's. He'd grabbed her so hard that she'd panicked and almost hyperventilated. But his arms had released her easily when she jerked against them. Her breathing had come back to normal by the time she'd been on the main floor and had seen him still on the upper landing at the railing.

She put Goose in reverse and eased down the rutted driveway, checking for cars, and then out onto the road. She headed back into town, opening a hand on the steering wheel and seeing it still trembled. She needed a coffee... or a drink. That might be better. Maybe they sold mimosas in one of the coffee shops in town.

Last night, Mitch had started out as a faceless house squatter, then became a bearded, stony-faced construction lout, and finally a legal adversary who was out to spoil her dreams. She thought she'd imagined his great smell and sexy jawline, but she hadn't. And he was the opposite of a lout. His black, wavy hair and strong brow looked almost aristocratic. His thick-framed glasses made him cool in a nerdy way, a look that always made her stomach flutter. His hands were huge and rough and....

She gripped the steering wheel harder.

"No, no, no," she said out loud. He was the enemy. She could not afford to be attracted to the enemy. She'd seen friends in high school and college turn stupid when they'd gotten emotional about a guy. She'd watched and she'd learned the most amazing lesson a woman could—you could get a lot out of a guy if you didn't let your emotions get involved.

You could have fun dates and get a guy's help with almost anything; you just couldn't care enough that when they cheated or broke things off, you were shattered. It had successfully kept her life on a very even keel since high school. But if the guy in question wasn't cooperating, sometimes you had to take action to get things started.

She'd tried to deploy that strategy with Mitch. She thought a little flirty talk would soften him up, but he hadn't responded at all. In fact, he seemed to withdraw, as if he knew what game she was playing. Even her made-up stories about her aunt hadn't moved him.

And then he gave her all that talk about the work that needed doing! He made it sound like the inn was about to fall down at any minute. More than half of what he said had to be fake, she decided. It looked like a solid place to her, not to mention drywall and painting had happened. From her research on construction renovations, this wouldn't happen if there were structural problems.

She rolled her shoulders a few times and tried to enjoy the scenery. The gray sky and gray water reminded her of her many visits to the Atlantic coast with her adopted parents. That was another odd, emotionless relationship she'd had to learn how to navigate, no different from Mitch. She only had to endure him long enough to have him kicked out of her house.

Goose the Subaru chugged relentlessly along, passing fields of grass that transitioned into tree-covered land, which became dotted with small homes. The road curved and dipped, and the main strip of the little town of Cranberry Hill appeared before her.

The town was very uniform and neat in its arrangement. Most of the buildings were white, and those that weren't, were a faded umber

NALA HENKEL-AISLINN

or gray. It definitely had the feel of a beach community. Cars parked at neat angles on either side of the road, and Katy saw a coffee shop called The Oasis on one side, and another called the Golden Lily across from it. Some business fronts, like the local credit union, had a shingled awning. Some, like the real estate office, had a faded hand-carved sign that hung on a metal pole. *A hand-carved sign for the inn is on my to-do list*, she thought.

Toward the far end of the strip, she saw a red-bricked building of two stories that had a large clock at the apex of its centered peak. She slowed Goose to read the sign mounted on the building. It listed several businesses, one of which was Carlisle and Associates. This was her stop. She parked a little farther up the road and checked her watch. She still had some time before her meeting and took a stroll and get acquainted with the small town.

The first thing she noticed was that every business had a bench outside, although nobody was sitting on them. There were three crossroads on the main drag. Peering down the side streets, she saw colorful signage for a glassblowing studio, a wool and rug making shop, and a chocolatier. She also saw a computer repair shop, two hair salons, and a bug museum. It would be fun to explore these later.

On the other side of the street was the real estate office, and she pulled open the door.

"Hello," said an older woman at a desk. She rose and met her at the counter, looking her up and down as she walked.

"Hi. I noticed your carved sign and wanted to know where you had it made," Katy asked.

"Well, the man who did ours does it for a hobby. It'll take too long for you to take home."

"Oh, I'm not a tourist," she said, and smiled as the woman looked her up and down again. "I own the house out on Beach Drive Road. The old Grant place," she said. "I want to convert it to an inn."

Katy could see the cold front sweep over the woman's features.

"The man we used isn't taking on any new commissions. I'm sorry," she said, in that not-sorry way.

"Oh, that's too bad," Katy said. "Thanks anyway."

The woman nodded and turned away.

BLUEPRINT FOR LOVE

Katy left, but as she walked past the window, she saw the woman on the phone.

"Welcome to the neighborhood," she muttered.

She passed a barbershop complete with the striped pole and got to the post office. She walked in the double doors and located the counter with various forms.

"Can I help you?" asked a man from behind the nearby counter.

"I need a change of address card."

"Oh, I can get you that," he leaned to open a drawer. "Are you moving to Cranberry Hill, then?"

"Yes. To the Grant House on Beach Drive Road."

She saw the man pause and look back at her with disappointment.

"That's... nice," he said.

"I'm going to turn it into an inn."

He pulled a small card out and placed it on the counter.

"That seems to be a popular idea," he said, no longer making eye contact.

"Thank you," she said as she picked up the card and tapped it on the counter. The man turned away to shuffle some papers, not responding.

She left and looked down the street. She'd expected it to be a challenge fitting in as the new person in a small town, but she hadn't expected the animosity. Either these people hated all newcomers, or they knew Mitch and she was the automatic enemy.

Crap, that's got to be what this is. I'm taking something from one of their own.

She walked past a bookstore, a hardware store, and thankfully arrived at the Golden Lily. She opened the door which rang a brass bell, and four conversations paused as she came in. Everyone wore bright colors, and her all-black outfit made her feel like a double agent. She felt self-conscious ordering her normal extra-hot, double-shot almond milk latte, and scanned the menu for something simpler.

"What can I get started for you?" asked the barista. He was a skinny young man with messy brown hair and a pointy chin. He wore a T-shirt that said **Dude. I'm just here for the lattes**.

"I know how you feel." Katy pointed to the man's shirt with a small smile. He smiled back. *Finally, a friendly face.* "I'll have a grande extra-hot, double-shot almond milk latte to go." She bounced a little realizing she hadn't had one in a few days.

"I dig someone who gets excited about their order," said the man with a solemn nod. Katy pointed at him and winked.

"Right?" She nodded in agreement. He made her drink expertly, and she had her first sip right there at the pickup counter. "Perfect. Thank you!" Katy left the coffee shop and headed to the brick building for her meeting.

The lobby was like stepping back into the '50s, with worn marble floors and the lingering smell of stockpiled paper, even though the space was empty. She examined the directory and found the lawyer's office, but was pleased to find offices for an accountant, a tax specialist, a graphic design firm, and the local newspaper. That would make it a one-stop shop for setting up and advertising her inn. They couldn't refuse her business, could they?

She skipped the elevator and walked to the end of the hallway to take the stairs to the third floor. Her footsteps echoed in the cavernous stairwell, and when she exited, the door made a muffled boom she could hear from the hall. Following the worn beige carpet in the beige hallway, she walked past two brown doors to a third that was labeled Carlisle and Associates in a plain font. She turned the slightly bent metal doorknob and entered... into a beautiful paradise.

She expected the office to face the street, but it overlooked a bay. The office was high enough that the wall of windows she faced showcased trees at the bottom and a gray water and sky in the distance.

Above the windows were gorgeous cream Roman shades. A wide-plank washed hardwood covered the floor, meeting a tall, white baseboard that transitioned into cool cream tone-on-tone wallpaper. Smack in the middle of the windows, a young woman sat behind a shiny white desktop with charcoal-colored legs. A large, silver Mac computer and two file folders were the only items on her desk.

"Are you Katherine Williams?" she asked with a smile, rising and walking around the desk. She wore in a mint flannel suit and had her hair pinned up in a smooth French twist. Her face was fresh and clean of any makeup.

"Yes. Well, Katy Williams actually. Are you Rally?" This woman looked too young to be a lawyer.

"No, I'm Brynne. Rally's in her office." As Katy shook Brynne's hand, Brynne nodded toward one side of the office. Katy hadn't noticed the clear glass walls to either side of Brynne's desk that sectioned out two elegant workspaces. The glass ran floor to ceiling, and two silver hinges held the glass door in place. One office was empty and in the other sat a brown-haired woman tapping at her laptop. No sound escaped her office, though. "You can go in. She's expecting you."

Katy walked over and pulled on the long, silver door pull. The glass moved like silk. Even though she was in Rally's line of vision, the woman kept typing. Katy pulled the door closed behind her and walked to stand directly in front of the typing lawyer.

"One second," she murmured, hitting a key with extra force and then peering closer at the screen, her eyes moving rapidly back and forth. "That looks good." She moved her mouse and clicked it. Katy heard the *whoosh* effect of an email being sent. "So, Katherine Williams." Rally rose and held out a slim hand. "I'm Rally Lawson. I'm administering the estate of your aunt."

Rally was tall and slim. Her light blue shirtdress matched the startling blue of her eyes. Her brown, natural-looking wavy hair framed her face, held in an elegant ponytail. Her handshake was firm, and she invited Katy to sit.

Katy pulled out the chair and shuffled around it, glancing down at her own black jeans and boots. "Nice to meet you. Um, everyone just calls me Katy." She glanced at the glossy white top of the desk. Everything in the entire office was austere. Other than low credenzas that lined every wall, there was very little furniture. "Is it okay if I put my coffee here?" she pointed to the desk edge closest to her.

"Of course." Rally briefly smiled and then opened the single file that sat on her desk. "So you're the heir to the Grant house."

"Yes." Katy put down her latte and opened her purse to pull out the letter. Rally held up her hand when she tried to hand it to her.

"I just need to see two pieces of photo I.D."

"Yes, of course." Katy fumbled her wallet out and placed her Illinois driver's license and her passport on the desk in front of Rally. But Rally made no immediate move to pick up the documents, continuing to look at Katy steadily with those pale blue eyes. Katy was mesmerized, and then felt her body go hot and clammy. *This woman is my lawyer. She can't change her mind now, can she?*

She shrugged off her jacket and took a sip of her latte. When she set the cup back on the desk, Rally straightened and looked down to pick up the driver's license and wordlessly make notes on a paper in the file. She did the same with the passport.

"All right, that's all done. Thank you." Rally pressed a button and after a few seconds Brynne entered the office. "Can you make certified copies of these, please." Brynne left with the documents, and Rally went back to arrange some papers in her file.

"If I can get you to sign here," she held out a page with yellow post-it arrows and passed her a pen. "And then here," she turned the pages as Katy signed them. Once done, she called her assistant back in to make more copies.

"We sent you a copy of the will. I assume you read it?"

"No, I... I received it, but I really didn't want to read it." She remembered how she'd burned it, actually.

Rally stared at her blankly, her slow blink telling Katy what she thought about people who didn't read legal documents.

"I have three certified copies of it for you." Rally held up a large brown envelope.

"Will I need them?"

"You will, if you intend to sell the property. Three should be sufficient, but you can come back for more if you need them. You'll also need a copy if you intend to keep the property and file a statement of claim with the State. That's a separate issue, though, since this is a more complicated situation than usual."

"Oh, well, I definitely want to keep the property. I want to open an inn."

Rally's eyes narrowed; her hand holding the envelope stilled in mid-extension to Katy. "That seems to be a popular idea."

Katy huffed out a short breath. "Tell me about it," she muttered under her breath, reaching out to take the envelope. "How do I file a statement of claim? Are you not able to do it?"

"Well, I could, but if you want legal representation, I'll have my partner Gordon handle it. It would be a conflict if I did it for you."

Katy's brows furrowed. "Why? You're handling the estate. Isn't that part of it?"

"Normally, it would be, yes. But I filed a statement of claim on the property for a third party, and I'm representing that party's interest in the property as it relates to a missing heir. That's what makes your estate settlement complicated. So it would be a conflict for me to represent you on that," Rally finished coolly.

"I know it's some guy named Mitch. You don't have to hide his name from me," Katy said. Rally leaned back and rolled her fancy silver pen between her thumb and forefinger, staring at Katy saying nothing. *So much for women banding together.*

"Fine," Katy continued, "I'd like to schedule a meeting with Gordon to do that, then." She smiled, tipping her head to the side. "I assumed from the letter I responded to that there was only the house. Is that correct?"

"Yes. There were other bequests—you can read it all in the will—but the house was the only possession bequeathed to you. If you had claimed it right away, it wouldn't have been put in trust with the State. That's standard procedure for all missing heirs in the State of Washington."

Katy didn't hear any censure in Rally's tone. She was all business. Maybe she'd imagined that little flash of hostility in her eyes.

"I wish I had come to my senses sooner too. There's just... I have some emotional baggage from the past, and it seemed easier to ignore it than deal with it."

"I wish you'd dealt with it earlier, too." Rally pulled a light pink business-sized envelope from the file, her voice lowering as she added, "For everybody's sake." She handed Katy the envelope. "This is a letter we've been holding for you from your aunt."

Katy's hand stopped short of taking what Rally held out at the mention of her aunt. *Aunt Penny had left her a letter?* After a moment, she closed her mouth, not realizing it had fallen open at the appearance of the envelope.

Conflicting thoughts flooded her, and she fought to keep her mind and expression blank. Rally leaned forward, watching her face carefully. She thought she saw the lawyer's expression soften, and then she really had to fight to keep emotion from changing her expression. She didn't do a good enough job.

"Hey," Rally said, putting the envelope in front of her and laced her hands together. Now she looked uncomfortable. "This is all going to work itself out. I'm sorry for your loss, Katy. I should have said that at the beginning. Sometimes I get lost in the paperwork and the work, and I forget why people are here."

"I thought all of this would be easier," Katy confessed. "The legal part is confusing. I should have learned more about how it all works."

Katy picked up the envelope and toyed with it, dread creeping over her. Rally reached out and patted her hand, then breathed deeply, back to business.

"Because it's a public document, I can tell you that Mitch Howard has filed a claim of right to the property and posted a significant bond. The State has permitted him to make certain renovations because by law they cannot let the property fall into disrepair. This is fairly standard. After all this time, nobody thought you would come forward. There are laws about how long property is held for missing heirs before the State can sell it."

"I moved around a bit in the last few years, and it took a while for your last letter to catch up with me." Katy recalled how the initial news of Aunt Penny's death had hit her—with anger.

She'd read the cover page and then burnt the first pack of papers on the stove, much to Summer's anger. She'd tried to stomp out the fire, but Katy had wrestled it away and burned it completely. Since they met in college, they'd never fought. But that day Summer had given her the silent treatment. It lasted for two weeks—an awkward, endless two weeks. Over two years had gone by before Katy had received a final notice about the inheritance. Rally's voice broke her reverie.

"I'm going to take my legal hat off," Rally continued. "Mitch is a very good friend of mine. He's had a dream for that property for years, and almost everyone in this town wants him to make it happen. I'm asking you to be very, very sure that this is what you want. I see many east coasters wanting to move here, and they all go home. Please... just be certain this is right for you." Rally stood up and walked around her desk to stand beside Katy's chair.

Katy's neck broke out in a sweat, the way it used to when she thought she was unprepared for a test. Right on cue, a roll of nausea swirled in her belly. *Was this friendly advice or a warning?*

"You should give yourself a little space to think everything through."

Katy stood, dropped her purse, picked it up, and tried to pull on her coat, which only made her drop her purse again. She stopped and sighed. "You're right; maybe something to eat would help." She tried to laugh it off, but the sound fell flat.

"Let me hold your purse," Rally offered and took it out of Katy's hand without waiting for an answer. Katy put her coat on, grabbed her mostly finished latte, and gripped both envelopes tightly in her other hand. "Go to The Oasis down the street. They have to-die-for scones." Rally draped her purse over her shoulder.

"Thank you," Katy said and meant it.

"You're welcome. Gordon should be in the office shortly after lunch. Do you want me to schedule you to meet with him this afternoon? He can walk you through how a statement of claim works, timelines, all of that."

"I think so," Katy replied uncertainly. "Let me have that scone, and I'll call you right back?"

Rally nodded with a small smile. It seemed like the first genuine smile she'd given her.

When she got outside, Katy took in a deep breath of the damp air. She looked up and down the street, imagining critical eyes singling her out as "that east coaster."

She'd thought it would be a simple thing—sign some papers, get her house and move in. She should have known better.

She squared her shoulders and headed down the street. In all her years, nothing had come easy. Why would it start now? She scanned the street ahead for the sign for The Oasis—big white letters on a green background. She charted a route for her feet and let her mind dip into memories.

Aunt Penny had been a fairytale figure to her. She wore fitted pastel dresses and heels and smelled like sweet flowers. She lived in a small apartment in Boston, and every night, she would wrap the couch in flannel cloud-covered sheets with a matching blue quilt and puffy pillow.

"Dream time, Katy-Girl," she'd tell her, holding the blanket up for her to jump into.

The memory faded, and she stared blankly at a door handle, and then jumped back when it opened and a chuckling couple walked out.

"Oh, sorry!" said the man, his movement freezing when he saw how close the door had come to hitting her. Both he and his female partner were holding white cups that had a bright green sticker that said The Oasis.

"That's okay." Katy gripped the handle and pulled the door wider so they could both exit. "I'm in a daze today." She shrugged and tried a little laugh. It almost sounded real.

Inside the café were a fair number of people compared to the quiet street, but she didn't really look around. Katy got into line and immediately saw the huge scones, lumpy and golden brown. Her stomach saw them too and gave a decent growl.

"One ham and cheese scone, please. And a latte. Sorry to bring in the competition." Katy raised her almost-empty Golden Lily cup. She dropped it into the nearby garbage can.

"Not a problem. It happens all the time," said Holly, whose nametag also suggested Katy **Get Sconed at The Oasis.**

"I like your nametag." Katy pointed, and the blonde woman smiled distantly as she scooped a scone onto a plate. *Another enemy.*

"Heated?"

"No, thanks." Holly handed her a plate with the massive scone on it.

"What was your drink? A latte?"

"Sure," Katy said. Suddenly, everything was too heavy—her purse, her coat, the decision about her latte... but especially the envelope in her hand.

She finished the transaction and shuffled to the nearest table, putting everything down and taking off her jacket. She moved plate and documents around until the pink envelope sat on the table before her.

Funny, but seeing what must have been Penny's handwriting spiked her anger. **For Katy Williams only** was on the front of the envelope. The flourish of the *K* and the perfectly uniform *A-T-Y*. Flawless, just like her image of Aunt Penny from all those years ago.

She'd locked Aunt Penny and that sliver of happy time in a vault. This letter wouldn't change the past, but it could sure screw up the present. If she let it.

4

Mitch was finally relaxing. He had his coffee and was enjoying a little banter with Suze, who was reloading the coffee station at The Oasis where she worked.

"So, what time do you get off again, Coffee Lady?" he murmured gruffly, letting a little Louisiana slide into his tone. Suze flashed him a wicked look as she filled up the wooden stir sticks. Suze was the perfect partner for him.

Physically, she was compact and strong, showcasing her love of strength training. She was studying to be a massage therapist, and her hands were so firm he thought he'd have bruises whenever she "practiced" on him. He never did, and he always felt invigorated. She had short, silver hair that curved up at the ends in electric blue spikes. Her round face was expressive and cheerful, which was exactly what he needed this morning.

Emotionally, she put no rules on their relationship. She was an easygoing companion and always gave him lots of room, which he appreciated. He didn't have to worry that his habit of getting lost in his own thoughts and plans would make her resentful.

"You know I get off when you do, good looking," she murmured back, exaggerating her lean to replace the stir stick cup so she could press her body against his arm.

Mitch had been framing his next line when his radar perked up. A movement across the street caught his eye. Sure enough, there she was. The Shatterer of Dreams. She carried a coffee cup and the brown envelope in one hand and strangled her purse strap with the other. Her gaze focused straight ahead, and though he craned his neck, he couldn't see what she was staring so intently at.

Go to the Lily, go to the Lily, his mind chanted. But of course she didn't. She stopped at the door and spun in place facing The Oasis. He almost ducked, but realized Suze blocked most of him from sight.

"What are you looking at?" Suze asked, turning to glance up and down the street.

"Ugh, the missing heiress is in town, and it looks like she's coming in."

"Oooh, Margo told me about her!" Suze hissed. "She went into the real estate office earlier."

"She did?" he asked. Had his planned worked so well she wanted to sell?

"Yeah, apparently she wanted a sign made for when she turns it into an inn."

Dammit.

Suze craned her neck to look across the street. "That must be her in the black. Sticks out like a sore thumb, doesn't she?"

"Yup." Mitch swallowed some of his hot black coffee.

He stepped back beside the coffee station. He wouldn't hide, but he wouldn't make it easy for her to spot him so she could come over and gloat. He knew the title transfer process was complex, but the part of his heart that he'd allowed to get excited about his inn was heartbroken at the sight of that brown envelope. He knew he had an option or two legally, but his irrational side was imagining she'd already received the deed to the property, when he knew it would take several days at the earliest. He took another sip.

"Mitch, dude!" called a male voice. He looked up to see Mark and his girlfriend Brenda wave at him on their way out. "Game this Saturday, right?" He pointed at Mitch.

"You bet!" Mitch answered. "Who are we playing again?"

"Mount Vernon."

Mitch winced. "Gonna be a tough one."

"They're all tough, man. We suck." Mark laughed and then pushed open the door—almost into Katy's face. Mitch winced but saw that she'd leaned back to avoid the hit.

"Oh, sorry," Mark said. Katy's hand was on the handle, and she pulled the door wider so Mark and Brenda could leave.

"That's okay," she replied, her face a bland mask. She murmured something he couldn't hear and then made the most pathetic attempt at a smile he'd ever seen. The couple walked out and Katy walked in, heading straight for the order line.

Something was off. The woman he'd met last night, and this morning had more... energy, he decided. She'd had a spark in her eyes last night, and more like a sparkle this morning. Not so much now.

"She's got the New York look down. The slick city woman," Suze said, continuing to wipe the station counter in lazy circles. "She probably buys yoga wear and never goes to yoga," she jibed, nudging Mitch with her elbow.

"Hm?" he asked, turning to her. "Oh, yeah. Probably."

"Don't worry. She doesn't look like the type that has staying power. Typical east coaster. Breeze in with her big ideas, have fun, and then escape back to their own kind when the ideas fall apart. Oh," she interrupted herself, glancing at him. "I didn't mean that your inn idea would fall apart. Just that she doesn't look like the kind of woman to have what it takes to make it happen."

"I hope she doesn't," Mitch said, looking back to see Katy put everything on a table and then arranged it all carefully, ending by placing an envelope in front of her. Her movements were slow and precise. "She looks weird, though. I wonder what Rally told her."

"Probably that she didn't stand a chance, that the whole town would support you and force the state to grant you the property."

"That's a nice thought, but that's not how it would work." He leaned toward her, planting a quick kiss on her lips. Suze quirked a brow at him and then grabbed his chin and planted a longer kiss on his mouth.

"I'll see you tonight? When we both 'get off'?" she infused as much innuendo into her words as they could hold. She gave the arm of his glasses a tweak and giggled.

"Absolutely," he said, and gave her arm a quick squeeze. But the heiress distracted him. Something was off with hers, and if it affected his hold on the inn, then it was a problem.

"Latte for Katy!" called Gillian. Mitch headed over to where the white mug sat on the counter.

"I've got this, Gillian. I know her." He walked over to Katy, who was standing up ready to retrieve her drink.

He'd expected something from her when their eyes met. Anger, satisfaction, smugness... something. But her expression had no emotion at all. It made it difficult to know the right approach to take.

"Latte delivery, courtesy of the squatter," he announced, and slid the mug on the table. He caught the writing on the envelope: **For Katy Williams only.** She was still staring at him, and now he got the opposite impression from before. That a million emotions were going through her so fast that they didn't have time to leave any traces on her face. "Yo, is there a Katharine somewhere in there," he prompted, waving a hand in front of her eyes until they zeroed in on him.

He pulled out a chair across from her and sat, watching her plop back down and brush her hair behind her ear. Then she picked up her mug and had a sip. And then another, longer drink. "Oh my God, that's what I needed. This would be amazing if it was hotter. I don't know why I didn't get my regular order."

"Your regular order. I'm curious, how many syllables is is in that?" he smirked. He saw a spark come back into her expression, and he wondered if he shouldn't have said something to keep her off kilter. She was his adversary, and he should exploit any weakness he could.

"I usually order an extra-hot, double-shot almond milk latte." She took another sip, and he watched the corners of her mouth turn up in the satisfaction only coffee lovers know.

"Huh," he wondered, counting it out on his fingers, "over ten syllables. Thanks for not letting me down, East Coast." He saluted her with his cup and took a sip. He watched her eyes move back to the envelope, but this time a frown settled on her face. Ah, dammit. He'd been so involved in what would happen with the property he'd forgotten that someone close to her had died. He might have been brought up poor, but he *was* brought up with some manners.

"I'm, uh, sorry for your loss," he said into his mug as he sipped his coffee. The silence between them stretched and Mitch fidgeted, not sure what to do when she didn't offer the normal "Thanks" response. She looked down, frowning, and he was relieved that it didn't look like she was about to cry. He retreated when any conversation turned emotional.

"Sorry. Thank you. She was my Aunt Penny. The distant aunt I told you about. I only knew her for a few months when I was little." She shrugged and crossed her arms on the table near the envelope. "I... really wasn't expecting to get a letter from her. It's... unexpected."

Mitch smirked again. "I thought you had fond memories of your aunt. Warm stories and all that."

"Warm memories and cold reality can co-exist," she stated, raising a slim eyebrow at him as she sipped her latte.

He scratched his beard, took another sip of coffee, and then folded his arms similarly to hers.

"Why do you think she left you a letter?" he asked.

"Many reasons, none of which I'm inclined to share with a stranger," she said with a raised eyebrow.

"Maybe it's a plea to sell the house to someone capable of restoring it to its original glory," he suggested with a nod.

"Or maybe it's a reminder not to trust smooth-talking men," she countered, her eyes twinkled at him over her mug.

"Hah!" He pointed his mug at her triumphantly. "So you think I'm a smooth-talker, huh?" He smiled as her eyes narrowed.

"Where I come from, smooth talkers are on the same level a snake oil salesmen."

"So a compliment," he agreed, and enjoyed the frustrated expression that bloomed on her face.

"Hey, Mitch," came a familiar voice from behind him. He turned and saw the big belly of Walt Coombs before he looked up and saw his friendly face. Every day of the year, Walt wore his fishing hat and vest. Today was no exception. "How's the inn coming along? Heard that woman turned up," he said, nudging Mitch's shoulder with his elbow. He said "that woman" the way you might say "rabid dog."

Mitch stood and shook the large hand he held out. "Pretty good, pretty good. Yeah, she did. How are you doing, Walt?"

"Not bad for an old guy. Say, I've got word of those Bakelite switches. There's a guy down in Seattle that's got a mess of them, but there' are a lot of different styles. He says you should come down, but I don't know why you couldn't just get him to send you some pictures."

Mitch could sense Katy's movement behind him, and he peeked over his shoulder to see her leaning closer to listen in. "I can come to your store later and get his number, unless you have it with you."

"Yah, come to the store. I've got those Sawzall blades you wanted. I'll be there, what... in a couple hours? Gotta go down the pier and see what's happening on the water. Always a good time to fish, ya know!" Walt laughed broadly and slapped Mitch on the arm. Mitch slapped him back and laughed.

"Howdy, good day, miss." Walt tipped his hat to Katy as he sauntered out of the café with his coffee and scone.

"Bakelite switches. Is that art deco?" Katy asked, leaning forward with interest.

"Yeah," Mitch said, dropping back into his chair. "From the 1920s."

"I love that period. I was expecting to see something similar to a Cape Cod home when I got out there this morning, but other than the shingles on the exterior, it isn't the same. The porch has those posts..."

"Craftsman style," Mitch said, leaning forward. "It's not an exact representation, but my plan is to restore the inside in that style."

"I noticed the windows on one side—are those original mullioned windows?"

"Yes." Mitch was pleased she'd noticed. "They're all original wood-paned windows. I was looking online at how to restore them instead of replace them. It's a little finicky, but I think I'll be able to do it." He smiled at the enthusiasm in her expression. It matched his own.

"Nice." She leaned back in her chair and nodded, but the envelope she'd been leaning on caught her eye. She scowled and grabbed it, folding it in half and shoving it into her coat pocket.

"All joking aside, if your aunt suggests you sell the inn, I can make you a good offer," he suggested, see how that test balloon would float. It sank.

"I have another appointment this afternoon, and it won't be to get advice on selling," she said firmly, but he noticed she fiddled with her earring as she spoke. His friend in college always fiddled with his ring when he had a decent poker hand and didn't know what to bet. He and his roommate made a lot of money on that guy.

"Are you nervous about the appointment?" he prompted.

"Why would I be nervous?" He watched her tug at the collar of her turtleneck and fiddle with her earring again. He saw her eyes following his, and she slapped her hands on her lap and glared at him. "Stop reading me," she said with a half-laugh.

"Sorry." He held up his hands with a short laugh. "Poker habits die hard. Where are you staying?"

"At a little motel out near the highway."

He nodded and looked into his almost empty mug. "Well, I think I'll get a refill to carry on with work. Lots to do! Lots and lots and lots."

"Yup, for me too." She nodded at him as he stood up, staying in her seat.

"Good luck with your meeting later," he said and raised his mug in her direction. He turned and motioned to Suze, who was now behind the counter, to refill a to-go cup with the dark roast drip. She blew him a kiss and winked. After a minute, he headed out the door, saying hi to a few other friends on his way out.

On the street, he headed to Walt's hardware store where he'd parked his truck. There was no way he'd be able to keep the inn if she wanted it. She was the heir, and it was just a matter of time and paperwork. He knew he would get his bond money back and every dollar he'd spent from the state, as his paperwork set him up as their contractor for property maintenance. That had been a nice little deal Rally had worked out.

But it wasn't about money. This was about his dream of creating something permanent with his own hands.

Something in that house—*his* inn—had called to him the second he'd seen it, abandoned and empty for years. He'd thought he wanted to build something from scratch, but the house in his imagination matched this one down to the last porch post and mullioned window.

The owner didn't want to sell, and when she'd died and a year went by without the heir responding to claim it, it had convinced him the heir was dead. He couldn't fathom someone receiving title to a home and not claiming it immediately—even if it was just to sell it.

When Rally had filed his claim, he'd spent the next year methodically ticking off everything on the list he had to do to get it up and operating.

He pulled open his truck door and climbed inside. He reached into the space behind his seat and pulled out his rolled-up architectural blueprints. He toyed with the paper edges near his signature, Mitchell G. Howard, Architect. He slid the elastic band off and unrolled each sheet until he found the one with the detail he'd drawn of the upstairs bathroom. It would have wainscoting and a pedestal sink, crown molding, and a black ceramic Bakelite switch—although the detail of the switch was in his mind and not on the blueprints. He remembered the sparkle in Katy's eyes when she'd mentioned it.

It was possible Operation: Overwhelm would work, and she'd file all the papers to claim her inheritance then turn around and sell him the house and walk away. She didn't look like she had construction experience, and for all her brave words, she might just want to unload the property and take the cash.

But something in her expression when he'd been talking about Craftsman style and the windows made him wonder. Her face had come alive as they chatted. It could be she felt as strongly about her dream as he did about his. There was also the fact that nothing in his life ever came easy.

He needed a Plan B.

He thought about that gleam in her eyes, and it was around that that the spark of an idea crystallized. Charm her. Dazzle her. Get her to trust him and then—WHAM—get her to sign the house over to him.

It was the most devious idea he'd ever had, and he'd only ever done it in the past for small things, like football tickets or free drinks. This was a house.

Hmm, he'd have to deal with his conscience later.

He weighed the obvious flaw in his plan—that he was attracted to her. He didn't want to be, but deep down he knew he had some kind of connection to her in a way he hadn't experienced before. A way that set off an alarm bell for him.

She definitely wasn't his type. She expected a formal relationship. She was an east coaster, and those women needed all kinds of commitment and boundaries and other things that tied guys down. That alone should act as a bucket of cold water if any romantic ideas came to mind.

That was the answer. He just had to remind himself over and over that she was a trap. Besides, he didn't have to try too hard to dazzle her. It was a skill he was born with. He'd just have to be wary of her cuteness.

He unrolled the blueprints farther and heard something drop between his legs. He moved the plans to look down on the floor, and he grinned. There was his to-do list! A good omen.

5

Katy pulled Goose to the side of the road, right where she'd parked the other night. She put him in park and turned off the engine. Stepping out of the car, a gust of Pacific Ocean wind hit her. Going to the back seat, she retrieved her black knit cap and pulled it on.

She walked along the road until she got to the driveway and looked up at the inn. For so long she'd seen it as a millstone. A reminder she'd been part of a family that didn't want her. She'd never been close to her adoptive parents, but she'd tried to distance herself mentally from her blood relatives. Summer had helped her see this inheritance as a business opportunity and not a source of pain.

Looking at it now, she couldn't think of it as a house; it was made to be more. The exterior was faded and chipped. They had painted the shingles, which she considered a travesty, but whatever. That was fixable. The white trim similarly needed a healthy touch-up. It looked in solid condition to her, although she wasn't an expert. The only reason not to trust Mitch's appraisal was because he had a monetary interest in it. Maybe even an emotional one. Therefore, she was reasonably sure most of what needed doing was not too serious.

Katy turned and crossed the narrow two-lane road. The grasses that separated the road from the beach were tall and pale yellow, bending in the wind. The tide looked to be on its way in. Below where she stood was a rocky ledge that dropped about ten feet to the sand. The sky above was a solid gray down to the thin line of horizon where it met darker gray water. The trill of her phone sounded, and she pulled it out of her pocket.

"Hello?"

"Is this Katy Williams?" asked a male voice.

"Yes, this is she."

"This is Gordon Carlisle from Carlisle and Associates. They booked you to see me this afternoon, but I finished my last appointment a lot earlier than I thought. Do you have time to see me now?"

"Uh, yes. Yes, that would be great. I'm on my way. I should be there in ten minutes."

"I'll see you shortly." He hung up.

Katy turned back to look at the house, her brain ticking through the mental image of her spreadsheet. So Mitch had already completed many tasks, and yet several. When she thought about it, she was way ahead of schedule.

She shoved her hands in her pockets and felt the envelope there. Her finger sought the impression of the heavy handwriting. It reminded her of the last envelope that had unexpected news.

Rally's law office had made three attempts to contact her. The first one, she'd burned, which started a fight with Summer. The second one, she'd burned without Summer knowing about it. But the third one, Summer had signed for at their front door, and then overpowered her by sitting on her chest and reading the letter to her. She'd skimmed the will and told her she had inherited a house from her aunt.

Summer had told her the plain truth—Katy was unstable if she could let childhood resentment impede this unbelievable opportunity. After a long night of talk and wine, Katy had seen Summer was right. Although she didn't believe in it, this was a kind of divine intervention. An opportunity to start and run a business and live rent-free. She'd jumped right into spreadsheet planning mode after that.

She crossed the street and climbed back into the calm of Goose's interior.

She pulled the light pink envelope out of her purse and tapped it on the steering wheel. She didn't want to hear anything from her aunt. It was as if she was holding open a door and saying to Katy, *"Come on back for more rejection."*

Katy was not someone who shied away from hard work. She let no one dictate her worth or value, and she was letting this envelope turn her upside down. Sitting up straighter in Goose, she flipped over the letter and tore the back open in one stroke. She pulled a single sheet of paper out and opened it to see her Aunt Penny's handwriting.

Dear Katy-girl,

I'm writing this in the living room of the house I'm leaving to you. This house was my husband Clinton's pride and joy, even though we haven't lived here in a very long time. He'd wanted to leave it to a historical society, but since Clinton was the reason I could not legally adopt you when you were little, I've decided it's only fitting that I leave it to you.

I hope you can forgive me. I've lived with regret and cowardice, even past Clinton's death when I should have written you. Now that it's my time, I have a small amount of courage to write this letter.

Despite the examples of your mother, your grandparents, and myself, I know you have a strong will and backbone, and that you will make a magical home here. Never let a man dictate your life to you, Katy-girl, or what you can and cannot do. You are strong! I saw that when you were five. Trust that every choice you make will take you where you need to go.

Love always,
Your Aunt Penny

"That's just perfect," she scorned, refolding the letter and shoving it into the envelope. She wanted to focus on the part where Aunt Penny had asked for her forgiveness. But she was fixated on the reminder she came from a family of cowards. Of people with no backbone.

Cramming the letter into her pocket, she started the car and used the inn's driveway to turn around. Her tires squealed just a little as she sped up toward town.

<hr />

THE STATEMENT TOOK NO TIME AT ALL, AND GORDON WAS KIND TO her. If he noticed she was a ball of contained anger when she arrived, he chose not to comment.

He was a thin, silver-haired man in a charcoal suit and a delightful purple paisley tie. He had a close-trimmed beard, similar to Mitch's. He had run in to Clinton and Penny several years ago and said they were a nice couple. He knew Mitch, and the progress he'd made with the renovations.

"So you want to run an inn!" Gordon leaned back with a smile once she had all her copies tucked in her purse.

"Yes, and thanks to Mitch's hard work, I might open by Christmas."

Gordon grimaced. "That's a quick timeline, but I expect if you work hard and find some good contractors to finish, you could make it happen."

"I'm definitely not afraid of hard work," Katy agreed; a measure of relief allowed her to lean back in her chair. Hard work had always been the answer to her problems and was usually what other people were unwilling to put in.

"Mitch is a hard worker, too. He wandered by that property some years back and has obsessed over it ever since. Enough that he moved out here with dreams of buying it. And the care he's taken in the renovations has been outstanding. Everyone in town is always talking about it."

"Yes. He seems very committed."

"I feel bad for him. But he knew this situation was a possibility when he petitioned the state," he pointed to her with his pen, "and the law is the law. Mitch is fair and honest to a fault. You don't have to worry that he'll argue with you when the time comes for him to vacate."

"Good," Katy said, but slumped in her chair. She could tell by

Gordon's voice that the town had plenty of respect for Mitch. Taking over the property would put a big target on her back. How long would that take to overcome?

"But don't think he won't pursue every legal avenue to change the outcome," Gordon said. "As is his right."

"Oh, I expect that," she agreed. The man she'd met seemed to feel as strongly as she did about the property.

"I imagine a few people around here will feel bad about the whole situation," he continued. "Hopefully they'll get to know the nice young woman you are by the time they find out Mitch no longer has a claim to the property."

"When do you expect that to happen?" Katy asked, thinking that would be one outcome of today's visit—a quick eviction.

"It will only take a day or so for the state to verify your claim. They do that electronically these days, especially since I added an expedite request. The actual paperwork will come in another week."

"I was hoping to move out of the hotel today," Kate thought out loud. She still wanted to, but didn't look forward to a potential confrontation with Mitch. "Do I *have* to wait?"

"Legally, once the electronic acknowledgement gets to my email, you have a right to be on the property. But it would be the neighborly thing to defer your move a few extra days until I receive the physical order. That way I can notify Mitch by registered mail and keep emotions on an even keel, so to speak."

"Hunh," she grunted. "Well, nothing worth having ever came easy, right?" she asked him. When his expression relaxed, she realized he'd been expecting her refusal.

"That's what they say." Gordon smiled and nodded. "You know... have you ever thought of hiring Mitch to finish the renovation? He's got a thorough knowledge of the house and the work it needs. That would definitely put him ahead of any other contractor new to the job."

Katy adjusted in her seat, uncrossing and recrossing her legs. "I don't know how... open he'd be to that. He and I haven't seen eye to eye on a lot of things so far."

"Hmmm," Gordon said, leaning on his desk and linking his hands together in thought. "I can see how that might be. Mitch has always been an independent sort. You know..." His eyes brightened, and he tapped his desk with his forefinger. "You could approach him to be a partner in the inn. His plans for the property are almost identical to yours, right down to the opening date."

"Uhhh," Katy began, a deeper part of herself rejecting the idea immediately. "I don't know, I'm an independent sort myself."

"I can agree with that, seeing as how you drove across the country alone to take on this new adventure. But my sense of you is that you're smart. Even though things might be uncomfortable for you and Mitch, both of you want the same thing. Working together might be the best thing to make this new business successful." He eyed her thoughtfully as he turned the pen over and over in his hand. "Plus, the town's real fond of Mitch. That would automatically put you in good standing with them."

Her heart sank. His words echoed her own misgivings.

"Maybe you can't share any information," she asked hesitantly. "But has Mitch ever partnered with anybody?" She watched Gordon's face, but it remained open and sincere.

"Not to my knowledge, but then that's what partnership agreements do. They lay the ground rules for how to work together. The key is for all parties to keep their eye on what matters, which is the smooth running of the business."

Katy would have bet that Mitch was even less of a cooperative sort than she was, but she couldn't afford to alienate Gordon by saying it out loud. It was bad enough that she'd have to win the town to her side if she wanted to be successful.

"I'll think about it," she said with a thoughtful nod. "At the very least, it definitely makes sense to continue the renovation work with someone who knows exactly what needs to be done."

"Good! Think it over. And having said all that, I'll tell you I've also known Mitch to be a proud man. If the partnership idea doesn't fly for you both, you can call Brad Denby." Gordon opened his middle desk drawer and pulled out a stack of various business cards. He flipped through until he found one. "He's a good man. Very reliable. He's done

BLUEPRINT FOR LOVE

a bit of work in Cranberry Hill, and I believe he's familiar with the Grant house."

Katy took the card from Gordon's outstretched hand. "Thank you. I might just do that."

KATY SAT UP IN BED WITH A JOLT, HER SLEEPING BAG CINCHED TIGHT around her face.

She glanced around, the weak morning light slowly revealing the simple furnishings around her. Right, she was in the musty-smelling motel room. She wiggled around until she could squeeze the clasp and loosen the sleeping bag enough to push it down. Her phone said it was just after eight.

She tapped a few buttons and listened to the ring tone.

"You can't be mad at me, because it's only ten o'clock there," Katy jumped in before Summer could even say hi.

"Good morning to you, too. Wait, you're not in jail or anything, are you?"

"No," Katy scoffed. "I'm still at the motel. But hopefully that was my last night. My new lawyer says I just need to get an acknowledgement from the state of my claim and that's good enough to evict Mitch."

"New lawyer? And who's Mitch? Wait," Summer interrupted herself. "I'm on a stake-out, so I might only have a couple minutes."

"Who are you staking out?"

"The accountant with crime family connections. He's supposed to show up at court and I want to get him on camera. Anyway, bring me up to date. Who's Mitch?"

"The squatter."

"Oooh," Summer said. "Why didn't the police kick him out when they found out you owned the property?"

"It's a long story, but it turns out he has a legal right to be there. Had a right, past tense."

"So everything's all settled once he's gone?"

"Mostly. He's done a lot of the renovations that needed doing, but there's still some work left to do. Gordon suggested I hire him to finish the renovations."

"Who's Gordon?"

"Sorry, he's my new lawyer."

"What happened to the old lawyer?"

"She's the one who filed Mitch's claim on the property. It would have been a conflict for her to file my claim, too. Although..." she gnawed on her lip as the next thought came to her. "There might be something between her and Mitch. She warned me to be sure I really really wanted to stay in town and keep the property. And she seemed almost territorial about him."

"I love the intrigue. What does this Mitch look like? Is he a model or something?"

"He's okay," she fibbed, swallowing before she continued. "Brown hair, glasses, a beard. Just a normal guy."

"What aren't you telling me?"

"Nothing." She swallowed again.

"Everything!" Summer accused with a laugh. "You're doing that weird swallow-with-a-click thing when you talk about a hot guy."

"I didn't!"

"Don't argue with a reporter. We're trained to catch things normal people don't. So this Mitch is hot. Don't tell me—he's super tall, dark hair, with that triangular build... broad shoulders, slim waist. Am I right? I'm right, aren't I? Nailed it!" she sang when Katy stayed silent.

"Yes to it all," she gave in, "but not only does my previous lawyer have the hots for him, he has a girlfriend. They were mooning at each other at the café yesterday. He's probably one of those guys who's slept with every woman in town."

"What do you care? You just need to do that cute, flirty thing and get him to finish the renovations."

"That's the problem. I tried. He's totally immune to me."

Now it was Summer's turn to pause.

"Summer?" she asked, when the silence lasted a minute. "Are you still there?"

"I'm just shocked, frankly. I've never known a guy to be immune to the Katy Williams dimples. How is that possible?"

"I don't know," she grumbled. "Anyway, it seems like a pipe dream to think I could pay him to keep renovating his dream house for someone else. Apparently he has the same dream I do."

"Huh, that is a lot to ask. Anyway, the upside is you're much farther ahead than you thought you'd be. I'm sure there's some contractor out there who'd want to take on the job."

"Gordon had another idea. That I ask Mitch to partner with me on the inn." Katy ran a finger along a seam in the down sleeping bag. "But that's a dumb idea. Right?"

There was a long enough silence that Katy thought their call had dropped.

"It's not a dumb idea," she said in a contemplative voice, as if it might be fifty-fifty. "It's just never been your game plan. Even in college, you ran two businesses and worked the coffee shop, always refusing any help from anyone."

"I know," she said, when in fact she didn't know. "It's just that everyone in this town sees me as the usurper and Mitch as the hometown hero. I couldn't even get a recommendation for a sign."

"My advice to you is follow your gut. Anything worth having..."

"... is worth fighting for, I know."

"You're saying the words, but somehow I don't hear your heart in them. What else is going on?"

"I got a letter from Aunt Penny," she said, thinking of the pink envelope still in her jacket pocket.

"Really," Summer said, her words awestruck. "What did she say?"

Katy leaned forward and hopped to the table where she'd draped her coat. Pulling out the envelope, she read the note to Summer.

"Wow. I can't believe she waited until she was dead to apologize. That's some kind of cowardly."

"I know. I carried it around all morning before I could read it. As much as it sucks to hear it now, it confirmed what I've always believed. To never let a man get in a position to control me."

"And she's right about the backbone. You've got the strongest one I've ever seen. Look at everything you did over the last six months to make your dream happen!"

"Despite having the whole town against me."

"It'll just make you even stronger," Summer declared.

"You're right. I made it across the country. I can make this work, too." Her old enthusiasm started to flow through her.

"That's the Katy I know! Oops, hey... I see my guy, so I've gotta go. Call me if anything gets weird."

"I will. Love you."

"Love you too, Katy."

Katy shrugged out of the sleeping bag, realizing she'd crawl in fully clothed. She'd just decided on a quick shower when her phone chimed.

Good news! Notice from the Secretary of State received. The property is yours, and you can pick up a set of keys from Brynne any time, read Gordon's email. **I'll notify Rally, who will notify Mitch. Would you like me to advise them you'd like immediate possession?**

Katy plopped down on the bed as she stared at the message. Yes, that's exactly what I want. Isn't it?

She shook her head and hit the reply button.

Great! Yes, please advise I'd like immediate possession. Thanks so much, Gordon.

She opted for a quick shower and then spent an hour getting caught up on work email. Her boss had reluctantly agreed to let her work remotely for a few months while she settled her aunt's estate. She hadn't told him the full truth yet about opening an inn, and the truth was she hoped to keep working another six months until the inn was turning a good profit.

She picked up the keys from Brynne just after noon, thinking to say hello to Gordon but he and Rally were out for lunch. She pointed Goose down the road to the inn, and ten minutes later, pulled into the driveway, the gravel crunching under her tires.

Mitch stood in the front yard, his hands jammed into his pockets as he looked up at the house. He turned when she pulled even with him, and she saw his brows lower into that familiar line. *Oh boy*, she thought. He did not look happy.

She didn't want a confrontation, but she wouldn't back down from one either. She pulled Goose onto a grassy strip to park beside what she assumed was Mitch's truck. She saw a tool chest and several boxes in the back.

She slung her purse over her shoulder and took a bracing breath, walking to meet Mitch as he sauntered to the middle of the driveway.

"Looks like you got all your paperwork in order," he said, his voice even but his eyes flinty.

"Yes."

"Rally called me this morning. I packed up most of my personal stuff, but there are a few things I'll have to come back for."

"That's perfectly fine," she said with a nod, pleased that he was looking at this rationally.

"Like the piano. I don't have a place to store it yet, so if you don't mind, I'd like to leave it here for a week."

"All right."

"And my chop saw is still in the barn. And my drill press. I couldn't fit those into my truck."

"Okay," she said.

He just stood staring at her, and she racked her brain for something polite to say that would end the awkward conversation.

"I... appreciate all the work you've put in here." No response. "I wish..." she trailed off, and he cocked his head at her.

"You wish what? Things could be different? That you weren't spoiling somebody's lifelong dream?" The sarcasm dripped from his words, making her seethe.

"You're not the only one with a dream, you know. In fact, we have the same one for this house."

"Really," he said with a dour laugh. "A lifelong dream that took you over a year to decide on? Sounds more like the whim of a rich girl who'd gotten bored with life back east and wanted an adventure. Well," he swung his are out in an arc, "here you go. Good luck with it."

His sneer made her spine straighten. Several comments bubbled up in her mind, and she even took several steps toward him.

"Thank you," she replied, giving him the smuggest smile she could.

His eyes flared, and she saw his jaw clench. He shoved his hand back in his pocket and stepped around her.

"Keys are in the kitchen," he said coldly over his shoulder, then he climbed into his truck and started it up.

She crossed to the porch and watched him back down the driveway and drive away. Not once did he look back.

A tingle spread through her as she touched the railing. *Her porch. Her house.* She turned the kitchen doorknob and walked inside.

She'd expected things to look as they had when she'd been here two days ago. But the kitchen was empty. The boxes, both opened and sealed, were all gone. As was the kitchen island. And he'd taken the beautiful upper moulding, the nail holes marking where it had hung. He'd also taken the boxes of tiles, although he hadn't removed what was on the floor.

He'd left one square of cardboard taped in the middle of the room. Written in black felt in a circle were the words "Good luck" and in the middle were the keys.

"That sneaky, son of a..." she muttered, picking up the keys and pulling out her phone to call Gordon.

6

Mitch flopped onto Suze's couch and crossed his feet on the top of his suitcase nearby. Her apartment was cozy and luckily had two bedrooms.

"Thanks again, Suze," he called as she fussed with something in the bathroom. The words came out testy, and he cleared his throat. He didn't need to take out his frustration on her.

"It's no problem. It'll be fun to have a roommate," she called out. "I've even got a spare toothbrush and I've got an extra washcloth here for you."

"I've got my toothbrush. I'm not a complete neanderthal," he said with a laugh. Something in her voice—a giddiness—was setting of an alarm bell. "It'll just be for a couple days." He'd been thinking a week, but not if she went all weird on him.

"Stay as long as you need. A month even," she said, walking back into the room and sitting beside him. "I can't believe after all the work you put in, she can just step in like that. It's not right."

"What's right and what's legal aren't always the same thing. Besides, I undid some work I hadn't reported on to the State. Which will add to her to-do list."

Suze propped her elbow on the back of the couch and turned to face him.

"She's going to walk through that house and freak out about all the things that need doing. You watch. I bet she's calling you by the end of the week to see if you want to buy it."

"That would be a best-case scenario, for sure," he agreed.

She reached out and fiddled with the zipper of his coat.

"So what do you wanna do? I have a half hour before my shift starts," she said, looking at him through her eyelashes.

"Actually, I have a lot of phone calls to make." Her flirty smile changed to a pout. "Maybe we can watch a movie or something tonight. If I don't have an early night, that is." He shrugged. He didn't know why, but he wanted to set some boundaries between them.

"Okay. I set up the futon in the other bedroom. I hope you don't mind that I have a few boxes and things in there."

"I don't mind at all. And I really appreciate you letting me crash for a bit. I promise not to get in your way."

"You can get in my way whenever you want," she said, poking him playfully in the chest. When her hand lingered, and she leaned in, he lifted it and gave it a short kiss.

"All right, I've got to get some things sorted out." He rose and lifted his suitcase. "Have a good day at work," he said with a smile, and strode to the bedroom.

He was about to call his first supplier when his phone beeped with Rally's ringtone.

"Hey, Rally," he greeted. "Don't worry, I vacated the premises."

"I heard. The new owner had her lawyer contact me about that."

"Yeah? What did she have to say?" he asked, laughing. He had an idea exactly what she said.

"She was disturbed to find the property... shall I say, in a less finished state than when she last viewed it. Did you uninstall some moulding and cabinets, by any chance?" she asked, her voice teetering between humor and exasperation.

"Only a few changes I haven't updated the State on. Those were the rules in my claim."

"You enjoy making my life difficult, don't you?"

"I'm abiding by the law. How is that making your life difficult?"

"Gordon is my boss, and Katy is his client. And he likes her, so when you're mean to her it puts me on the side of the enemy."

"That's not very objective, for a lawyer."

"He says he admires her spirit, coming across the country to be the new kid in town trying to start a business. I have to admit, I admire her a little, too."

"Hey," he accused with a frown. "You're supposed to be on my side."

"I am, but speaking as someone who wants to have a good working relationship with my boss, maybe you could let up a bit.

He sank down on the fluffy quilt covering the futon.

"That goes against every instinct, but I'll try. I'm glad you called, though. I was just about to call you. Do I have any legal options at all? Even some goofy law from a hundred years ago about east coasters not owning west coast property." He pressed his fingers to the bridge of his nose as his amusement from a few seconds ago melted in the face of reality. "I can't lose this place, Rally."

"I only know the legal ways. Make her an offer and buy it."

"She looks like she has no intention of doing that."

"Probably even less, now that you've removed some finishings she liked."

A little shot of pride made him smile.

"At least she has good taste," he allowed.

"You don't know how she'll feel in a week or a month. Maybe offer to help do some renovations. Get on her good side. She seems nice, but I don't know if she knows anything about running an inn. She might get cold feet, and there you'll be ready to take it off her hands."

"Yeah, maybe," he said. But Rally hadn't seen the gleam in her eye when they'd talked about windows. Or the look of pride and excitement she'd had when she looked over the house the other day.

"Just don't go shutting off the electricity or anything," Rally said, making his heart sink as he thought about the two phone calls he'd made that morning. "Mitch," she warned when he stayed quiet.

"It's likely nothing will change until tomorrow. Utilities are notoriously slow," he offered weakly, regretting his rash revenge.

"You will be the death of me. Honestly, if we didn't have history..."

"I promise from here on out, I'll try to get on her good side. And hey, I appreciate all the help you've been through all of this."

"What are friends for?"

They hung up, and he dug out his to-do list from his pocket. He'd arranged for some plumbing and electrical to happen next week, and he'd have to call that off.

"Hey, Nate," he greeted when the plumber answered his call.

"What's up, Mitch? I don't have you scheduled until next week."

"That's the thing. I have to cancel."

"What's wrong?"

"The heiress showed up. I'm officially out of the house."

"No!" Nate said, genuinely sounded distressed. "Man, that's a shame."

"Tell me about it. I knew it could happen, but after all this time I didn't really believe it."

"That truly sucks, buddy."

"You might not miss out on the work. It's possible she'll find you in the phone book and call you up. If she even realizes what stage the house is at." He rubbed his forehead as he started to imagine all the things she might screw up.

"No way. I work for you on that house or I work for nobody. We've worked on too many projects for me not to have your back."

"I appreciate the thought, Nate, but don't say no to good-paying work on my account. Although," he said, with a grin, "if you wanted to charge her double, I wouldn't try to talk you out of it."

"Huh," Nate grunted a laugh. They chatted a bit longer then Mitch ended the call to have the same conversation with his electrician.

"No bloody way!" Pete exclaimed when Mitch filled him in on the news. Pete also swore he wouldn't work for her and asked for her name just so he could make sure he was turning down the right person. "I can spread the word around, if you like. Make it hard for her to get anything done."

"Thanks for the thought, but maybe we should just let things lie. I might make her an offer and buy it outright from her. I would have had to buy it from the State, anyway."

"Well, let me know how else I can help. And if I hear anything from my other suppliers that might help you out, like if she's talking about selling, I can let you know."

"I appreciate that, Pete, thanks."

He dropped his phone on the bed and lay back on the mattress, trying to slow down the thousands of thoughts flying through his brain.

He'd never thought the heiress would show up. And when she did, he didn't think she'd do anything but sell the house. He hadn't expected her to be a young, pushy wanna-be business owner. He wondered if she would call up mommy and daddy to arrange for all the serious work to be done so she could relax and be an innkeeper.

Although, her Subaru looked and sounded like it had seen better days. He frowned as he thought about the dirt-caked car that had pulled into the driveway, loaded to the roof with boxes and bags. He would have guessed a rich girl would have hired movers and flown to Seattle, maybe even on a private jet.

"Rich people can be weird," he said, shrugging at the ceiling. He put all thoughts about wealthy people aside and turned his mind to his next move. He'd let her rattle around in the empty house for today and stew on things. Let the overwhelm sink in. Then he'd pop by and try to make amends. Maybe even bring her that multi-syllable latte she liked. He smiled at the direction "Operation Overwhelm" was going.

"Part two, overwhelm her with my charm," he said to the ceiling with a chuckle.

7

The piercing cries of seagulls roused Katy from sleep, and she shifted slightly on her comfy air mattress and camping cot to enjoy the sound. She grinned as it sank in that this was her new reality, living near the ocean in her own home.

She sat up, feeling her trusty sleeping bag cord tighten around her face. The light was dim, and she guessed it was earlier than seven. She wiggled an arm up to loosen the cord and realized how cold her nose was. As she pushed the bag down over her flannel PJs, the frigid air enveloped her.

"What the heck," she muttered, swinging her legs off the cot and pushing the puffy nylon bag down to the floor. She searched around with her woolen-socked foot for her boots and slipped them on. Despite her t-shirt and flannel PJs, she grabbed her blue sleeping bag and wrapped it around her as she walked into the hall.

She checked the thermostat on the wall near the stairs.

"Forty-four!" she shouted and shuffled back to the sparse bedroom she'd chosen to hunt for her cap and jacket. Just as she zipped up, she heard the crunch of tires on the driveway.

She clomped down the hall and the stairs to see a white truck slow and stop near the corner of the house. She glanced down at the white kitten faces on the pink background of her bottoms and shrugged.

"Excuse me, hello," she called, waving to the man in a bulky brown coat with reflective strips around the arms. He carried a long metal rod in his hands.

"Good morning," he called back, glancing back with a smile.

She shuffled more quickly to keep up, seeing the decal on the driver's door of his truck. **County Water Department** it read.

Mitch strikes again.

"Can I ask what you're doing?" she asked, although she already knew.

"Service termination. Customer closed his account and I'm turning off the water."

"Is there any way I can talk you into leaving it on? I promise I'm going right back into the house to set up a new account."

"Nobody'll be in the office for a couple hours," he said, stopping to peer down at the ground. When he found what he was looking for, he pushed the rod down and flipped up a plastic cover. "I'm not allowed to do anything without a work order," he said with a hint of apology.

"Is it normal for you to be doing this outside of business hours?" she asked, crossing her arms and rubbing some warmth into them.

"Not always, but I live near here. I got the service order emailed last night, so it made sense to stop by on my way to work." He flipped the rod around and dropped it into the exposed hole, turning it in his hands a few times. She heard the squeal of metal on metal. He replaced the lid and looked back at her with a smile which she returned with a hint of exasperation.

"Can I count on you to be so diligent when I get my account set up today?"

"Maybe," he said, hoisting the rod on his shoulder and walking past her to his truck. She turned and shuffled after him, pausing when threw the rod in the back of his truck.

"I take it you know the guy who was working on this house, am I right? Mitch?" she asked.

"Could be," he replied, shrugging but a tiny smile curved his lips up. He was so genial, she couldn't help but smile back.

NALA HENKEL-AISLINN

"Well, my name is Katy Williams. And now you know me..." she looked at his name patch, "Jonah. My aunt owned this house, and I'm planning to open an inn here."

He nodded and then looked surprised when she stuck her cold hand out for a handshake. He took it, though, and gave it a firm shake.

"Nice to meet you, Katy Williams."

"Now that we're acquaintances, I expect to see you this evening on your way home from work," she said, looking him in the eye and giving his hand an additional shake.

"It's very possible," he said, the small smile turning into a grin. He released her hand and climbing into his truck.

She walked further to the house and climbed the stairs to the porch, turning to watch him back out. She wondered if he smiled because she didn't give him crap like others might, or because of her worn Hello Kitty flannel PJs. When he was on the road, he paused and rolled down his window.

"Have a great day!" he called out.

"You too, Jonah," she yelled back and gave him a wave. She looked down with a chuckle. *Had to be the PJs.*

She had her hand on the kitchen doorknob when she heard two horns honk. Turning back to the road she saw Mitch's truck passing Jonah's and then ease into her driveway.

"The troublemaker returns," she mumbled, crossing her arms. He'd be disappointed when he saw she wasn't panicking over a night without electricity.

He drove up slowly, his truck swaying as the tires dipped in and out of the driveway ruts. He pulled off to the side, parking beside Goose. She watched him reach to the passenger seat for something before he climbed out of his truck.

"Before you fire a cannon at me," he said, holding up one hand up to halt her from speaking. The other held a cardboard tray with two Oasis coffee cups. "I didn't expect the county to turn off the water so fast. It took days for them to turn it on for me."

He stepped gingerly toward her, holding the tray out as if it was a slab of meat meant to calm a tiger. It worked. She danced from foot to foot and waved him close enough to grab the cup he angled toward her. Enemy or not, no electricity and no water meant no morning coffee.

"Extra-hot, double-shot almond milk latte, right?" he asked with a wide grin and a twinkle in his eye. She popped the lid to inhale the aroma, her lips curling into her first sip.

"That's right," she sighed, unable to make any smart aleck reply she might have.

"Uh, you really get into your coffee," he said gruffly, his expression going blank.

"Don't you?"

"Not... like you." He cleared his throat and took the other cup from the tray. He expertly flicked the tray into the back of his truck.

"You must be up to something if you're willing to order such an east-coast drink," she teased. She took in his tall form, almost her height even though she stood several steps higher than him.

He looked similar to the other times she'd seen him, with a plaid flannel shirt and a puffy vest, form-fitting jeans and heavy-duty work boots. His rolled-back cuffs exposed dark hair, strong hands, and a silver watch on one wrist. She struggled to see why he looked different and realized it was because he was smiling. A real smile, with no hint of his usual sarcasm or smugness. It was nice.

"I swear the only thing I'm up to right now is expressing regret. I... didn't react well yesterday when Rally called me about your claim coming through," he said, his smiling going lopsided as he rubbed his neck and looked away from her momentarily. "Actually, I was an idiot. Please accept my apology latte."

She took another sip of the magical drink and closed her eyes with a sigh. She couldn't be angry at anybody when this delicious fluid warmed her belly.

"Apology accepted," she said, and he held up his cup in acknowledgement. He didn't leave, so she did the thing that seemed most natural. "Would you like to come in and see what I've done with the place?" she asked, raising an eyebrow.

"I was hoping you'd offer," he agreed, and strode forward to hop up on the porch. He even pushed the door open and gestured for her to precede him, making her heart flutter. She liked this Mitch, even if he had some kind of agenda. After turning off the water, he couldn't have many more tricks to play.

She walked to the wall where she'd pinned her layouts and spreadsheets.

"This is my master plan," she announced. He adjusted his glasses and stepped forward with interest, his eyes scanning the pages she'd tiled together into a sort of blueprint.

"That's a copy of an original blueprint," he said with surprise, his finger tracing the faint lines of the printout.

"It's amazing what you can find online. If you look in the corner, you can see the stamp where they submitted a copy of the original floor plan when the back bedroom was added on in the fifties. So technically, it's a copy of a copy of the original."

"That' great. And it looks like you've been busy," he murmured, pointing to her drawings and notes.

"I wanted to know how things had changed from this plan and the only way to do that is to measure. My friend, Summer, gave me this cool laser level that measures distances between points. I had fun going over every inch of this place and updating the plan."

He straightened and looked at her with a strange light in his eye, jangling her nerves.

"I don't mean that as an insult or anything. I love that you widened the entranceway from the dining room to the other rooms, and the closet you added to the master bedroom. And stole some space from the upstairs bedroom to make the bathroom roomy." Her words trailed off when he just stared at her. The tension in her only eased when he adjusted his glasses again and looked back at the wall, scanning all her inspiration images.

"And these are some of your plans for finishings?" he asked, gesturing to a close-up of a doorway casing.

"I love the wide-plank wood around doorways, and I found some images of heritage homes online and printed these out. Although I don't know for sure if they're a fit for West Coast style or not."

"They're exactly what I had in mind, too," he murmured, his eyes roaming the wall. They stopped at the Bakelite switches and he looked at her. "You'd thought of these before you came?" He asked her, his eyes widening.

"Actually, I printed those out yesterday." She pointed to the printer on the floor in the dining room. A folding chair holding her laptop stood beside it. "I think they're gorgeous."

He thrust his free hand into his back pocket and leaned back.

"I gotta say, East Coast, you surprise me." His words had admiration in them, and she squinted to see if it was real. "What?" he asked, noticing her stare.

"I'm waiting for the 'but'. Compliments from you are not what I usually expect."

"It's real," he assured her. "And since we seem to have similar good taste, it's like I'm complimenting myself, so…" he trailed off with a sardonic grin, making her laugh.

"Now *that* I expect," she laughed. "And for the record, I'm more Midwest than East Coast." She paused and then took a chance that he'd be open to a friendly question. "And I'm guessing you're not a Pacific Northwest guy. My guess is… Louisiana?"

His eyebrow shot up in surprise.

"*Ça bien*, Katy. Small-town Louisiana. How did you guess?"

She blushed when she remembered overhearing his flirty conversation that first night.

"You have an accent sometimes, and it reminded me of a vacation I had in New Orleans when I was in college."

"Ah, a spring break party trip, right?" A hard light came into his eyes, and she wondered what he was imagining. Nothing nice, from his expression.

"Sort of. Did you never go to a fun place for spring break? Pile into a car with your fraternity buddies and a trunkful of beer and bourbon?" she asked, hearing the hard edge in her voice.

He looked at her and she saw something flicker in his eyes. His mouth quirked up in a half smile.

"Sort of," he agreed. He turned back to the wall with a long sigh. "You have some well thought out plans here. Good for you. It should be a breeze finishing things off, provided you can find a contractor."

He cast his eyes around the room, as if taking it in for the last time, and something in her wanted to reach out and stop him from leaving. Which was weird, because yesterday she couldn't get him off her property fast enough.

"You should probably make sure they agree with your vision wall before you hire them, though," he continued, taking a few steps to the door. "A few trades thought I was crazy for not completely modernizing everything. Much as I hate to see it, they'll probably take one look at you and think they can walk all over your plans."

"Would you... consider finishing... the renovation?" Her words sputtered the same way her steps stuttered as she followed him to the door. She regretted it the second she saw his back stiffen.

Damn, damn, damn. Her mind raced to find anything she could say to take the words back. Or at least paper over them so they didn't undo their fragile truce.

He spun around, looking at her with incredulous eyes. The tension was a physical thing that rolled off him and surrounded her.

"I'm sorry, that's a dumb idea," she said, mortified at the hopeful lilt that crept into the last word, making it a question instead of a denouncement.

He turned away, scanning the room again. He walked through the area the island had occupied, spun, and walked back. He rubbed a hand over the back of his neck, his face mirroring a dozen thoughts that seemed to buzz through his brain.

A small spear of hope kindled in her. Would he agree? Her fingers rose to fiddle with her earring and she instead pushed some hair behind her ear, not wanting him to read her nervousness again.

"Katy, I..." he began, his voice gruff. He closed his eyes and pinched the bridge of his nose in that way she was getting familiar with. "This place has been my dream for so long. It's breaking my heart just to stand here, knowing that it's in your hands now. I'd love nothing more than to see my plans... your plans come to life. But there's no way I'd have the heart to see it through."

He didn't meet her eyes, his eyes looking near her knees.

"I'm really, really sorry," she rushed out, her hand on her chest. "That was a stupid thing to ask. I understand completely..." He spun and walked to the door, cutting her off.

She followed him, wanting to stop him from leaving but not knowing what she could say or do to make that happen. He startled her by pivoting, stopping her a mere few feet from him.

"Here," he said, holding out a card. "I don't think you will, but if you change your mind about selling the house, call me first. Before you call a realtor. I promise to make an offer above the market value."

She looked at the white card hovering between them and reached out to take it. The minute he let it go, he turned and walked out the kitchen door. She watched through the window as he drained his coffee in a gulp and threw the cup in the back of his truck.

He started the engine and gave her a short wave and a grim smile as he backed down the driveway. For the first time, she was ashamed at the narrow opinion she'd had of Mitch. He was someone with a dream, just like she was. He hadn't turned his back on this house the way she had, acting like a privileged princess who could afford to walk away from an inheritance.

She blew out a long sigh and let herself wallow for a full minute. Then she headed upstairs to change and get back to work.

※

Three hours later, she slumped in her low chair and plugged her phone into its charger. Setting up an account with the water department had been slightly more complicated than she expected, but she figured it out. She'd even cheekily requested Jonah come to turn on the service. The other utilities had been easier to arrange by comparison.

Her quest for a contractor was less successful. Everyone was booked solid through spring. She hadn't wanted to call Brad Denby, Gordon's recommendation, when she found out he was two hours away. Paying someone four hours a day for travel made her nervous, but he'd been her last hope.

As she settled in to responding to some work email, her phone buzzed. She recognized Brad's number.

"Katy Williams," she answered.

"Hi, this is Brad Denby. You called me?" His laid-back Aussie twang echoed what she'd heard on his voice mail.

"Hi, Brad. Gordon Carlisle recommended I call you. I'm renovating the old Grant house, and I'm looking for a contractor. Actually," she paused, deciding to lay it all on the line and hope he had a heart. "I'm desperate for a contractor. Do you have any availability before the next millennium?" She finished on a laugh.

"Actually, I do. I'm familiar with the house, too. The previous owner was a friend of a friend, and he had me come out a few years ago to make a roof repair."

"That's perfect," she said, not even caring that he'd probably overcharge her based on her desperation. They planned for Brad to walk through the house in a few days and she ended the call.

Just as she added the appointment to her calendar, an urgent email came in from her boss. Scanning the body and all its exclamation marks made her groan. She stood up and stretched before settling back in to do several hours of damage control for a client's urgent request.

8

The cold air of a clear November dusk gave the main street of Cranberry Hill an eery pink glow. Mitch pulled open the door to a small bar at the end of the street, stepping into an even darker atmosphere. He grimaced, thinking how it matched his mood.

"Hey, Mitch," Harv greeted from behind the bar as he pulled out a stool.

"Harv," he greeted shortly. The lanky man threw a coast down on the bar and cracked open a Heineken, setting it in front of him.

"On the house," Harv said, waving him away when he reached for his wallet.

"Appreciate it," he said, tipping the neck toward the bartender then taking a long pull.

"It's a bitch of a thing, that woman showing up," Harv said, loading some pint glasses into the washer behind the bar.

"Yup," he said, not really wanting to talk about it. The heart break he'd mentioned to Katy that morning was hitting him.

"Everyone's in town is pissed about it," Harv continued. "Some guys were talking about running her off."

"No," Mitch said immediately, his voice sharp with anger. He scowled at Harv, whose eyes widened. The thought of Katy alone in the house and any of Harv's goon friends showing up sent a shaft of fear through him. "I've made my peace with her, and if I check in and hear about anything, I'm coming to find you," he finished, pointing a finger at him.

"Okay. No problem, Mitch."

"Spread the word," he demanded, this time making his point by punching a finger on the bar.

"Sure thing," Harv said, and cracked open another Heineken for him. "Also on the house," he said, his voice a little shaky as he put the second bottle beside the first one.

Mitch pulled in and blew out a long breath, some of his anger and fear dissipating.

"Thanks. Maybe you could also spread the word that Katy's a nice lady, trying to do right by a heritage house. Same as I was. She deserves a fair shake from this town."

"You got it," Harv agreed, giving him a nod.

Mitch finished the first beer and set the bottle where it would be easy for Harv to grab. He thought back to the morning and his meeting with Katy.

He'd been cocky, thinking he'd show up to find a shivering, helpless woman. His first twinge of regret was seeing Jonah drive by, having already turned off the water. But that had melted away when he'd seen the heiress on the porch, smug and mocking as she faced him. A small spark of respect had leaped in him, looking over her practical yet whimsical kitten-face PJs, snow boots, knit hat and parka.

She'd had not a scrap of makeup on and seemed okay with that. Definitely not his idea of a privileged east coast trust fund baby. But a switch had flipped in him when he saw her plans on the wall.

Her sketches of the new room dimensions, her notes about colors and fixtures, the pictures and swatches to back everything up—all of it had blown him away. He kept all his plans and ideas locked in his head, parceling out tasks on his to-do list. Not only was her vision laid out in color, it's like it had sprung from his own brain. And that was before he'd seen her print-out of the Bakelite switch.

For a fleeting second, the term "soul mate" made sense to him.

He'd looked at her expressive face, full of excitement about her plan. He'd seen the raw passion in her eyes, which mirrored what he'd felt with every board he'd cut, and a sense of kinship buzzed through him like he'd never felt.

When she'd made her hesitant request, his first instinct had been to say "Hell, yes!" But right on the heels of that thought came fear. His lifelong instinct was to keep women at a distance. They were only ever trouble. And this one, with this project, could inflict some serious damage on him. He didn't know why, because she wasn't his usual type, but deep down he knew some of his instinct had melted away.

"Hey, Marsh!" Harv called, as the bar momentarily lightened when the door opened and closed.

"Harv, draw me a stout, will ya?" Marshall called, and seconds later a heavy hand whacked Mitch on the shoulder. "I'd ask how it's going, but I already know," Marshall said, pulling out a stool beside him.

"Yup," Mitch agreed, wondering how many times he'd have this conversation.

"Let me know if you want me to come down on her with some bylaw infractions. I'm good at writing obscure citations. You'd be surprised at what's against the law in Cranberry Hill," Marshall suggested.

"No," Mitch said, looking at his friend. "What's up with everybody in this town?"

"Don't go there, man," Harv warned Marshall, sliding him a pint glass with a grimace. "He already chewed my ass about my offer to drive her away."

"Yeah, but I was joking," Marshall said, sipping his dark ale.

"Yeah, I was, too," Harv said, but looked uncomfortable as he turned away.

Mitch looked at Marshall, noticing his jeans and jacket.

"You're not on shift?" he asked.

"Not until late tonight."

"Do me a favor. Add the inn to your standard route." He glanced over at Harv, who was chatting with two rough-looking characters. "I'm worried about people taking this inheritance interloper thing too far. And let me know if there's any trouble. I feel responsible."

"Sure thing, I'll check in tonight and let you know if anything seems off," Marshall agreed. "But I'm sure it's mostly talk. You're well-liked around here, Mitch. Everyone wanted to see you turn that property into something."

"This town needs to get behind Katy, now. She's the owner." He hated that he sounded pouty, but there it was. "I've seen her plans, and they're great. Not that different from mine."

"I'll spread the word," Marshall said with a nod. "If people know you're okay with it, that you support her, they'll support her, too. You'll see."

"I hope so," he said, taking a long drink of his beer.

"Crystal wants to see the new Marvel movie this weekend. Why don't you and Suze come with us?"

"I don't know," he said.

"C'mon. Tony Stark will shake you out of your funk."

He frowned at the idea of being in a funk. Pouting over a few beers, fine. But a funk?

"Okay, that sounds like a good idea." He pulled out his phone to text Suze. "She's got work, but if she can't make it, I'm still..." He didn't have time to finish when Suze's response buzzed in his hand.

Love to, sweetie!! Suze replied. *Sweetie?* Since when did she call him anything like that? Since he'd moved in she'd texted him more and more. It was almost stifling.

"She can go," he said with a frown. "Hey, do you know anyone around here that's renting an apartment, or has a basement suite?"

"No, but I can ask around. Are things not working out at Suze's place?" Marshall asked with a laugh.

"Not exactly. I haven't had a roommate since college, and I'm figuring out why."

"Man, I felt the same way before I moved in with Crystal," Marshall laughed his eyes looking off as he remembered. "She pushed for it, and I didn't want us to break up over it, so I did. But now?" He took a long drink of his stout. "It's heaven. I love coming home to her."

"Why?" Mitch asked, genuinely stumped. It had been something he dreaded with Suze, her cheery greeting starting to grate on his nerves every time he walked through the door. He liked it better when she was at work, which created a low-grade churning of guilt in his gut.

"I don't know. It's comforting, I guess. She doesn't do anything in particular, it's just a sense of having someone there who loves you. Like getting into a warm bed," he said with a self-conscious laugh.

"Wow, that's downright poetic, Marsh."

"Mock me all you want, but it's how I knew."

"Knew what?"

"That she's the one. I'm going to ask her to marry me, man. This weekend. And I'm nervous as hell about it."

Mitch's eyebrows almost shot off his face. He knew Marshall to be a serial dater. He should have guessed the writing was on the wall when he moved in with Crystal, though. That had been a shocker.

"Congratulations," Mitch said, which had Marshall looking at him with skeptical eyes. "No, really. That's great. I can definitely see little red-haired Marshalls running around."

"Yeah, me too. That was another thing. I'd never thought about kids until I met Crystal. She's never talked about it, but after we'd been living together for a while, my thoughts started going there. I started thinking about weird things, like how close our place was to the elementary school. Shit like that." He shook his head as if he was still trying to wrap his head around it.

"Huh," Mitch murmured. An emptiness settled over him. He was usually relieved when a friend announced they were getting married. Happy for them, but glad he knew that wasn't for him. Now he was confused. Losing his house had messed him up more than he thought.

"I wish I could set you up with someone who made you feel that way," Marshall said.

"If you want to help me out, set me up with some design work. Now that my innkeeper days are behind me, I'll need some way to pay the bills. And if you're a God-fearing man, maybe say a prayer."

"For what?"

"That Katy changes her mind about selling." He smiled grimly at Marshall as he finished his Heineken.

9

Katy floated awake to the sound of seagulls, but also the sound of rain. The difference today was that her nose was warm. The electricity had come on late last night, just in time to rescue her laptop was about to die.

She swung her flannel legs off the cot and sat up to stretch her arms overhead. She'd been up late fixing her employer's client's campaign that had gotten royally screwed up somewhere between the art department and the newspaper. The wrong ads had run nationally, and tempers had flared.

Her phone chimed, and she groaned, seeing several new emails.

Call me ASAP! said the latest one from her boss. She'd slept through several earlier ones and her heart sank. She needed to be up by five if she wanted to convince him working remotely was a benefit and not a hassle.

"Hi Gene, sorry I missed your earlier email. Did you get my message about the extra make-goods the papers will run for Hawthorne?" She'd negotiated a sweet apology from the newspaper chain, and she hoped it hadn't fallen through.

"I saw that. Good work. But I need you in the office tomorrow.

Hawthorne's people are coming in for a debrief on the whole fiasco and I need you there."

"I... can't, Gene. I'm sorry, but I'm not done with things here." She bit her lip.

"I thought you'd completed the paperwork?"

"I did, but a few things have come up with the house." If he pushed, she supposed she'd have no choice. She crossed her fingers and her legs and closed her eyes. She let her breath go when she heard Gene sigh.

"I guess I can swing the meeting without you. But I'll need you to Skype in. I'm worried."

"They can't fire us, Gene. We've grown their business twenty-eight percent. That's unheard of in their industry." Hawthorne was a time-share condo business, a sector that had seen a severe downturn in the last few years, but their business in particular. They were reluctant to let go of a business model that had stopped working ages ago.

"My head tells me that, but my stomach knots are still nervous."

"Don't worry, I'll call in ten minutes early. When do you need me?"

"Meeting's at nine," he warned. She did the math in her head.

"I'm setting an alarm an hour early so I can go over my notes and the campaign stats to date. Don't worry, Gene, I'm on this," she reassured him.

"I hope so, Katy."

She ended the call and cracked open her laptop. She started assembling the campaign results and felt her belly drop. Despite some ads that were supposed to be running already, the numbers were bad. Terrible. She'd seen clients fire agencies for results not even half this bad.

She made some notes and fired off a few emails. She had to scramble to find some alternatives to drive their social engagement numbers and push people to the promo. She liked one idea in particular and copied her boss and client contact with the idea. Everyone seemed receptive, and she executed the idea.

It was some hours later when she reloaded the stats. Better. She breathed a sigh of relief and got dressed. On a whim, she tried the tap in the bathroom. She cheered when the pipes gave a wet burp and then gushed water. Jonah hadn't been by yesterday afternoon, but he must have stopped by while she was working.

"Sweet," she exulted when the water turned hot on her fingers.

She gave herself a luxurious hand cloth bath from the sink and got dressed. She had grandiose plans of brewing some coffee when her phone rang. The screen showed her Gene's number.

"Hi Gene. Good turn around in the numbers, isn't it?" she greeted.

"Very good. But too little too late, I'm afraid."

"What? They're not that far off from our targets," she said. "They might exceed expectations in a couple days."

"They fired us, Katy."

She wasn't sure what dropped lower, her heart or her butt on the edge of her cot.

"What?" she asked, her voice a hoarse whisper.

"We're out. They appreciated your efforts, but word came from higher up. They're going with a New York company."

Her cheeks puffed out with a long sigh. Hawthorne was their biggest client and the only one she worked on. She wondered what project they'd be shifting her to, realizing she'd have to make a trip back to get up to speed on a new account.

"I'm sorry to hear that, Gene. I know landing them put you on the map. I'm sure other company's are looking at us because of it."

"I have to let you go, Katy," he said, the words rushing out.

"But... what?" For a second she swore she heard wrong. "Won't I just take on another client?"

"We're too lean to keep you on. Bethany and Claire are managing our other clients. There's no room on the payroll with Hawthorne gone, and we brought you on board to work on their account only." His voice sounded as miserable as Katy felt.

"I don't know what to say."

"This will give you time to deal with your aunt's house. And I'll give you an amazing reference, because you're amazing at your job. Truly, you are Katy. I know you'll land on your feet."

"Is this immediate?" she asked, her heart thrumming at the thought of her income disappearing.

"I'm afraid so. In the next hour they'll have revoked our access to all their social media accounts and monitoring dashboards. But I'll having Jill get a final paycheck to you this week." He paused, and she heard a few clicks from his keyboard. "Good grief, Katy, you've taken no vacation in three years!"

"Yeah," she said, thinking how she'd never wanted one.

"Well, your accrued time will be on your final pay. Including a month's severance. You've more than earned it. I'm sorry this happened."

They talked for a few minutes more, but she couldn't say what they'd said. All she could hear was her heart pounding.

She walked into the hall and to the stairs, sinking down to sit on the top plywood step. She squeezed the rough edge of the wood, focusing on calming her breathing so she didn't hyperventilate.

Money would be a problem before long, but the bigger weight on her shoulders was losing her job. She'd been working... it seemed like her whole life. Her first job was born in her foster parents kitchen making fancy coffee for her parents' bridge club on Friday nights. She was ten years old. It had expanded to include making beverages for her father's alumni group on Tuesday nights.

Her parents had been embarrassed by her "entrepreneurial pursuits," as they called them, but the money was impressive. Not a small amount for a ten-year-old child.

Money had become a way to be valued and provide security. When selling coffee had morphed to an after-school care program when she was fourteen, she made heaps of money. All along the way, she called the shots. Every idea she had was successful. Even this job had been her approaching the agency with the idea to pitch Hawthorne.

And now she'd been fired.

That was the scariest thing. She was untethered from the thing that guaranteed her security.

"I just need a new plan," she said to an empty dining room below her.

She jumped up and raced to her bedroom. She grabbed her laptop clumped back downstairs. Dragging the folding chair into the kitchen, she situated herself in front of her vision wall and flipped open the computer.

She flexed her fingers and then looked at her screen. She tapped to select the "Inn Business" folder in her browser and scrolled to her online banking link.

"Show me the numbers, baby" she murmured as she logged in to her account. Next she popped open her renovation spreadsheet. She had a lot of blanks she'd wanted to have filled in by now, namely the contracting fees.

She logged into the utilities accounts she'd set up, two of them able to show her some historical data. She started filling in some blanks and overestimating others based on some web searches on renovation forums.

"Shoot," she said, tension tightening her belly. If these numbers weren't too far off, keeping everything going here would be a challenge. In three months it would be impossible, if she didn't have revenue flowing in.

She'd planned to drive a half hour to the closest Home Depot to pick up a mini fridge and microwave, but ditched that idea to search something out on Craigslist. She spent the rest of the daylight hours negotiating, driving to pick up the items and then seeking a grocery outlet store to stock up on some staples for meals.

Later that night, after locking up, she dragged herself upstairs to get ready for bed. Within minutes she was cozy on her cot, finishing up some loose ends for her boss. She'd start a job hunt tomorrow and wanted to make sure his reference would be nothing but stellar.

Just as she turned up the volume on her laptop's classical music playlist, the sound of a rattling vehicle floated up the stairs and under her bed. She tapped the volume down and could make out the sound of an engine. Then she jerked off the cot, a crash of shattered glass driving her heart into her throat and her body to its feet.

She kicked out of the sleeping bag and ran to the bedroom door, pressing her ear against it and listening.

Laughter of two voices and "Screw you, princess!" echoed, then some banging and the rev of an engine. It sped away, but she continued to listen to the silence for another two minutes, just to be sure.

She pressed a hand to her chest, the fast vibrations of her beating heart easy to feel. She grabbed her coat and looked around the room, not seeing anything that could be used as a weapon. Her mind flashed to the only thing that might work, and she turned the doorknob and flew down the hall to the bathroom.

She pulled on her coat and then wrapped two hands around the aged bath curtain rod and shoved, the metal pole slipping free of the rusted holder.

She creeped down the stairs, holding the rod in front of her. She paused now and then to listen, not wanting whoever they were to catch her off guard.

Walking through the dining room, she flipped on the bare bulb of the overhead light and saw what had happened.

Shards of glass glinted on the floor in the living room. They made a trail from the large window to a brick that lay on the floor. A piece of glass that hung in the window loosened and fell to the floor, startling a gasp out of her.

"Damn," she muttered. She stepped closer to the brick and saw something white on it. When she stood over it, she could read the message someone had scrawled in what might have been white out.

Go home, it read.

Her arms dropped from their ready position until the bath rod rested on her thighs. She lost the fight against angry tears, which blurred her vision and spilled over to her cheeks.

A gentle squeal of brake sounded, and she hurried to the dining room, flipping off the light. She pressed herself against a wall, hearing tires crunch up the driveway. Peeking around the opening to the kitchen, she saw movement through the kitchen door window. It was a light-colored vehicle, and when the engine died, she heard the faint sound of a dispatch radio.

Her heartbeat settled a little when she saw a figure get out with the unmistakable silhouette of a sheriff hat. But then her hands started to tremble.

"Hi Katy, I thought I'd... whoa, are you okay?" Marshall said after she'd opened the door, her trembling hands turning into a shaking body and her hand covering her mouth, embarrassed that she was about to cry.

"I'm... I'm..." she stuttered, backing up when he stepped inside and closed the door. She gave up trying to talk and waved him to follow her into the living room.

"Huh," Marshall said from where he crouched over the brick. "Mitch was right to have me check in on you."

"Mitch asked you that?"

"He was worried that someone might..." he looked up at her and she had the impression he was editing his next words. "Cause some trouble."

"Why would he think that?"

He didn't answer her though, looking at the brick.

"This makes me think it's Cody. He's a local troublemaker. He's done a message on a brick before. I'm surprised I didn't see him when I drove up, if this just happened."

"Does Cody drive? Because I heard a car drive away after this crashed through the window."

Marshall shrugged.

"No, but he's got a few friends who do. One second," he said, pulling out his phone and tapping. After a pause she heard a faint, deep voice that kicked her heartbeat up a notch.

"Hey Mitch, it's Marshall. You were right to have me check in. I think Cody just chucked a brick through Katy's front window."

, she'd be angry that he called Mitch, but she was relieved. Out of everybody in town, Mitch would care most about what happened to the house, even if he didn't care much about her. Marshall chatted with him for another minute, most of the time just making agreeable noises.

"He's on his way," Marshall said. "He'll bring some cardboard and tape to cover that up. You won't be able to get a glazier out until tomorrow. He's offered to stay over, too, in case Cody and his friends get brave enough to come back."

She nodded and hugged her arms around herself, her eyes fastened on the brick. The words on it dredging up all the voices in her head that had plagued her on the drive from Chicago.

"Show me what you've got going on in the kitchen, Katy," Marshall said, tugging on her sleeve and turning her away from the glass on the floor. She shuffled after him, her feet too heavy to take proper steps.

Marshall stood in front of her vision wall, scanning all the pictures and layouts, whistling in appreciation.

"I gotta say, you look way more organized than Mitch ever did. All he had was a scrap of paper and a roll of plans. You've put a lot of thought into this."

She knew what he was doing, and she let him. Maybe touring him through her thought process would get that nagging voice to shut up.

By the time she'd made a carafe of coffee and was laughing about Marshall's opinion on the latest Avenger movie, another set of headlights swung into the driveway.

"Hey," Mitch called, right after rapping on the door and opening it.

"Hey, man," Marshall said. He finished his coffee and set his mug on the board Katy had found and used on two boxes for her coffee station. "I should get going now that reinforcements are here. Katy, don't forget to call your insurance company in the morning. I'll keep you updated on what I find out when I talk to Cody. I know where he hangs out, and I'll head over there now and see if he's around."

"Thanks, Marshall," Mitch said. He stepped over to stand beside her, looking at her even though he spoke to the deputy.

"Thank you for everything, Marshall," she said, giving him a weak smile as he left the kitchen.

"Are you okay?" Mitch asked, his voice low and warm. She hated that she wanted to cry all over again.

"Yeah," she said, her voice wobbling.

"Hey, hey," he said, and pulled her into a hug. "Where's the spitfire who wanted to arrest me not so long ago?"

Her face pressed against the rough knit of his sweater, cool from the outside air and smelling fresh and woodsy. Her head fit under his chin, which he rubbed against her. His hands had been squeezing her arms, but now they slid to her back, holding her.

"She's having a bad day," she confessed.

"Because of a brick? A brick's nothing. Cody and his friends spray painted some colorful ideas about genitalia all over the side of the house when I first moved in. Then a week later they pushed over some fencing. Then they starting stealing tools. Before I locked it up, they'd dragged my drill press halfway onto the road before giving up."

"I don't have insurance," she confessed, letting out a shaky sigh. "I called a few and haven't heard from anyone yet."

"That's not a big deal. I know someone who can come and replace the window. I bet for cheaper than an insurance deductible would be." He patted her back in emphasis, which made her clench his coat as a bubble of emotion rose in her throat.

"And I lost my job today," she wailed, helpless to keep the gulping sobs inside any longer.

"Oh, *cher*, shh. *Pauve ti bet*," he murmured. "My poor little thing, she had a bad day for sure." He'd been holding her before, but now he pressed her closer, as if he could wrap her up and absorb some of her sadness.

It was so nice to let her guard down with someone else. Someone who seemed to understand the setbacks she faced since he'd had the same dream.

"Thank you," she murmured, pulling away when she thought she'd gotten herself under control.

"Yeah?" he asked, leaning back to look at what she was sure was her puffy, drippy and red face. She lifted the long edge of her Hello Kitty top to dab her eyes. "There you go. I see your kick-ass self coming back already." He patted her arms in emphasis and then turned to the door. "I'll bring in some things to cover up the window and then have some coffee. I think I should stay here tonight…"

"Yes," she said, stopping him from needing to justify his thought. She didn't want to stay here alone tonight.

While Mitch went outside, she pulled her foldable chair into the dining room where she could sit while he taped up the broken window. He came back in and made fast work of the task. Then he brought in a broom and cleaned up the glass., he brought in a huge duffle bag and dropped it beside her chair.

"I've got my air mattress and sleeping bag, and I'll sleep down here so I can jump into action if Cody comes back."

"Okay," she said, and got up to pour him a mug of hot coffee. "Do you take anything in it?"

"Nope," he said. And then "Thanks," when he took the mug from her.

"Thanks for asking Marshall to check on me. I figured it would take people around here a bit to get to know me, but I didn't think they'd throw bricks through my window."

"Most of them wouldn't. And when they get to know you, they'll love you."

"Love me?" she asked, some of her old teasing spirit coming back. "That might be a stretch."

He shrugged, looking uncomfortable for a moment. "How about like you a lot?"

"I can settle for that."

"And then tomorrow, I can help you with insurance."

She sighed, thinking about her dwindling bank account but knowing she couldn't cut corners on insurance.

"What's wrong?" he asked.

"Nothing, just going over my budget in my head. It's a bad habit."

He frowned at her, then unzipped his duffle bag. As he unrolled his air mattress and sleeping bag, he started talking.

"You know, I've been thinking about our... situation."

"Our situation? The situation where you want me to sell you the inn?"

"Not exactly," he said, fastening a hose to a small square block and flipping a switch. A fan whirred and his air mattress started to inflate. It was the size of a twin mattress and three times as this as her sleeping pad.

He inflated inflated and nudged it against the wall opposite her and spread out his sleeping bag. Lying on it facing her, he picked up his mug and looked at her.

"I'll help you finish the renovations."

She was shaking her head before he'd finished speaking.

"No, no. I have to figure out my budget before I can get anybody here to quote on finishing the work." She made a mental note to call Brad back. He might not want to make the drive if she couldn't afford him. Those four hours a day for travel time suddenly seemed like an automatic disqualification.

"Look, you need to get this place finished and open for business.

My goal was Christmas, and from what I saw on your wall, your goal was the same."

"I'm going to look for some work tomorrow. I can work from here on my computer, so living off the grid by the ocean shouldn't be a problem."

"How are you going to manage a new job and all the work that needs to happen here?"

"You were doing it," she pointed out.

"I have two year's worth of expenses banked, not to mention the State reimbursing me for the improvements."

"The State will reimburse you?"

"That was part of the agreement," he said, and then he made a face that made her think he was holding something back.

"What? What aren't you telling me?"

"Well, the State will bill you as the new owner."

"What?" she exclaimed, her heart sinking.

"I submit logs of the work being done and my receipts. They keep it all and it's added to the purchase price if they sold it. But you inherited, so it's likely the paperwork hasn't caught up to you yet."

She groaned and slumped deeper into the canvas chair. It made sense, and if she was getting a regular paycheck, she'd just add it onto her spreadsheet.

"Which is why you should take me up on my offer. I'll continue with the renovations and give you the receipts. Once you're open, you can pay me back. Even in installments, if that works better."

She looked up at him with a frown.

"Why would you do that? I'd think you'd be trying to talk me into selling and moving instead."

He sighed and frowned down into his coffee cup.

"There are a few reasons, I guess. First is that I want to see this project through. I think we have the same aesthetic, and nobody could jump in and hit the same completion date," he looked up at her with a self-deprecating smile. "At least in my humble opinion."

"Go on, the next reason?" she said, unable not to return his smile. *Careful, Katy, he's turning on the charm.* She arranged her expression into something more professional, as if this was an interview.

"And second." He looked off into space as if trying to find the right words. "I don't like to see someone bullied. A few of the people in town are maybe a little... too on my side. And that doesn't seem fair."

"Hm," she said, nodding in consideration.

"It's been a stressful day. Just think it over. No pressure. But you're right," he said, a huge grin spreading across his face.

"About what?"

"I'd be okay if you wanted to sell and move, too."

10

Mitch measured and adjusted the long piece of wood on the saw stand. Reaching up, he grabbed the saw handle and squeezed the trigger, pulling the blade of the chop saw down and up in a clean motion. The sound echoed around the big, drafty barn and then faded to nothing when he flipped off the power switch.

The few days he'd spent at Suze's place stressing about the inn, stewing about the heiress and hanging around town being idle had eaten at him. Even though he'd stored most of his materials, cutting these few pieces of crown moulding had set something right inside him.

He didn't like to think about last night. Marshall's call had interrupted a ridiculous argument he'd been having with Suze about letting her wash his clothes.

"You're kind of pissing me off," she'd said, grabbing the clump of socks and underwear out of his hands. "I'm doing laundry tomorrow, anyway. And these were on the floor."

He'd had to grab them back and throw them in the spare room, closing the door and standing in front of it.

"They were on *my* floor, in the room you said I could treat as my own," he defended.

She'd just narrowed her eyes and stared at him.

"Are you trying to keep something from me?" she asked.

"Yes. My dirty underwear."

"You act like I'm crossing a line."

"You are. I like my personal space. I thought I said that when I moved in."

"Yeah, but it's just underwear. I'm doing mine."

"I don't go into your bedroom and gather up your underwear."

"But you could," she said, giving him an innocent smile. "If you wanted to."

His phone couldn't have rung at a better time, but when he saw it was Marshall, his heart almost stopped.

"What's wrong?" he said, before any word of greeting.

Marshall explained, and his heart double-timed from fear to anger.

"I'm on my way," he said, and ended the call. He went into his room, pulling his duffle bag from the closet and shoving most of his clothes into it. It already held his air mattress and sleeping bag and adding his pillow filled it.

"What's wrong?" Suze asked from the doorway.

"Cody threw a brick through the front window of the inn," he explained, hoping Suze wouldn't start another argument about it. "I'm going to check it out and stay there in case Cody comes back and tries something else."

He shouldered the bag and looked at her. She nodded and looked concerned.

"Is Katy okay?" she asked.

"Sounds like it."

"I'm sorry about the laundry thing. I promise to respect your boundaries." Her face was full of regret, and it eased a small amount of his frustration.

"I appreciate it," he told her. "I'm sorry I got upset. I'm a bachelor through and through, and not used to people doing nice things for me. So thank you for the thought."

"No problem," she said, giving him a relieved grin and a quick kiss as he left.

He tipped the two pieces of baseboard from his saw stand and swung them to the sawhorses behind him where three other boards were stacked.

He looked out the open barn doors. It had clouded up and was pouring rain.

A grove of pine and fir trees separated the barn from the house. A dirt path connected the barn and house through the trees, resulting in an oasis of peace where he did most of his prep work.

On either end of the structure were huge doors that opened and could allow a semi-truck to drive right through. The cement floor was rough but level, the dust was contained, and he had enough height to swing around the long pieces of wood he needed to cut. The barn even had a loft that he could convert to more rental space once he'd finished work on the house, thanks to the solid structure of the building.

Well, a loft Katy can convert.

He hadn't seen her that morning, preferring to sneak out and satisfy his idle hands with some work. He hoped she'd take him up on his offer. Even though it was illogical to offer to help someone else realize his dream, the work was therapeutic.

"So much for Operation: Overwhelm," he said to the falling rain. He'd had her right where he wanted her last night. Sad, defeated and within inches of throwing in the towel. But instead of pouncing something had risen in him, wanting to help.

"You talking to yourself, boss?" asked a voice from the opening on the opposite end of the barn. Mitch turned to greet his friend, a local who kept to himself but did odd jobs where he could find them.

Tandy sat on his beat-up bicycle, rain hat and poncho covering his slim body. His face and hands were lined and the stubble on his head, whenever he lifted his cap high enough to see it, was pure silver. Despite his thin frame and age, he had the stamina of someone younger than Mitch.

He'd been invaluable to Mitch, seeming to show up when he needed an extra set of hands. And though he never talked about himself, Mitch thought he must have worked construction at some point. He was too comfortable in all his tasks, using the most efficient way to measure, cut and assemble that could only come from experience.

"You caught me," Mitch smiled, tucking his pencil behind his ear and walking over to the slim man. "This project must drive me mad."

"Well, we're all a little mad, I think. It's human nature." Tandy smiled, lifting and lowering the old Yankees cap he wore under the poncho, as was his habit. "I haven't seen your truck around in a while, but I seen a green car here for a coupla days. Got some trouble?"

"Not trouble, exactly. More like a complication. How much time do you have today?"

"All day," Tandy said, lifting and lowering his hat again.

"Come with me. I put the rest of the crown moulding in my storage unit and could use a hand bringing it back," he said.

"Ayuh," the older man agreed, climbing off his bike and rolling it in the barn to lean it against the wall where he often put it.

They walked down the path through the trees, getting a slight reprieve from the rain, and Mitch handed Tandy his truck keys.

"Crank the heat, will you?" he asked. "I'll let Katy know where we're going. I'll fill you in on everything on the drive."

Tandy nodded and continued on to the truck while he hopped up the stairs.

"Katy?" he called up from the bottom of the stairs. He heard feet drop to the floor and a door upstairs open.

"Up here," she said, and something tightened down in his stomach. Her voice sounded sleepy, and he didn't want to picture her hair mussed and eyes sleepy.

"I'm going to bring some crown moulding back. I should be more than an hour."

She hesitated and then said "Sure," although she didn't sound sure at all.

He headed out before she could draw him into a conversation about the renovation. He realized he wanted to do this more than he realized.

"That must be the niece," Tandy said once they'd started driving down the road.

"Yeah. She's the niece."

"What's she like?"

"Organized."

"Is she nice?"

"She's annoying," he said after a moment's thought.

Tandy hooted his high-pitched laugh and slapped his leg.

"You got trouble, boss," he said, laughing more.

"Why?"

"You like her. And you don't like women."

"I just said she was annoying. How do you figure I like her?"

"It's the way you said it."

"I like plenty of women. All women, actually," he said, glancing at the man who still shook with quiet laughter.

"And none of them annoy you. This one's getting under your skin, ayuh." He grinned.

He wanted to deny it, but Tandy was right that almost everything about Katy got under his skin. But it was because she was ruining his plans, not because of any special feeling. He'd feel the same if it was a man. *Would you?* asked a little voice inside, making him frown. *Would you help some guy finish the renovations?*

"Where have you been staying these days?" he asked, changing the subject.

"I was at the cabin for a few days, but now I'm staying over at Dan's place."

"Man, you have got to tell me where this cabin of yours is. I always hear you talk about it, but I can't find it."

Tandy leaned back and gave another hoot of a laugh. "It's in the trees on the bluff, boss! Can't see it, but it's there."

"I hiked as far as I could into those trees and couldn't see anything."

"You got to look the right way," he teased, which made Mitch shake his head. "You're not ready to find it yet. When you are, start looking from the other side."

"You're talking in riddles," he said, to which Tandy shrugged and looked out the window.

Tandy talked a lot about this mysterious cabin he always visited.

He'd told him it was just down the road in a forest of madrone trees, but he hadn't been able to find it. Part of him wondered if Tandy had made it up, or remembered something that was long gone.

Their trip to the storage unit took longer than expected. Two moving vans had parked on either side of his unit, and they had to wait for one to finish loading and leave before he could access it.

They loaded up several pieces of crown moulding and covered it with a blue tarp. He grabbed a tub of sparkling putty and tools and a few other items before he locked up and they left.

When they pulled into the driveway, he saw a dark green truck parked where he had been. **Denby Contracting** read the sign on the passenger door. He passed by the truck and Katy's Subaru to get as close to the path to the barn as possible.

"Uh oh," Tandy said with a laugh Mitch put the vehicle in park. "Competition's here."

"Brad Denby is not competition," he said, but his jaw clenched.

Brad Denby was an Australian surfer turned contractor. He charmed his clients and then cut corners to widen his profit margin. His work was okay, but Mitch had learned to double his site visits if any of his clients used him. They'd gone toe-to-toe a few times when Denby had strayed from his blueprints by even a fraction.

"I wouldn't trust a pretty lady of mine around him, all the same," Tandy said, his eyes twinkling.

"Tandy," Mitch said, squeezing the bridge of his nose. "She's not my pretty lady."

"But you think she's pretty," he said with a nod.

"I don't... she's not..." He sighed. "Can we just drop talking about her? Please take the moulding to the barn." He fished around in his pocket for his worn list. "If I'm not back, start cutting these lengths."

"Ayuh, boss," Tandy said, taking his list.

He left the man to work and headed to the house, not sure why he felt the need to be present when Katy was showing Denby around. She'd reached out to contractors, and since he knew Denby was friends with Gordon, it made sense she called him.

He could see Katie and Denby through the kitchen door, Katie's hands moving in animated conversation as they stood in front of what she called her vision wall. Her back was to him but on the other side of her, Denby have faced the door. His eyes shifted to Mitch and back to Katy, the corner of his mouth lifting. *Smug jerk.*

"Hi," he said when he tapped and opened the door simultaneously. Katy spun to look at him in surprise, her hands lowering and then clutching each other in front of her.

"Hi, Mitch. This is Brad Denby..."

"Hi, Mitch," Denby said, lifting his hand in an acknowledgement. He hated the way his accent made his name sound one inflection away from 'leech'.

"Yeah, we know each other," Mitch said, lifting his hand to return the greeting.

"Oh," Katy said. "I forgot I called Brad a few days ago."

Out of the corner of his eye he saw her twist her hands back and forth, but he couldn't look away from Denby, who stepped closer to her.

"Katy sounded in dire need of a contractor, and you know it's hard for me not to help a lady in distress," Denby explained, splaying his hand on his chest and flashing Katy a mega-watt smile. She swung a grateful gaze to him.

"I appreciate you coming all this way. Mitch has done all the work so far. Like I said, he's offered to continue."

"And like *I* said," Denby emphasized, bending at the waist in her direction, "I'm happy to help. I can even defer some payments, since you're in a bit of a bind with your job."

"That's very kind of you," Katy said, and gave a funny laugh when Denby turned and bent his elbow toward her.

"Why don't you show me around," he murmured, giving her another blast of a smile when she looped her arm through his.

"I'd love to. It's a gorgeous house."

He hovered in the kitchen, not wanting to trail after them, but not comfortable leaving Katy alone with Denby. He planted himself in front of the vision wall, letting their voices as they walked downstairs to the basement guide his eyes on the layout pinned to the wall.

"These beams are an issue, I believe," he heard Katy say, a lilt in her voice turning the statement into a question. He heard Brad murmuring in response but couldn't make out what he said. Katy's voice trilled in that goofy laugh, and he rubbed his neck.

There was more mumbling as they moved around in the space and then thumps as they walked back up the stairs.

"... and that's how the no-donut rule came into effect," Denby finished, walking into the kitchen and flashing him a grin.

"I have a hard time believing *anybody* doesn't like pastries, but I guess it's possible," Katy said from behind Denby.

Mitch knew the incident Denby was talking about, but he wouldn't rise to the bait the man was laying out.

"Brad says the beam structure looks solid. That's great news, right?" she said to him, her eyes challenging.

"Of course they are," he said, looking at her with mock confusion. "Why wouldn't they be?" He enjoyed watching her shoot him a withering smirk.

"Can I show you the upstairs, Brad?" Katy said sweetly, pointing to the dining room and the stairs. "Feel free to go back to your work out back, Mitch."

"I would, but I want to take a few baseboard measurements," he said, folding his arms to hide the fact that his closest tape measure was in his truck.

"Before you finish the floors?" Denby laughed, raising his eyebrows at Katy. "That's an architect for ya."

Mitch raised his own eyebrow at Denby. The Aussie was laying it on thick with the accent, which seemed to be working based on Katy's body language.

They both looked at him, but he remained silent. He didn't trust a hack like Denby not to talk Katy into all sorts of design changes, and if his presence helped stop it, he wouldn't budge.

"Okay," Katy said with a shrug. She walked ahead of Denby into the dining room.

"Good to see ya, mate," Denby said, his sly wink adding fuel to the slow burn on Mitch's temper.

He stood there while the two of them tromped up the stairs, talking and laughing from time to time. Feeling like an idiot, Mitch jogged out to his truck to grab his tape measure and some paper.

Back in the house, he measured the wall in the dining area. He'd added a notch for a built-in book case, and it was the only place he didn't have exact measurements. After that he measured random things and made notes, all the while straining to listen to their conversation.

He heard nothing that showed Denby was trying to get her to change her design, but he heard a lot of his signature flattery. Mostly, Katy kept directing him back to her questions, which fixated on the existing plumbing and insulating around the existing windows.

"I appreciate you taking the time to look the place over, Brad," Katy said as they walked into the kitchen.

"Not a problem. I know you said Mitch offered to finish the job," Denby said, talking to Katy as if Mitch was leaning against the wall five feet away, "but if he gets off schedule I can step in and help."

"Thank you, that's very kind. Could you send me a quote, just so I have some hard numbers?"

"Absolutely," he said, and they pulled out their phones to exchange contact information.

He knew he was glowering, but he couldn't help it. Denby was coming on way too strong, and he wondered what the man was up to. He knew how to push Mitch's buttons, but he rarely went this hard.

"Have you been busy?" he asked the man, gritting his teeth when Denby held up his phone to take Katy's picture.

"I like to have faces for names in my address book," he told her with a grin. Katy smiled and slid her phone into her back pocket. "I've been busy enough," Denby answered him, and followed Katy when she led him to the kitchen door.

"Thanks again," she said.

"I'll email you some numbers today. Make sure you get something in writing from this one, too," he said, pointing at Mitch without looking at him.

Katy tipped her head and smiled, not in agreement but not dismissing his suggestion either.

"All right. I'm off to grab a donut on my way back," Denby said, including Mitch in his broad wink.

"He's a talker," Katy said after she'd watched Denby walk all the way back to his truck.

Mitch stood in the middle of the kitchen, not sure what was keeping him from going back to his work in the barn.

"I'll get you something in writing, if you need it," he said, irritated at the sudden rise of tension in him.

"If you like," she said with a shrug.

"And for the record, my issue with Denby was around his lax safety rules for his crew."

She nodded, her expression neutral.

"It had... very little to do with donuts," he finished.

Her face broken into an easy smile.

"Something tells me Brad might have a world view of flexible rules," she said. "But he's right about one thing. We should have something in writing that says both of us stay in this until the end. We should be able to count on each other, for scope of work, deposits, terms of payment, that sort of thing." Katy straightened away from the door, her voice sounding strained. "I don't want you to think I'm going to abandon the project."

Some tension in him eased. She was proud. He couldn't fault her for that.

"I won't walk away, either," he said, his voice gruffer than usual. "So I guess you better give me your email address."

11

Not only did Katy type in her email address, she added her phone number. "I already entered your email from your business card," she explained when she didn't hand him her phone.

"All right," he said, shoving his phone back into his work shirt pocket. "What are you up to now?"

"I'm going to work on a supply list for when I'm ready to open. Linens, mattresses, furniture, stuff like that," she said. "There were a lot of things I couldn't fit into Goose, and I didn't think he could haul a trailer."

"Goose?" he asked.

"My car. I named him Goose."

"It sounds like there's a story there."

"Not really. Just a night of wine and *Top Gun* with my best friend, Summer," she said with a laugh.

"Well, that makes perfect sense. Although... doesn't Goose die?"

"Only in the movie. In real life, Goose just breaks down every few thousand miles," she said, tucking her hands in her pockets.

He gave her a satisfied nod and then just looked at her for a few seconds.

"Okay," he blurted, and turned to leave the kitchen.

She walked to the door, looking through its pane as his tall figure walked to his truck and then beyond to the path that led to the barn.

She wandered to the dining room where her chair, laptop and printer sat. Instead of sitting to get to work on her list, she went into the living room. Standing in front of an unbroken window, she mused about what had just happened.

Did two hot guys just fight over me? Well, one hot guy, she corrected herself.

Brad didn't do any fighting, but he did a lot of provoking. He got under Mitch's skin. And she picked up on a jealousy vibe from him. *Interesting.* There was something delicious about thinking Mitch was jealous. Over her.

"Snap out of it, girl," she told her reflection. She made a point of never musing about guys, hot or not.

The buzzing of her phone interrupted her thoughts.

"Hi, Gordon. How are you?" she said when she recognized his number.

"I'm fine, but I think you should sit down. I received the final accounting of maintenance from the state."

She plopped down on the wide window frame.

"Okay, I'm ready."

He quoted a number that knocked all the wind out of her.

"Katy?" he asked, after she stayed quiet for several seconds. "You didn't pass out, did you?"

"Not yet. Geez," she sighed, covering her eyes and squeezing her temples. "That's all and half again what I have in my savings account."

"It's a large amount," Gordon agreed.

"Is it accurate?"

"They sent copies of all the receipts, and all the purchases look reasonable. I called the manager to double check, and he said none of the purchases were outside of the norm, so they had no reason to question it."

"Can I request a review?"

"You can, but they'll still demand payment. They'll just hold it in escrow until the review is complete, which could be a few months."

She covered her mouth now, hopelessness rising and threatening to overwhelm her.

"What about a payment plan?"

"They don't do payment plans."

She jumped and muttered a few choice curse words as she paced the living room.

"I agree," Gordon murmured.

"When do I have to pay?"

"Upon receipt of this notice."

"Can I just not pick it up?" she asked, half joking but half serious.

"This phone call is the official notification, I'm afraid. Although I can fib and buy you a few days to get some financing together."

"I wish I could get financing. My credit cards are close enough to cover what I'm short, and now that I don't have a job I doubt I could qualify for a loan." Her mind raced as she tried to work the problem. "Do you have any suggestions? I'm open to pretty much anything."

"I have an idea, but I don't think you'll like it."

"It's not selling, is it?" She asked, and tried to modulate her voice. "Sorry, I know you're just the messenger. But I refuse to give up."

"That's not what I was thinking. What if you found a business partner? It doesn't have to be Mitch," Gordon rushed on before she could speak, "I know I mentioned that before and you seemed hesitant. There are one or two people I could approach who fund real estate ventures."

She blew out a long breath, turning his words over in his mind. Now that she was stuck with this new dilemma of the State's bill, partnering with Mitch didn't seem so impossible.

She preferred the idea to partnering with one of Gordon's associates, who would be a complete stranger. And someone who might not agree with her vision and just see the house as a property to be fixed and sold. Inns could be risky businesses, as she'd found out when she'd been researching them.

"Can I have today to think things over?"

"Of course. Take a couple days. The hard copy from the State is being mailed, and we can look at the receipt date of that as the legal notice date for the debt."

"Thanks, Gordon. And thank you for your advice. I appreciate it."

Katy hung up and did what she always did when faced with a decision. She paced. From one side of the long living room to the other, pausing to look out at the gray sky and ocean every few minutes.

Then she pulled her chair into the room to face the window and cracked open her laptop. She started a fresh spreadsheet, putting 'Partnering with Mitch' at the top and one column with 'Pros' and the other with 'Cons'.

The pro side filled up with comments like 'shared aesthetic and vision' and 'familiar with the project' and 'permits already organized in his name.'

The con side had only two items—'working with someone I'm attracted to' and 'Mitch is hot'.

"That's the same thing," she mumbled out loud.

She started a new column with the heading 'Things for a partnership agreement' and started listing all the things she worried about. Like assigning an objective third party to settle design disputes and a rough list of responsibilities. For example, he should do as much of the work as possible, but report to her so she could maintain a more formal production schedule. And there should be a master budget with immediate accounting of all receipts.

When she looked over her work, a weight lifted off her shoulders. This was a solid guide for any kind of partnership.

She opened her browser and searched for partnership agreement templates. Finding two she liked, she spent the next hour reading both of them over and making more notes. She only stopped when her hunched posture put a cramp in her neck.

Closing her laptop lid, she stood up and placed the computer on her chair. She stretched and then walked around the covered piano. She hadn't touched it since she'd arrived, but now she folded back the canvas on the long side and pulled out the bench tucked underneath.

Her foster parents had insisted on a year of piano lessons, which hadn't stuck. She had not a single musical bone in her body, but she loved music. She was jealous of anyone who could sit down and play anything, gathering people around to sing. She wondered if Mitch played, or if this was just an instrument handed down through his family.

She opened the cover and slid her fingers over the smooth ivory keys. She pressed middle C, the soft tone muffled by the canvas cover. She closed the cover and replaced the canvas. It felt too much like spying.

She retrieved her phone and found his contact record. She tapped his email address and started tapping.

I have an idea I'd like to talk to you about, she typed, and pressed send.

I'll be done here in another 20 mins, he replied.

The twenty minutes were an agony for her, as she changed her mind, changed it back, and then changed it again.

"It's not failure to partner with somebody," she argued with herself. She wondered if Summer's rich boyfriend could make her a loan. But that idea made her queasy. She didn't like Nick and partnering with him felt like a bad idea.

"All done," Mitch called after opening the door. He stomped his feet on the porch and she heard the door close behind him.

"I'm in the living room," she called out, and put her laptop on the rounded end of the piano, the lid partially open.

"What's up?" he asked, shouldering out of his coat and draping it on the far side of the piano. His dark hair was damp and curled against his neck behind his ear, and his cheeks were flushed red from the cold air outside. She could imagine the fresh smell of sweat and cold air mixing from where she stood.

"Katy?" he prompted, his hands on his hips.

"What? Oh. Right, well, I've been thinking and I have a proposition for you."

"Okay."

"You don't have to decide right away. Or even... by this weekend. And you can totally say no, you won't hurt my feelings or anything."

"All right."

"But just let me finish before you ask questions."

"Okay."

"I've been thinking, and maybe... what I mean is, I want to suggest a partnership. You and me. On the inn."

He just stared at her, and though she tried to read his expression, it was blank.

"An official partnership, with an agreement that we get Rally and Gordon to approve on our behalf," she waved a hand between them, and then kept talking, realizing her greatest worry was that he would say no. "We'd spell everything out so there were no misunderstandings, and we'd keep..."

"That sounds good," he said, with no hint of emotion. As if he agreed that ham sandwiches sounded good for lunch.

"That sounds... what?"

"That sounds good. But I tell you what. I'll pretend I want to think about it, then tell you on Saturday that it sounds good." This time he smiled. It was a nice smile, she decided, neither gloating nor pitying. She was grateful for that.

"Okay, then. That was a lot easier than I thought it would be."

"Easy for you, or for me?"

"For me," she said with a short laugh. "Definitely for me."

"It was easy for me, too. I mean, I'm sure it will be easy for me once I decide. I'm thinking about grabbing some lunch. Did you want to come along?"

Every cell in her body said yes, as she took in his broad shoulders and twinkling eyes, but her practical side won over.

"I have a lot to do here. And I have some ham in the little fridge that I should finish. Thanks, though," she said, disappointed when he seemed okay with her decision. She gave herself a mental shake.

Business partners and nothing more, she scolded herself. Besides, he has a girlfriend. His attitude to Brad had more to do with their working relationship than jealousy.

"I'm going to clean up in the upstairs bathroom, if that's okay?" he asked, pointing a thumb toward the stairs.

"Sure," she said, watching him walk to the stairs and take them two at a time.

Instead of making a sandwich as she'd planned, she turned back to her laptop. After a few clicks, she'd emailed her idea to Gordon along with a question about preparing her own agreement to save on legal fees. Gordon replied, agreeing with her.

She settled into her chair and got to work, waving when Mitch returned and said goodbye.

12

Mitch leaned back in the theatre seat, trying to get comfortable as the giant superheroes and villains on the screen battled each other. Suze sat to his right, riveted to the screen and clutching her neck whenever Thor appeared. Marshall and Crystal sat to his left.

It was a movie he'd wanted to see for weeks, but his thoughts kept drifting to thoughts about Katy. *Thoughts about their partnership*, he corrected.

He hadn't seen her much for the last couple days. He'd gotten into the habit of getting up early to do errands. Thursday, he'd brought the kitchen cabinets back, and yesterday morning he'd had Tandy help him lug his bigger power tools back. Both times when he'd returned to the inn she'd been out running errands, a sticky note explaining that on the door. He suspected she was keeping her distance, but he wasn't sure why.

This afternoon, Saturday, she'd caught up with him in the barn.

"I'm officially presenting you this partnership agreement for your consideration," she said, looking nervous as she handed him a brown envelope. A glance inside showed several pages held together with a thick clip.

"I'm glad you gave this to me in person, instead of... I don't know, posting it on the kitchen door with a sticky note," he commented, not meaning for the words to sound as harsh as they did.

But her eyes just twinkled.

"Don't think I didn't consider it," she murmured.

"Am I that scary?"

"This whole partnership idea scares me. I'm not used to having to rely on other people. It's like... marrying a stranger."

"Really?" he said, taking a closer look inside the envelope. "Is there a ring in here, too?"

She looked like she might poke him but thought better of it.

"I'm going to a fabric store to look at samples, but if you want we can look at it tonight?" Her small smile brought out the dimple he'd been avoiding all week, and he almost said yes.

"I... can't," he said, drawing out the last word as he remembered his movie date with Suze, Marshall and his girlfriend, Crystal. She nodded and stared at him, expecting him to explain, but a strange reluctance kept him silent.

"No problem," she said after several quiet moments passed. "Maybe tomorrow?"

"Yeah."

"Okay," she said, tucking her hands into her coat pockets. "See you later."

As a business partner, she was surprising. And intriguing.

"I love Chris Hemsworth!" Suze whispered hotly in his ear, startling him. The whole audience laughed. He laughed along, not hearing what the funny line was. He tried to glimpse his watch without being obvious, but there weren't enough bright sequences in the movie for him to see it. Marshall had suggested they grab a bite and a drink after, but something about Katy being alone in the house bothered him. Nothing had happened since the brick through the window, and Marshall had assured him he'd given Cody a serious warning, but he still had this low-grade unease.

Suze leaned into him again, laughing and squeezing his arm. He smiled at her, pushing thoughts of Katy and their partnership aside. He focused on Suze and all the reasons he'd first started seeing her.

She was his kind of woman. They'd connected right away and hooked up right after. Without explicitly saying it, they'd agreed to be exclusive, and that had been as serious as it got. It was a good fit for him. She may not care one way or the other when he got carried away talking about his plans for the inn, but she was a good companion and fun to be with. Every friendship had tradeoffs, right?

Even though she drove a beat-up Subaru—that she'd named, no less—he still believed Katy was a high maintenance kind of woman. She had an innocent, wide-eyed vibe, and he wondered if she'd had many serious relationships. She looked young too, but she was obviously a college graduate. At least she seemed smart enough to be.

It intrigued him she knew marketing. That would definitely fill a gap in his knowledge—he was crap at marketing and networking. He could tell, with her personality, she'd be great at that. He could picture her talking to their guests, sitting on the porch while he was doing some yard work.

What am I doing? He heard the record needle screech in his mind. *I'm on a date with another woman!* He forced himself to pay attention to what Robert Downey Jr. was doing.

Two hours later, after a coffee and danish with Marshall and Crystal, he and Suze were in his truck. He'd pulled up in front of her place, but made no move to turn off the engine.

"Aren't you coming up?" she asked, perplexed.

"I should check back at the inn," he said, saving himself from saying "check in with Katy" at the last minute.

"Oh, okay," she replied, sliding up against him and running a hand down his chest. "How long will you be?" she murmured. She pressed a soft kiss on his mouth and looked at him with sultry eyes.

"Uhhh, I might just stay over. I'm sorry, but she and I have a lot to go over tomorrow, and it's already late..." He squeezed her roaming hand to emphasize his apology, but also because its movement was annoying him.

"Okay," she said, making a face at him. "But you're the one missing out. Chris Hemsworth gets my engine going." She planted a firm kiss on his lips and slid back to the passenger door. She zipped up her coat and slung her purse over her shoulder.

Opening the door, she darted through the rain to the narrow door that gave access to the stairs to her apartment. Mitch waited until she was inside and then returned her wave and drove away.

He drove faster than usual, eager to get home. *To the inn*, he corrected himself. As he rounded the curve, and the house came into view, he saw that the main floor lights were on and his heart gave a little jump. *Unless she left them on and went to bed.*

He pulled into the driveway and saw Katy through the kitchen window. A pink bandana held her hair back, and her black coat covered what looked like a plaid flannel shirt. He parked the truck and jogged through the drizzle to the porch.

"I think black winter coat and PJs is a good look on you," he said after he closed the kitchen door and got a full view of her matching plaid bottoms.

"Thanks," she replied from her crouched position by the mini fridge as she looked through its contents. "Summer said if I didn't own plaid, I'd get kicked out of Washington State."

Mitch rocked his head from side to side as he weighed her explanation. "Most likely," he agreed.

"Did you have a nice night?" she asked, taking out a green juice and facing him. She gave it a good shake and then banged the bottom on her hand, making the lid pop.

"Yeah, we saw the new *Avengers* movie."

"Oh, those are great. Chris Hemsworth is the perfect mix of funny and hot."

Mitch rolled his eyes. "That seems to be the consensus." He took off his coat and hung it over the sidewall of the island he'd moved in the other day. He stretched his arms over his head to stretch and wandered into the living room toward the piano. She followed him.

"I thought you would be a lot later than... 11:30," she commented, checking the phone from one of her jacket pockets. She unscrewed the cap from her drink, licked the inside, and dropped it in her other pocket. She took a sip from the bottle and smacked her lips in appreciation.

"I was tired." He uncovered the piano and pulled out the bench, lifting the lid and lightly touching the keys. He played a few chords and then hit a single note a few times.

"Can you hear that?" he asked, playing a chord again. She shook her head and leaned an elbow on the piano. He played an excerpt from a Strauss waltz, the airy notes floating in the room. "It's a little flat. I'll have to get it tuned."

He continued to play. Despite his claims of tiredness, his mind felt sharp and his fingers itched with the energy to play. Katy turned to lean both arms on the piano, resting a cheek in one palm while her other hand held the juice bottle.

"Your fingers don't sound tired."

"Yeah, weird, isn't it?" He made a silly face and marveled at his second wind.

"Did you take piano lessons? You play really well."

"You may not believe this, but I was the five-year-old sensation of Point Coupee Parish, Louisiana." He unleashed his Louisiana drawl on the last four words and added a zydeco flourish on the piano.

"A sensation?" Katy's eyes sparkled. "Do tell."

"Well, one time after church, I wandered up to the front where the old piano was. According to my mama, I climbed on the bench, looked at the sheet music, and just started playing. Somewhere in my storage unit, I still have the newspaper article. 'Five-year-old Musical Sensation' was the headline." He switched from Strauss to another song, forever burned into his memory.

"Wow!" Katy leaned closer, craning her neck so she could watch his fingers fly expertly over the keys and shake her head as she listened. "What are you playing? It sounds familiar."

"'Beautiful Savior.' It's the song I played that day."

"Do you remember that day?"

"I feel like I do, but I probably only remember the fuss afterward. And the newspaper photo. They had me pose in front of the piano, holding the sheet music."

"What happened after that?"

"According to my mama, teachers were falling all over themselves to take me on as a student. So I took lessons for several years, and then I got a music scholarship to the University of Virginia. Which I turned into an architecture degree." He played some very serious, heavy Wagner.

Katy frowned. "But why? You're so good."

"There's a big difference between a freak skill of recognizing and playing characters and patterns on sheet music and bringing those notes to life. Technically, I was born with this skill. But I couldn't infuse the music with life. Much to the dismay of every teacher. I was too wooden, they said, to be a great performer. And what I knew... I just knew. It wasn't something I could teach."

"Do you compose?" Katy wondered, her juice forgotten and her chin now resting on her arms so her eyes were almost level with his.

"Oh no," he said immediately. "To create music, you have to be in touch with something inside yourself, in touch with your emotions and be able to translate that into music. That is definitely beyond me. However—" He played a little ragtime and morphed that into a Beatles song. "—I'm a hit at parties."

She smiled and her sleepy eyes pulled at something inside him. "Why architecture?" she asked, the words ending on a yawn.

He remembered the exact moment he'd fallen in love with building structure. "My first summer at the University of Virginia, there was a trip to Washington D.C. It wasn't so much my first sight of a single building, although I have some favorites; It was a more instant understanding of what buildings could represent. The power they could have on your emotions. I never had that feeling about music. Even for simpler projects, when I'm walking through a house to get a feel for what the remodel could be... I feel a singing deep inside me. That probably sounds dumb to you." He looked over at her to see her eyes closed and a soft curl had fallen in front of one eye.

He stopped playing and leaned toward her, close enough so he could easily reach forward and lift the curl back. The strand was so soft. He placed his hand in front of hers on the piano's top. Her light breathing tickled the small hairs on the side of his hand. Without thinking, he leaned even closer. He just wanted to smell her hair. The fresh, sweet scent hadn't left his memory since he'd pulled her against him on the stairs. But somehow, on the way there, his lips ended up on her forehead, and then her cheek, and as she lifted her head, he caught her questioning "Wha—" with his mouth. For the briefest of seconds, her lips moved in time with his, gently tasting and pressing. And then they were both standing straight up and staring at each other in shock.

"That was all me," he said in a rush. "I apologize. I got caught up in the moment; it won't happen again. Really, Katy, I mean it. I'm sorry." He watched her eyes go from sleepy to startled to confused to... something he couldn't define, but if he guessed by the way she touched her lips, he would say she wasn't outraged.

"That's okay. Let's just agree, from here on out, we're business partners."

"Yes. Agreed. Business partners." He held out his hand, which he noticed wasn't steady.

"We can be friends too" she amended, reaching out to shake his hands and then pausing, "but *business* friends," she said, raising her eyebrows to prompt his agreement.

"Absolutely. Business partners and business friends." They shook hands, and Mitch sat back on the stool, looking down at the keyboard and trying to calm the jitters that raced through his body. *Get your head in the game, man,* he chided himself. He couldn't slip up like that, not if he wanted to make this partnership work.

"I'm going to go to bed. Goodnight," Katy said, and she picked up the rest of the green juice and shuffled through the doorway to the stairs. He listened to the cadence of her footsteps on the stairs and to her room. Her door gave a muted *click* as it shut. The rain pattered harder against the roof, and the distant sound of the ocean hissed. He touched his own lips, wondering at how they tickled. *Dammit.*

13

Katy smiled as she felt the hands on her face, the lips on her mouth. She backed away to look at Mitch, and as she started to speak, a blues piano riff came out of her mouth. She stopped and tried to talk again, only to have the same piano riff come out again.

She opened her eyes and saw the white ceiling over her. Her phone played the blues riff again beside her pillow.

"Hello," she mumbled, disgruntled that the phone cut her dream short.

"Hi, Katy. It's Rally. Do you have a minute?"

"Yup. Go ahead." Katy awkwardly unzipped her sleeping bag and kicked it off. Either her flannel pajamas had kept her too warm or where the dream was going had raised her body temperature.

"Mitch emailed this morning to say you two are forming a partnership and asked if I'd represent him. Do you have Gordon representing you?"

"Yes, I do." Katy rubbed her eyes and held the phone away while she yawned. Looking at the screen, she saw it was 9:00 a.m.

"Did you give Mitch a digital copy? If not, it would be helpful if you could email one to me."

"I can do that." Katy thought for a moment and decided to be honest. "It was just a template I bought online. I wanted to save a few dollars."

"That's not a problem," Rally responded without hesitation. "But there are a few things about conflict resolution that they might overlook. I'll send Mitch a list of questions for you two to consider, which may not be in your agreement. Are you comfortable with that?"

"That's fine, thank you," Katy said.

"Great. There are also a few steps to setting up a partnership LLC, but you don't really need to pay me or Gordon to do it. The Washington State business center website has all of that information."

"Thanks, Rally. I appreciate it." Katy hung up and grabbed her laptop, searching for the partnership agreement and emailing it to Rally. Afterward, she stretched her arms overhead, enjoying the feel of all her muscles waking up. Maybe a few sun salutations would shake the last of her sleepiness away.

She raised her arms straight up and then bent over until her hands were flat on the floor. She paused until she could feel the back of her legs stretched out and comfortable and then jumped her feet back until she was in a plank position. Then she slowly lowered until her chest brushed the ground, pushing up so her shoulders and head were high. After a ten-count she reversed the steps and started over again.

Her mind drifted to her dream as she continued her yoga routine. That kiss last night hadn't been *all* his fault. She'd felt him move her hair and kiss her forehead, her cheek. She'd been moving her head so she could kiss him full on the mouth. His shocked response had caused her to jump back more than his kiss had. She felt guilty that she'd let him take the blame and then scuttled away so she could fantasize where it might have gone. She had not fallen asleep right away. Just looking at her empty sleeping bag made her imagine seeing him in it, if they had let that kiss develop into something more.

"No, Katy, no," she warned herself. She needed a distraction. Maybe she should call Brad and ask him out. She was sure he wouldn't turn her down. The thought of it, though, wasn't all that exciting.

Crap, she thought. She didn't want to have romantic feelings for Mitch. It was a distraction from their project. Besides, he was dating Suze. She thought about that for a second.

Maybe for Mitch, the kiss had just been a weird late-night confluence of feelings. Maybe Suze had shut him down and he was dealing with his own frustration?

She pulled on her clothes, feeling no closer to a solution. She checked her email on her phone and there was the one from Rally. After a quick read-through, she was impressed. Rally had given them a lot of questions to answer, which hadn't been addressed in the agreement she'd downloaded. She finished pulling on her thick socks and short boots and went to find Mitch.

She only had to follow the sound of the saw to find him in the barn. He wore a red flannel shirt under a green puffy vest and clear safety goggles wrapped around his glasses. Even buried underneath work clothes, he was sexy. She waved her phone at him to get his attention, and he flipped the switch to turn off the saw.

"Hey, good morning," he said. He stood stiffly by the saw, lifting his safety glasses. Then he leaned against the saw table. And then he stood up straight, shuffling his feet.

"It's okay; you can relax. Last night's kiss was as much my fault as yours. Let's put it behind us and move on."

Mitch blew out a sigh and relaxed. "Sounds good."

"Rally sent me a list of questions we should consider for our partnership, and they sound fantastic. I think we should go over them and add them to the agreement.

"How do you want to handle that?"

Mitch leaned against the saw and rubbed his jaw. "How about we go over all that at lunch today? A working lunch."

"Sounds good," she said. "My plan was to work up an advertising schedule, but other than that I've got nothing going on."

"Tandy will help me with trimming out the living room this morning. That should take us right up to lunch."

"Okay. I'll make sure I'm not in your way. Is that the man I see riding around on his bike?"

"Yup, that's Tandy. He's a local who's been helping me out. He's a good guy."

"Ah. Nice. Well, I'll let you get back to work." They both stood for a moment, and Katy had a strange sensation of not wanting to turn away. Mitch lowered his safety glasses in place and continued to stare at her. She stared back for a moment and then turned and headed to the barn doors. After she walked through, she heard the hum as the saw started up again.

She settled herself into the camp chair that she'd dragged to the far corner of the front room, facing the big windows and the gray ocean sky. Her work quieted the butterflies that had swirled in her tummy the moment she'd walked into the barn.

She opened a copy of a campaign calendar she'd used for a lodge in Northern Michigan. They were offering a winter package for the first time to see if they could launch an off-season revenue stream. She thought it could be comparable to what they wanted to do for the end.

What *they* wanted for the inn. Their inn. *Quit mooning*, she berated herself.

She dug out some stats for the lodge's campaign. She knew it wouldn't provide direct relevance to running an inn on the West Coast, but it would give her some knowledge about what customers were interested in for vacationing at Christmastime. She reviewed the campaign report to see what recipients had clicked on and made some notes on a separate spreadsheet for herself. Well, for herself and Mitch.

The thought lit a frisson of excitement in her and her feet tapped a little staccato beat, making her laptop bounce. She'd never been in any kind of relationship, friendship or otherwise, where she and her partner were so strongly on the same page about something. So invested in the same thing. And in the inn, it connected with who they were; At least it felt that way to Katy. Her attraction to him made her nervous. She usually kept the upper hand in romantic relationships and guarded her feelings so they couldn't control her. So opposite to her aunt, it turned out. She was determined to stay in control with Mitch, which meant no romance.

Lunchtime rolled around in no time, and Mitch came in to get cleaned up.

"How's the work coming?" he asked, poking his head around the corner of the living room.

"Great. I have some interesting insights to share with you about it."

She smiled. She noticed movement behind Mitch and saw Tandy hovering in the doorway.

"Tandy, this is Katy. Katy, this is Tandy," Mitch made introductions.

"Hi," Tandy said, tweaking his hat and looking shyly at Katy. She stood up and put her laptop on her chair.

"Hi, Tandy, it's nice to meet you." She approached Tandy and held out her hand. He stepped inside to shake her hand then returned to the threshold of the doorway.

Mitch pointed him to the mini fridge. "There's some egg salad in there and juice. Help yourself to whatever you want."

"Thanks," Tandy replied, removing his hat and stepping gingerly into the kitchen. "I forgot my lunch."

Mitch glanced over to Katy. "I'll change my shirt and then we can go." Katy nodded and went back to pack her laptop into its sleeve. Mitch ran up the stairs, and Katy returned to the kitchen.

"Have you lived in Cranberry Hill for a long time?" Katy asked.

"Ayuh," Tandy said with a nod, "I was born here. I was in the army for a spell, but I came back."

"I'd love to learn more about Cranberry Hill. I've never been to the West Coast, but I'm looking forward to making it my home."

"Ayuh, you'll love it." He tweaked his hat and gave her a smile. "If you can stand the rain."

His weathered cheeks looked like they had permanent stubble, and the worn baseball cap was loose on his head. He peeked in the fridge and took out a juice. He turned away to look out the kitchen window as he drank. Katy respected his shyness and stepped outside to wait for Mitch on the porch.

Mitch and Katy drove to a restaurant called the Reach in Mitch's truck. Mitch gave her a short history of Cranberry Hill as they drove.

"This property here, behind the inn, used to be a cranberry farm. The owners were hit by a disease that killed half the bushes. It used to be a big operation until then. That was maybe… twenty years ago, I think. Tandy could tell you more. Harvesting technology changed and with the drop off of their production, they couldn't afford to keep up. They tried to adjust their business to farm blueberries, but it was a hard market. The business just died. The family still owns the property, but they only use it as a summer home. The fields are overgrown and aren't likely to be used for anything for quite some time."

"What do you think of the 'Cranberry Hill Inn' for a name? Seems fitting." Katy smiled at Mitch and then turned back to watching the scenery as they drove the winding road toward town.

"It does seem fitting," he agreed.

They pulled into the Reach's parking lot about thirty minutes later. It was fairly empty, and they sat at a table at a window. They placed their order and Katy pulled out her laptop.

"I'll take notes as we go."

"Sounds good," Mitch approved, sliding his mug to the edge of the table as another server came over to pour his coffee.

"Hi, Mitch," she said with a wide smile. "How are you?"

"I'm great, Bailey. How've you been?"

"Pretty good. We miss you Thursday nights," she singsonged, rocking on her feet as she waited for his response.

Mitch shrugged. "Not only am I renovating, but I'm about to go into business with Katy here. Katy, this is my friend Bailey."

"Hi, Bailey." Katy smiled and got a glimpse of a smile before Bailey turned her attention back to Mitch.

"You can't get free even one night?" she wheedled.

Mitch looked at Katy. "We had a poker group on Thursday nights," he explained. He looked back to Bailey. "Nope, not even one night. And then once we open, I won't even have time to go out for lunch." He laughed, sliding the coffee in front of him and turning his attention back to Katy.

"Darn. Oh well." She shrugged. "Enjoy your lunch," she said, including Katy in her look this time, and strolled back to the coffee station.

"Is there anyone in town you haven't dated?" Katy murmured and then clapped a hand over her mouth. "Sorry about that," she said, grimacing. He had such an easygoing way and a confidence in himself that she knew he would be a magnet for any woman. She couldn't begrudge him that, but she needed to keep some of those thoughts in her head.

"Don't worry. Honestly, you're probably right." He laughed, and Katy laughed with him.

They spent more than two hours going through Rally's questions. Their discussion covered the detailed job duties they each would be responsible for, how they would handle decision-making and conflicting opinions, the percentage of the company they would own, the amount of investment each would have in the partnership, and how they would handle dissolving the partnership.

Katy shared a little of what she'd learned from the email marketing campaign for her client, which Mitch seemed interested in. She'd also sketched out a bullet-point list of what needed to happen for marketing if they wanted to soft open at Christmas but have one or two rooms booked for New Year's. They also looked at a rough budget Katy had started. Mitch filled in some materials costs they'd still need to allow for.

"I'm glad you're handling the marketing and bookkeeping part. That is definitely not my strength," he said, relieved.

"And I'm dangerous with anything sharp like a saw, so I like our division of duties too."

Katy saved her notes and closed her laptop. "Wow, we covered it all. That was almost too easy," she murmured, knocking on the wooden tabletop.

Mitch leaned against the booth's seat, swirling his third cup of coffee as he looked at her. "Can I ask you something?"

"Shoot." She nodded.

"Why did you wait so long to claim your inheritance? I don't want to pry; I'm just genuinely curious."

"You're not prying. It's a long story, though."

He made a point of looking around the empty restaurant.

"I don't think anyone's in a rush to get a table," he said.

"True. Well, Aunt Penny was my mom's sister. My mom died when I was little. My grandparents wanted nothing to do with me, so my Aunt Penny took me in. I have some wonderful memories of my short time with her, but then she handed me over to social services. For years, I'd always wondered why Aunt Penny didn't want me. I hated her for it. When I found out she died, I didn't care. I'd spent years telling myself I didn't want her either. So I rejected anything that had to do with her, including the inheritance. Summer helped me see it differently. She knew I wanted to start my own business and this could be it. I'd helped our landlady turn her home into a boarding house, so I thought I could do that with the inn."

"I can't imagine a family not wanting to take in their own in a situation like that. Especially a young child."

She sipped her coffee and debated telling him everything or keeping the last thing to herself. The worst thing. His expression wasn't smug or even curious. It was caring.

"My mother was a drug addict. She died of an overdose, and my grandparents didn't want anything to do with her. That included me. That's how I ended up with Aunt Penny for a short while. Years later, when I was getting ready to go to college, I decided to look my grandparents up. I had a pretty big chip on my shoulder, and I wanted them to know I was going to school on a full scholarship without their help." Katy looked down at her hands on the table, remembering doing the same thing years ago as she sat across from the old, dour-looking couple in a roadside café.

"What was their response?" Mitch asked, eyebrows pulled down in a line over his eyes.

"I think they were relieved I didn't want anything from them, first of all. Then they made it clear they didn't think either of their daughters amounted to much, but maybe I would make something of myself. I had envisioned things going differently, but then every young person's dream is to make the villain in their story feel regret, isn't it?"

"Probably," Mitch agreed, but his expression remained somber. "I wonder why your aunt didn't keep you. It sounds like you never reconciled anything with her before she died."

"She wrote me a letter when she was dying."

"The envelope that day in the café," he said, as the puzzle pieces fell into place.

"Yeah. She explained how her husband, who she'd been dating when she'd taken me in, didn't want an instant family. He'd said I was a deal breaker, basically. Hence she left me the inn as a way to apologize, I guess."

"I guess that's one way to do it. I looked into Clinton Grant when I found out he owned the house. Your aunt inherited a massive estate when he died. She really didn't leave anything else to you?"

"Nope. She left all her other holdings to her charities and the foundations whose boards she sat on. Only the inn came to me."

"Shit," he said, shaking his head. "That's messed up."

"Yeah. My birth family is.... There are just some people you'll never understand. At least I'm nothing like them. Or like my Aunt Penny. I've always had the philosophy that I'm never going to let a man have that kind of power over me. Ever."

"Hear, hear!" Mitch tapped her coffee mug with his own. "I like independent women. So, what happened after your aunt gave you up, if your grandparents didn't want you?"

"I was in a few foster homes, but finally settled in for the long term with a doctor and his wife. I grew up in Boston. It's funny, because they were well-to-do people, but I rejected all of that. I was always introduced to their friends as their 'foster daughter.' So I applied to a tiny college down South and got a scholarship, because I wanted as much distance from them and their money as possible."

"I can't blame you. It can't be fun to always be reminded you're adopted."

"It's not," she acknowledged.

"Do you stay in touch with them?"

"Oh yes," she said, sipping from her coffee. "We're on good terms. We've never been incredibly close, and I think we're all happy with that."

Mitch leaned forward, his eyes searching her face. "So let me keep track of this. Not a rich east coaster."

"No," she agreed.

"Not from a privileged family, exactly."

"Not in the way that matters to others, no."

"Independent and resourceful."

"I like to think so."

"And business savvy and intelligent."

"Definitely yes to that." She smiled.

"Sounds like a perfect business partner to me," he said and smiled broadly.

"I agree. Aren't you glad you didn't charge me with trespassing?" she asked, making him laugh. "What about you? What's your background?"

"Let's see. You know about my skills at the piano. My architecture degree." He paused as he had a sip of coffee, his eyes fastened on the dark liquid for a moment. "I grew up in a shack in Louisiana. We had nothing that wasn't borrowed or found or traded for. When I went to college, I told my friends my father was a fisherman, but in reality he dredged a small tributary off the Mississippi and sold whatever he found. Sometimes it was old crawfish traps, sometimes metal things he could sell as scrap. I have an older brother who moved away as soon as he could. I haven't heard from him in forever. My mother had work on and off as a waitress. She'd bring home leftovers from the restaurant which tided us over when we didn't have enough food."

Katy was rapt. She wouldn't have guessed in her wildest imagination that someone had as broken a childhood as she did. "Are you still in touch with your parents?"

"My dad died the year after I went to college. He drowned and his body washed up near where he kept his boat. My mom remarried and had kids with the new guy almost immediately. I was never really welcome around their house, which was fine by me."

Katy watched his face, devoid of expression yet his eyes were bright and intense. Their server came by and refilled their coffee mugs. "Look at us," she said, "two lost souls who figured out how to plant their feet on the ground."

"I don't know about lost. We both seem to know what we want. How about... instead of lost, we say we're untethered from the past?"

Katy watched him sip his coffee as she mulled over the feelings she had about her own past. She wasn't sure she could say she was untethered from it. Her aunt's letter had stirred up some murky feelings for sure. "Untethered," she mused out loud. "I'll drink to the possibility." She tapped her mug against Mitch's.

The ride back to the inn was quiet. When they got to the house, Mitch asked her to go with him to look at something in the barn.

He switched on the work lights and pointed to a shadowy corner. "I rigged something up, since I had the wood," he explained, gesturing to a structure near his workbench. Katy stared at it until the form took full shape in her mind.

"A desk!" she exclaimed, looking at the rustic combination of wood slats that made up the surface and sides.

"I broke down the pallets that the appliances had come on. I figured you'd need something to work on, since you'll be running marketing and accounting." Mitch shrugged, and Katy couldn't help but walk around the desk and look at it from every angle. Some little bubble of emotion swelled within her, and she couldn't make eye contact with Mitch for almost a minute.

"I love it. Nobody's ever made anything for me before. Thank you," she said, embarrassed when her voice came out low and gruff.

Mitch lifted a shoulder again, but said nothing. Katy walked over to him and silently wrapped her arms around him in a hug. He carefully hugged her and then stepped back. After a second, he walked around her to the desk. "Which room do you want it in?" he asked.

"Can you put it in the living room? I love looking out at the water while I work," she asked. He effortlessly picked up the desk and walked out of the barn with it. Katy trailed after and then darted around to open the kitchen door for him.

"Thanks," he murmured, and angled the desk to get it through the doorway without scraping the doorjamb. She followed him to the living room and pointed to the back wall when he looked at her questioningly. She quickly slid the camp chair behind it and sat down. She sat a bit lower than the surface, but smiled as she ran her hands over the desktop.

"You got the wood so smooth," she admired, taking off her coat and rolling it up to sit on it. "If I add another pillow, the height will be perfect. Thank you, Mitch! It's lovely." This time, she thought she saw Mitch's cheeks redden a little.

"Oh, by the way, here's a rough schedule I've been keeping to." He handed her a folded, handwritten list of to-do items with deadlines. "Maybe it would be helpful to make a spreadsheet to keep us on track.

I've already lost this once, and it's the only copy I have." Mitch held the paper by the corner, letting go as soon as she touched it.

"I'll make up a master schedule around this and print it off for you," she said, gesturing to the printer on the floor.

"That would be great," Mitch said, his eyes on her lips. They tingled in response, and before she could catch herself, she bit one as if it would stop the sensation. His body stiffened, and he backed away.

"Don't..." he said, and she knew exactly what he meant.

"I'm sorry," she said, covering her mouth with her hand.

"That's okay. But I'll be honest with you. I find you attractive as hell, and to keep my focus, I think sometimes I just have to walk away." He inched closer to the kitchen but hovered there, as if he needed her agreement before he could leave the house. His gaze only went as far as her feet.

Katy's cheeks warmed. Part of her wanted him to stay, but she knew he was right. They had to put any attraction aside and focus on the inn. On their partnership.

"Got it. Let's agree that if either of us just leaves a room, there's no deeper meaning to it. Agreed?"

"Agreed." Mitch's voice sounded strained, and he spun and walked away. Katy turned and looked at her desk and hugged herself tightly.

14

Mitch crossed off 'baseboards in living room' from the job list Katy had printed out for him. The last four days had passed with them seeing very little of each other.

When Tandy had helped Mitch install the last of the crown molding, Katy had been out looking at thrift shops for furniture they'd need. When she was in the living room completing the online registration of their partnership LLC, Mitch stayed in the barn prepping materials for the next tasks. Tomorrow, he was expecting the countertops for the kitchen, and she had plans to shop for curtains and other window coverings.

They communicated back and forth by text, asking and answering questions with ease.

But oddly, all the times they'd sought each other out to discuss something face-to-face, it had turned into a disagreement.

"The switches for the bathroom should be white. Aren't most bathrooms white?" she'd asked when he'd double-check with her on the brown Bakelite switches.

"I thought you liked these. They're cheaper and they'll go with the stained wainscoting."

"Stained? I thought the wainscoting would be painted white. Isn't bathroom wainscoting always white?"

And it had gone the other way too.

"Why don't we have shutters or roller shades for the front room? It looks better. Cleaner," he'd suggested.

"Curtains are softer and make a room feel more cozy."

"But in the afternoon, shades will be better at blocking the sunlight, and the room will be cooler."

"We're on the ocean. Why would we want to block our guests from watching the sunset?" she argued.

He didn't know if it was sexual frustration or plain annoyance he felt when he'd watch her act cheerful and bubbly with everybody else but be cool and distant when she talked to him.

"Is something wrong?" he asked her once, after they'd met with a local guy who agreed to grade their driveway.

"No. Why?" she asked in the cold voice he'd gotten used to.

"You seem angry."

"Well I'm not." Her voice was short and clipped, and he only barely bit back saying "See!"

It had left him feeling pissy, so he'd texted Suze to see if she wanted to grab dinner one night—which was tonight. He knew it was petty, but Suze's instant reply of **You bet, lover!** made him feel better.

"Mitch," Tandy called from the barn opening, bringing him out of his daydreaming. "I finished painting the main bedroom downstairs."

Mitch took off his safety glasses and pinched his nose then looked back at his job list. He found the task and crossed it off. "That's great, Tandy. If you have time today, do you want to cut in the paint on the walls in the upstairs bedrooms? The two closest to the bathroom?"

"You bet. Also Katy says to tell you Rally and Gordon are here." Tandy dipped his head at him and returned to do more painting at the house.

Mitch gritted his teeth in frustration. Soon she'd be sending Tandy to communicate all the time. He unpinned the job list from the wall and tucked it into his work shirt, turning to walk up the path to the house.

He paused on the porch as he heard Katy speak his name.

"Mitch is amazing. I can't believe how far we got this week," she said. "We'll be ready to advertise for a New Year's getaway."

Mitch smiled to himself, squaring his shoulders a little.

"Mitch is great," Rally agreed.

"He's a true craftsman with finishing," Gordon added.

As their talk turned to what furniture Katy was planning to use throughout the house, Mitch entered through the kitchen door. "Hello, hello," he called. The women and Gordon returned to the kitchen, and Rally walked over and hugged him.

"The place is looking great! And Katy's got the LLC set up. I think the Cranberry Hill Inn is the perfect name."

"Kind of a no-brainer," he said, smiling at Katy, but she looked away. Mitch sighed.

"Here's the draft agreement. You two did well at answering all the questions, so this is very thorough." Rally handing them each a document.

"Read it through and mark any changes you want to make." Gordon handed them red pens.

Mitch leaned against the wall, skimming over the document's five pages. He thought about saying they should add a section about civility, but didn't think it would go over well.

"This looks great. I have no changes," Katy said.

"Mitch?" Rally asked.

"Same for me. This looks good to go."

"In that case, we just need to sign each copy." Rally swapped their red pens for blue ones, pulled out a third copy, and prepared her seal. After they'd signed all three copies of the agreement, she pressed the seal onto the last page of each, and handed them their copies. "I'll file this one with the state, and we're all good."

"We'll send you an email about managing your LLC—annual meetings and such," Gordon said, shaking Mitch's hand. "But you're ready to roll. You must contact the state for an employee identification number if you'll have staff."

"Thank you, both of you!" Katy's voice was just short of a squeal and she hugged Gordon and then Rally. Mitch hugged Rally, and when Rally looked from Mitch to Katy, Katy rounded the kitchen island to hug Mitch. First, it was tentative, but then he felt her excitement take over and she hugged him fully.

"We should celebrate!" she said to the three of them. "Maybe go out for dinner tonight?"

"Sorry, I'm meeting up with some friends tonight," Rally said.

"And my wife is dragging me to a play in Seattle. I'm picking her up in about an hour," Gordon said. "And I've got to run if I want to make it out of the office on time."

Gordon and Rally congratulated them again and left.

Katy spun to face him, looking disappointed.

"I guess that just leaves us. Mitch," she said, holding up a hand when he tried to speak. "I need to apologize for how I've been this week. I haven't been dealing well with this... attraction thing between us. At least not as well as you have, and I'm sorry for being such a pain. I promise I can have dinner with you without acting like a child." She smiled up at him, twisting his gut.

"I've got a date with Suze tonight." As each word left his lips, he watched Katy's expression sink from eagerness to ice. He wished could undo the words.

"Oh," she murmured with a little dignified nod. At that moment, Tandy came downstairs with two cans of paint.

"Mitch," he called as he walked down the stairs into the living room. "These are both green, but they look different. Which one do you want for the bedrooms?"

Mitch looked at the swatch on the top of the cans. "This lighter one is for the bedrooms. The cans of the darker green can come down here."

"Tandy, tell me you're not busy." Katy touched his arm before he could go back upstairs. "Our business just got off the ground, and I want to celebrate. Would you like to go to dinner with me?"

Tandy glanced at her hand and then at her, and Mitch watched a light blush creep over his cheeks. "Oh, I'm not one for fancy dining."

"We don't have to go fancy. Just tell me what your favorite food is and we'll have that."

"Well, I really got a thing for the chicken they sell at the Gas and Go. And maybe some orange soda."

"Done!" Katy smiled at Tandy, but as she turned away, her gaze slid past Mitch without making eye contact, and her smile faded to the barest upturn of the corners of her mouth. She disappeared through the dining room and after a moment he heard the scrape of her chair on the floor.

Dammit, Mitch thought. Should he cancel his date with Suze? Katy's icy eyes weighed on him. He planted his hands on his hips, staring at the opening to the dining room. This was what he wanted to avoid—emotions that interfered with work. That interfered in his careful plans. He had no reason to feel guilty. They'd agreed to not let feelings get in the way, and that's what he was doing.

***

He walked into the Willard's Bar and Grill six hours later. He scanned the dim interior for her familiar face.

"Hey, gorgeous!" She waved from a table in the far corner. When he got there, she rose to give him a long, wet kiss. She even wrapped her leg around his calf and pressed herself full against him.

"Oh, wow, hi," he mumbled between kisses when she let him come up for air. He disentangled himself from her leg, when his first instinct had been to force her away from him. His intention had been for a freewheeling sexual encounter, but from his first sigh of her he knew he couldn't follow through.

"Let's sit down," he suggested, tugging her hand to direct her to her chair, worried she might jump into his lap and continue the make-out session.

"Sorry, I'm just amped up to see you. It's been a while," she said, her eyes darting all over his face and his body, and then drilling into his eyes.

"Yeah, I know. Sorry about that. I'm swamped with everything."

"I know. I get it. Let's eat and then leave, so we can make up for lost time," she suggested, squeezing his thigh under the table. He put his hand on her hand to still it and then lifted it to the tabletop. He looked at her. Her energy felt odd to him, and as he watched her face, he noticed a frantic look he hadn't noticed when he walked in.

"Suze. What's going on?" he asked. He liked Suze. He could tell she was being driven by some emotion, and he hoped his own inner impulse to work out a little sexual frustration, which disappeared at the touch of her lips, hadn't fired her up.

She pulled her hand away and rubbed her temples with her fingers. He could see the wild energy spiral out of her, and she relaxed against the back of her chair. "I don't know," she said. She leaned forward to rest her face on one hand and put her other hand on his on the table. She gave him a weary smile. "Actually, I know. And I feel sick about it. Can I be honest?"

"Of course," he replied, concerned. Serious was the last thing either of them were with each other.

"I met someone. I'm really into him, but he's not into me. I thought he was, but... no. And when you asked me out I thought... you know, I could... work out some of my frustration." She finished on an embarrassed laugh. "That's really terrible, isn't it?"

Mitch couldn't help the laugh that came out. "Suze, we think a lot alike."

Her mouth dropped open. "You too?"

"Oh yeah. Big time."

"With Katy?"

"Yup." He leaned back, ran his hand through his hair, and looked around to get their server's attention. "Can we get two shots of Buffalo Trace and two beers?" The server left, and he turned his attention back to Suze. "I thought the same thing about tonight until you kissed me. I'm so relieved you're feeling the same way, because what I think I really need—maybe what we both really need—is to talk to somebody."

Suze agreed, and talk is what they did. Through an appetizer, dinner, and a shared dessert, they shared their similar stories. She'd had an instant attraction to a guy one day, a guy with a hot accent.

"Was it by any chance an Australian accent?" he asked.

"Yeah, how did you know?"

He told her about knowing Brad professionally, skipping any mention of donuts.

"What a small world," she said with wonder. "Is he a good guy?"

She asked and then threw up her hands. "I don't know why I care, since he's not into me." She shook her head. "Tell me about you and Katy."

"Well," he started, thinking back to the first time he'd met her. "I thought she was everything I hated—a rich, spoiled east coaster, looking to dabble in running her own business. And then it turns out she isn't rich or spoiled. And that she has business smarts. And now she's sexy to me in this whole other way that I wasn't expecting. She's gotten under my skin, and I never let women under my skin."

"Don't I know it," Suze said with a kind smile.

"I'm baffled, because I don't want to jeopardize our partnership, but I don't see these feelings going away soon."

"Hmm." Suze mulled as she sipped her coffee. "Is there something wrong with having both?"

"Just experience. I've structured my life around independence. Why change something that works?"

"I don't know. For love, maybe?"

As he drove home a half hour later, he thought about that word. *Love.* He'd never believed in it, at least not for himself. His stomach roiled as he got closer to home. Maybe he just needed to work more in her presence so they could find an easy companionship, because he definitely needed their partnership to work out. They could be great partners running a great business.

The house was dark when he rounded the bend. He pulled into the driveway and parked. Avoiding the puddles, he walked up to the porch and unlocked the kitchen door. He saw the remnants of Katy and Tandy's chicken dinner boxes on a piece of wood they'd put across the island to serve as a counter. Beside it were two empty bottles of orange soda. He heard a noise from the living room and walked around the doorway to see what it was.

He saw Katy in the faint light through the front windows. She sat sleeping in the camp chair, wearing her flannel top with her sleeping bag over her lap. On her desk, she'd spread out one of her bath towels. On it was a flashlight, a bottle of wine, and two plastic cups. He kneeled beside her and brushed a curl off her forehead.

"Mmm," she murmured, turning her head toward his touch. Her

eyes opened, and he lost all awareness of his surroundings. "You're home."

"I'm home," he agreed, keeping his hands clamped onto the canvas of the chair arm and back. Part of him wanted to scoop her up and carry her upstairs and another part wanted to bolt from the inn.

"I wanted to celebrate, even though I made you mad," she said.

"I'm not mad," he replied.

"I've been trying really hard to just be friends, but it kept... not working."

"It seemed like you didn't want to be friends at all."

"I do. I want to be more than friends, even though we agreed we shouldn't."

He couldn't respond to that. He thought even moving his vocal cords would break this magic spell. The truth was he didn't know what he thought or what they should do. With any other woman, he would have leaned in for a kiss, gauged her response, and then moved on from there. There weren't even signals he had to interpret, she put it all out there: she wanted him. All he had to do was take her upstairs. He'd done this a million times in his life, yet as he kneeled there beside her, he couldn't move.

"Mitch, please kiss me?" She lifted her arm, her flannel sleeve sliding down to show her slender forearm as her hand came to rest near his shoulder. Her pale skin gleamed in the moonlight that shone through the front windows. Her eyes were sleepy, seductive.

He reached for the far leg of the camp chair and shifted her so she faced him. He inched toward her, her legs under the sleeping bag shifting as he drew closer. His hands slid over the sleeping bag and around her hips to her back.

She sighed and her head tipped back, her eyes wide and fastened on his lips. She moved her hands up his arms, to his shoulders, and then one hand curved around his neck, pulling his head closer as the other lifted his glasses up and off. "I've daydreamed about this," she whispered against his lips.

And then his lips sank into hers and it was perfect. Every woman he'd ever kissed, there'd been a period of change, of lips getting to know lips, how they fit and how they moved. The mind getting involved, trying to make sure she enjoyed the kiss, trying to anticipate movements, trying to gauge when to deepen the kiss. He had a plan of seduction he followed, and it had never let him down. But her response threw his plan out the window.

Her lips mirrored his, and it was as if they were moving in magical choreography. The smell of her, the feel of her as his arms surrounded her, the shivers of her body, they were all lines of music that thrummed through him. These thoughts were alien to him, and he wondered what magic flowed through his veins.

And then it felt like too much. Something in him was careening out of control, and it scared him. He broke the kiss off, stunned, his mind and pulse racing. "No." The word stumbled out, more directed to the intensifying emotion he felt rising in him than to her or the kiss.

"Yes," she insisted, moving with him as he backed away. He stopped her by gripping her upper arms and holding her in place.

"I don't know what's happening," he said. He was drowning in a situation he'd normally have full control of, and he heard his breath puffing out in shorter, panicked gusts.

Katy sat up, put her cool hands on his cheeks, and looked into his eyes. It was as if she could read all his emotions. "Breathe," she whispered, not moving any closer. "Just breathe."

He did, and the frantic thrumming in his body gentled. Her hands left his face and rested on his arms, her thumbs moving in soft circles on his biceps.

"We don't have to do this," she stated. Some tension left his body, and he sat back on his heels, pulling her into his chest and tucking her head under his chin. Looking into her eyes was too much for him.

"I'm fine," he lied, tracking his heart rate and willing it to slow. This panic disoriented him. That had never happened to him before. "You're a sweetheart, but I don't think I want to get into a serious relationship. In fact, I just broke things off with Suze so I could focus on the inn."

"What if I don't want a serious relationship, either? I'm attracted to you, Mitch." She pulled back to make her point. "I'm not in love with you, or anything Hollywood like that. I just, at my animal level...

want to jump your bones," she finished with an angelic smile and a flutter of her lashes.

Not love, he thought, *just sex*.

Mitch felt something unwind inside him, and his breathing settled into a normal groove. Nothing serious, no happily ever after, no promises he didn't want to make and definitely couldn't keep. They were on the same page and his previous panic was probably because he thought they weren't.

She shifted to wrap her arms around his neck and press her body against him. A sizzle of wanting slid through his body. Whatever anxiety had come over him a few minutes ago disappeared. A night of fun with a beautiful woman, with no strings? He was up for that.

15

Katy snuggled against him. She wouldn't waste this opportunity. She'd hung out with Tandy all afternoon, and all he'd wanted to do was talk about Mitch—how he was skilled at construction, how smart he was with renovations, how kind he was to let Tandy help him and earn some money.

As a result, she'd had Mitch on her mind all day, but in her own context. Mitch and how his broad shoulders moved when he was hammering up drywall, how his muscular legs flexed when he crouched to lift a piece of plywood, and how his black wavy hair fell over his brow as he marked measurements. She'd been trying to ignore the attraction all week, but now it reared up and demanded action. That's when her rationalizations had begun.

My rule has been no mingling of business and pleasure, but I can manage this, and, *we'll just hook up once and then this will be out of my system.*

So when she'd been at the Gas and Go buying the chicken and she'd seen the selection of wine, something cracked inside her and she'd decided tonight would be the night she seduced him. She hadn't been too worried about Suze. It seemed like they were more fun than serious. But she wasn't sure he'd fall in with her plans to hop under her sleeping bag. He'd been giving her the cold shoulder all week, which had compounded her frustration.

But now, watching his eyes glaze as she pressed against him, and then watching them blaze when she slipped her hand under his shirt to his back, her heart raced.

"*Ça bien, cher*," he whispered against her lips, kissing her again.

His hands reached around to grasp her butt and lift her with him as he stood. He'd trapped her sleeping bag between them, and when he turned to the stairs, she kicked it to the floor.

"No love, no relationship. One night of lust, and then back to business," Mitch said as he climbed the stairs with her.

"Absolutely, just two adults having a night of lust. And maybe another night or two, but nothing more." she agreed with a giggle, kissing the corners of his mouth and then his full lips when he'd finished agreeing with her. "And as adults, you should know I've been on birth control since I was in college. I'm also free of any STDs. You?"

"Same," he said after a long kiss, "except for the birth control. I have protection though."

He continued to climb the stairs, pausing at the top to consider which room to use. He'd moved his bed to a room down the hall from hers.

"I think my mattress is more comfortable," he murmured, his voice getting gruff when she pressed closer.

"Okay," she breathed, her heart thudding faster with his every step.

※

MUCH LATER, SHE LAY UNDER MITCH'S ARM AND LEG, WARM BUT agitated as if all those vibrant cells were shaking her into new thoughts. She looked at the fall of his curly hair as it lay on his forehead.

His broad shoulder tilted to cover her and his muscled arm was heavy across her waist. These were things that had attracted her to him, but now she saw them in a new light. She couldn't shake the impression of being both literally and emotionally trapped by him.

Her breathing quickened, and she worked to calm her thoughts and her diaphragm down. *This is not the way to respond to amazing sex,* she scolded herself. *Just slow down, get a good sleep, and deal with it in the morning.*

And she did, but not in the way she thought she would.

16

Mitch stared down at the curly-haired woman lying in his bed. She snuffled on every breath, almost inhaling the flop of curly hair that had fallen over her face. He wondered if she'd deny she snored or embrace it.

His limbs moved heavily as he pulled on his thick flannel work shirt over his T-shirt. What happened last night? He'd been ready for some fun, non-committal sex, but didn't expect the mind-shattering experience they'd shared. At least... he assumed it was mutual, based on how she was sleeping now.

As he watched her lie there, her flannel PJ top back on, weird anxiety built in his chest. He looked away to find the rest of his clothes. Avoiding the creakiest floorboards, he picked up his boots and sock-footed out of the room.

"Morning, boss," Tandy greeted when he entered the barn.

"Morning." Mitch walked over to review his task list hanging from a nail.

"Late night?"

"Sort of."

"Me and the lady had a nice chicken dinner yesterday," Tandy said, filling a tool belt with screws.

"That's nice."

"She's nice. Bossy though."

"Oh yeah? I didn't notice." He gave Tandy a small smile.

"What's on the list for today?"

"Can you fill the nail holes and joints in the crown molding? If you use the blue stuff, it'll dry in a couple hours. After that, touch it up with the white gloss."

"Sure thing." Tandy moved off to find the tools he'd need and headed to the house.

Mitch made a note on the task list and then stood back. He had no energy, no enthusiasm. That definitely wasn't like him after great sex. Or even mediocre sex. Sex was sex, and it was always a good thing for him. But now he felt... off.

His phone rang, and he found out the countertop delivery would be delayed. *Great*, he thought.

He checked the time on his phone and then dialed a number.

"Hey, Mitch. How are you?" Rally answered.

"Good," he said.

"What's up?"

"Oh, just checking on things on your end." Mitch drew a line in some sawdust with his boot, waiting for her to respond.

"What's happened? Has something bad happened?" Rally sounded worried.

"No. Why would you think that?"

"You sound weird. Unhappy. Or down. I've never heard you sound down before."

"I sound weird?" he stalled.

"Yeah. Something happened, so don't try to BS me."

Mitch paused and let out a long sigh.

"I think I did something I shouldn't have done," he said.

"Oh my God, Mitch, what?" Rally sounded panicked, and in any other circumstance it would have made him laugh.

"I slept... with Katy." He waited for her response, which was a long time in coming.

"You had sex? With Katy? That's it?" she asked.

"Yes."

"You didn't kill her or anything? Your mopey voice is only because you had sex with someone?"

Now she was just being irritating. "Yes, and it's a big deal, because we're just supposed to be business partners. But she was waiting for me with wine and was in her flannel pajama top. It was entrapment," he finished, and then rolled his eyes at the outrage in his voice. *I sound like an idiot.*

Rally was quiet for a moment and then got even more annoying. "You're falling for her," she said. "I never thought you would let that happen. Nothing has ever affected you, not when we were together or in the years since. Not a woman or a job or... anything. Ever."

"I'm not falling for her. I'm realizing I've made a dire mistake, and I'd like your advice on how to undo this."

"Oh, there's no undoing this. Well, you could hide away somewhere and in a few years it will get more bearable," she suggested.

"You're being ridiculous. And no help at all, so thanks for that."

"I specialize in law, not relationship advice. What's wrong with falling for her, anyway? I like her."

"She has a ridiculous foo-foo coffee order, she named her car Goose, and she's not my type. I like women who are more grounded. Practical. Not so... excitable. Plus, we have to work together, and romance should never complicate working relationships. I'm sure there'are a dozen *Forbes* articles about that."

"I can see your point about the coffee thing. The other stuff, I'm not buying. But as your friend, I have a question. I've seen you break things off with quite a few women. You've never asked me for advice. Never needed it, from what I could tell. Why do you need it this time?"

Mitch ran his hand through his hair. "Because," he started, walking to the barn door and looking at the trees, at the sky. "Because... I had no connection with the other women. I mean, I still need to have a relationship with this one. I can't afford for the 'let's cool it' conversation to go sideways."

"Why do you think it'll go sideways?"

"Because I don't think she'll want to end the sex side of things."

"Oh, you were that good, were you?" she teased.

"Yes. I *am* that good." Mitch couldn't hold back the smile.

"At least your ego sounds healthy."

"Seriously, though. How do I break that part off without it affecting anything else? And don't say 'just talk to her honestly.' I need the actual words. Tell me what to say." He grimaced at the pleading he heard in his voice.

"Hm," was all Rally offered before his phone beeped.

"Damn, I've got another call," he said. "Can I call you back?"

"Sure," Rally said, and he disconnected to accept Walt's call.

"Hey, Walt. What's the news?"

"Hi, Mitch. The switch guy called and says he's got enough in to fill your order. He can ship them, but if you want them sooner than a week, you could drive down. Just call him."

"Sounds good. Thanks." Mitch hung up. Instead of calling Rally back, he meandered to the house. The morning air was damp, and he looked down the driveway at the misty sky that hung over the ocean.

Rally was right; this had never been hard for him before. He'd never had to ask anyone's advice about women. He just needed to man up and tell her straight. Maybe start out with something flattering, like how incredible last night had been. Because that was the truth.

He couldn't remember such intensity since... well, some time. He couldn't place it yet, but there must have been a time when he had such an intense experience. Anyway, he could follow that up by saying he needed space. Or maybe that he needed to step back. Or time, he needed time to... to what? He almost walked into Tandy coming out of the house.

"Sorry, boss," Tandy said when the door almost hit him.

"That's okay. Have you got everything you need?"

"Yup. Just going to grab your kneepads, but other than that, I'm all set. What are you working on?" he asked.

Mitch looked inside, toward the stairs. Thinking about Katy sleeping upstairs.

"I'm going to drive to Seattle to pick up some switches. I could get them shipped, but I'd rather have them today than next week." He grimaced at his need to justify his decision to drive to Seattle. To justify avoiding Katy a little longer.

"Okay." Tandy nodded, heading toward the barn.

"Oh, can you let Katy know? I think she's still asleep, and I don't want to wake her. But she'll probably wonder where I am." He didn't tell Tandy she was sleeping in his room. He could figure that out later if she wasn't up yet.

"Yeah, she's nosy that one. I'll tell her." Tandy walked away, waving a hand to say he'd handle it.

Mitch walked to his truck and sat in it for a moment. Since when did driving round-trip for four hours make more sense than spending ten bucks for shipping?

17

Katy's eyes flickered open. She could tell by the gray light that it was past morning and probably close to noon. The lightweight sleeping bag and super comfy mattress also told her she was not in her own bed. Delicious memories floated back, but something else less delicious followed close behind them. She climbs out of Mitch's bed and went back to her room and her phone. Sitting on her less-comfortable air mattress, Katy hit a speed dial button.

"Hello?" answered Summer.

"Can you talk?"

"Yeah. The accountant I'm staking out is scheduled to testify today. The lawyers ran out of delays. But not much is happening yet, so I've got time. What's up?"

"Oh, you know... this and that." Katy played with the zipper of her sleeping bag.

"You didn't call me for 'this and that.' What's really up?"

"Well, Mitch and I... you know... we slept together."

"Woo hoo! Finally! Was it hot? You don't have to tell me, but... was it hot?" Summer's words burst out of the earpiece.

"Yes, it was hot. And a mistake."

"No way is hot sex ever a mistake, but make your case and let's see if you can change my mind."

Katy drew in a deep breath, deciding where to start. "Mitch is great. He's awesome! He's this incredible architect, but he also knows a lot about construction, and the work he's done on the renovation is beyond amazing. And everyone in town loves him."

"It sounds like you're introducing a contestant on the Dating Game. Get to the sex!"

"I can't even describe it. Something happened that's never happened before."

"If this is going to get weird, I might not want to hear it."

"It's not weird. It's like…. How can I explain this? It's like seeing in black and white your whole life, and then suddenly seeing in color."

"Oooh. Wow, that sounds amazing."

"Yeah," Katy agreed.

"You sound sad. What's the problem?"

"It's overwhelming. I don't want intimacy to get in the way or take over our working relationship. Because that's the most important thing."

"I get what you're saying. Seeing in color can be addictive," Summer said with a laugh.

"Exactly. And I have this gut feeling that if I don't cool things down, things could get complicated."

"Complicated how?"

"Like... with feelings and stuff."

"Ew, feelings. You're right—don't taint a great night of lust with feelings."

"Summer," Katy scolded, "take this seriously!"

"You know, if I didn't know better, I'd think you were falling for this guy."

Katy sat up, her back rigid. "Why do you think that?"

"You already admitted you could have feelings for this guy. Feelings equal love."

Katy's mouth opened and closed, but she couldn't think of an argument for that comment.

"Plus, when I asked you about the sex, you told me about how awesome this Mitch is. That's Infatuation 101."

"No it isn't." But Katy's stomach dropped. "Is it? I'm so confused."

"That's another thing! You're the queen of *not* falling in love. Never in my life have I known you to have a problem with a guy. You're my hero in that respect."

Katy sighed and laid back against the pillows on her air mattress. "That's what I thought before last night, that I could keep it light and fun. Stay in control."

"So what's different?"

"Ugh! That's the thing. I don't know! I have this tension in my stomach like I did something wrong. Or like that time I ate that bad burrito," Katy said, and both women chuckled at the memory.

"That's easy then. Lay off the burritos for a while until your stomach gets back to normal. Or do what I end up doing—get so wrapped up in your job that the guy you're with gets frustrated at the lack of attention and breaks things off."

"Is that what's happening with you and Nick?"

"Maybe. Something's definitely off, but we're talking about you."

"The only problem with that idea is this guy is part of my job."

"I didn't say it would be easy. Ooo, I see something happening. I've got to go. Update me later on how it's going. Hang in there, girl. You'll figure it out. You always do!"

Katy disconnected and stared up at the textured ceiling. Summer was right; Katy had never had to formulate a strategy to deal with a guy. And she was the only person in the world who never had "guy problems."

She knew when her interest in a guy was over and that it was time to break things off. Her philosophy was guys are fun, and if you're not having fun with them, there's no point. She'd never seen the purpose in staying with someone who became boring or possessive, which all guys did at some point, in her experience.

"Lay off the burritos," Summer suggested. *The problem was, that burrito was so heavenly*, she thought.

A SHOWER HELPED HER PUT A BETTER PERSPECTIVE ON THINGS. AND it gave her time to prepare a script.

"'Last night was great, Mitch,'" Katy said in the shower as she rinsed the conditioner out of her hair. "'And now back to business, just like we agreed.' Hmmm. 'No commitments and no strings, right?' Yeah, that's better. Maybe I should shake his hand too."

After she dressed, she went downstairs to a silent and empty house. He must be out in the barn. She breathed a sigh of relief and opened her laptop to get some work in. It was some time later when Tandy startled her by opening the kitchen door.

"Sorry to disturb you," he said, tipping his hat at her.

"No problem, Tandy." She checked the time and saw how late it was. "Late lunch, huh?"

"Yup, and I left my sandwich in the fridge." He pointed to the mini fridge that occupied the spot where the full-size fridge would go. He walked over and took out a brown paper bag. "Mitch said to tell you he went to Seattle to pick out some light switches."

Katy frowned. Then she shook her head. She should be relieved. More separation between last night and when they saw each other next would give her time to get her feet on less emotional ground. Tandy was looking at her, his sandwich paused halfway to his mouth.

"You angry about something?" he asked.

"Oh, no, Tandy. Sorry, my work has me distracted." She hoped he'd buy that explanation for her scowl.

"Ayuh." He nodded, taking a big bite. "I'm going to get back at it," he said, and walked out the kitchen door, pulling it closed behind him.

Great, now I'm scaring our only worker.

Katy paced around the living room, linking her hands behind her butt and lifting her arms for a good stretch. Then she repeated it from the front. She tried to figure out where this annoyance was coming from. Sure, Mitch headed out saying nothing to her. What was the big deal about that?

Shouldn't he tell you what he's doing, as a sign of respect for a business partner, and not send Tandy with the message? she debated with herself.

No, he's just running an errand. He didn't even have to have Tandy tell me anything. We had no meeting planned for today, so it doesn't matter, she argued back.

So why are you angry? the other voice taunted. She turned that over in her mind.

Was it because Mitch was doing the equivalent to a dine and dash? Would he freeze her out the way some jerks did once they had sex? She had no idea, since she'd only known Mitch for a few weeks.

"I'm *not* angry," she said to the room, hoping muttering the words out loud would make them true. Wong.

She crossed over to her desk to grab her phone. She'd stop being annoyed and get things back on a business basis like she'd practiced in the bathroom. She opened a text thread with Mitch and thought for a moment. And then another moment. She typed, deleted, and retyped.

Looking forward to seeing the light switches! I'll keep working on the marketing plan, she typed and hit Send.

She regretted the exclamation point after the first sentence Then she berated herself for texting at all. She never texted him.

"Why am I acting like a teenager?" she shouted to the empty room. She put her phone on the windowsill, walked the twelve feet over to her desk, and got back to work. Her new mantra was *Business without lust*.

18

"It's only a dollar more per switch if you want the white. These are reproductions, but here's an authentic one so you can compare," said Rick, who stood behind the counter at the electrical supply store. He pulled out an aged and chipped switch. Mitch's gaze slid between the switches Rick had put out on the counter. A brown one, a white one, and now the authentic one. "You can fix up the original, but I only have seven right now. It might take a while to get enough in to fill your order. Plus they cost about $10 more each, depending on their condition."

Mitch continued to look down at the switches. He picked up one, then another. Then he picked up the heavier antique original. "Weighty," he said, and Rick smiled.

"They come with oak faceplates, which are really nice. Unfinished though. So you'll have to stain them if you want a color other than the natural grain." Rick waited for a response, but Mitch just nodded. "Most people get the brown switches. That was most used back in the '30s and '40s."

"Hm," murmured Mitch. *Not Katy, though. She wants white for the bathroom.* He grimaced. That's the last thing he needed now—thoughts about Katy. "Is it okay if I take a photo?" He held up his phone.

"No problem. Gotta make sure the wife approves, right?" Rick winked.

Mitch was horrified. "No! No, I just want something to remember the difference between the repros and the original." He took a photo of each, and then the three together. "Can I see the switch plates? How many of those do you have in stock?"

"I've got enough for a 200-piece order, which is a lot more than you need," Rick said, as he disappeared into the rows of shelving behind the desk.

While he waited, Mitch looked at his phone, thumbing back to Katy's text. **Looking forward to seeing the light switches!** she'd texted. He could hear the accusation in her words, especially with that exclamation mark.

Damn, he should have told her himself he would get them, that way they could have talked about where they stood. Now he had to deal with the game-playing shit he wanted to avoid, these vague texts. He'd thought she'd be above them. And they *weren't* married, so he owed her no report of his comings and goings. *It was just sex!* he railed at the universe for the hundredth time.

But was it? asked a quiet voice inside him. He'd been pushing that voice away the whole drive here, but now it had found a corner of his brain and hunkered down. *It was more than sex. This woman is more than just a night of fun.*

No, he argued back. His whole life, Mitch got laid. He didn't make love. He didn't "get intimate." He got laid. And when his yearnings had run their course, he broke things off, and either made a new female friend, or never saw the woman again. He figured the split between friend and stranger was 90/10, because he never got involved emotionally and did his best to make sure the woman knew it. He was honest about everything up front.

That's what was so infuriating to him. He'd been honest with her. They'd been honest with each other! This was a casual thing. No commitments. What he couldn't figure out was why she was making it more.

Is she? asked that quiet voice.

"Yes!" he said out loud and then looked around to make sure

nobody heard him. That text, for one thing. She *never* texted him, yet here she was the morning after, following up on him. Each letter in her message felt like a rope cinching him down.

Other women have done this, like Suze. And you ignore them or break things off. Why can't you ignore this one? came the voice again.

He picked up the white Bakelite switch and began clicking the toggle on and off. *Because she's my partner*, he answered. *We're in business together. I'm going to set things straight with her so we can run the inn properly.*

"Here's a few of the plates. Nice, huh?" Rick asked.

"Very nice. I'll take three of the white and the rest of the order in the brown. And face plates for all of them."

"Great. I'll ring that up."

When Rick turned to look after his order, Mitch looked down at Katy's text message and hit Reply. He sent the image of the three switches and typed, **Just finishing up.** And then jammed his phone in his back pocket.

❦

AN HOUR LATER, MITCH SAT IN HIS TRUCK AT HIS FAVORITE TRUCK stop diner on the outskirts of Seattle. Before he went in to grab lunch, he gave Rally a quick call.

"How did the conversation with Katy go?" she asked, not even saying hello.

"Uh, I haven't done it yet."

"Have you been hiding from her all day?"

"No," he said, "I had to go to Seattle for parts."

"*Had* to go to Seattle, huh? I'm calling BS on that one."

"Look, I've thought it through, and I'm going to talk to Katy and tell her we can't be... intimate any more. Like this: 'Even though the sex was amazing, I don't think we should be intimate any more.'" To which Rally laughed. "What's so funny?"

"You sound like you're ready to hurl every time you say 'intimate.' Just say sex."

"Most women want to call it intimacy, don't they?"

"Don't guess. Be true to your own feelings. Katy might surprise you, though. I think she appreciates honesty. She's less of a prissy east coaster than I thought she'd be."

"Yeah, I'm thinking that too. Anyway, you asked earlier why this was hard for me, and it's because my radar is saying she wants there to be more between us. So I want to let her down easy."

"Well, your radar hasn't let you down before. My only advice is don't rush the conversation. Let her have her say for as long as she wants to talk. I still think you're overreacting, but you've spent more time with her than I have. Let me know how it goes."

"Okay," he said, and disconnected. He stayed in his truck, thinking over his next steps. Now that he knew what he wanted to say, he wished he was already back at the inn. But that was over an hour away. He could call her. He pulled her up in his contacts and stared at her number, his thumb hovering over it. His stomach started knotting up again. After several seconds, he tapped on the Message button.

Heading back after I grab a bite. I was thinking about last night. Great as it was, maybe we should only focus on being business partners? Let's talk tonight.

Mitch read and reread the message. He analyzed every word, wanting it to be complimentary, yet open-minded. Brief but practical. He hit Send and then sat still, watching and waiting for the Delivered message to change to Read, and then dreading that it would. He hit the Sleep button and went into the restaurant.

After he got a seat at the counter and placed his order, he put his phone on the counter. *This is ridiculous,* he thought, picking it up. He saw that his message was still just marked with Delivered. Which made him wonder where she was and what she was doing.

She went almost everywhere with her phone. She was always looking at it and googling something, or looking up stats, or chatting with her friend, Summer. Now all of a sudden she didn't have her phone nearby.

Or maybe she's ignoring him. That could be it. Making him cool his heels. It's just... that didn't really seem like her. *I've only known her for a week, give or take,* he thought. It's good to find this out now.

When his server placed his burger and fries in front of him, he dug in and tried to clear his mind of anything except the work he had to do in the bathrooms.

❦

OVER AN HOUR LATER, HE GOT OUT OF HIS TRUCK AT THE INN AND locked up the vehicle. He checked his phone and saw that she'd read his message while he'd been driving, but hadn't replied. *Huh*, he thought with mild annoyance, even though he'd argued with himself that broaching the topic via text was less than admirable.

"Hello," he called when he opened the kitchen door. He heard a keyboard clacking from the living room and headed over there.

"Oh, hey," Katy said with a yawn when he walked into the room. "I'm just finishing up some ad copy. My old boss had a freelance project for me, and the money was too good to say no to. Just... one... second." She continued typing and then saved her work with a triumphant click on the keyboard.

"That's great," he said, amazed again at her skill. She was good, to be sought out like that.

"I saw your text," she told him, closing her laptop and walking around her desk, "and I agree. Sorry I didn't respond to it, but it was a complex project." She made a face that people the world over make when overwhelmed by work.

"No problem. I'm glad you feel the same about last night."

"Absolutely." She nodded. "I thought it would be something we could handle, but I think it was a huge mistake. The biggest mistake I could have made, really."

"Yeah, it's not ideal when we're in a partnership. But... I mean, I don't know if I'd say 'the biggest mistake.'"

"Oh, no," Katy rushed to correct him. "I just meant biggest for me, not you. For you... well, I don't know what it was for you, but it's not something you want to continue, right? Which puts us on the same page. Let's just focus on the inn." She brushed a curl behind her ear and put her hands on her hips. And then dropped them to her sides and then put them back on her hips.

Mitch paused, wondering why her words didn't put him at ease. "It was awkward for me, but not the biggest mistake I've ever made," he ventured.

"Awkward is a good description! Everything felt wrong to me this morning, and having this thing between us—" She gestured back and forth with a hand, her face taking on a distasteful expression, which set his teeth on edge. "—it felt all wrong."

"What thing?" he asked, folding his arms across his chest.

"Well, the intimacy. What you texted."

"I didn't say anything about intimacy. I said last night was great—"

"And it was!" Katy hurried to reassure him, like he was about to explode and she needed to diffuse him.

"But I didn't feel any *intimacy*. It was sex. And I just think we shouldn't have sex any more. And you're right—intimacy would have been a big mistake. Huge! Now I get what you're saying." Mitch injected a sigh of relief into his voice, although oddly he felt none of it. "Let's move on with the inn." She looked frozen, her mouth open as if she'd been about to say more. He wondered if his rejection of her belief they'd been intimate had stopped her.

"You're right. It was just sex." She didn't move a muscle, but he sensed her backing away from him. Coldness crept into her voice. "Although a text was a little harsh to broach the subject, don't you think?"

"Hey, you said our hook-up would be a casual thing, and texting is a casual thing. I wanted to put it out there before anything got complicated." He didn't know how the angry tone crept into his voice, but it was out there now.

"There's casual," she said with a smirk, "and then there's professional. If I had known you wouldn't be professional about this, I would have thought twice about partnering with you."

"You can still think twice about it; we've agreed on the terms of dissolution."

"Oh, you'd like that, wouldn't you?" Her face was red and her eyes shimmered. Part of him wondered how the conversation had gotten so heated. The other part wanted to push her even more.

"I would, actually! I broke things off with Suze to focus on the inn, and now you've lured me into another entanglement."

"I've *lured* you?" Her voice raged. "*You're* the one who carried me up all those stairs. I was the one reminding you we didn't have to go through with it."

"Like I wasn't going to go through with it with you in your flannel top and barely anything else!"

"Yes, I'm an irresistible siren who tempts confused and innocent men—with flannel!"

"Look, why not reach out to your foster parents for a loan and buy me out?" He regretted the heated words when he saw her head jerk back. He rubbed a hand over his beard and turned away from her expression, his anger receding.

"Was that your plan? To piss me off so completely that I'll sell? Hats off to you, I guess." He turned back to see she was collecting her laptop and phone from the desk. "How about you buy me out? That way I can go back to Chicago. It's not like I was fitting in with the locals, anyway."

He was about to disagree, trying to tell her that Rally liked and respected her, when her phone rang. She looked at the caller I.D. before answering.

"Hi, Carson," she greeted with a question in her voice, her eyebrows pulled into a frown. He watched her listen to a muted voice that he couldn't hear. He watched the color drain from her face, and his heartbeat kicked up, pumping away all his anger. "She's.... Is she okay?" Another pause. Then she covered her mouth and murmured, "Oh my God. I'm on my way." She brushed past him, and he had to hurry to keep up with her as she bounded up the stairs to her room, still talking to someone named Carson.

"I don't care. I'm coming out there. That's nonsense. There's nothing here to keep me. I'll see you at the hospital."

Mitch followed her into her bedroom and watched her look around the room. Her eyes skittered over everything as she turned in a slow circle. Her face was twitching with emotion, breaking apart as he watched, and he wanted to hold her close if she'd let him.

"Katy," he said, his throat thick with his own emotion. His arms hung by his sides. If this had been anyone else, he would have stayed downstairs in the living room, choosing to avoid any hint of emotion. But his legs had led him here, and his mind scrambled for words.

"I have to go," she mumbled, pushing a hand into her hair as she continued to look around.

"Go where?"

"To Chicago. Summer... Summer's been shot."

"Oh my God," he hissed, and couldn't stop himself from walking over to her and putting his hands on her arms. She jerked her arms to dislodge his grip, shocking him with her aggression.

"Don't." One word, clipped and cold, froze him where he stood. Finally, the sheen that had been building in her eyes broke and ran down her cheeks in two streams.

"Let me drive you to the airport." The words were gruff and barely made it out of his clenched throat. He knew what her answer would be before she said it, but he hadn't expected her word choice to stab him so painfully.

"I can't be in a car with you. I'll drive myself." She crouched down to pick through the clothes in her suitcase, making a small pile and then shoving them into a shoulder bag. She looked up at him, making steady eye contact. "Can you leave? Please."

Mitch stood still, unmoving, lost. She rose and faced him, waves of anger coming from her that made him half-step backward toward the door.

"I'll leave," he said. "Just let me know how I can help. What can I do?"

With every step he took away, she took one forward until he was in the hallway and she stood in the doorway. "Call Rally and tell her to draw up papers. I'm selling you the business. The inn... all of it." She slammed the door in his face, and he stood there, listening to her gut-wrenching sobs on the other side of the door.

19

Katy slumped against the backseat of the cab as it sped down I-90 toward Chicago's Northwestern Hospital. It was a steel-cold morning and tiny snowflakes were trying to become a storm. She re-read Carson's texts that had flooded in when her plane had touched down.

Summer's doing great. She's on painkillers. They want to operate soon, was the first one.

Summer's on the 3rd floor room 24B, was the next.

Summer's just gone into surgery. Might be a few hours, was the last one.

"Are you visiting family for Thanksgiving?" the cab driver asked. Katy swung her eyes from her phone to look at her in the rearview mirror. She met the kind, wrinkled eyes of an older woman. She wore a green knit cap and black jacket.

"Thanksgiving?" Katy asked.

"Yeah, this Thursday is Thanksgiving." The woman disappeared from the mirror as she checked to make a lane change and then returned a bit to make eye contact.

"Oh. I guess so."

The cab driver nodded. "Those red-eye flights really knock you out, don't they? You were smart to get in early. They're saying the snow is going to turn mean."

"Hm," Katy mumbled with a nod, not even sure what she was agreeing to. *Thanksgiving is this Thursday*, she thought with some wonder.

She'd been in a whole different world out there in Cranberry Hill. *No more though*, she thought. She needed to look for a multi-room fixer upper out here. Maybe around Naperville, where Summer lived. Mitch would get the inn, but she'd make him pay a decent price. As the image of Mitch rose in her mind, she shut it down.

The driver was saying something again, but Katy couldn't listen.

"I'm really beat," she interrupted, smiling an apology at the driver's eyes in the mirror. "Do you think you could play some music? Something without words would be great," she asked.

"Of course," she said, and flicked through a few stations until classical music flowed out of the speakers. Katy tried to thank her, but drifted off to sleep.

※

THIRTY MINUTES LATER, KATY WAS STRIDING THROUGH THE hospital lobby to the elevators, and going up to the third floor. A few hallways later, and she was at Summer's room. As she entered, she saw Carson slouched and snoozing on one of the yellow vinyl guest chairs.

"Hey," she nudged him, watching his eyes open. He was such a replica of Summer, with his golden hair and eyebrows, gray eyes, and a wide smile. She noted a few extra lines on his forehead from the last time she'd seen him.

"Hey, Katy," he greeted, moving to wrap her in a gentle hug. Katy buried her face in his scratchy wool sweater and felt a well of emotion pour out of her in loud gasps. "It's okay," he said over and over as her body shook.

"Is she okay?" she asked when she could get the words out. Carson's eyes were red and damp.

"Yes. The bullet kicked an artery which is what they're fixing now. It tore up the back of her leg a little. Some muscle, which they'll repair.

But they say it's nothing she can't recover from. She'll need crutches or a cane for a while."

"Thank God," Katy said, breathing to steady her racing heart.

"Summer said she's pissed she'll never be a swimsuit model." They both laughed.

"That's our girl." She smiled. "Was it hard to get time away from the restaurant?"

"No. But then I didn't ask. I just left." Carson shrugged and Katy stared at him, surprised.

"Wow! Way to go... I think?" She looked at him.

"That place has ruled my life for too long. Honestly, I've been thinking about getting out of it for a while."

"But... you got your star there."

"I know a Michelin star seems like a big deal, but then the hours and the pressure and the snobbery take their toll. And then something like this happens, and you realize it's all bullshit. I'm hoping they'll fire me, to be honest."

"But they won't fire you, because you put them on the map," Katy said, giving his hand a squeeze. "You're their star chef, literally."

"There's two other talented chefs in the kitchen, but you're right. They're a couple years away from being great. That won't stop me from quitting though. Probably next year, I don't know."

Katy smiled at him and then leaned in to hug him again. "I support whatever you decide, my brother from another mother."

He hugged her back and then got up and pushed her into his chair. He dragged another chair from beside the empty bed across the room and positioned it to face her. Then he pulled a thin blanket from the foot of Summer's bed and draped it over her. He sat down and lifted her feet onto his knees, making sure the blanket covered them.

"Hey." She looked around the room. "Where's Nick?"

"Ah, well it sounds like good old Nick's family had some kind of connection to the shooting. At least that's what Summer thinks, based on a couple questions the cops asked her. I don't know more than that."

"Holy shit!" She didn't want to believe it, but she'd thought there was something a little shady about that guy.

"Anyway, you should sleep." He patted her feet. "You look dead. Summer should be in recovery by now, and back here soon. I won't let you miss any chat time with her if she's capable of it, I promise."

Katy had been about to make him swear, but the coziness of the blanket and her feet on his knees wouldn't let her do any more than nod. Off she drifted.

※

SHE WOKE UP TO LAUGHTER. HER EYES CRACKED OPEN, AND SHE SAW Summer leaning back against the raised hospital bed and Carson sitting beside her, poking her face with the straw that was in a cup of water, saying "C'mon, show me what you got. Is that it? That's all you got?" as Summer tried to grab the straw with her teeth.

"Hey, girl" Katy yawned, pushing herself up and letting the move turn into a long stretch.

"Katy!" Despite obvious exhaustion, Summer pushed herself up straighter and held her arms out, waving her hands to encourage Katy to hop on her bed. Which she did.

"Oh, I'm so glad to see you," she whispered into Summer's white-blonde hair. She felt frail to Katy, and her eyes welled up again. She squeezed them shut and let the tears slip out onto her cheeks. She leaned back to look at her best friend. "And looking so elegant in your pastel green hospital gown."

"You know me. I always have to be runway ready." Summer gripped her hands, not letting her move off the bed.

"You look good but as your honorary sister, I have to be truthful. Your breath is harsh."

"It's the glamour of being in surgery. Which, by the way, check this out." Summer pulled back the covers to show her leg, swathed in thick bandages and bolstered by a round pillow under her knee.

"Impressive." Katy nodded, but couldn't summon a smile. "I'm so glad you're okay. What happened?"

"I was on that stakeout and we got lucky. The guy appeared. One minute, I'm following him with my microphone, and the next minute, I'm lying on the steps of the courthouse and I can't move my leg. Then

I'm in the emergency and the doctor's telling me everything's great, but I've been shot."

"Oh my God." Katy shook her head, holding Summer's hand up to her cheek. "Why...? I don't understand why it happened."

"From what I gather from the cops, the accountant I was trying to interview was the target. I got in the way." Katy could do nothing but shake her head and be grateful it wasn't worse. "And Nick's somehow involved, but I don't want to think or talk about it any more. It's bad enough I'm going to have to give a longer statement in the next couple of days."

"Okay, we don't have to talk about that. What do you want to talk about?"

"Tell me what's happening with you and the inn and the hot guy," she said, settling into her pillows and grinning.

"What hot guy?" Carson asked. "I knew about the inn, but not a hot guy."

"When Katy got to the house, there was a hot guy squatting in it. Turns out he wanted to buy it, because Katy almost didn't claim the inheritance. Long story short, she and the hot guy did the deed, and now I want to hear all the details she wouldn't tell me on the phone."

"Ooo, this sounds good," Carson said, also getting comfortable on the bed. Katy looked at them both, the topic of Mitch feeling like a bruise she'd just bumped.

"Well," she said, shifting her eyes around the room as she tried to abbreviate the story as much as possible. "I'm going to be selling the inn to the hot guy."

"What? Why?" Summer's voice was almost a wail.

"Yeah." Carson frowned. "You drove across the country in Sad Excuse Goose to claim that house. What could Hot Guy have done to make you want to sell it?"

"Hey, Goose is my trusty wingman, and I take offense at your criticism." Katy shook her finger at Carson, who just rolled his eyes. "Things got complicated between us, we argued, and I realized I couldn't be partners with him. End of story. He wanted to run the inn on his own anyway, and I'll get enough to buy a property here, so it's all good."

Both Summer and Carson stared at her with their cool gray eyes, measuring her expression, which she tried to keep neutral. "Nuh-uh," Summer said. "Nice try. Your mouth says one thing, but your eyes are telling me it's the opposite of 'all good.'"

"No one wanted an outsider to start a business in that town. Someone even threw a brick through my window. Well, the lawyers were nice, but that's about it."

Summer's face said she was having trouble comprehending it. "But... you had amazing sex with the hot guy Mitch. You said you felt weird, but I thought you just really liked him. I don't get why you have to sell the inn."

"It doesn't matter. When I get the money for the inn, I'll buy a place here. And you can be my first long-term tenant, now that it looks like Nick will be out of the picture. And if you need a wheelchair ramp or a special elevator...."

"Bite your tongue," Summer threatened, dipping her fingers into the cup of water Carson held and smattered Katy with drops.

"What did you guys fight about?" Carson asked her.

"We both agreed that the sex part was a mistake, and then he got angry."

"Really?" Carson asked.

"Yes. Well, he said we should just be partners, and I agreed and said it had been a big mistake, and then he said—"

"There it is," Carson said, nodding.

"There what is?" Katy asked.

"Nobody wants to hear that they're a 'big mistake' when it comes to sex. You might as well have kicked him in between the legs."

Katy waved her hands and shook her head. "It doesn't matter; it's done."

Summer looked at her. "I don't know. There's something in your voice that sounds off."

"Hey, was he there when I called?" Carson asked. "Because you sounded upset when you answered the phone."

"Yeah, he was there."

"Did he hear our conversation?" he continued, Summer following their conversation like a tennis match.

"He heard my side of it."

"And what did he do?"

"He followed me upstairs." Katy sighed, wondering where Carson was going with this.

"What did he say when you got off the phone?"

"Why does it matter?"

"I'm curious. What did he say?"

"I don't remember. I think 'Oh no' or something like that. I think he offered to drive me to the airport."

"Hm, that's a nice gesture. How long of a drive is that?"

"Two hours, and there was no way I'd sit in a car with him for two hours."

Carson started shaking his head. "Katy, this sounds like a nice guy. Your whole life, you've never dated a jerk. Maybe your argument was a misunderstanding and a little ego... do you think?" he cajoled her, and she frowned at him.

"She sounded totally smitten with him when I talked to her," Summer informed him, and they both looked at Katy.

"Maybe he had mixed feelings about hooking up with you, but maybe he was really into you and didn't know how to handle it. Not all guys are bad. I mean, take me." He smiled, flicking his hair and looking off into the distance in his best male model pose. Both women laughed.

"Yeah, why couldn't I have fallen for you instead?" Katy asked, still chuckling. She stopped when she noticed neither of them were laughing along. They just stared at her. "What?" she asked.

"So you *did* fall for him!" Summer said. "I never thought I'd live to see the day. Katy, you're in love, girl!"

20

A mist hung over the driveway as Mitch exited the kitchen holding his second huge mug of coffee for the morning. He kept his eyes down on the weeds and gravel as he walked to the barn, not wanting to look at the space where Katy had always parked Goose.

He assumed she'd gotten to Chicago safely. He thought about texting, but he didn't. She wouldn't have acknowledged it, anyway. He rubbed his eyes as he thought about the way she'd left. She hadn't let him help her at all, not even to open the door for her. He'd watched her taillights disappear down the driveway and onto the road. He must have stood at the window for an hour. Then he'd roamed the house aimlessly most of the night, his mind replaying their argument and the phone call.

"I'm selling you the inn. The business. All of it," she'd said in a dead voice before slamming her door in his face. They were the words he'd wanted to hear almost from the instant she'd fallen at his feet that first night. And now it was the last thing he wanted to think about.

"Morning, boss," Tandy called as he walked into the barn.

"Morning," he growled, and then cleared his throat and said it again in a more human voice.

"You keep up with the late nights and you'll cut a finger off or something," Tandy warned, going back to stacking trim boards on the far side of the open area.

Mitch watched him for a while. His lanky frame reminded him of his father, at least what he could remember. They were similar physically, which he hadn't noticed before. They were both men of few words, although his father's words were mostly critical of him.

Tandy liked to help and was a hard worker. His father was a hard worker, but preferred his own company. Mitch had always felt his father resented having to take him on the boat when he was little. The day he died, Mitch had been at a piano recital. He'd done very well, taking second place behind someone four years older than he was. He'd been excited to tell his dad, even though his dad thought playing piano was a useless skill. But his dad hadn't come home that night. Or ever again.

"Boss?" Tandy asked, looking at him with concern.

"What was that?" Mitch prompted, shaking away the cobwebs of memory.

"Something's wrong. I noticed the lady's car is gone. Where'd she go?"

"Back to Chicago. Her friend got hurt."

Tandy walked over to him, looking at him intensely.

"What?" Mitch asked him, frowning when Tandy got so close he almost backed up.

"What really happened?"

"She's decided to sell me the inn."

"Why would she do that?" he questioned, surprise on his face.

"She... says we don't get along. That the partnership wasn't working for her. Something like that anyway." Mitch took a long sip of the hot coffee and looked away from Tandy's stare. "We're two very different people. It's probably for the best," he finished.

"Hm," Tandy grunted. "You and me, we're two very different people. We get along."

Mitch didn't know what to say, so he just shrugged.

"Of course," Tandy said with a knowing smile and an elbow dig into his arm, "you don't feel about me the way I can tell you feel about the lady. Is that why she left?"

Mitch ran a hand over his chin and around to the back of his neck. "I don't know. I just don't know." But it was hard to swallow his coffee around the lump in his throat. *What the hell?* he thought. Maybe he did need sleep, because the coffee sure as hell wasn't improving anything.

"I think it's time," Tandy stated, tapping his forearm with a long, crooked finger.

"Time for what?"

"To go to the cabin."

"I don't see how going to your cabin will solve anything." Mitch's chest was tightening in that way he was becoming accustomed to. He hated it.

"At the cabin, there's nothing except the sounds of the earth and nature. It helps a body find peace. You've lost your peace, boss," he explained, as if it made perfect sense. "Also, you need to get away from here and move. You have no energy, no drive. Go to the cabin," he finished with a firm nod. He even gave him a little push on his shoulder.

"But I don't know where it is. You've never told me."

"Start down on the beach at the cliff's edge. Follow it around, all the way around. You'll see the way from there."

Mitch looked at his serious face and thought, *Why the hell not? I'm good for shit around here today*. "Okay, I'll go. Will you be okay here?"

"Ayuh." He nodded and took Mitch's mug out of his hands. "You won't need this, but I do." And he took a long drink. "Get on now. And don't think so much, boss. Just listen."

Mitch watched Tandy take another long drink and then turn back to his work. "Just listen," he'd said. That was a relief. He'd spent the whole night thinking, and it hadn't got him anywhere.

"Go!" Tandy shouted, still facing away from him, and the sharp tone startled him into movement.

It didn't take too much time for Mitch to see what Tandy meant by starting at the cliff. Hidden half a foot below where the water washed up against the rock was a wide ledge. He should have gone back to change out of his work boots, but something about going as he was felt right. It might have been the lack of sleeping talking, but this was a journey, and he meant to follow Tandy's instructions to the letter.

He cleared his mind and listened to the surf. He started inching around the cliff wall, slow-shuffling his feet and dragging his hand along the rough rock wall for balance. His soles seemed to have a good grip on the rough rock, and soon he was around the curve with nothing but the cliff in front of him and the ocean roaring behind him. He glanced back to see good-sized waves being broken quite a way out. *Must be a reef out there*, he thought. At the very least, he wouldn't be washed away.

He sloshed along until he arrived at a crack in the cliff wall. He looked inside the darkness and saw light deep inside. It was two bodies wide, and he continued to shuffle along the ledge which took him right into the crevasse. The air was salty and cold, but at least the wind had lessened. His feet splashed through the water, echoing up the rock wall and back down to ring his ears.

Minutes later, the crevasse opened into a lightened area and the rough rock smoothed out. It seemed to rise as well, and his feet were now only inches into the water. He tried to empty his mind of all thoughts, just listening to his feet splash and far-off seagulls. He trailed his hands over the smooth rock and startled when one hand slipped into a hole.

He noticed it wasn't just one hole; it was a series of natural-looking grooves that had been made in the rock. He looked up, following the recesses all the way up. "You'll see the way from there," Tandy had said. Without questioning it, he started to climb.

After a few minutes of climbing, the wall angled down, so he was more crawling instead of climbing. The walls on either side of him curved around him like a tunnel. At the top, it opened out onto a flat plateau covered with a soggy moss. He turned and was overwhelmed by the endless expanse of ocean.

The gray of the water merged with the gray of the sky so seamlessly it made him dizzy. He stepped back to regain his balance. Then he turned to look at the next wall of rock that faced him. No handholds there, but there were two thick ropes that ran from top to bottom. He followed them down to where they disappeared under a flattish piece of driftwood. He pried at it and it popped off, exposing a water-filled hole. Inside was a folded rope ladder with one of the lines tied to it. He pulled the other line and watched as the ladder was hoisted smoothly up the rock wall.

"Well, well." Mitch smiled for the first time in a while. When the ladder stopped ascending, he looked around for something to anchor the rope to. He saw nothing strong enough to hold it, so he felt inside the water-filled hole and found a hidden anchor pin. He ran the rope through and tied a snug anchor hitch knot. He tugged on the ladder and then tested his weight on it. It didn't budge.

He was halfway to the top when it started to pour. He was extra careful the rest of the climb and finally reached the top plateau. Stones were at either side of the ladder, and another metal anchor was buried into the rock where the pulley hung. He gripped the stones and stepped onto the flat plateau. This one was wider than the one below and turned into a forest of pine and madrone trees.

The hiss of the ocean was more distant, and he turned to be treated to an even more amazing vista. He stared until the rain soaked into him, forcing him to turn and follow a path through the trees, wondering what mystery he'd have to solve next. But there was no mystery. A generous path guided him through the trees then it narrowed until he reached a clearing. There in the center was the cabin.

The building was a hallmark of turn-of-the century log construction. The squared-off timbers were darkened with age and interlaced at the corners. Soggy grass covered the low-pitched roof. An overhang at the front protected the doorway. Two windows—no glass—were on either side of the entrance. Inside, he saw that the other three walls had a similar window centered in each. There was a rustic table and a chair. On the table was a plastic bag. Curious, he opened it and found two rough blankets and two small pillows.

He replaced the pillows and blankets in the plastic bag and paced the interior of the small cabin. It was a single room and smelled of rain, earth, and moss. His feet shuffled across the rough wood planking of the floor, and above he could just make out trusses of the roof in the dim light. He lifted a chair and carried it to the doorway. He sat down, the overhang giving him about a foot of dry space where the rain couldn't reach. He sat and stared at the ocean.

"Don't think so much. Just listen," Tandy had counseled. But this was the perfect place to think. Something had changed last night, and he wasn't sure if it was with Katy or their partnership or with him. She'd been angry for sure. Was she angry when he'd gotten there? He couldn't remember. Maybe. The one thing he saw when he closed his eyes was her face when she said Summer had been shot. Even more than her coldness when she told him she would sell him the inn, the image of the agony on her face stayed with him.

He shook his head and stood up to walk around the small clearing. The rain fell in a steady thickness, hitting the leathery madrone leaves in sheets and flooding his ears with waves of white noise. The rain drenching the leaf-and needle-covered ground released a rich smell as Mitch's boots disturbed the ground cover. He walked the perimeter of the clearing, and then he followed the path back out to the cliff.

The clouds were low, as if the heavy rain had pulled them down, shuttering his previous view of the ocean. The wind gusted, pushing him back to the path. He returned to the cabin and then explored behind it. A path tried to break through the thick, fragrant junipers and sentinels of fir and pine, just to end weakly at thick overgrowth. He returned to the cabin. He walked inside. Then back out. He looked at the path to the cliff, and then he looked at the chair. He sat down.

Listen.

This time, he obeyed. It took a while, but he finally succeeded in letting go of the restless energy that had walked him all over the clearing. He let the sounds and smells of his surroundings take the place of random thoughts that would pop up in his mind. He found he had to do this over and over, but after some practice, the moments of quiet grew longer and longer.

When he opened his eyes, the light was different. His body relaxed completely against the aged chair back. He closed his eyes and saw Katy as she looked the night he was playing the piano. He blinked and saw how she'd been curled up under his sleeping bag. Why was she something he would want to keep at a distance? And now that he'd won—he had the inn—why wasn't he out celebrating? Why hadn't he even emailed Rally to start the paperwork?

He'd told Katy he was protecting their business partnership by breaking things off. The truth was, he didn't know how to have a relationship with someone, and he wanted to end the intimacy before she figured that out. He had prided himself on navigating life relying only on himself, finding success on his own terms. He needed nobody and had assigned emotions and relationships to those who needed a crutch. Now it was obvious why he was sitting in the rain outside an abandoned cabin instead of celebrating. It wasn't the inn that mattered, nor the business. *She* mattered. And now she was gone.

Those words hurt. He let them play out in his mind. *She's gone. I let her go. Pushed her to go, really, because I was scared.*

The light was brighter, an interesting balance to the heaviness in his chest.

Listen. The word drifted through his mind. This time, he heard something intertwined with the rain and wind that flowed around him. It was a note, and then several notes, and then a chord. It was all around him, but it was inside too. He hummed along, wondering if it was something he'd heard before. He took his phone out and opened his voice recording app, tapping the red circle. He hummed what he was hearing, and when he was done, he saw he'd recorded several minutes. At the top of the screen, he saw it was midmorning and that he had two bars of coverage. Without a thought, he pulled up Rally's number and called her.

"Rally, I need you to do me a big favor."

21

Katy's hands twisted Goose's steering wheel as if it needed to be wrung out. Goose's three days at the expensive Airport Park and Ride had set her back almost $50, and now she was caught in Thanksgiving Day traffic through Seattle. In a hellish downpour. Summer had questioned her about traveling on Thanksgiving, but once Katy had her plan thought out, she hadn't wanted to wait another day. But now, with nothing but a drive between her and seeing Mitch, she felt sick to her stomach. It's funny how confidence can disappear over the course of a five-hour flight.

Her phone rang, and she gave it two quick taps to answer and turn on speakerphone. "I haven't chickened out, Summer," she spoke before her best friend could say hello. "At least not yet."

"Good. Do you feel nauseous?"

"Why would I feel nauseous? I'm only exposing all my vulnerabilities to someone who might want nothing to do with me." She shrugged, her voice approaching a level of frantic only dogs could hear.

"Yes, you're exposing your vulnerabilities. But I think he wants *something* to do with you. Why else would the lawyer say he's got an interesting proposal about the inn, but you have to be there in person to review it?"

"Ummm, because I'm about to find out he's a sadistic jerk who needs to be in control?"

"There's the sense of humor I know! *My* best friend Katy would not hook up with a sadistic jerk. Or even a regular jerk. Your radar is too good for that. And the proof is he could have arrested you when you trespassed, and he didn't."

"He probably thought about it."

"No way. You're too cute for anyone to want to arrest."

"Summer... this is crazy. I could have made my case on the phone. Or on Skype. What was I thinking?"

"No, no, no. You were right; this is a face-to-face thing." There was a shuffling sound and Summer's next words were muffled. "She's waffling. Time for reinforcements." And then Katy heard Carson's voice on the line.

"Katy, you stay on that highway and drive to the inn. You admitted you've got the feels for this guy, so now you have to tell him. At the very least, you don't want to walk away from your dream because you had cold feet, do you?"

In the background, she could hear Summer say "Good one!"

"And why did I listen to you and get all dressed up?" Katy looked down at her purple knit dress and high boots. She'd even found a YouTube tutorial so she could put her hair up in a fancy chignon.

"It's your armor," Summer said at a distance, and then there was more scratching and shuffling as the phone was passed again. "You're a confident businesswoman, Katherine Williams. Plus, you're a knock-out in that outfit, and I bet Mitch hasn't seen you in anything fancier than leggings and turtlenecks."

Katy started wringing Goose's steering wheel again. "Uunnnggghh... I want to believe you."

"Remember your plan. It's a great plan—you're going to put everything on the table. He might not feel the same way, but then again, he might. Regardless of his feelings, you're going to be okay. Okay?"

"Okay," Katy said, nodding as she focused on the traffic and breathed deeply. "Okay, okay."

"You're equating loving someone with giving up control," Carson said in the background. "When that person loves you back, you're not giving up anything. It's worth being scared."

"All right, all right. I'm going out there to have an honest conversation. I'm ashamed of how I left things. Regardless of how this turns out, I need to apologize. Once the air is cleared, I'll be able to focus on the inn and what will happen with it. Right?"

"Right!" they both shouted into the phone.

"Can I get back to driving so I don't get a ticket for talking on my cell phone?"

"Yes!" They said their "I love you's" and hung up. Katy navigated the rest of the clogged I-5 in silence.

IT WAS STILL RAINING AS SHE AND GOOSE APPROACHED THE INN. SHE saw it in the distance, pleased despite herself to see some scaffolding up and one exterior wall painted a pale yellow. As she rounded the last bend, she saw a low sign installed at the driveway opening. **Welcome to the Cranberry Hill Inn**, it read, and she bit her lip. The sign was exactly how she imagined it, but she hadn't been there to help erect it. *Trust the plan*, she told herself.

There were no vehicles in the driveway. She pulled into her usual spot and stepped out of her car, running to the cover of the porch. Once she got there, she saw Tandy's bike, and to the left of the door, the old wicker couch she'd found in a thrift store. Someone had found gray striped cushions for it. It looked exactly like she'd hoped it would —inviting and friendly. She sat down to test it out and only moved when the damp air started to give her a chill.

She headed over to the door and peered through its window. The lights inside were on and she saw that the countertops had arrived. They looked fabulous too. She pulled at her scarf vaguely as she looked down at the doorknob. She decided to knock.

"Coming, coming." She heard Tandy's voice inside. And then he was at the door, peering out at her. "Hello, Katy! Come in." He swung the door in and swept his hand wide to invite her inside. "You look nice," he said as she walked by. Her black wool coat reached her shins, and Tandy pointed to it, and said, "Not the best for the rain."

"No," she agreed, "but thank you. You look good too." Her throat tightened at seeing him again. Where was all this sappy emotion coming from?

"Thanks," he replied, blushing and tweaking his hat as he liked to do, and then gestured to the counters. "What do you think of the countertops? They just came in yesterday afternoon. It was close!" He shook his head.

"Close to what?" she asked, but he was already waving her toward the living room. Baseboard and crown molding gleamed white in the warm light from the new light fixtures. "Holy...." She turned as she entered the room.

"And we got the curtains you ordered put up. Cody came and helped us with that." He smiled as he gently moved a hand over the fabric.

"Cody? The boy who stole tools from Mitch?" She remembered that Mitch had mistaken her for him when they first met.

"Ayuh, he's a good kid deep down though. Mitch knows that."

Katy couldn't keep her mouth closed from all the surprises. An old wingback chair was in the far corner with an antique reading lamp beside it. The gleaming piano that had once been covered by dusty old canvas was angled perfectly to fit the corner of the room. A reading light was perched on its top, shining down on some sheet music resting on its shelf. She wanted to look at what he'd been playing, but Tandy was already moving to the stairs.

"There's one more thing Mitch wanted you to see, up here," he called as he mounted the stairs. Katy followed him up to the bathroom where he clicked the white Bakelite switch on and off. The backsplash and floor tiles were done, but the wainscoting was in pieces leaning against the wall. "White switch," Tandy said with a smile. "We didn't have time to get the board on the wall yet." His head tipped in an apology.

"White," she agreed, and then flicked the light on and off when he gestured for her to try it out. "Where is Mitch?"

"He's waiting for you at the Reach. He said you knew where it was."

"I do. I... just thought I'd be meeting him here."

"Nope," he said happily.

"Huh," she murmured, "I could have stopped there instead of coming all the way to the inn."

"But then you wouldn't have seen all our work. Did you see the sign out front?" he asked with a proud smile.

"Yes, it's beautiful."

"You should go," Tandy said, and waved her out of the bathroom and down the stairs.

When she pulled into the restaurant's parking lot, it was packed. That seemed odd for Thanksgiving, but she supposed it could be travelers, since the restaurant was close to the highway exit. She circled through it, but there were no available spots. She ended up having to park out of the lot on the side of the road, and with no umbrella, even though she ran fast, she was drenched when she stepped into the restaurant.

"Hi!" greeted the hostess. Katy took off her wet overcoat, and the woman took it from her, hanging it up.

"Hi. I'm meeting someone...."

"You're Katy," the woman said, smiling.

"Yes." Her hair was dripping, and her dress was even clingier than it normally was as her coat had soaked through, but she didn't think anyone would notice.

"Right this way," the hostess said, and starting walking through the crowded restaurant. As Katy followed her, she noticed someone wave and saw Rally at a table full of women. Katy smiled and lifted a hand to wave back and then saw Gordon at another table with a woman who had to be his wife. They both waved at her. She saw Marshall standing in the back, his arms wrapped around a smiling blonde woman. He gave a whoop when he saw her, and she waved at him.

She almost stumbled when she noticed everyone was looking at her, strange and familiar faces alike, and she tried not to tug at her dress or fix her soggy hair as she followed the hostess. She ended up at a table near a low stage. It was a table set for two, and the hostess pulled out a chair for her.

"Here you go," she said, and then inclined her head to the chair which Katy promptly sat down in. At least she was away from most of the stares.

Then a spotlight shone on her. And a voice came over the speakers on the stage.

"When I met this woman... well, she wasn't this wet," Mitch said, and the crowd laughed. "But she *was* this beautiful. And it only took a day in a secluded cabin to realize I want more than a business partnership with her."

Katy covered her mouth with a shaky hand and was relieved when the spotlight moved to shine on a stool and keyboard on the stage. Mitch stepped into the light, and her heart almost burst. He wore a black suit and a silver tie, and his normally unruly hair had been neatened with a comb. But seeing him adjust his glasses and watching his brows settle into the familiar line over his eyes as he sat down sent her heart racing.

"By the way, if you haven't met her yet, this is Katy, everyone," he introduced, putting the microphone into a holder on the keyboard. "And Katy... meet Cranberry Hill."

"Hi, Katy!" greeted everyone in the room, and she glanced over her shoulder and gave a quick wave. It was hard to take her eyes off Mitch, and while her brain raced trying to figure out what was going on, she wanted to remember every second of it.

"Someone asked me once if I composed music. I said no, because I've always believed you have to be in touch with the truest part of yourself... and really trust that part in order to create music, or poetry, or any kind of art. I never believed I had that ability, and that was okay by me.

"And then I met someone who forced me—although she didn't realize it—to look deeper within myself. She forced me by walking away, and I had to take a close look at who I was and what I wanted. I had to figure out who I wanted to be.

"As I was doing that, a melody popped into my head. If you can't tell I'm nervous by my shaking voice, you can probably see by these." Mitch held up his trembling hands. "I've never done anything like this before. I'm not a speech-making, lounge-performing kind of guy, but once in a lifetime, you meet someone and, well... then you just have to go there.

"So in case I haven't been sappy enough, this song is called 'For Katy.'"

The restaurant erupted in applause, which faded quickly as Mitch played.

Katy didn't hear a single note. Her eyes were fastened on Mitch the entire time, memorizing the way his black hair waved and how a piece fell across his forehead when his head bowed down to follow his hands over the keyboard. She studied his high forehead, his dark brow, and how it made a straight line when he was confused or concerned. Or concentrating, like he was now.

She examined his straight, aristocratic nose, and how his lips moved when he had sassed her by saying "Good luck with that, Katherine" or seduced her with "Ça bien, cher." She watched how his wide shoulders moved in his suit jacket, and how they'd felt when she'd held on to him and he'd carried her upstairs.

So she didn't hear him playing as she sat at her table, her hair still dripping and her hands resting on the wet knit dress that covered her legs. But deep down, in the place she'd gone to when she'd finally admitted to Summer and Carson that she really felt something for Mitch—that's where she heard the music. It brought her to her feet and walked her onto the stage to sit beside him.

Days and weeks later, whenever she ran into someone in Cranberry Hill who'd been there that night, they'd tell her that when he'd finished playing there had been huge applause, but that she and Mitch only had eyes for each other. That she'd started to speak, but he'd turned off his microphone so nobody could hear what they said. And that they stared into each other's eyes and spoken quietly for several moments. And then kissed, which had resulted in another loud cheer.

What Katy remembered was this:

"I heard that here." She put her palm on her heart as Mitch turned off the microphone. "That was the sappiest, most beautiful thing I've ever witnessed."

Mitch put his hand over her hand and then moved it to cover his own heart. "All I know is I don't want to do anything, anywhere, unless you're a part of it. If that's what love is, then I love you."

"That sounds an awful lot like how I feel." She exerted pressure on the palm covering hers and pulled herself closer until their lips touched. Even though she was told later that people cheered, she was pretty sure her heart was singing louder.

EPILOGUE

Katy patted the dirt around the last hellebore and leaned back on her heels to admire the row of flowering shrubs she'd just planted in the front garden. The purple blooms were perfect against the backdrop of the lattice work of the porch. She crawled forward to grab the empty plastic pot, when arms wrapped around her from behind and lifted her high.

"Hey!" She laughed, feeling Mitch's chest against her back and his kisses on her neck.

"You're literally a dirty girl," he said, his lips moving against her skin.

"Heck yes, I am," she agreed, hugging his arms as he held her.

"It's fitting that the first time I met you, you were prowling, and then the day before our wedding, you're prowling again. Old habits, huh?" He set her down and turned her, brushing some dirt off her nose.

"I wanted a little color for the front yard. The turf you rolled out last week looks so good I wanted to contribute." Despite the April sun, the morning air was chilly, and she snuggled closer against Mitch's thick work jacket.

"Get used to her controlling ways now, Mitch," Summer called from across the lawn, where the arbor and white folding chairs had been set up for tomorrow's small ceremony. Summer was maneuvering around on a cane as she slowly but systematically set up the chairs.

Mitch looked into Katy's wide brown eyes, partly hidden by a curl of hair. He unzipped his jacket so he could pull her closer and wrap it around her back. "'Controlling ways'... that sounds like fun."

"Good grief," Summer groaned, watching them kiss for the millionth time that morning. "I'm surprised you two get anything done, let alone finish my loft," she called over, and then made her way around the house to where the other chairs were stacked.

"How did it become 'her' loft?" Mitch smiled at Katy.

"Good question," Katy answered, just as Mitch's phone trilled.

He pulled it out of his back pocket, his face lighting up. He tapped the screen to answer the video call. "Landis, how're you doing, man?" He turned the phone so Katy could be in on the call too.

"Pretty good. Not as good as you, though."

"This is Katy. Katy, this is my buddy, Landis. He's terrible at returning messages. In fact, we've gone year-long stretches where we only played phone tag. We were roommates in college."

"Hi, Landis. Nice to meet you face-to-face." She waved at Mitch's impossibly hot-looking former roommate. He had golden hair, silver eyes, and *GQ*-chiseled features. It was hard not to whistle.

"Nice to meet you too, Katy. Hey, I'm sorry I can't make it tomorrow."

"No worries, man. I know you CEOs have the candles burning at both ends," Mitch said.

"That's the truth. But I promise to make it out there soon, okay? I really want to see this place of yours." Landis smiled.

"Sounds good. Take care, man," Mitch ended the call.

"*Goodness*! I didn't know you had a sexy pirate for a roommate. You're so lucky I didn't meet him first."

"Oh yeah? Well, I'll make sure to delay his visit until I know you're absolutely, irrevocably, inextricably under my spell."

Katy wound her arms around his back, pressing against him from chest to knees. "I don't know if I can hide the fact that I already am.

Besides, he looks like Summer's type—when Summer's ready to date again." Katy's eyes sparkled.

"No way. Landis and Summer would be like... trying to mix hemp oil and fancy bottled water. Besides, I think might be committed to some socialite he's had an on-and-off thing with."

"Oh. Even if he was available, that doesn't sound like Summer's type."

"Are you talking about me?" Summer called as she dragged three more folding chairs from around the side of the inn.

Katy walked over and took them away from her. "Are you in the running for the Martyr of the Year award?"

"I'm not an invalid." Summer followed Katy, who leaned the folded chairs against the first row that was set up.

"Let Mitch bring a few stacks of chairs on his wheeled thing. Then you can set them up without having to walk so much." She watched Summer put her cane on a chair and start unfolding the three Katy had just set down. "And you *are* an invalid. I don't think you're supposed to be spending hours on that leg yet."

"I know when to cool it with the leg. In fact, I'm about to agree to Mitch bringing over stacks of chairs so I don't have to walk as much. See? I can be rational." She smiled sweetly at Katy.

Katy walked over to her and hugged her tightly. Summer hugged her back just as fiercely. "I just worry, that's all," she admitted.

"I know. I appreciate it," Summer said.

"I'm sorry your brother hurt his knee and can't make it," Mitch told her as he walked over to join them. "He helped convince Katy to came back, so I'm forever in his debt."

"Seems the Richardson clan can't avoid the injuries lately," Summer sighed. "He's sorry he has to miss it too."

Katy and Mitch held hands as they wandered across the lawn and down the driveway of the inn, letting Summer continue to unfold chairs.

"Well, *cher*," Mitch said, tucking her against his side as they turned to face the inn from the road. "We did it."

"Yeah, we did," she agreed happily. The shrubs she'd crawled beside months ago had been trimmed and were covered in bright green buds ready to bloom. The lawn had been torn up and replaced with sod. The driveway had been leveled and covered in gravel. The inn stood before them, a creamy yellow with white trim, soft curtains in the windows. The rooms had been empty this week, but were booked full of guests following their wedding and honeymoon.

"I always knew it would work out, but I had no idea the depth of satisfaction I'd have, or that it would take another person to make that happen," Mitch said, dropping a kiss on her hair.

"Same and same, baby. Same and same," she whispered.

Thank you for reading **BLUEPRINT FOR LOVE**! I hope you cheered when Mitch and Katy found their happily ever after. But Katy's found a new skill—matchmaker!

IT'S A CASE OF OPPOSITES **DISTRACT!**

Summer is a dedicated journalist, but after a dangerous run-in with a crime family, seeks refuge with Katy and Mitch at the cozy Cranberry Hill Inn.

Landis is on the look-out for the next media property to buy. And Summer's newspaper checks all the boxes.

He just didn't expect Summer to check all his boxes too!

"I'm loving the amazing characters in these books, and this is another great one in the Cranberry Hill Inn series."

—*Amazon Reviewer*

Click the image to download!

Join and receive the
Cranberry Hill Series Prequel
"Operation Vengeance"
FREE!
Click to download now!
https://BookHip.com/NNSLJV

ALSO BY NALA

Maple Cove Dog Lover's Society

Small Town Shepherd (Sam & Brody's story)

Beauty and the Bulldog (Vi & Noah's story)

Foxhound Foes (Rylee & Matt's story)

Billionaire Beagle (Olive & Xavier's story)

Westie Besties (Quinn & Levi's story)

Second Chance Corgi (Eliza & Phil's story)

Cranberry Hill Inn Series—Paperback Books 4–6

Everything for Love (Rally, Cassie & Garret's stories)

For contests, prizes & free reading, join my Reader's Group by visiting https://www.subscribepage.com/l4m3s1

LEAVE A REVIEW

Reviews are powerful tools when it comes to getting my books in front of other readers. Not only do they help other readers figure out if they might like the book before buying it, reviews help independent authors like me get more attention for their work.

It would mean a lot to me if you could spend just a few minutes leaving a review on my book page here.

Thank you!

COPYRIGHT

All the characters in this book are fictitious, and any resemblance to actual persons living or dead is purely coincidental.

Copyright © 2018 by Nala Henkel-Aislinn

All rights reserved.

No part of this book may be reproduced, or stored in a retrieval system, or transmitted in any form or by any means, electronic, mechanical, photocopying, recording, or otherwise, without express written permission of the publisher.

Published by Nala Henkel-Aislinn

Edited by Hot Tree Editing

A CRANBERRY HILL *Clean* ROMANCE

Deadline on Love

NALA HENKEL-AISLINN

DEDICATION

To my husband, partner, love of my life, and Alpha Reader (naturally), Eric.

To Taylor, Dara, Keegan, Piper, Al, and Dave.

To my wonderful friend and Alpha Readers, Eric, Regina and Wendy.

1

Summer Richardson sat curled up on her deck in her favorite papasan chair. The chair faced west where, if she was lucky, she could watch a late summer evening crimson sunset after a long day of work.

Right now, though, instead of enjoying a chilled glass of pinot and unwinding, she stared moodily at the tablet on her lap. Her fingers alternately slid and tapped on the screen, scrolling through and opening photo after photo of possibly the most arrogant-looking man she'd ever seen. Although she'd never met him, she could see private jets and nail-buffing privilege etched into every feature of his smug face.

Landis Blake was the CEO of Blake Media. Summer had overheard her boss agreeing to release financial information to his company, which could only mean the small-town newspaper she worked for might actually be sold.

"You can just tell," Summer called through the screen slider to her brother, Carson, who was manning two woks in the open kitchen. "He definitely pays someone to style him to look like a pirate in a tuxedo." She shook her head with distaste, fixating on a particular image that ground her gears.

In it was Blake, leaning slightly forward as he buttoned up his tuxedo jacket. His hair was slicked back, but with the perfect strand breaking free across his forehead. His jaw had a shadow of stubble that was light enough to say "sexy corporate raider," but not so dark that it said "morning after whiskey flights at the supper club." His mouth quirked up at the corner in what Summer could only interpret as condescension. *I look pretty damn good, don't I?* that face prompted.

Summer uncrossed and recrossed her legs on the papasan chair, kneading her upper thigh a little where an old injury still troubled her if she sat in one position too long. She tapped and zoomed and minimized and tapped, huffing in disdain.

"I also think he's paying for *GQ*-type lighting," she called out again. "I mean, nobody looks this good naturally."

Carson looked from one wok to the other as he dried his hands on a tea towel. He twisted the dial on a timer, and then grabbed his cane from where it hung on the edge of the counter and came out on the deck.

"Scoot over." He waved his cane at Summer's lanky body and waited for her to unfold herself and make room. As she plopped herself higher onto the curved pillow, she looked up from her tablet.

"What's up with Pete?" she asked, looking at where Carson's prosthetic right leg should have been. He'd lost his leg almost a year ago after a broken bone had revealed osteosarcoma. When the prosthetic arrived, Carson had waited three weeks to try it. He'd said he needed to get to know it before "they" could work together. The day he announced he'd christened the leg "Pete" was the first day he put it on.

"The vacuum valve needed to be adjusted." Carson dropped onto the papasan and took the tablet out of her hands. "Don't worry, I'll have it back before game day."

"You better," she said, leaning into him and watching his finger scroll through the images of the Blake Media CEO.

"You're positive Gage is going to sell?" he asked.

"Yeah. Since June had her stroke, he's mentioned it a few times. But I thought he would sell to one of the two indie publishers here, not some spoiled, East Coast, rich boy." She frowned and looked up at him as he leaned away to look down at her.

"That is not the objective journalist I know my sister to be," he admonished. "The only facts I have so far are that he looks like a movie star, and…" Carson lifted the tablet closer to his face and scrolled through a few more screens of photos. "Good grief!"

"What?" Summer asked, pushing closer to look at what he found.

"Well, if I'm not mistaken…I think this guy has five different tuxes. Five!" He looked at his sister with mock outrage. "That's reprehensible!"

"Oh, you." Summer whacked Carson's shoulder.

"No, you're right. He's a privileged no-good east coaster. Although, to be fair, we're east coasters as well."

"We have scruples!" she defended.

"Did your sources give you some info on this guy's…. What's his name again?"

"Landis Blake." She made a face as she said his name. "I bet when he gets bored he flies around the country buying art."

Carson whistled. "You really have it in for this guy."

Summer shrugged, unable to disagree.

"Do you have some evidence to back up Landis Blake's lack of scruples and indiscriminate art buying?" he asked.

"Not a lot. Blake Media is a private company. A few disgruntled employees filed suits about unlawful dismissal when his father ran the company. And there's been some recent talk about unfair labor practices in a printing plant in Georgia. There might be a strike." Summer lifted her hand up to fuss at a hangnail on her thumb, getting ready to bite it, when Carson pushed her hand down.

"Don't bite your nails," he scolded, and then he mussed her white-gold hair, which was so similar to his own. "I don't know what to make of Five Tuxedo Guy, other than he goes to a lot of fancy events and has G-R-E-A-T taste in women." Carson tilted the tablet toward Summer, and she saw the curvy redhead draped over Landis in many of the photos.

She sighed and leaned away from her brother until she felt the orange warmth of the early evening sun bathe her face. He had a point. Not about the nail biting—because that usually helped her work through a dilemma or get past a stuck point in a story—but about her strong reaction to this guy based on a few texts from her contacts and a stream of internet images.

"I don't get why you care if Gage sells the paper. Will you lose your job there?"

"It's possible, if they change the format. It's what happens when big media companies buy up little papers to use as news feeders. It happened at Blaine News right after I left. Everything was fine for about three months, and then they went from twenty-three staff to four, and those four basically monitored the police line for the St. Charles affiliate. Unless someone important was shot, there was no more local reporting."

Carson checked his watch, handed Summer her tablet, and used his cane to help lever himself up from the cozy chair. "I can't blame Gage if he wants to sell. He's not getting any younger, and with June needing more around-the-clock care, he probably wants to spend more time with her." He walked into the loft to the kitchen, and Summer rose to follow, only pausing for a moment to knead her thigh and stretch her leg.

"I can't blame him for that, either. But he's been at that paper since he was delivering it when he was fifteen years old. It's where he met June, and it's become their baby." She followed Carson, who went around the counter to the stovetop facing out to their deck, and Summer sat at the counter facing him.

"Exactly," Carson agreed as the timer chimed. He turned it off and took turns stirring each wok. "He's been there, what... over forty years, I bet. And with June needing rehabilitation, I bet he could use the pile of money selling the paper would bring."

Summer paused while she thought that over. She knew Gage had been having a scary few months since June's stroke. It hadn't even been the stroke so much as the complications that came with it—her fall when it happened, the headaches, and then the dangerous edema.

"True, but the paper's been doing really well since Christmas. We almost tripled our subscriber base. And the online version we launched before Easter has been huge."

"Ah, well, all that is great, but it probably made *The Cranberry Hill Chronicle* a sweet acquisition target as well."

Summer slumped. He was right. She'd seen struggling media properties get acquired by bigger companies, and also successful ones like the *Chronicle*. She'd just thought she'd have more time to enjoy the small-town reporter beat she'd created for herself.

She lifted the tablet to look back through the images Carson had left off at. Landis Blake, sleek chestnut hair combed back, looking up at the camera with gleaming silver eyes while buttoning the jacket of one of his too-many tuxedos. The guy was one part Jason Statham and two parts hot Italian soccer player. Something in her bristled as she examined his chiseled features. *He's probably never had to really work at anything*, she thought.

"Hey, frowny, dinner's ready."

Summer looked up, brows lowered and forehead creased. "I'm not frowning."

"Sis, we may not be twins, but your face is telling me the whole story. You're looking at this hot guy and thinking 'this is one arrogant, privileged, elitist media mogul' and you're prepared to hate him for one reason, and it's related to a guy you told me I'm never allowed to mention."

Summer smoothed out her expression and set the tablet down. "For your information, 'mogul' is out of fashion. I'm much more scathing than that. I think he's an elitist media oligarch." She reached along the counter to pull over the placemats and place settings she'd set up when she arrived home. Carson used a potholder to wave more of the smell over to her. "Mmmm," she murmured, eyes closed. "That smells heavenly. Why did you make two?"

Carson reached for two bowls and gently ladled a generous helping from one of the simmering woks. He closed his eyes as he hovered his face over the steam from the bowl and then handed it to Summer.

"Green curry with kaffir lime and eggplant. Yours is half-star spicy, and mine is four-star spicy. I know you're a baby about spice. And fair warning—be prepared to be amazed at your brother's culinary genius." He ladled a helping for himself and walked around to sit beside her. They reached for each other's hand and closed their eyes, quietly taking turns to say a few words of appreciation about the day. It was a habit they'd picked up after Summer got out of the hospital and flew to the West Coast to join her brother.

"You can mention Nick," Summer said, stirring her curry and leaning over to enjoy the aroma that wafted up from the white bowl. "I'm over the worst part of those two years, I think. I just don't want to be blind again. Nick was my first big mistake in making assumptions about people from rich families, and I think using more discretion— Good*ness*, this is amazing!" she yelled after swallowing her first taste of the curry.

Carson gloated, merely nodding as he continued to eat.

"I meant to ask, what's with all the Thai food lately? I thought the Trestle used local foods to make local dishes." Summer had to force herself to chew and swallow each bite and not continuously load her mouth non-stop.

"Oh... I guess..." Carson fidgeted and looked away. "I just got to remembering my trip to Thailand last fall. The foods really stuck in my mind. By the way, this should be served with rice but we're out."

"This does not need one extra little thing, but I'll see if Katy has any rice. I remember her buying a twenty-pound bag not too long ago."

"Oh!" Carson snapped his fingers. "Another thing. Katy needs some biscuits and muffins for tomorrow morning. I've got both doughs made; I just need to pop them in the oven. I'll do that right after we eat. Could you take them over to her later on?"

"Sure. I thought they weren't booking the inn this close to the baby's due date."

"I don't know about that, but apparently it's a friend of Mitch coming up from Seattle. I think she said he was Mitch's roommate in college."

Summer and Carson both spooned another bite of the creamy curry sauce and vegetables, closing their eyes as they savored it.

"What's this thing?" Summer asked, pushing a ping-pong-sized green ball around in her bowl.

"That's the eggplant. Isn't it cool? The tiny green things that look like giant peas are eggplants, too."

"Wow, that *is* cool." Summer grinned at her brother. "Thailand is obviously a vegetarian-friendly country. You have my permission to continue with your Thai cuisine experiments."

"Why, thank you, sis." Carson inclined his head, and they tapped their spoons together in a silly salute.

TWO HOURS LATER, AFTER FINISHING DINNER AND CRACKING JOKES in the kitchen while Carson baked, Summer carried a large basket full of muffins and biscuits down the stairs of their converted barn loft. She winced as she stepped off the bottom stair onto her left leg and set the checkered cloth-covered basket down. Pulling up her cargo shorts cuff, she glanced down at the puckered and undulating scar that started at the outside of her thigh and disappeared around the back of her leg to a few inches above her knee.

She leaned forward as her physiotherapist had taught her, put both her hands on the bottom of the scar, and gently kneaded the taut muscles. Sitting or standing in one place too long always caused these shortened muscles and ligaments to tighten up painfully. It only took about ninety seconds before the pain lessened. She did a few leg lifts and a few slow stretches, shook her leg out, and hefted the basket again to make her way to the inn.

Summer followed the scattered stones of the flagstone walkway through the tall cedar and fir trees that separated the inn from the barn. The stand of trees was dense enough to block the view of the inn from the loft, but at ground level, where the branches were sparse, she could see the quaint hip-roofed house about a hundred and fifty yards away. The inn and its property sat on a hilly crest, and Beach Drive Road—the only road out here—curved around it, giving drivers an unrestricted view of the sparkling Pacific Ocean before the road angled back inland to the small town of Cranberry Hill.

Summer breathed in the woodsy smell as she walked, listening to her sandaled feet slap against the flagstones. She remembered when Katy and Mitch planned this walkway, and when they'd figured out the old barn was in good enough shape to renovate it and add the loft. She smiled when she remembered how Katy would call and tell her about the arrogant mule of a contractor she was butting heads with over the ownership of the property and everything that came after. Including their simple but beautiful wedding.

She slowed her steps, her smile fading. She only thought about the specifics of the last two years when she was alone. She hadn't lied to Carson about being over the "Nick Incident," but she still felt some incredulity when she thought about everything that happened in that time span. She'd experienced trauma, surgery, and recovery, as well as her brother's fight with bone cancer. Also, her best friend Katy had started a new business, a new relationship, and would soon welcome a new family member. The fact they had each come through such trials to build this peaceful life close to nature, and each of them were doing what they were meant to do, felt like a magical dream. She didn't want it to ever end.

"Hey, girl!" Katy called from the porch as Summer emerged from the trees. "Ahhhh, you come bearing magic! You give that handsome brother of yours a big hug from me." Katy was snuggled into the soft cushions of a wicker couch on the side porch of the inn, her pregnant belly overwhelmingly large even from a distance.

"How's little mamma tonight?" Summer climbed the two steps up to the porch and set the basket down, putting her hands on her slim hips. "You look like you're relaxing, so three points for Katy."

"Only three?" Katy's bottom lip popped out before curving back into its natural smile. "Do you know how impossible it is to be thirty-eight and a half weeks pregnant, running a business, and managing a worried husband?"

"You're right! I forgot you're the first woman ever to have a baby, and a career, and a husband. How do you do it?" Summer smirked and plopped down on the other end of the couch, taking in her glowing best friend and college roommate with a big smile. Physically, they were exact opposites—Katy with soft curling hair the exact color of fudge, her brown eyes matching her hair, and a petite, curvy body, compared to Summer's surfer girl coloring and swimmer-lean tallness. "Well, I've decided when I have kids, I am not going to get as big as you. Are you sure there aren't two in there? Like, really, really sure?"

Katy's face crinkled as she lovingly caressed her large baby belly. "I wish there were three in here! Summer, I have so much love for this baby I don't know where I'm going to put it all." Tears glistened in her eyes, and she reached out to hold Summer's hand. "I'm so glad you and Carson are here. You'll be able to put up with my love overflow, right?"

Summer gripped Katy's hand the way her words gripped her heart and beamed at her as tears rose in her own eyes. "Absolutely, forever, plus a universe."

"All right, then." Katy wiped each eye with the back of each hand and took a dainty sip of her iced tea.

Behind Summer, the kitchen's screen door opened with a creak and closed with a bang, startling both ladies.

"What's going on here? Another cry fest? I thought that was supposed to stay between week two and week twenty." Mitch walked over to squeeze Summer's shoulder and plant a lingering kiss on his wife's lips. "How are my two wee ones?" He knelt down beside her to murmur quiet words against her rounded belly. Katy and Mitch shared dark, curly hair and brown eyes, and Summer couldn't wait to see how adorable their baby would be, and whether he or she would inherit Katy's business savvy, or Mitch's musicality.

"They weren't really tears, just a little weepy seepage. And that's probably going to last until our child is at least forty." Katy ran her hands through Mitch's ebony hair as he continued to murmur into her naval. "Don't listen to anything he tells you about Mamma," Katy told her belly with a laugh.

"Too late, she heard everything, and she's already on my side." Mitch beamed up at his wife, placing his hand on her cheek. Summer watched as Katy in turn placed her hand on his cheek. They had found something with each other that she would've sworn only existed in old-time Hollywood movies. She'd be squirming uncomfortably if she didn't find it so beautiful.

"So, Mitch," Summer broke in after a considerate pause. "Do you want to earn some points too?"

Mitch gave Katy's belly one more kiss and then stood up to face Summer. "Absolutely."

"There"—she pointed with a flung-out arm—"are your breakfast goodies for your guest. And if you would be so kind as to portion out a pound or so of rice for me from the giant sack you bought last week, I would be ever so grateful. I will pay you back with some of Carson's *amazing* curry he made tonight. And..." Summer added as she saw Mitch's eyes light up, "I'll grant you ten points."

"Done!" Mitch scooped up the basket and went into the house.

"I still don't know how I only got three points," Katy complained. "I think growing a human in your belly should give you an automatic twenty points every time."

Summer leaned back into the cushions. Her line of sight took her eyes out to the ocean, watching the waves in the distance shimmer from the sun that was hidden behind the house but almost fully set.

Katy patted Summer's thigh, and Summer obliged her by lifting her foot up and placing it on Katy's leg. Katy squeezed Summer's foot in the way she knew Summer loved. "What's up, girl? You seem a little out of sorts."

Summer exhaled on a long *Phhhhhhh*, looking away from the wonderful emptiness of the ocean to her friend. "Did I tell you Gage might sell the paper?"

"No!" Katy's mouth and eyes opened wide then settled back to normal as she shrugged. "I guess I can understand it, though. With June. She's not bouncing back like everyone hoped, is she?"

"Gage is upbeat, but no, I don't think she is."

"You can't be worried about losing your job there, though. Right? I mean, it's no secret to anybody that your arrival is what exploded circulation for the paper. I bet nobody would want to buy it if you hadn't shown up."

"No, I'm not worried about work. I could freelance today if necessary. It's just... I don't know how to explain it. Everything is perfect right now. It's not that I'm afraid of change, but...."

"Whoa, hold on there. For the record, you have *never* been okay with change." Katy tapped Summer's foot in emphasis.

Summer frowned. "I don't think that's true. Moving here and then getting Carson settled in was a big change."

"True, but you still came up with a hundred excuses why you couldn't do it. You wanted Carson to move in with you back in Blaine

County. As many miles as there are between us and Chicago is how many hours it took us to convince you!" Katy finished on a laugh.

Summer couldn't deny that was true. "I guess what's really bugging me is the guy he wants to sell it to. It's one of those monster media companies that chew up little guys so they can expand their empire." At that moment, Summer paused. A little whisper of an idea had popped into her brain and stopped her flow of speech. *What if...?* Summer looked down at her thumb and worried the small hangnail there with her finger.

"Who is it?"

"Huh?" Summer's attention snapped back to Katy, "Who's who?"

"The monster media company. What company is it?"

"Blake Media. They own some small radio stations and newspapers on the East Coast. I guess technically they're not a monster, but they seem to be heading that way."

"Hmm." Katy's forehead furrowed. "Blake Media. That name sounds familiar. Who's actually running the show?"

"Landis is the CEO. His father passed away some years ago and handed it over to his wife until Landis was old enough to take over. His mother, Evelyn Blake, is the president." She wiggled her foot when she noticed Katy's hand had stilled. Katy resumed applying pressure to different parts of her foot as Summer continued. "I'm trying not to be a reverse snob, but honestly—don't those names just reek with privilege? They're not going to care about a mom and pop paper like the *Chronicle*. They sure won't care about the role the newspaper plays in Cranberry Hill. They probably just want to shore up their balance sheet by swallowing it like a great white shark. What's the matter?"

Katy's eyebrows had climbed halfway up her forehead and her smile had a plastic look to it.

"You're not going to believe this, but... I think I know Landis Blake."

"What?" she exclaimed.

"Well, not *know*-know him, but know in that kind of way where your husband maybe... went to college with him... just a little bit."

Summer shot off the couch to look down at her. Katy rubbed a hand across her forehead and then covered her eyes. "Mitch went to college with Landis Blake?" Summer asked.

"They were roommates." Katy peeked through the hand over her eyes. "And Mitch invited him to stay at the inn, because he had some business... to look into... in the area." She peeked through her fingers at a now-pacing Summer.

"*What?* He's the guest you needed muffins and biscuits for tomorrow?"

"Ye-es." Katy waved her hand toward Summer's hand, trying to grab it, and gave it a squeeze when she caught it. "This is not a big deal, okay? Landis had other things to do in Seattle and told Mitch a month ago that he was going to tie in a visit here. He updated Mitch last night about staying a bit longer because of other business."

Summer squeezed Katy's hand before slipping away. "I'm sorry I'm all flustered. I promise I'm not going to create an awkward scene, but let me go for a quick walk along the beach just to settle my nerves down." She peeked through the kitchen window to the clock—8:40 p.m. "What time are you heading to bed?"

"Not for a while. Come back for a hug when you're done, okay? Although I'll take one now, too." Katy waved Summer over.

Summer leaned down and gave Katy and her belly a gentle hug. "One for now, and I'll bring you another one in a bit."

Instead of stepping off the porch and walking down the driveway toward the beach, Summer opted to walk down the long porch. Inside the next window, she saw Mitch. He held up a zippered linen bag, pointing to it and Summer, asking a silent question. She gave him a thumbs-up, and then tapped her wrist and held up a hand to say "I'll be back in 5." Mitch gave her a thumbs-up and a smile.

She walked down the front porch steps, along the matching flagstone walkway, and crossed the empty road. About ten feet to the right were worn wooden steps that led down to a grassy field that precipitated the beach sand. Lifting a foot at a time, she removed her sandals and let her feet sink into the dry, hot sand. She'd always loved to swim, but she'd never considered herself an ocean lover. Until moving here.

She walked directly toward the water, fixing her eyes on the orange horizon, which quickly bled to a splendor of blues as night rolled closer. The wind pushed against her in weak, salty gusts, which told her the tide was on its way out. She turned her mind to the turmoil in her belly.

Sometime over the last hour, what had been a whimsical thought a week ago had become a possible plan of action. That maybe, possibly, *she* could buy the paper. Not on her own, of course. But with a partner, or a partnership group. Or even find someone else who had money and wanted to buy it.

She'd wanted to broach that with Katy and see how any of those scenarios could work. Katy was a business graduate and a successful business owner. But she'd also worked at a large company and had a lot of insight into the corporate world of buying and selling businesses.

But now she had no time to mull these ideas over. The fox was landing in the chicken coop this very night, and she hadn't had any time to lock the chickens away. Despite the hollow feeling in her gut, she smiled at her unintentional wit. She was right about Landis being a fox—in looks and probably in his business dealings. For the first time in a couple years, she was grateful for the lesson Nick had unwittingly taught her. Not to trust men with money. Especially handsome men.

She finally arrived at the water's edge. The dry sand had merged into hard undulating ridges and now melted beneath every step she took into the gentle surf. The cool water covered her feet, moving up her ankles, and the gusting breeze lifted wisps of moisture to mist her knees and thighs. Summer stopped walking.

Breathe. She closed her eyes and saw the word appear and repeat, floating over the image of the horizon and water in her mind. *Breathe and release and breathe and release.* She pictured every cell of her body relaxing, opening, and letting go of little gray strands of tension that floated up and away from her.

Two years ago, recovering from the shooting, she'd thought she'd been handling everything pretty damn well. A witness that tied the shooter to a small-time crime family that had connections to her boyfriend? No problem, Nick explained everything. Finding out she'd need three surgeries and walk away with a hefty scar? Also no problem, it would add character. But finding out Nick's family was involved in her shooting? That's when her hair started falling out.

"You need to talk to someone," Katy had pleaded with her on the phone. "Even without your hair falling out, you've been through a serious trauma. Talking is a way to deal with it."

So Summer had followed up with a therapist, who had been beyond amazing. She had helped her develop this calming visualization, and so far, it had a one hundred percent success rate at balancing her troubled mind.

After a few minutes, in which the ocean had slunk away to merely lick at her toes and the sky had turned a navy blue, Summer squared her shoulders and let her mind work away at her idea until it was time for Katy's second hug.

2

Landis Blake relaxed his grip on the steering wheel of his rented Mercedes as the stress of Seattle city traffic faded behind him. It helped that his cell hadn't buzzed in about ten minutes, too.

He pressed the Talk button on his steering wheel.

"Tell me what you would like me to help you with," came the mostly-human automated voice system over the car's speakers.

"Play some blues music," he requested, checking his mirrors as he changed lanes to pass a slower car.

The voice system made a sad sound, and answered, "I'm sorry. What was that?" in a caring voice.

"Play the blues," he said in a louder voice. Although the Mercedes CLS Coupe his assistant Melanie had managed to wrangle for him was gorgeous, the car's voice-activated system needed a massive upgrade.

"I'm sorry. I didn't understand. What would you like me to do?" The friendly voice was starting to grate on Landis's nerves.

"Play. The. Blues." Landis tried again, loudly emphasizing each word.

This time, the car pinged an affirmative tone, and answered, "All right. Playing the blues music." The honky-tonk tinkling of the piano intro to "Must Have Been the Devil" drifted out of the car's magnificent sound system and right into his bloodstream. His back muscles responded by melting deeper into the seat and that alone was worth whatever this rental was going to set him back.

Three songs later, his guidance system alerted him. "Your exit is on the right. Take this exit."

Landis eased the car over, slid to a pause at the four-way stop, and then turned the car toward the setting sun. Just as the driving guitar chords of "Whiskey Flavored Tears" started, they faded and paused to let his mother's ringtone fill the car.

"Yes, Evelyn?" he answered after tapping the Talk button on the steering wheel to answer the call.

"The pressmen at the Charleston paper are coordinating a strike vote, maybe as soon as Saturday." The car's speakers made it seem like his mother was right there in the passenger seat.

"I know. Have you heard anything about how it might go?"

"No."

Landis paused, waiting for more. He held up a hand to the dashboard panel that said he was connected to "Evelyn-Mother," inviting her to elaborate. "So?" he had to prompt when she remained silent.

"I just wanted to make sure you remembered."

"I remember. Is there anything else?"

"Did you get the Wyeth?"

Landis gritted his teeth. He wanted to forget how unsatisfactory the negotiations with the art dealer had been. "It remains to be seen."

"Huh. That must be disappointing for you," his mother said, not unkindly but not with any particular emotion either.

"It is. Evelyn, was there anything else? It's been a hellish day and my head is splitting. I'm hitting some dark curving roads, and I'd rather concentrate on that for a while."

"I'm just trying to ascertain why you thought this trip was necessary. Right now. When we're facing a possible strike."

"We covered this already. When I planned this trip, there was no strike vote being planned. And the Wyeth exhibit is heading overseas in a week." Landis's hands tensed around the steering wheel. Was this the fourth or the fifth time they'd had this conversation?

"All right, dear," Evelyn said after Landis's silence extended a few beats. At least she was not slow on the uptake.

"Thank you. It's very late in New York. You should go to bed and let me get to mine. And stop worrying."

"It's my job to worry, Landis. Details get missed when nobody's watching the store." She had a regal tone when she was condescending. He wondered if he sounded like that at times. He often felt a lack of patience with his executives lately.

"I can't tell you what to do, Evelyn. I've learned that much. Go ahead and watch the store; just don't make anybody crazy. I'm taking one meeting tomorrow, and then I plan to be unreachable for the next forty-eight hours. If an emergency happens, like a body part falls off, let Melanie know."

Evelyn let out an abrupt "Huh!" of disdain, which brought a smile to Landis's face.

"Thank you, Evelyn. Goodnight."

Landis disconnected before she had a chance to respond. She was a driven, independent woman, and though he'd been abrupt, there was a mutual loyalty and respect that meant they never had hard feelings over honest talk. Their relationship thrived on efficiency and didn't need any extra emotions to sustain it. Business rivals in the past thought he and his mother had a cold, dysfunctional relationship that could be exploited, but they'd been disappointed.

The music swelled to fill the car after the call ended. As Landis steered into the first curve and the evergreens crept closer to the road, he drank in the deepening orange of the sun on the horizon and punched the volume-up button until the raucous Chicago blues filled the car with sweetness.

※

Twenty minutes, four phone calls—none from Evelyn—and a raging migraine later, Landis slowed as he approached the driveway to 2525 Beach Drive Road. The house was as pictured in the printout Melanie had tucked in his briefcase, a gabled two-story bungalow with Craftsmen finishes, light gray siding, and white trim. A hand-carved sign sat low and close to the road. It read *Welcome to the Cranberry Hill Inn.*

Landis slowed to a near stop to make the sharp turn into the driveway. The gravel crunched as his sleek rental inched closer to the house. Assuming he should park in line with the two vehicles pulled off to the right in a grassy area, he rolled the Mercedes to a stop beside a green Subaru. The other vehicle was a battered pickup, the color of which he couldn't discern in the dusky light.

He looked in his rearview mirror and noticed a glowing light on the porch and two figures seated on the outdoor couch. One stood and walked to the edge, sliding his hands into his pockets. Mitch.

Landis had every intention of greeting Mitch, but as he unfolded his 6'4" self from the car, he let out a loud groan instead. Without conscious thought, his hands reached over his head and stretched. It helped his muscles but didn't do much for the pounding in his head. He'd been wearing his dark blue business suit for more than fifteen hours, and all he wanted was to shuck it for a T-shirt and shorts. And a cold beer, if he was being completely honest.

"Hey, buddy!" Mitch called, then turned to pull his very pregnant wife to her feet from the wicker couch she'd been sitting on.

"Hey." Landis waved back, trying his best to inject some life into his voice. He reached inside the car to pop the trunk, and then walked his tired body to the back of the car to haul out his briefcase and overnight bag. "Sorry. I'm later than I thought I would be."

"That's okay. Late night arrivals aren't unusual for us. How was the drive?"

"Seattle is nuts. It's a beautiful city, but the traffic is crazy. It's on par with New York, except in New York there's a language and a flow to it. Here, it just stops. For no apparent reason." Landis rubbed the back of his neck, hoping a firm hand would drain some of the pressure from inside his skull. To his ears, he sounded like a whiny baby, and he didn't want that to be his first impression after the many years since he'd last seen Mitch. He especially didn't want Mitch's wife to think poorly of him, although as he shuffled toward where she stood on the porch, her eyes looked mostly sympathetic.

"Landis, this is my wife, Katy. The amazing woman who tried to steal my inn away and somehow ended up with both the house and my heart."

"Hi, Landis. It's nice to meet you in person." She shook the hand Landis extended to her.

"It's really nice to meet you too, Katy. The few times Mitch and I have spoken over the last year, he's made me extremely jealous. And congratulations on the baby."

"Thank you. We're very excited, and impatient to get through the next two weeks." She patted her belly.

From the shadows the house threw across the driveway came the crunching of footsteps on gravel. Landis turned to see a slim figure approaching, but the dusky light was too dim to make out more than a white blouse and blonde hair. Katy turned toward the figure and gave an excited wave. He saw her eyes dart to him and back again, and he groaned inwardly. The last thing he needed was well-meaning friends trying to set him up with anyone.

"You don't have to take that," he said a little too sharply when Mitch took his bag.

"No problem," Mitch replied, slapping Landis's arm in a greeting. Both men turned and watched Katy step off the porch to join the woman in the driveway, both of them putting their heads together to talk quietly. Landis couldn't control his eye roll. "She's cool," Mitch assured, nudging Landis to follow him up to the porch. "She was Katy's roommate in college."

"I just don't need to meet any friends of friends who would be 'perfect for me,' if you know what I mean. I get enough of that from Evelyn and her friends." Landis groaned, wishing he could just get into the inn and to his room.

"I'm pretty sure there's no plan to set you up, but now that I think about it"—Mitch grinned and stopped with his hand on the screen door handle—"it would be pretty funny to see. The liberal crusader meets the uptight corporate executive."

"Whoa, whoa, whoa... uptight? Where does that come from?" Landis laughed but stopped as his head pounded even harder.

"From all the mergers, meetings, and other things that kept you from visiting." Mitch arched an eyebrow at him, and Landis's mouth quirked at the corner.

"You might have a point. Look, I hope you don't mind, but my head feels like it's about to crack open. Can we catch up tomorrow when I feel more human?" Landis stepped closer to the screen door, but Mitch didn't move, looking over Landis's shoulder.

"Mitch, did you bag that rice for Summer? She's ready to take it home," Katy asked, walking into the light from the porch with her arm linked through the woman's arm.

"Yup, let me grab it from the counter. Landis, this is Summer, by the way. She lives in the barn loft in the back, and she's our local liberal crusader." Mitch winked as he stepped into the inn to get the bag Katy had asked him for.

Landis couldn't stop the groan that slipped out of his lips. His head doubled-up on the pounding, and he momentarily dreamed of just continuing in the house behind Mitch without saying anything. But manners won over and he reluctantly turned to say hello.

Many things cluttered Landis's mind as his eyes skimmed over Summer. First were the pale gray eyes that sparkled. Second was the golden skin that shimmered like she had just stepped from the ocean. A very close third was her long sea-swept hair that fluttered around her shoulders and down her back in a white gold curtain. Lastly, but most strikingly, was her look of disdain. Or should he say disgust? It was there and beaming directly at him, and it sparked annoyance in him. When he put out his hand, she shuttered the look and grudgingly extended her own hand. He was able to grasp long, cool fingers, but that was all. She pulled away so fast he wouldn't have thought the handshake happened at all.

"Nice to meet you," she muttered quickly, stepping back and more firmly into Katy's side.

"Yeah, same." Landis wasn't able to keep a tinge of sarcasm out of his voice. He saw Katy shoot a look behind him and turned to see Mitch holding the bag of rice. Mitch looked from Katy to him to Summer and then back to Katy. Nobody was saying anything, and Landis tried not to let the awkwardness annoy him further.

"Thanks, Mitch." Summer stepped past Landis to take the cloth bag Mitch was holding out. Landis was surrounded by a sweet scent that swirled in her wake, and jerked back from her. He shook his head, wondering if, despite her look of disdain, this was some kind of ploy. In his world, most women had some kind of agenda.

Summer caught his expression and head shake, and he could see her stiffen and the look of disdain come back to her face.

"I'll talk to you tomorrow, Katy," Summer said shortly, as she stepped off the porch and headed toward a path that ran through the trees beyond where the cars were parked.

"Okay." Katy waved a distracted goodbye to Summer's quickly departing back.

"Are you hungry?" Mitch asked him, as Katy turned back to loop her arm through Mitch's and stood looking at Landis strangely. There was definitely a setup being planned between him and this Summer woman. He could spot those a mile away.

In response to the question, Landis's stomach let out a low growl. "I guess I am. I don't think I've eaten since breakfast... fifteen hours ago." That's what this disorientation was. Not a weird reaction to the smell of an angry woman. Landis felt marginally better.

"Come on in, my friend, and we'll get you set up with... some scrambled eggs, or a sandwich? What do you prefer?" Mitch asked, guiding Katy with one arm and holding the screen door with the other. Landis followed behind the pair, going through the door and into the kitchen.

"A sandwich sounds great." Landis ran his hand through his hair then rubbed his stubbly chin tiredly. "I want to apologize if I seem crabby. I've got a few situations that have developed in the last while, and they're all becoming critical this weekend, it seems." Mitch pulled a pre-made sandwich out of the fridge and set it on the island. The three of them gathered around.

"Is one of the situations buying *The Cranberry Chronicle?*" Katy asked, gnawing on her lip and watching Landis intently.

"Well... yes, actually. But that's a good situation. It looks like a slam dunk based on the financials I've seen."

"I don't want to throw a wrench into your good situation, but you may have some competition."

Landis turned the plate in front of him, eyeing the meat-stacked marble bread sandwich hungrily. "This looks amazing. Thanks." Landis nodded at Mitch and took a healthy bite. He glanced back to Katy to see a wicked gleam in her eye and a tiny smile at the corner of her lips.

"Oh yeah? Who's the competition?" he asked around a mouthful of sandwich.

"Summer."

"Summer. The woman I just met."

"Yup!" Now Katy fully smiled.

"Summer... what?" Mitch asked.

"Summer wants to form a consortium to buy *The Chronicle*."

"Form a consortium?" The sandwich was sending instant energy to his brain and already dulling the throbbing at his temples. He took another bite and nodded a thank you at Mitch, who'd filled a glass of water and placed it in front of him. "That's a big move," he admitted to Katy. "Does she know what's involved to pull something like that off?"

"Summer is friends with most of the businesses in Cranberry Hill. And with a lot of the residents. She thinks they'd be willing to keep the newspaper local," Katy said, fixing an innocent look on her face.

"Summer thinks this? Our Summer?" Mitch questioned Katy, who simply shrugged again and nodded.

"I think she could do it," she added.

"By this weekend?" Landis paused for a long drink of water. "Because after I talk to Mr. Halcourt and settle on some of the details, I'm ready to formalize an agreement and transfer a large sum of cash directly over to him. Can she move faster than that?" Landis raised a brow at her, his headache almost completely gone. Was it the sandwich, the thought of thwarting Miss Snooty, or a good business battle? This weekend was getting more interesting by the second.

"Maybe. Or maybe she just needs to let her boss know what she's thinking and squash your deal."

Landis frowned. "What boss?"

"Gage Halcourt, editor and owner of *The Cranberry Chronicle*. And honorary dad to his star reporter, the woman who singlehandedly led the paper to its first significant profits over the past year and a half—

Summer Richardson." Katy couldn't stop the triumphant ring that sounded with her last words.

Mitch whistled as Landis's frown deepened. "That's all true, buddy. Gage treats Summer like the daughter he never had. He's adopted every idea she's had, and they've all worked."

Landis took another bite of his sandwich and mulled this over. The thought of this challenge sent a shot of energy through his body. He thought of Summer's look of disdain at meeting him, and where he already was in terms of negotiating with Gage. He felt his familiar game face slide into place. This is where he lived, negotiating deals and pulling together complex details to everyone's satisfaction. Summer stood no chance.

Katy's expression faltered slightly as she looked at him, and she tucked herself a little closer to Mitch as Landis stood and leaned toward her with a fierce look.

"Game. On," he said, and picked up the last of his sandwich and his bags.

"One sec while I grab your key." Mitch hustled around the corner to the front desk. Katy eyed Landis uncertainly. Landis took pity on her. Katy and Summer were obviously good friends, and despite this being business—and when it came to business, it was every man or woman for him or herself—he wanted to reassure Katy.

"Look, this is just a business deal. I'm not out to ruin anyone. In fact, my personal belief is that both sides of any business arrangement can get what they want if they put in the work. It's not a zero-sum game for me. If Summer is this amazing reporter, odds are Blake Media would renegotiate her contract to make sure she stays put—or negotiate out of her contract in a way that is equitable to everyone."

Katy looked a little uncertain, absent-mindedly rubbing her belly. "That sounds fair."

"I don't believe in scorched earth. But I know the media business, and although she might try valiantly to buy the paper, I think she'll fail, which won't help her opinion of me. I could tell when we met that I didn't impress her much."

A laugh burst out of Katy. "You're not kidding! She got one look at your fancy Mercedes and called you an elitist media tycoon." She immediately slapped a hand over her mouth. "Don't tell her I told you that!"

"Told Landis what?" Mitch walked into the kitchen and handed Landis a key.

"That I'm an elitist media tycoon," he replied, and laughed when Katy shouted, "Hey! No telling *anyone!*"

Landis chuckled then took the key, his bags, and his sandwich and walked into a dining room and lobby area, where a wide staircase led guests to the rooms on the second level. Mitch and Katy trailed after him.

"You don't look like that elitist Monopoly guy"—Mitch considered Landis's appearance—"at least not yet. Maybe once your hair goes gray. And you grow a bushy mustache."

Landis paused at the bottom stair, looking at Katy. "You said Summer was responsible for the paper's recent profitability. Is that because of sales skills, or strictly because of reporting and content?"

"She would say the last one, although she has an amazing way with people. I've seen her get the thriftiest business owners to buy ads and sponsor sections."

"Hm, interesting," Landis mused, then tipped his head to both of them. "Thank you for waiting up. Thank you again for the sandwich. And thank you for the heads-up in my business negotiations. I'll see you in the morning." He climbed the stairs with a certain spring in his step. He glanced back at the couple, who were chatting vigorously. Katy had a slightly worried look on her face, but Mitch looked like he was barely containing his laughter.

In his room, Landis set down everything except the small remains of his sandwich, which he demolished in two bites. He took out his laptop and started it up. While he waited, he unbuttoned his shirt and retrieved his toiletry bag from his suitcase.

His room shared a bathroom with the room across the hall; however, he knew from Mitch he was the only guest for tonight and through the weekend. Flipping the toggle on the round, Bakelite-period light switch, Landis took his time admiring the restoration they'd done to the Cape Cod-style bathroom, from the white, antiqued wainscoting to the finely patterned golden brocade wallpaper and period light fixture. He made a close inspection while he brushed his teeth. Man, they'd nailed the heritage look but with a modern feel.

After he finished washing up, he headed back to his room. He couldn't imagine working on a hands-on project of this scope with any of the women he knew. The whole concept would be alien to his mother, who would rather hire someone to hire someone to manage the work. And Stella would be impossible. Although incredibly smart and business savvy, she proved the stereotype of fiery redheads. He stood in front of his laptop, scanning his email. There it was, an updated financial report from Melanie on *The Cranberry Chronicle*.

He opened the password-protected document and paged directly to the income statement. Gage Harcourt had directed his accountant to update the document to include the three previous years' figures, and after what he'd learned from Katy, he was eager to look at the numbers. Sitting down, he scanned the columns and, sure enough, there it was in black and white. Income spiked almost two years ago and has continued to grow month after month. And all based on sales, not a cash injection in sight, as was sometimes the case. A quick flip to the balance sheet showed that the newspaper was well capitalized and modestly run. This was a no-brainer. If Gage wanted to sell, he was buying. He didn't really need a face-to-face meeting to finalize the deal, but his gut told him Gage would never sell the paper without it.

A light caught his eye through the window. He got up to look out at the trees, where the light was shining. That must be the barn loft. Where Summer lived. One thing he knew—he had to keep her at the paper if he wanted to see continued growth. At least for the first year. There was a steady rise in advertising revenue on the balance sheet, but no corresponding spike in marketing costs, so it was likely that Katy was right; Summer was the driving force that turned the paper around. And she couldn't stand him.

Landis's mind flashed to the silky, sparkling hollow at the base of her throat, and the hair on the back of his neck tingled. She'd worn a thin, silver chain with a slim silver bar that hung right there, in that hollow. He thought of the sheen of her skin, and how salty it would be...

Wait!

Landis turned abruptly from the window. He didn't need distractions. It was clear Gage wouldn't be a challenge, but getting Summer to stay with the paper would be. He needed to see her contract and find out what her specific role at the paper was. This was no big deal. He did this all the time. But as he set the alarm on his phone for 5:00 a.m., he wondered why his hands felt a little sweaty.

3

Summer lay in bed, staring at the ceiling. She'd been up all night plotting her strategy to build her consortium. The idea had started when she'd first found out Gage had sent financials off to some company, but it had been a whim to imagine herself taking it over. Now it seemed like an imperative.

After she settled her mind down last night, she'd been able to sketch out a rough plan that included talking to Gage, assessing interest in the few contacts she had, and then expanding that circle to include the newspaper's business partners and some key people in Cranberry Hill.

She'd been eager to broach the idea with Katy to see if she could punch holes in it, but when she'd seen the silver Mercedes logo on the slinky black car and the GQ cover model who was Landis Blake, her idea ramped up from planning stage to ready-to-fire.

When Katy had come out to greet her, Summer waved her over and blurted, "I'm going to buy the newspaper!" Then she rambled on with all her thoughts, probably in an incoherent mess. Katy was caught off guard, but very quickly caught up with her enthusiasm. Which, if she looked at her flurry of babble honestly, was probably ninety percent mania and ten percent solid, fact-based elation for a business idea.

"Oooh," Summer groaned, and jumped out of bed and into the chair in front of her computer. All those emails she'd sent in the heat of her excitement. She wanted to gauge the appetite of the few local business owners as soon as possible. But... did she really send them out at... "Oh no, 2:12 in the morning! And 2:27... and 2:51...." She groaned again.

She quickly read through all she told them, nodding at some of what she wrote, wincing at bits. She also cringed at her overuse of exclamation marks, a personal pet peeve. She leaned back.

The cat was out of the bag, as they said, and since her email program didn't have a "retract sent email" feature, her idea was out in the world. She pacified herself with the belief that this uncharacteristically impulsive act would be interpreted as a once-in-a-lifetime opportunity, and not the act of a manic woman.

She combed through her handwritten notes that were strewn across the desk. Somewhere in the paper mess was a checklist of next steps. After about a minute, she'd found no less than three lists. Summer sighed.

Her computer told her it was 6:32 a.m. If she hurried, she could beat everyone to the office and have an hour to chat with Gage, who was naturally an early riser. She convinced herself that she didn't have to have everything in order; she just needed to convince him her idea was sound. And get him to back off any final decisions about a Blake Media acquisition. Summer bounced up and headed to the shower, running through conversation starters in her mind.

Twenty minutes later, she deflated as she stood in front of her closet. All her clothes said *Pacific Northwest Bohemian Hipster*, except for the sweatpants and leggings, which spoke for themselves. Did she really purge all of her *Wannabe Anchorwoman* suits?

Katy's closet would be chockfull of seven kinds of business wear, but no way was she going to wake up her friend. Plus, with their height difference, the resulting short skirt length would send the wrong message. Making the best of it, Summer pulled out a lightly embroidered white peasant blouse and a somewhat muted wrap skirt.

Tiptoeing out of the loft and down the stairs, Summer opened one of the main barn doors, which creaked horrendously, and pulled out her bike. Throwing on her cloth backpack that held her notes and the few printed pages of her plan, she started off down the back trail and took the fork that would lead her to Beach Drive Road and Cranberry Hill township proper.

It was a glorious morning. The first tide of the day was fully in and the sea salt air swirled around her as she rode. No one was on this stretch of the road this early, so she could ride down the center line as she headed east into the sunrise and town.

Summer loved that she knew this town so well. Being the only reporter in such a small community meant she got to meet everybody and learn their stories. She didn't even mind the fact that everyone learned her story. And her brother's. And their history. She knew whenever she and Carson were in town together that people affectionately referred to them as "the orphans." It wasn't meant to be hurtful, just a nod to the fact that no Cranberry Hill citizen had ever lost parents in a car accident.

She loved knowing the history of the abandoned cranberry farms and fields—they couldn't keep up with the investment in new harvesting technology. And that the biggest scandal was when the local hardware store took twenty-four hours to refund the purchase of three gallons of paint that had been tinted incorrectly—new employee and inexperience.

She knew that, of the two cafés in town, the Golden Lily made the best pour overs, and the Oasis had the best scones. She'd sold ads to them both after featuring them in a lifestyle column. She also knew all five firefighters—Brian, Stephen, Carter, Jax, and Phil—at the neighboring Chutney Fire Department after meeting them in several community slow-pitch games. They each took turns visiting her for their monthly community PSA for the paper.

But strangely, one thing she loved most was the land. How Beach Drive Road swept you in and away from the crazy urban world to the raw ocean, hooked around the inn's generous plot of land, and then gently guided you back in, past a cliff of dramatic madrone trees and over rolling hills that one by one revealed the bits of the sleepy town that lay ahead.

All the storefronts had been kept classic '50s, with only updates of paint. She may or may not have been influential in a few town hall meetings when improvements were discussed. She had a vision for the town and was not ashamed to use her influence to encourage refurbishments to follow a plan. A few of the townies had suggested she run for county council, but politics were definitely not her thing.

She pulled up in front of the newspaper and got off her bike. She walked it around the side of the building where the bike racks were and froze in her tracks. There sat a black Mercedes in all its squat opulence and prestige. She'd taken the back trail from home, and therefore hadn't seen which cars were still parked at the inn. Somewhere in her belly, a fuse ignited, and she could hear the practical, analytical Summer jumping around and trying to stamp out the lit end of it.

She robotically locked up her bike, trying to induce breath and release, but it wasn't working. She felt raw fear at having to go into Gage's office and try to out-business the consummate New York businessman at his own game.

What were you thinking? she argued with herself.

I was thinking I'd hit on a pretty good idea, she argued back.

Liar! You were thinking Gage is not *a businessperson, and he would be so wowed by your amazing proposal that he would accept it immediately and give you all the time you needed to make it happen. Happily ever after. The end.*

It *was* an amazing proposal, and any business owner would see it made sense.

But Landis wouldn't. He'd know it for the cooked up frenzied act of... what? A madwoman? A desperate woman?

Why are you desperate, Summer? What are you desperate for?

She inhaled deeply, willing calm to enter along with the pull of air and spread throughout her body. This self-talk wouldn't help anything. She had to settle down, march into Gage's office regardless of who was there, and pitch her idea to him.

If her voice shook, fine. If she threw up in a recycle bin, also fine. If Landis jumped in and outmaneuvered her with fancy business language, okay. The only thing that mattered was presenting her case from her heart and letting whatever happened next happen. Although she really didn't want to vomit in a recycle bin.

She waited a moment to see if the voices in her head would come back and argue some more, but they seemed to be in agreement with her course of action. Before anything could change, she charged into the building.

She got out on the top floor of the three-floor building and walked down the narrow hallway to the door with "This is your Cranberry Hill Chronicle" into the glass. She took a last deep breath and opened the door.

Across the open work area of six desks was the semi-walled-off area where Gage had his office. Her throat closed up as she recognized the tall figure of Landis rising from a chair. The sound of the door caught the attention of both men, and Gage and Landis turned to look over at her. She straightened up and slid her cotton backpack off. Reaching inside, she pulled out the pages of her proposal, and loosened her grip on them so they wouldn't shake so much

"Well, I guess I should be leaving." Landis reached out a hand to Gage. "Thanks for your time this morning. I'm in town until Sunday, if you want to talk things over in more detail before then. I know it's a lot for you to consider."

Gage shook Landis's hand with a smile. "Not that much, really. You'd be surprised at how close we are on terms already."

Summer felt her heart sink to her feet. She forced them to carry her across the office just as both men headed her way toward the elevator.

Don't give up, Summer.

"Good morning, Summer," Landis greeted, his expression politely blank. He zipped the bottom of a camel-colored light sports jacket. As he stepped closer, a hint of cologne teased her senses, and she took a step back. An unruly part of her wanted to shove him against the wall for trying to entrap her with his scent. *What a rich, entitled...*

"Summer! You're here early." Gage smiled, walked up to her, and gave her shoulders a friendly squeeze. "I'm glad. I want to talk to you." He headed back to his desk.

Landis stared at her intently, his silver eyes drawing her in. She stared back, lifting an eyebrow and straightening her shoulders. After a heartbeat, he turned to walk to the elevators, and said, "Enjoy the day."

She turned and followed Gage with heavy footsteps.

"Sit down, my dear. I have some news." But Gage himself didn't sit. With his curly gray hair, mustache, and round glasses, his eyes glittered like an excited scientist who'd just pulled off the best experiment ever. Summer stayed standing too, sensing she would lose some kind of edge if he was above her.

"I had something I wanted to talk to you about, too." She lifted the meager pages she held in her hand, looking from Gage to his desktop, and saw a brown envelope and a blue folder. A sticker on the folder said **Offer of Intent.** Wow, not only was he fast with the deals, he was fast with the professional stationary.

She looked down at her loose papers and gathered as much enthusiasm as she could to inject into her next words. "I know you've probably just received a pretty amazing offer—"

"The most *amazing* offer. Truly, my accountant made a guess at what I could expect, but this... well, when I call him and tell him, I think he's going to fall out of his chair." He scratched the back of his neck and shook his head in disbelief, rocking back and forth from his toes to his heels.

"Before you make any final decisions, I think you should be open to other ideas." Summer tried to make her smile genuine, but this was getting worse by the second. "It's never, ever a good idea to act rashly, even if it's a most amazing offer."

"My dear Summer, this offer affects you too!" Gage said excitedly, dropping into his chair and picking up the neatly bound document in front of him. Summer slowly sank down across from him.

He took on an official demeanor as he flipped to the title page.

"This is an offer of intent for Blake Media to acquire 1798469 Holding Company LLC, dba the Cranberry Hill Chronicle Newspaper... um, let's see." He tilted his head back to get a better look at the page through his bifocals. "It goes on with more legal jargon I'll get Gordon to go over, but here's the part about you." His finger moved farther down the page and he looked closely at it so he got every word right. "'Summer Richardson shall be promoted to the position of Editor with a salary commensurate with the current Editor position, to be increased by 15% within 90 days should all parties find the position satisfactory.' And then it goes on to define duties and whatnot, but isn't that the most incredible thing?"

Gage dropped the document back on his desk with a dramatic flourish, pulled off his glasses, and threw them on top for effect. He leaned back in his chair to stare at her, ready for her to be amazed as well.

And she was amazed. Amazed that Landis Blake had the balls to try to buy her off.

"Editor? I can't be an editor. I'm a writer, Gage. I don't know anything about putting a newspaper together, about all the things you do to keep this place running!" Summer sat back with a curious feeling.

What she said was true, and yet here she was about to make a case for owning the Chronicle as the papers in her lap detailed. She brushed the feeling aside for now.

"Also, I question the generosity of that salary. Nobody in their right mind would offer that to a newcomer, someone with no experience whatsoever." She scoffed, folding her arms. "He might be addled. You should have your people look into his mental stability."

Gage only hooted at that and waved her words away. "Summer." He leaned forward, elbows on his desk as he picked up his glasses to shake them at her with each of his following words. "You run the paper right now. In fact, since the day you've walked in here, you've exhibited an innate understanding of what it takes to make a paper successful. And then you just plowed ahead and did it." He beamed at her.

"I don't know what you mean." She was confused. All Summer remembered about her first weeks here were writing her head off and meeting deadlines.

"You met with people, wrote hundreds of stories, and people fell in love with you. And you happened to sell ads along the way. *And* got us on the map when regional events needed a fresh perspective. That's never happened for the Chronicle before. Now, from my side of the desk, that's called meeting with our key stakeholders, creating content guidelines, and acting as our principal sales manager." Gage leaned back, steepling his fingers as he watched his words sink in and various expressions flash across her face.

"But that was just.... I didn't set out to do any of that." Summer couldn't argue with anything Gage said, but she wanted to try.

"Of course you didn't. It came naturally to you. That's why I know you're the perfect person for the editor's chair. Honestly, I thought years ago that one day I would sell the paper, but there was nobody local that I knew for a fact could step in and do what you've done." Gage got up and walked around to lean on his desk and face her. Summer stood, her papers useless in her hand.

Gage pointed to the papers. "Landis said you may have an idea about taking over the paper, and it seems like you have some sort of a plan there. But I'm telling you right now—you were made for this position. You've got the chops, young lady. And even better, you can still write if you want. Goodness knows I've taken advantage of your writing skills to shirk that duty myself."

"No, no, don't say shirk. You've been there for June, and that's how it should be." Summer looked down at the papers in her hand. "My idea... is not as good as the Blake Media offer. Um, can I have time to think it over?"

"Of course you can! But please, don't overanalyze it, Summer. Tell Carson and Katy about it. They'll lend an objective ear. I have a feeling the idea you have there is likely very similar, just with a lot of added headache, mostly for you." Gage smiled, and Summer could read a small speck of pity in his eyes as he held out his hand. "Let me look at what you've put together, though. In the name of fairness."

Summer reluctantly handed over her pages and watched him walk around his desk and place them beside the glossy blue offer. Her face felt warm when she saw them side by side, and she turned abruptly to head to her desk.

"One more thing, Summer." Gage was back to business, looking through some papers in his in-basket. "I need you to go out to Harrison's Farm. They're having a very belated estate sale, but word is they're selling a rare Van Gogh that Linus kept hidden. Can you imagine that? A hidden masterpiece? I want you to go scout it out. Here's some contact info for an art dealer in Seattle that can give you

DEADLINE ON LOVE

some pointers if Viola lets you look at the painting." Gage handed her torn piece of paper.

"Why wouldn't she let me look at it?" Summer stepped back to take the paper from him. "I had tea with her at the junior high school track meet in March. She'd probably let me look through her underwear drawer." Summer frowned. She looked up from the paper to see Gage simultaneously beaming and shaking his head at her.

"Do I need to say more about why you'd make an excellent editor? Now get going before Viola gets too busy to show you anything. I'm heading to the hospital but need to make a to-do list for Hank before I leave. About the painting," he called as Summer started to walk away. "If it turns out to be interesting, I want to put it on the front page of next Wednesday's issue. If not, let's just give it a write up for page three's Happenings column." Summer gave Gage a half-hearted salute and headed across the office to the elevator.

She stabbed the down button as her thoughts turned to Landis. What was he up to with this job offer? Probably lulling her into a false sense of security for whatever probationary period was noted, and then he would cut her loose for some junior reporter who would do the job for half the salary. She'd spend some money to get a good lawyer to look over this agreement. Someone from back in Chicago. Gage's lawyers here probably weren't devious enough to smell out really dirty tricks.

❧

PUSHING OPEN THE GLASS DOOR OF THE OFFICE BUILDING, SHE stepped out into the morning sun, her legs warming in the light. Wait. What did Gage say? *"Landis said you may have an idea about taking over the paper..."*

"Son of a bitch!" She marched around the building to get her bike and stopped cold when she saw Landis standing beside the driver's door of his car, hands on his hips and facing away from her down the street. "Contemplating the next business takeover in Cranberry Hill?" She stared at him angrily then rooted around in her backpack for her lock key. He turned around abruptly, looking surprised.

"Not exactly. Look, let me give you a lift home. We should talk." He walked over to the rack, looking down at her as she unlocked the bike.

"I'm not going home. I've got to work to do." She put the U-lock back in its holder and stood to look at him with mock sweetness. "As in real work at a real job. I'm not flying around the country buying things. Besides, I thought you'd be in a hurry to fly home. Mission accomplished and all that." She lifted her bike seat to pull it out of the rack, but Landis took hold of the other side of the handlebar and seat, setting it back into the rack.

"Then let me drive you to wherever your job is. I want to talk to you." Landis released the U-lock from its holder and held it out to her. "Please?" His lips compressed and she wondered what game he was playing now.

"Wow," she deadpanned, "I bet that word was hard for you."

"Not when I want something." He stared at her and she waited for him to say more. He didn't, just continued to what he probably thought was a smoldering look. *Egotistical jerk.*

Summer slit her eyes at him, which caused a corner of his mouth to quirk up.

"Are those your reporter eyes, meant to stab me in the heart?"

"You can't stab something that isn't there."

She'd wanted to confront him about how he knew of her plan, but she'd wanted the bike ride to Viola's farm to give her time to sort out her argument. Maybe it was better just to jump into it.

With a grunt, Summer bent to lock her bike in short angry movements. He backed up and opened the passenger door for her. She got in, and he bent over before closing the door.

"Here are two other words that will shock you—thank you." He smirked as she scrunched her face at him.

4

Landis pulled up to the main road, letting the simple task of navigating distract him from his nerves. *Why am I jittery? The deal is basically done, and all I have to do is damage control to make sure it stays that way.*

"Which way are we going?" he asked.

"Left," Summer bit out, staring straight ahead.

They drove in silence for a minute. "Then where?" Landis asked.

"It's on this road. I'll tell you when to turn." She looked out her window.

He drove for another minute, feeling her tension, which was in turn making *him* tense. "And how long until the turn?"

An exaggerated sigh from Summer. "Twenty minutes."

His grip tightened on the wheel. Tension in someone else was usually good news for him. It meant he'd found a weakness and just had to pay attention to use it to his advantage. But this... this was not comfortable at all.

He needed the two of them to be on better terms, even if it was just for politeness's sake. He didn't want her to blow up, and then blow up the deal. But she had this irrational dislike of him, and it hurt his pride a little that she didn't respond to his intense stare the way al women did. Maybe hurt more than a little.

Maybe her dislike was distrust. He puzzled at this, trying to find the right way to approach it.

"I want to come clean with you," he started, "Katy may have let it slip that you were thinking of setting up a consortium to buy the paper."

"'May have let it slip'?" she accused, her eyes flickering to him and then back to the road.

"I think she's on your side and thought that, by telling me, maybe I'd back down on my offer. Look, the best business deals are the ones where everybody wins. And everybody wins in this one." He glanced over at Summer, who had just folded her arms over her chest. "Do you really have a deep yearning to raise capital, handle the legal paperwork, take on all the headaches that come with owning a newspaper, *and* deal with the job of running that same newspaper? Is that really what's in your heart?"

He watched Summer cock her head to one side and then slowly turn to look at him. Her eyes were cold crystals, and her direct gaze did something funny to his breathing. Her folded arms loosened until her hands met in her lap and clasped together, and then she faced the road once more.

"If I'm being honest," she said slowly and evenly, "no. That's not what's really in my heart. I'm not a businessperson like... like Katy is," she finished.

She wasn't going to give him any credit for knowing business. Well, that was fine. He sensed her settle a little more into her seat, instead of how she'd been sitting, straight as a post without touching the seatback. That was a good sign.

"Mitch is an old friend, and I've only just met Katy, but she seems nice. And the two of you are friends, so I don't want the business I have with the Chronicle creating bad feelings for anyone. Can we make a truce here?" She was quiet and still for so long that he glanced over at her to see if she'd heard him.

She was facing ahead, but he saw her eyes flick over to him and then away, and her teeth quickly bit her bottom lip and then released it. His gut squeezed, and his pulse kicked into a faster gear. The lip bite pulled his attention to her pale-pink lips, and when her tongue darted out after it, his heart rate amped up another ten beats. *Dammit, man, get a grip.* He didn't need any complications, so he held out his hand.

"Truce?" he prompted.

Summer paused then reached out and gave his hand a solid shake. Her skin was smooth and cool, the bones in her hand and fingers long and delicate.

"Okay, truce," she said, but her words were stilted. "You're right. I don't want bad feelings between us to affect Katy. She doesn't need the added stress of arbitrating between friends so close to the baby's due date."

"Agreed. Can I go one step further and say we should try to find some friendly ground? I'd prefer our truce to become a lasting peace treaty."

"You can try," she allowed, her tone saying she thought it unlikely.

"Here's something that will put you forever in my good books." Landis pressed the Talk button on his steering wheel as Summer watched him curiously. A *ping* sounded from the stereo.

"Tell me what you would like me to help you with," said the audio assistant.

"Play Little Walter Jacobs," Landis requested.

"I'm sorry, what was that?" she responded.

"Play. Little. Walter. Jacobs." Landis enunciated each word.

"I'm sorry, I still didn't understand. To request an action, you could say 'Play a station,' or, 'Navigate home.' Please try again." The same *ping* sound followed.

Landis pressed cancel on the car's video screen. "It's infuriating." He shook his head.

"Maybe you're not loud enough," Summer suggested.

"You want to take a shot?" he asked, and she nodded. "I think the microphone is up here." Landis pointed to a thick plastic piece the rearview mirror was mounted to. "Ready?"

"Are *you* ready?" Summer asked and leaned toward the mirror with a wicked smile. Landis pressed the talk button again.

"Tell me what you would like me to help you with," prompted the automated voice.

"Play Little Walter Jacobs!" Summer yelled into the mic, almost bursting his ear drums, and then fell back in her seat with a laugh.

"I'm sorry, what was that?" asked the voice.

"Play Little Walter Jacobs." Summer lowered her voice down into a rough grumble.

"I'm sorry, I couldn't find Lilly Water Jenkins in your contacts. Please try again."

This time, they both laughed.

"This car is obviously broken." Summer scoffed.

"See? Even elite media tycoons have problems," he chided.

Summer smirked at him. "Well, I'm glad you're owning your elite tycoon-ness. Is this car connected to your phone?" When Landis nodded, Summer held out her hand. "Let's do this the old-fashioned way."

Landis took his phone out of this shirt pocket, held it up for face recognition, and then passed it to Summer. "You realize what a leap of faith I'm taking by handing you my unlocked cell phone."

"Oh, I appreciate it all right. Now, let's see. Where's your mom in your contacts? I have a tall tale I could tell her about her son." She chuckled as Landis made a grab at the phone. "Just kidding! Sheesh. I'm sure there's no story wild enough that she wouldn't believe."

"Ouch. Is your opinion of me really that bad?" Landis joked, glad some of her animosity had faded.

Summer put down the phone and turned slightly to face him. "I'm sorry. We agreed on a truce and I'm just being... petty."

He looked at her earnest face, hair fluttering around her beautiful features, and for once her lips curved down in regret and not a smirk.

She sat there in what he guessed was the most formal clothing she owned—a white blouse and colorful skirt—and he wanted to scoop her up in his hands like a little bird and protect her. No woman had ever made him feel that, not even the women he thought he'd been in love with. *Wait, where did that thought come from?*

"Apology accepted," he said, and faced back to the road to get his thoughts back on business.

Summer went back to looking at his phone. "Huh, you really are a blues fan. I thought the Little Walter Jacobs was a fluke."

"No, ma'am, I'm a big blues fan."

"Mostly Chicago blues, though," she said as she scrolled through his song selection, "which I guess I can forgive."

Landis was flabbergasted. "Forgive? What are you talking about? Chicago blues is everything. What tops it?"

"Mississippi blues, of which Chicago blues is derived from." Landis picked up a tinge of condescension in her voice.

"And you're an expert, how?"

"I was raised in Tutwiler, Mississippi. When I was twelve, my parents died in a car accident and my brother and I moved there to live with my aunt and uncle. When I was a little older, my brother and I would hitch rides up to Clarksdale for the Juke Joint Jamboree. It doesn't get more bluesy than that." Summer raised her eyebrow at him.

Landis whistled. "No, indeed." He paused before going on. "I'm sorry about your parents."

"Thank you. It happened a long time ago, and luckily Carson and I have lots of good memories." She shrugged.

"A Juke Joint Jamboree sounds amazing."

"It was. And sometimes dangerous, because we were too young to be hitching rides. But I'll never forget it. The music embeds itself in your soul."

They spent the next ten minutes discussing music, listening to songs, and sharing their top ten concerts.

Landis was surprised at some of the things he shared with her. Things he'd never told the handful of girlfriends he'd had, because they hadn't seemed to care to know. Summer wanted to know everything about any event he mentioned. He wondered if it was genuine interest, or just her journalism habits taking over.

"Oh, turn left up there by the green mailbox." Summer pointed up the next hill, where a green box on a post marked a driveway that was surrounded by trees. Pink balloons were hanging from it.

"It's not too early?" he asked, but Summer just huffed.

"These are farm folk. They've been up for hours."

Landis turned the Mercedes off the road and drove up the long driveway that opened out into a wide yard. Straight ahead was an ancient red barn, and to the right was a big century-old farmhouse.

Strewn around the yard were tables filled with kitchen items, glassware, books, and other items. Racks of clothes stood off to one side. In and around the barn were farming implements from hoes and rakes to a harvester and a tractor.

Landis and Summer exited the car at the same time. She rummaged in her backpack and pulled out a notebook and pen. A few people were carrying items out of the back of the barn and from the house, arranging them on the ground near the overflowing tables.

"Hey, Viola!" Summer called to an elderly stooped woman. Viola wore a pink cotton dress and a light white sweater. Her face was covered by large-framed glasses that were connected to a silver chain that ran around her neck.

"Summer!" Viola greeted her with a lift of her hand. "Come for the sale?"

"Well, I've come to see one thing you might be selling," Summer coaxed kindly, going up to Viola, hugging her, and getting a hug in return.

"Now, now, now, who told you that?" she teased. When Summer shrugged, Viola glanced over at Landis. "Who's your fella?"

"This is Landis. He's friends with Katy's Mitch."

"Hello, friend Landis. Nice t' meet you." Viola held out her hand for a dainty handshake, which Landis obliged. "Now, young lady, give me a few minutes and then I'll take you to see what the big hoopla is about."

She disappeared into the house, and Landis followed Summer as she moved from table to table, perusing the goods on display. Sometimes she commented on an item or asked one of Viola's helpers a question about something that was for sale.

Kindness and caring poured out of Summer as she spoke with the people. It showed in the way she picked up an ancient rusted eggbeater, or a delicate piece of crockery. It showed in the patient way she listened to the older man in the barn, who had trouble finding the right words. And it showed in the way she touched a shoulder or an arm when asking a question or responding with a shared delight.

He also found he couldn't keep his eyes off her body. She was nothing like what he normally looked for in a woman, which was lush, round curves. Her body was lithe and strong and tanned, with modest curves. Yet the shape of her toned calves and her elegant neck ignited something in him. He couldn't look away nor let her get too far away from him. He felt possessiveness he didn't know what to do with.

"Okay, c'mon," Viola called to them from the front steps of the house, pulling Landis out of his musings. They all went into the house and up four flights of stairs to an alcove that housed the access to the attic. A knob hung from the ceiling where it could pull down the hidden attic stairs. "There it is," Viola said, pointing to the wall inside the alcove and moving aside so they could get closer.

Landis and Summer stepped into the space and peered at the wall. In a frame was a charcoal sketch of a farmwoman standing but bent down, her back facing the artist and her face hidden in a bonnet. She was hoeing a hole to plant a leafy vegetable that was in a basket beside her on the ground. Around the figure, the artist had merely made cross-hatches and other nondescript markings. In the bottom right corner, also in charcoal, was written **Vincent.** Landis looked at Summer, who looked back at him with wide eyes.

"Wow, this is beautiful, Viola." Summer leaned closer, taking in every detail and then making some notes. Landis leaned with her to get a better look as well, but quickly became distracted by the fresh scent of her perfume. "You're not going to sell it, are you?" she asked.

"Oh, I'm selling almost everything. Gonna move to Mount Vernon. They got me a spot in one of those independent living places."

"But you could probably take this with you, if you wanted to." Summer gently touched the carved wooden frame. Landis watched her slim fingers slide gently over the curves and notches.

"Ach, I don't much care for that kind of art." Viola waved her hand dismissively. "I like bright colors. But if this could fetch a pretty dollar, I'd be happy. Do you know anything about it?"

"Not yet, but I can call someone who might. Do you know anything about where it came from?" She took her phone out of her backpack and took a few pictures.

"Just that it belonged to Linus's dad way back. Nobody ever talked about it, but one of the nurses who came to look after Linus saw it and said it might be worth something."

"Huh, well, it might. But it might not. Do you mind if I make a phone call?" She tipped her phone toward Viola, who gave one nod.

"Go right ahead. I'm going to go back outside and keep arranging."

Landis leaned in to look at the paper Summer fished out of her bag. "Who are you calling?" He was thinking of his contacts and who might be best for this type of identification.

"Gage gave me the number for an art dealer in Seattle. Troy... Haversham? I think?" She held the paper out to him. "Do you think that's what it says? Gage's writing is atrocious."

"Yes. I've spoken with Troy before. I wish he'd been the one arranging the Wyeth exhibit. I would have gotten further," Landis muttered, and shook his head with a "never mind" when she looked at him questioningly. She looked back at her phone to call the number, when Landis's phone rang.

"Hi, Melanie," he answered, stepping away from her and the painting.

"I promised Evelyn I'd remind you about the strike vote tomorrow, and she promised she wouldn't call you a hundred times and hound you about what your next steps will be if they vote to strike."

"Thank you for that. And don't think I don't know this is your tricky way to get me to figure out next steps for Evelyn." Landis rubbed the back of his neck, and then turned to see Summer disconnect from her call with a grunt of frustration before trying a second number as she paced farther away from him. "Melanie, do you have the number for the Master's Curator at the Met?" He lowered his voice and faced away from Summer.

"Hang on." There were three beats of silence as Melanie searched. "Alison Horvath is actually an assistant curator but specializes in the masters."

"Can you find out if she's able to authenticate a Van Gogh sketch? And if not, could she recommend someone?"

"Okay. Do you want a phone consultation, or for someone to come out to wherever the artwork is?"

"Let's start with some photos and then take it from there."

"Sounds good, boss."

"That's great. Thanks, Melanie. I'll call you back later about the next steps if there's a strike." Landis disconnected and turned back toward the sketch on the wall. Summer was looking at him oddly, her own phone by her side.

"Did I hear you say something about the Met?" she asked.

Landis took several photos with his phone, some very close, including various angles of the signature, and some from farther away. "Yes, I was at the Gala last year. My mother met the curator, and... well, why not use contacts if you've got them?" He shrugged and looked at her with a grin. Her eyes were back to being frozen chips of ice.

She walked past him and down the stairs. Landis followed, puzzling over her change as they exited the house and found Viola by the sales tables.

"Viola, we're heading out." She gave the older woman a warm hug. "I'll let you know if I find anything out about the sketch. And let's make sure we get together for tea before your big move, okay?"

Viola stepped back but took Summer's hands in hers. Landis could see a sheen in the older woman's eyes. "Thank you so much, dear. And whatever you find out is fine. If it's a work of art, or just a silly doodle, I appreciate you taking the time."

Summer squeezed Viola's hands back. "Good luck with your sale."

Landis gestured to the car, intending for them to walk together, but Summer stomped past him, refusing to make eye contact. He watched her stiff figure walk to the car and halt suddenly, as the door she tried to open was locked.

He walked slowly to the car, feeling the first flares of anger. Reaching into his pocket, he took out his fob and pressed the button to unlock the doors. She wrenched open the door and dropped into her seat, slamming the door closed.

He felt his anger kick higher. He'd done nothing wrong. He'd tried to help her, for chrissake! He slid into the car and pressed the start button before he buckled his seat belt. He saw Summer was already buckled in, her backpack on her lap, and was looking so fixedly out her window he imagined she'd get a crick in her neck in no time.

Fine. He'd ignore her right back. He wasn't going to ask what was wrong, or if she was okay, or if she'd had luck contacting someone—which, now that he thought about it, seemed likely. Maybe that's what had her irked. Well, if she couldn't accept help when she needed it, maybe he should reevaluate her suitability for a promotion.

He backed the Mercedes out in a wide C and abruptly shifted into Drive to head back down the driveway. Summer took hold of her door handle at the sharp acceleration but didn't say anything.

As Landis pulled onto the road, his phone vibrated, and Melanie's call rang through the car's audio system. "What's up, Melanie?"

"Alison Horvath recommended you contact Baxter Reed. He specializes in Van Gough provenance. Should I call?" He could feel Summer tense up at Melanie's question.

Good, Landis thought spitefully.

"Yes, but leave my number so they can call me back directly. Anything else?"

"Just the strike, although you said you'd call later about that."

Landis felt an uncharacteristic surge of frustration well up, and it came out in his next words. "You know what? Lock 'em out. They've been threatening a strike for a while, even after we gave them a cost of living bump. So if they vote to strike, lock them out."

"I'll let Vic know. And Evelyn."

He tapped the Disconnect button on the dash screen without saying goodbye.

"You're just fixing everything today, aren't you?" Summer flicked the drawstring of the backpack on her lap back and forth in sharp movements.

"It's not a fix. A fix would be a calm discussion that would bring an end to strike talk, but labor laws restrict owners from doing anything once union talks begin. Locking them out is a maneuver to break a strike if it happens."

"Does it make you feel powerful to be able to barge in, take charge, and change people's lives in an instant?"

"It makes me feel efficient," Landis answered calmly.

"That's not efficiency. That's escalation."

"So now you're a labor negotiator. Interesting."

"I've covered strikes before and locking out workers who feel the need to strike is petty and vengeful."

"Vengeful. Okay. I'm curious. How would you describe the call to the Met? Because I can tell I did something you think is wrong, and I'm confused about how helping you out has made you angry."

Landis could hear hot frustration creeping into his voice, and he tried to ratchet his emotions down. In his whole life, he'd never had to raise his voice to make a point. To the contrary, his voice usually got low, quiet, and cold.

"That wasn't helping! That was taking over! The rich guy with his fancy connections helping out the small-town reporter girl. Did it make you feel powerful?" Summer's words blasted around the interior of the car.

"I can't win with you, so I'm not going to try." *Breathe deep, buddy.* Landis shifted his body in the seat, suddenly aware how tense every muscle had become.

"Is that how Blake Media runs its papers? They don't trust staff to do their jobs, and they lock out employees who may have a legitimate gripe with management?"

"It doesn't matter what I tell you. You've got me cast as the bad guy. That's pretty slanted for a reporter who should have an unbiased point of view."

"I call them as I see them, and I'm glad I'm getting a sneak preview of what the rule of law will be as editor. If I take the position, that is." Summer bit the words out and looked coldly out at the road.

Landis twisted his hands on the leather steering wheel, annoyed the two of them were back at square one. But then her words sank in, and he set his mind to unraveling the situation. It took a minute for him to be able to trust that his next words would sound calm, but they did.

"Look, it wasn't my intention to take over your research. I truly just wanted to help, because I thought I could. If you don't want me to pursue authenticating the sketch, I won't. Or I can have this Reed guy call you instead. Just… don't make a rash decision that could ruin the deal I'm trying to make with Gage. At least think of him in all this." Landis hoped his voice sounded rational. He wasn't fully sure what tone would set her off again.

"What rash decision? And I would never do anything to hurt Gage." Summer gripped her backpack in two fists, and he had a wild thought she was about to whack him with it.

"Like not taking the editor job. Or quitting to spite me," Landis said earnestly. "Gage will never sell unless you take over as editor, and he told me there's no one else he has confidence in to do it."

He let the silence fill the car. He felt surer of himself now, as if they were in a boardroom and he was negotiating. This was a business objection. A problem to solve. All he had to do was wait.

The first sign that she was cracking was when her hands unclenched from her backpack. He didn't have to wait long for complete victory.

"I wouldn't quit." Her voice was gruff, and some of his triumph drained away. "I'm going to take the editor job." She hugged her arms around herself and leaned back into the seat, closing her eyes. "Can you drop me off at the paper? I want to get some work done. And talk to Gage if he's still there. I should tell him my decision right away and not make him wait."

"Sure." Landis stared straight ahead at the sun-bleached road, oblivious to the rippling summer grasses they cruised by and the glimpses of ocean they had when the dips in the hills allowed them.

He won. And yet, this did not feel good. This was what he'd wanted when they started out—a truce and the assurance she wasn't going to carry on with this pipe dream of a consortium. But the woman beside him seemed to have shrunk to half her size, and it prevented him from fully enjoying the moment.

5

As Landis pulled up in front of the paper, Summer lifted her watch with a heavy heart to check the time. Not lunchtime, but she could feel her stomach moving around, getting ready to growl. Maybe she should snack. She needed something to boost her energy.

"Are you hungry?" He slid the shifter into park and looked at her in a way that made her uncomfortable. As if he was trying to see into her brain.

"No!" She cleared her throat and worked to modulate her next words. "I mean, not yet. I want to get my notes organized and write a draft of what I know so far." She reached for the door handle, stopping Landis when he was about to get out as well. "No, you don't have to. Thanks." She swung open the door and climbed out.

"Hey, do either of the cafés up the road have Wi-Fi? I wouldn't mind getting caught up on some work as well."

"They both do." She bent down and pointed down the street. "The Golden Lily has the best coffee, and the Oasis has to-die-for scones." She did her best to smile naturally.

He continued to look at her for a long moment before his mouth nudged up into a small smile. Deep creases surrounded his mouth and his eyes crinkled like Clint Eastwood's. "Thanks."

She stood up and watched his car pull up thirty feet to park in front of the Oasis, and then she scurried into the paper's building before he caught her staring.

As she walked to the elevator and went up to the office, frustration set in. Frustration and embarrassment, all aimed at herself. She'd acted like a pouty child. Landis had been a hundred percent accurate; quitting the paper had been at the top of her whirling thoughts. And why? Regardless of how she felt about corporate and union relationships, her reaction had started with his casual connection to the Met and the ease he had doing her job for her. The strike phone call had just amplified her feelings.

Swinging open the Chronicle door, she walked through the cluster of desks to the one with her computer on it.

"Hey, Summer," said Hank, leaning out of the alcove where the coffeemaker and mini fridge were. Hank was a twenty-three-year-old computer operator who gave off a much older vibe. His hair was thinning, he wore wire-framed glasses, and he often related situations to old *Star Trek* episodes. He was responsible for the computer layout of the newspaper and making sure the printing press operators had what they needed.

"Morning, Hank." Summer pulled her notepad out of her backpack and dropped it on her desk. "What's up with you?"

"Just setting up some ads for next Wednesday's paper. Gage went to the hospital. Man, he was pumped up this morning." He went back to shaking powdered creamer into his mug, grabbed a spoon, and walked back to his desk. "He was trying to hide it, I think, but he was vibrating with energy. I wonder if he got some good news about June."

She watched him stir his coffee as he dropped into his chair. She waited for something appropriate to fall out of her mouth that wouldn't give away the news Gage was obviously keeping to himself for right now. As the editor, she was going to have to manage Hank. She was going to have to deal with problem their off-set printer might have. Or would Blake Media handle that? She was going to have to sell all the ads....

It was as if a trapdoor had opened and all her energy dropped out of her body.

"Maybe," she told Hank weakly. "I have to call him later, so if I hear anything, I'll let you know."

"Great," he said, swinging his chair around and putting on his headphones. From her desk, she could hear the scratchy sounds of death metal he liked to listen to while he composited.

She pushed all thoughts out of her head and opened a new article template on her computer. Reaching down, she pulled open a drawer and took out two of her emergency granola bars. Looking at her notes, she got to work.

Two hours later, she was satisfied with both of her drafts. The unfinished piece told the story of the discovery of an amazing local treasure, and all it needed was the authentication details and next steps before she could call it done. The other article wistfully shared the story of a long-time citizen leaving Cranberry Hill, and the melancholy feelings she had when she looked at a lifetime of belongings on Viola's wooden tables.

Change is everywhere, she thought, and her heart felt heavy.

Summer shut down her computer, swept granola crumbs into her hand, and tossed the metallic wrappers into the garbage. She went over to the alcove and dumped the crumbs into the compost pail on the counter. In the garbage, she saw where Hank had tossed a plastic fork and knife. She rinsed them off and put them in the blue recycle bin beside the compost pail.

"Hank." She waved her hand to get his attention. He pulled off his headphones. "Plastics go in the recycling."

"Oh, right. Sorry."

"I'm heading out. I'll call Gage from home. Is everything all right with the edition? Nothing you want me to tell him?"

"No, everything's great. He said to wait on you for your story, but you've got until Monday, noon. That enough time?"

"Yup. I might have it by end of day today. See you later."

"Later." He put his headphones back on and turned to his monitor.

She exited the building and looked down the street. Landis's car was still parked in front of the Oasis. Walking in the opposite direction, she rounded the building and unlocked her bike. She opted to ride down the back alley. For reasons she wasn't sure of, she didn't want him to see her heading home.

The alley took her behind all the businesses on the main stretch. She wove around crates and cars, and between the communal recycling bin and the smelly decomposing compost bin. At the end, she veered back to the main road and reversed her way home from that morning, this time with the ocean in front of her and the sun overhead.

Summer pedaled lazily, the emotions of the day flooding back and making her limbs heavy. Really, the emotions of the last twenty-four hours. She tried to look at it objectively, as if it were a story.

A newspaper owner wants to sell his company. His main reporter doesn't want him to. She decides maybe she should buy the paper. Then the owner says someone else bought it and wants to make her editor for a huge increase in salary. No stress about raising capital or managing partners. She'd be doing everything she was doing before, maybe with a few tasks shifting in priority, and she'd be making a ton more money.

She chewed on that for a bit. On the surface, it looked pretty straight forward, really. Nothing that should make her angry. It actually sounded like a dream. If she thought over the last six months, she could see she'd been ready to do more. Maybe that's why she started to "suggest" local shop owners run ads in the Sunday edition. Why she started planning stories further ahead than she needed to, even creating themed pullouts around local events.

No, instead of rolling with the new direction Gage was considering this morning, she'd let Landis Blake's stunning face on her tablet color her perception of Blake Media's offer. She'd done the one thing a good journalist never does, which is make assumptions.

She'd created a whole piece of fiction for Landis—a corporate dilettante doing charity events with hot arm candy as he fretted about how to stay young while spending Daddy's money. She let a "Huh" out loud, because she'd been there.

Nick Calvetti, who "ran" a financial investment firm so well he could spend days golfing and nights at charity events with Summer as his arm candy, had been her template for judgment. Because she'd had her attention on her career goal of anchoring a network news show, showing up at galas with Nick and getting acquainted with the social circles he put her in took precedence over seeing the kind of person he was, and who his friends were. Her colleagues had tried to connect some dots for her, but she'd ignored them.

It wasn't until after the shooting and her move to the Pacific Northwest that she'd been able to look at everything with clearer eyes. The bottom had fallen out of his family's shady enterprises, and even though she'd been on the fringe of that family for less than a year, she was deposed by a lawyer in Seattle whose line of questioning let her know how fine the line between wealth and corruption could be. And how close she'd been to falling down a dangerous rabbit hole.

Summer steered her bike onto the path that led to the back of the barn. She circled wide to where the flagstone path headed toward the inn but couldn't see any vehicles in the driveway. She had the whole property to herself. Pedaling into the barn, she swung her good leg off and immediately felt her left thigh cramp up.

She tried massaging it, but it was no use. When her leg got this bad, it needed a hot bath. This was the last thing she wanted on a hot day like today, but other than the dreaded pain meds she tried to avoid, it was the only thing that worked.

Hobbling up the stairs and into the loft, she shuffled her way to the bathroom and ran the water. She dumped in a good amount of Epsom salts, opened the bathroom window, and tilted the blinds to partially closed.

She got the water as hot as she could stand it, and then stripped off her "business" clothes, giving them a mocking salute as she draped them on the hamper. She caught a glimpse of herself in the full-length mirror on the back of the door, her butterscotch-tinted skin marked in white where her favorite bathing suit was outlined. From one angle, her legs were nicely muscled from riding her bike everywhere and swimming whenever she could, but from another angle, her scar created an unnatural ripple.

She stepped closer to examine it. It had taken months for her to even look at the scar. In the early days, when her home nurse would change the dressing, she dry-heaved as her vivid imagination painted the picture of a gaping, oozing wound. Which was ridiculous, because it was stapled shut. Her reaction had embarrassed her.

She was supposed to be a news reporter who could handle any situation with a level-headedness and emotional distance that would let her get an objective view of whatever the issue was. And there she'd been, almost throwing up on her pillow.

Summer shook her head to get rid of the thought and looked more closely at the scar. The bullet had done a good job at shredding part of her muscle, so the scar drew a line over a puckered landscape of underlying tissue in humps and valleys.

When she'd finally been able to look at it, she'd become obsessed with it, examining every crosshatch and line until they were memorized. Comparing its progress day to day, wondering if the red line would fade to pink then to white, but it had stayed a faded magenta color.

When she couldn't sleep at night, she'd sometimes run her finger over the familiar path of it, this new thing that was a part of her and yet completely alien to her.

She turned around to face herself straight-on in the mirror, her eyes traveling up the subtle curve of her hips, the long expanse of her stomach to her modest breasts. She thought of the full breasts of the redhead that had been in many of the photos with Landis. He would definitely think these were too small. He had large hands.

It had been one of many things she'd become fixated on in the car today. His hands weren't as smooth as Nick's had been, which had been a surprise to her. She'd joked to Carson about Landis hiring a lighting crew, but she could tell by the various photos she found of his charity events that it wasn't the case. Nick, on the other hand, had hired photographers to take pictures of him in his office, golfing, even getting in his car. Summer exhaled in disgust. She hadn't seen that as fake and staged at the time, just something wealthy businessmen did to get ahead. She shook her head and sighed.

Turning to the tub, she put her hand in the water and drew it back quickly. It was ready. It took several minutes for her to get her entire body into the tub, but once she was in up to her chin, the hot water worked its magic. Her thigh relaxed, her body calmed, and the steam gave her a wonderful facial as a bonus. She only lounged a few minutes before getting out.

As she wrapped a big white towel around her body, she heard tires crunch on the gravel and instinctively recognized the sound of Katy's Subaru they'd nicknamed Goose. To confirm it, Katy's high-pitched voice floated through the trees, and Summer could tell she was on her way over for a visit. She hurriedly dried her hair and pulled on her bathing suit and lacy cover-up.

"Whoa, have there always been that many stairs?" Katy asked as she walked into the loft, out of breath and holding her belly.

"I promise I didn't have any added." She took Katy's hand and pulled her closer for a hug.

"Going for a swim?" Katy pulled at the edge of her cover-up.

"I think so. Unless you need help with anything." Summer took in Katy's excited expression. "What's going on, Mamma?"

"I've got breaking news." She held up an ultrasound image, and Summer excitedly jumped up and down.

"What? I thought there'd only be the one scan."

"They had concerns about the placenta attachment, but it's all good. So they asked if I wanted a picture of the baby since they were looking at it, and how could I say no?"

Summer took the photo from Katy, grabbed her hand, and pulled her over to the couch facing the large windows. "Oh, Katy, look at her face!" The ultrasound showed a 3D image of the baby's head and shoulders.

"We don't know it's a girl," Katy chided, leaning over to watch Summer's forefinger trace the outline of the baby's face.

"*I* know it, and you're going to regret playing it safe and painting the baby's room yellow."

"I love that yellow color!"

"This baby girl is full of energy and creativity, and by the time she's five, she'll be asking you to paint it purple," she predicted, handing the photo back to Katy. She took it, kissed it, and put it in her shirt pocket. "How are you feeling? And how is Mitch? She's only a couple weeks away, if you make it right to your due date."

"I know. I'm a bundle of nerves, but Mitch is calm as can be. Which helps me."

"You know what I always say. You're not the first woman to have a baby. Everything will be great."

"I know." Katy shifted slightly to face her. "So tell me how it went this morning. Did you talk to Gage? What did he say?"

"Landis Blake beat me to it. He made Gage an incredible offer that included making me the editor." Summer laced her fingers into her best friend's and gave her astonished face a grimace.

"*What?* Are you kidding me?" Katy's eyes sparkled, and she tried to rock her pregnant body forward to give Summer a hug. "I can't.... Can you lean over here and hug your big-bellied friend?" Summer gave her a big hug and leaned back. "Are you happy about it, though? It's not what you'd planned," Katy added.

"To be honest, at first, I was angry. I was up all night putting my plan together, and I didn't even get a chance to present it. But after a while, I realized it's the perfect solution for Gage."

"And yet... you're not overjoyed. What am I missing?"

"Landis. His involvement... complicates everything."

"Because he's rich and you're a snob?" Katy asked innocently, laughing when Summer whacked her leg with the small pillow from the end of the couch.

"Well, partly." Summer lifted her knees and feet to curl up on the couch. "Today, he stepped on my toes while I was doing my job, and it makes me worry about what the working relationship will be like. You know how independent I am when I work."

"True, I don't know any good journalists who aren't. How did he step on your toes?" Katy asked.

"He overheard a conversation I was having and reached out to his own connections to do some research." She plucked absently at the lace fabric that covered her thighs. "It's not how management acts, let alone a CEO, and it makes me wonder how he runs his other publications."

Katy rubbed her belly as she listened to her. "I see how you'd wonder about that. However, I bet it's something you could sort out pretty quickly. Plus, you'll basically be a continent away from him, so maybe this is a one-time thing."

"True," she murmured, still frowning.

Katy watched her face, waiting for more. "So...?" she prompted when Summer didn't speak.

"There's something else,"

"Yes?" Katy nudged again when Summer paused longer and started to gnaw at her thumb.

"I think I'm distracted by him. He's... more than good-looking. He's sort of... electric. God, I sound like a dork." She shifted on the couch, putting her legs back down. "There was a point, before he got arrogant, when we were getting along. We actually laughed together, and there was this feeling... staticky is the best way to describe it. And I actually liked him. Or liked the possibility of him being normal, for an elitist."

Summer's voice drifted to silence as she remembered the sound of his laugh and how the lines around his mouth got deeper when he smiled. Her stomach flopped, and she rubbed her forehead.

"Honestly, that's not like you. To not give a stranger a chance."

"Right?" Summer held her hands open in agreement. "I like everybody." She let out another sigh. "He's only here for a couple days, so I should just make the best of it. Except... let's face it; he's hot. And now he's going to be my boss, in some capacity. Probably not directly. There'll most likely be at least one layer of management there. Hm...." Summer mused, her brow furrowing in thought.

"Oh my God, finally!" Katy exclaimed, clapping her hands together as if in prayer.

"Finally what?"

"You're finally attracted to someone, is what! When you didn't end up dating any of the firefighters, I lost all hope."

"Nobody's caught my interest. Although it got close with Phil, but I can't be with someone who isn't obsessed with reading."

"So you're saying Landis has caught your interest?" She tapped Summer's foot with hers.

"Uuugh! Don't make this weird. Landis is mildly interesting, and attractive, but complicated. He's a New Yorker. He's the wealthy capitalist, and I'm the hardworking socialist. There's nowhere for anything between us to go."

"It doesn't have to go anywhere long term. It could just go somewhere fantastic for the really, really short term."

She watched Katy grin. Then push at her foot and grin even broader.

"What, is this some trivia game I'm not getting? Just say what you're thinking," Summer begged.

"Have a fling! A hookup!" She drew out the last word as she nudged Summer's knee. "He's here until Sunday night. Make a move and see what happens, is all I'm saying."

"He's dating that redhead. At least, according to all the photos, it's likely. And I don't know why, but I don't get the vibe that he's a 'fling' kind of a guy. Who even says 'fling' anymore?"

"I don't think he's dating her. At least not currently. Mitch said something that made me think Landis is currently a free agent."

Summer shrugged uncomfortably, picking at the edge of her cover-up again. "I'm not good at that stuff. Give me a fire or a political scandal, and I can question the fire chief or mayor, but put me in a room with a good-looking man and... I don't have any game. I don't know what to say, except to ask a lot of too personal questions."

"It's easy. You just imagine a super sexy scenario with him, and then the next time you're with him, look into his eyes, let that daydream run through your mind, yaddah-yaddah, and then you jump on him."

"What? You can't 'yaddah-yaddah' the most important part." Summer looked at her friend, who was nodding confidently with her hands crossed over her belly.

"The yaddah-yaddah is him picking up your vibe and then making a move. It might be starting a conversation. Or taking your hand to help you out of the car. But he'll step closer to you and maintain eye contact the whole time, and that's how you'll know. Trust me, you'll recognize it when you see it. And then your gut will know you can jump on him, and that's when you do it."

"That does *not* sound like good advice. Is that what happened between you and Mitch?" She leaned back suspiciously as Katy laughed.

"Mitch and I couldn't *stand* each other at first, but then we grew on each other, started to have great conversations... yaddah-yaddah. And now I'm about to have our baby." Katy held up her hands and grinned.

Summer couldn't help but smile. "I don't even know if Landis is interested."

"He's interested."

"How do you know? Did he say something?" Summer leaned forward, feeling a little flutter in her gut as she awaited Katy's answer. *What is this, high school?* she wondered.

"He didn't have to. I could tell," she confided.

"How could you tell?"

"Body language. When a guy's not interested, his body turns away. When a guy's interested, his body stays turned toward what he's interested in. Last night, even though you sounded huffy and it seemed like he didn't care, his body faced toward you, and his eyes followed you after you left. Big tell."

"Where did you come up with that?" Summer scoffed.

"From watching hundreds of couples at the inn. Trust me, I know what I'm talking about. Anyway, Landis only has to be interested enough for a hookup, right? You're not looking for forever." She tapped Summer's knee and then squeezed it. "Right?"

Summer looked up and out the window. *What am I looking for?* She hadn't thought she was looking for anything, other than keeping everything the way it was. Her world was pleasant and serene, and for once not filled with chaos. Now chaos had shown up on two legs.

The sound of a loudly decelerating engine followed by crunching gravel drifted through the open window.

"Carson," they both said, recognizing the sound of his small pick-up truck. Katy waved Summer to stand up so she could pull her up off the couch.

"You know what's weird?" Summer asked as she pulled her ungainly friend to her feet. "Landis's car's engine and doors make no sound at all. They sort of whisper. It's kind of creepy." She watched as Katy waddle to the door.

"It's stealthy, which is also kind of sexy. Get your mind in the game, girl," Katy chided.

"Enough about a hookup already." Summer waved her toward the stairs.

"When are you going for your swim?" she asked.

"In a bit. I should update Carson on the job, now that he's home. And *maybe* I'll mull over this yaddah-yaddah you talked about." Summer hugged her friend and then stepped down two stairs ahead of her. "Let me get in front so I can break your fall, since you probably can't see the stairs over baby girl," she told her, to which Katy rolled her eyes.

Carson met Katy at the bottom of the stairs. He oohed and aahed over the baby photo and then hugged Katy goodbye. Summer hugged her too and watched her trundle down the path to the inn.

"What are you doing home? I thought you'd be at the restaurant all day," Summer asked, giving Carson a quick hug hello.

"I was. But we ran out of cilantro and mint, so I drove back to raid the herb garden." He walked into the barn and motioned for her to follow him. "Pete was ready, so I picked him up on my way back." He tapped the artificial leg he was wearing.

"Ah, okay. Will you be here long?" She watched him pick up the crate they used as a gardening caddy and add a hand spade and rake to it.

"It's a light night for reservations, so I've got a few hours before I have to head out. I'll have time to throw some burgers on the grill for sure. I want to eat before I go back."

"Perfect. That'll give me a little time to have a swim." She waved him off as he headed back toward the inn and the herb gardens that were planted on its far side. She headed back up to the loft for a towel and remembered one task she needed to complete.

She grabbed her cell phone from the kitchen counter and dialed Gage's number.

"Hi, Summer!" His voice was more cheerful than she'd heard it in a long time.

"Hi, Gage. Are you at the hospital still?"

"Yes, we got to meet June's occupational therapist today. She gets to come home in a week!" Gage exuberance lit up Summer's heart.

"That's incredible! I'm so happy for both of you."

"I have to say, Summer, when I told June about the deal with Blake Media and you being editor, she lit up like the Fourth of July. Her spirits have been flying high all day. Oh, but I don't want to pressure you for your answer yet."

"No pressure, and I'm happy to say I accept. I didn't realize how ready I am for the new challenge. And Gage, I'm honored you think I'm the right person for the job."

"You are. Don't forget it." They said goodbye, and she looked out the window. Regardless of how it came about, Landis's offer was definitely the best thing for everyone.

At the thought of Landis, a what-if scenario flooded her mind. Seeing Landis's tanned, strong hand on the gearshift from that morning made her breath skip and flutter. Instead of his hand moving back to the steering wheel, she imagined it sliding over to her knee then up her thigh... Summer's breath fluttered all over again. *Super sexy scenario indeed,* she thought. *I really do need a swim.*

6

Landis followed the winding road back to the inn. It had been a productive few hours in the very comfortable Oasis café that Summer had recommended, and he was satisfied that for the next few hours, nothing was going to blow up. He might even enjoy the weekend.

Gage had practically insisted he come play in their softball game tomorrow. Summer played first base, and apparently they had a need for a heavy hitter. He had been flattered that Gage made that assumption, even though he had little time for sports the past few years. Or a vacation. Or dating.

He frowned. He couldn't remember the last time he'd taken a break for anything that wasn't business related, and dating had fallen to the bottom of his list after the last few encounters fell flat. Every woman in his social circle was identical to the next, and identically boring.

Landis slowed and pulled the car into the driveway. He grabbed his briefcase from the floor in the back seat and headed to the porch. That's when he heard the metal sound of something digging in dirt and rocks. Curious, he set his briefcase down and walked toward the path to the barn, and then realized the sound was coming from his left, on the other side of the house. He followed another path that opened up to a broad garden that spread out along the north side of the inn.

A man in a T-shirt and shorts, with hair one shade darker than Summer's, was clearing a swath of small weeds away from a row of what looked to be spinach. He looked back at the man's hair and wondered at the fact that he knew Summer's hair right down to its shade.

"Hello, there," Landis greeted, sliding his hands into his pockets. The smell of sun-warmed dirt drifted over to him and it was heavenly.

"Oh, hi." The man dropped his hand rake, shed his gloves, and got to his feet. He was a beefier version of Summer and was no doubt her brother. When he stepped forward, Landis noticed one leg was a prosthetic from below his knee. He hopped easily over the rows and held out his hand. "I'm Carson. You must be Landis."

"Yes, I'm Mitch's friend."

"I also heard you're the elitist media tycoon." Carson laughed. "At least, my bohemian socialist newspaper reporter sister told me that."

"I'm just an average guy trying to make his way in the world," Landis said innocently, hunching his shoulders modestly and grinning.

Carson laughed harder. "Aren't we all?"

"You probably don't need help, but I haven't dug in a garden since I was a kid, and I forgot how much I loved it until I heard you doing it." Landis took off his shoes and socks and looked at Carson.

"Sure. I've got an extra rake here. I'm just skimming down the rows to catch any weeds before they take hold." Carson handed him the tool from the crate. "If you want to start on that end of the garden, we can work until we meet in the middle." He continued to stand, stretching his back.

"Sounds good." Landis walked to the far side of the garden, about twelve feet away. The dark soil felt good against his feet. Again, he wondered how many years had passed since he felt that. "Does this garden fully supply the inn?"

"Pretty much. There's a second garden farther down the fence line beside the road. It supplies the herbs I use at the restaurant I work at."

"Which restaurant is that?"

"The Trestle Table. It's about ten miles farther down Beach Drive

Road. It's a farm-to-table restaurant, so the menu changes a lot, depending on what's in season around the area."

"Sounds great. Maybe I'll get a chance to eat there before I leave."

"Maybe." Carson smiled. He bent over to stretch his hamstrings, and then checked the top of the prosthetic where his leg fit into the socket. "I got this adjusted, and I probably shouldn't overdo it until I know it's good. This leg makes even simple things a little more complicated than before." He dropped his hand rake and picked up a long-handled version to use instead.

"I can only imagine." Landis watched Carson continue to rake then turned back to his own row to scrape a small pile of weeds out, placing them on the grassy edge of the garden. "Can I ask how you lost your leg?"

"Cancer. Osteosarcoma. It was just above my ankle, in my tibia. It had been sore and swelling for a while, and I thought it was because of a baseball injury. And then in one game I slid home right into the catcher's shin pads, and it broke. That's when they found out the swelling was cancer. It had weakened the bone enough to break it."

"I'm sorry to hear that."

"It's all good now. Mine was caught early, and since the surgery, there's been no evidence of disease. It's taken a while, but it's kind of cool being part robot. It makes me more intimidating." Carson smiled evilly.

Landis chuckled. "You still play ball?"

"Oh yeah!" he said, digging and working the ground with his rake. "We've got a game tomorrow. Do you play?"

"I have before. Gage Halcourt invited me. He said you guys needed a heavy hitter."

"Yeah, we do. That's great. We're playing the Chutney Fire Department, and those guys are blasters. We're good, but they out-homerun us every time."

"I'm glad to help out, although I'm rusty." Landis pulled a particularly stubborn weed out, its root twisted and long.

"You'll be fine. It's all in fun. Mostly. Summer gets pretty serious sometimes," Carson added, darting a look at him.

"Oh yeah? Why am I not surprised?"

"The thing about Summer is, she's got a big heart. I'm her big brother, but she looks out for me like a mamma bear after her cub. Everyone in her orbit becomes her family, and she can sometimes see danger where there isn't any. So if she gets a little growly, that's probably the reason."

Landis stopped working to look at Carson's earnest face. "That's a nice trait to have in a sister."

"It is. I'll tell you one more thing. She had a rough time dating someone who came from big money and lived a fancy life. It made her... careful. Maybe you've already felt that, if you've spent more than half an hour with her." He looked at Landis inquiringly.

"You could say I've felt that."

"Don't let it throw you." He scraped out a weed and tossed it down.

"I won't." Landis smiled, and got back to weeding.

In a short time, they were done. Landis brushed off his hands and knees and leaned from side to side to stretch his back. He felt invigorated and said as much.

"Nothing like getting your hands in the dirt," Carson agreed, dropping tools and gloves into the crate. Clanking glass drew their attention to the edge of the house, where Mitch was leaning over the front railing. "Katy's got beer in the back if you want to grab one."

"That sounds great!" Landis called, waving to Mitch.

"Rain check for me. I've got dinner service tonight." Carson picked up his toolbox and stepped over the rows to where Landis stood. He held out his hand for a shake. "It was nice to meet you, Landis. Thanks again for your help."

"You're welcome. Thanks for letting me. I needed it." He gave Carson's hand a good shake and released it.

"See you tomorrow at the game."

"You bet." He watched Carson walk around the edge of the copse of trees and out of sight to the other garden. Landis made his way to the back of the house and to the porch where Katy sat on the couch. In front of her was a metal pail filled with ice and beer.

"Hey, gardener! Thanks for the weed work. Your payment awaits you on ice." She made a small flourish toward the pail on the floor of the porch.

Landis plucked one up, found the bottle opener that was attached to the pail with a length of twine, and took off the cap. He moved a pillow over and sat at the opposite end from Katy. "You're very welcome, and thank you for the payment." He took a long draw and released a satisfying breath.

"Everyone has seen this but you, and my rule is that everybody has to see this... so take a look." She held out a square piece of glossy paper. He was careful to hold a corner in case his fingers were still dirty. On it, he saw the head and shoulders of a sleeping baby with one tiny fist curled up under its chin.

"That's amazing!" Landis quietly exclaimed after a minute of staring at the photo.

"Technology, right?"

"Well, yeah, but also the fact that you and Mitch made this little human." He brought the photo closer to his face so he could examine every detail.

"Don't you make me cry. I've done enough of that today," Katy warned.

"Sorry. I've never seen an actual photo like this before." He handed the photo back. "I'm happy for you and Mitch, truly. You found each other, and now you're morphing into a beautiful family. You can't ask for more than that." He lifted his beer in tribute, and Katy picked up her iced tea and clinked her glass against his bottle. They both drank, and Katy looked back down at the photo.

"I'm proof that amazing things happen when you let love in. You know, when I met Mitch, I thought he was an arrogant idiot," she confided.

"Hey, we have something in common. I thought that about him when I first met him, too," Landis joked. He watched Katy's eyes move from him back to the photo and soften. His smile faded, and he felt a hollow place near his throat open up. "When did you change your mind about him?"

Katy looked off, her eyes distant as she roved through memories. "When I was able to stop being afraid." She looked back to him with a serious but gentle smile. "We all fear something, and relationships amplify that, I think. Suddenly, here's someone you like, and you want them to like you, and you have to admit your fear to them. That's challenging. But when you can let go, you free up room for love to come in. At least, that's the best way I figure it." She shrugged and took another sip of iced tea.

He looked down at the beer in his bottle, reflecting on everything that had happened between him and Summer that day, and him and women in general. What Katy described sounded so alien, like what they make movies about—unreal.

"When I first got here, I thought you and Mitch were trying to set me up. Like a blind date," he confessed.

Katy hooted out loud. "I've given up trying to fix Summer up with anybody."

"I've dated a lot. I guess you could say I've had a few relationships, but honestly, it just felt like extended dating. And then we'd get bored and drift apart."

"Dating is practice. I see it as the time you spend figuring out what you really want." Katy watched Landis turn the beer bottle back and forth in his hands. "Or maybe it's more accurate to say letting the right person come into your life and letting the wrong ones drift out. I think it's trying hard to make something work that messes things up."

"That sounds about right," he agreed, sipping from the bottle and trying to count how many years it had been since he'd spent any significant time with another woman, looking for anything close to the spark he'd felt with Summer today. Stella didn't count.

"That's good. Maybe you're ready to let someone who might be right drift in," Katy suggested.

"Today, I spent some time with Summer. And I wanted to ask you—"

"Hold up." Katy held her hand up, cutting him off mid question. "If you're going to ask me something about Summer, I have to plead best friend privilege. There are certain things you'll have to find out directly from her."

Landis smiled. "Fair enough." He thought he had a safe question to ask, when his phone beeped. He took it out of his shirt pocket to see who it was—Stella. He mouthed *Sorry* to Katy, who smiled and waved him ahead with his phone call.

"Hey, Red, nice to hear from you. What's going on?"

"I'm flying to Tokyo tomorrow, and wanted you to look at something that came up in a purchase agreement. Just some wording that has my spidey senses tingling. I have a layover in Seattle, and Evelyn said you were staying with friends, so I thought... why not see if there's room at the inn?" she finished with a laugh.

"Sure, I'll look at it. Not sure how much help I can be. Let me check with the incredible innkeeper here and see if she's got room for a short-notice single...?" He turned to look at Katy with raised eyebrows, and she saluted back with her glass and an affirmative nod. "Innkeeper says you're good to go. What time will your flight get in?"

"I land at 6:30 p.m."

"Ok. You'll probably roll up here around eight-thirty or so." Landis gave Stella the address and asked her a few questions about the purchase agreement before they ended the call. "Oh, Stell, one more thing. Don't rent a Mercedes. It makes the locals testy." He winked at Katy, who shook her finger at him, and then he disconnected the call.

"C'mon, my car made *one* local testy," he said, and they both chuckled at the truth in that.

"So... Stell? Is that short for Stella?" Katy asked.

"Yes, Stella and I go way back. Our families moved in the same social circles, I guess you'd say. In college, we dated for a while, but we just made better friends than lovers. We did make a pact, though. If neither of us found love by forty, we'd get hitched, make some babies, and let our parents rejoice that we were keeping all their money in the family."

Landis finished the last swallow of beer and put the bottle down beside the couch.

"It's funny. Stella has always seemed like the perfect woman to me. She's incredibly smart, she's funny, she's caring, she's family oriented, she's gorgeous, and yet... and yet the feelings between us were very sterile. At one point, I thought, if I can't feel real love for the woman that checks off every box on my list, why bother?" Landis looked over at Katy, who was nodding and smiling.

"That's a very good question, Landis. Why bother?"

He eyed Katy, her words echoing in his head. He looked out at the ocean, at the blue-gray of the Pacific, and suddenly Summer was there in his mind. "All right, things to ponder," he said, grabbing the empty bottle and standing up.

"Indeed," she echoed, rubbing her belly lovingly. "If you don't have plans, stay for dinner with us. We'd love to have you."

"That sounds great, thanks." He smiled at her glowing face and stepped closer, hesitating. "May I?" he finally asked, looking at the miracle under her hands. She nodded and he held out his hand, letting her guide it to the top of her round stomach.

"Wait," she said when he was about to pull away. "The tiger is about to move." And he felt it. At first, a flutter, and then a rolling lump, as if the baby was turning over, and a smaller knob—a foot?—slid under his hand. He met her eyes, feeling wonder shine from his. "I know, right?" She squeezed his hand to say she shared his wonder.

Landis thanked her again, retrieved his briefcase, and went up to his room. Stripping off his clothes, he found some shorts and a T-shirt and dug out his Adidas from his suitcase. He needed to run off a few miles worth of questions.

7

Thumping footsteps up the stairs pulled Summer's attention away from the laptop screen she'd been staring at.

"Hey, kiddo." Carson dropped a basket heaping with herbs on the counter while he moved various things around in the fridge so he could place the basket inside. "I was going to get cleaned up and then make some burgers. I thought you were going for a swim?"

"I was," she said absently, "but I received a call about a story I'm trying to finish and got caught up in some research." She closed her laptop self-consciously and set it on the low table. It had started out as Van Gough research and drifted over to thoughts of Landis. And then maybe a little more research on him than on her story. Summer walked over to plop on one of the stools on the nook side of the kitchen island.

"I met your nemesis." He flipped on the faucet and washed his hands.

"My nemesis?"

"Landis Blake." He towel-dried his hands and then opened the fridge again. "I thought I saw iced tea in here. Want some?"

"No, I already had a bucket load. Where did you see Landis?"

"Outside, while I was weeding. He dove right in and joined me."

He poured iced tea into a glass and smiled at her surprised expression. "He even took off his shoes and walked around barefoot in the dirt. Said he loved it." Carson took a long drink from his glass and set it down, looking at her expectantly.

She shifted on the stool, knowing what her brother was getting at. "Okay, I might have misjudged him."

"Maybe he's different at home." He held his hands up, allowing a tiny bit of her judgment to be right. "But the guy I met seemed genuine and open."

"He is. He came with me to Viola Harrison's estate sale this morning. He was kind and patient. He even used his connections in New York to help me with a story." She watched her hands draw invisible circles on the counter. "Which I may have given him a hard time about, but only because it's overstepping editor and owner boundaries."

"Wait... editor and owner boundaries?" Carson asked with a confused look.

"Oh, he and Gage agreed on the sale of the paper this morning. And apparently, I'm going to be the new editor." She held her hands up as if to say "Surprise!"

"What? Summer, that's awesome!" He ran around the counter and wrapped her in a big hug. She hugged him back hard. Tears stung her eyelids. "Hey," he said when he'd pulled back, his smile shifting to a concerned look. "Are those tears of happiness, or something else?" He sat down on the stool beside her and they swung around to face each other.

"They're tears of confusion. I wanted everything at the paper to stay as it was, and then Gage wanted to sell. And then I thought that would be okay, but then Landis came along and Blake Media seemed all wrong to buy it. And then Landis sort of acted like an ass last night, but this job offer makes a lot of sense." She was rambling and saw the confusion on Carson's face and tried to explain. "I toyed with the idea of buying the paper myself, so Gage wouldn't have to sell it to some entitled corporate raider. I stayed up all last night planning, but I didn't even get to pitch my idea..."

"Wait, you wanted to buy the paper?"

"...and then this morning, I thought Landis might be okay, but then he acted like an arrogant jerk, but I guess maybe he thought he was helping me out. And now he's going to be my boss and I have weird feelings about that." She shuddered out the last few words, angrily swiping at her eyes. Tears were weakness.

She saw Carson's mouth opening and closing as he tried to keep up with the multitude of things that had spilled out of her.

"Oh, my sister, I have not seen you this emotional since you first saw me walk with Pete." He hugged her again. "I think I'm missing a lot of the moving parts here, but you've worked for weirder people than Landis Blake. I don't know why it would be any different. Plus, he'll be on the other side of the country, won't he?"

"The weird part is the feelings I have. About him. From this instant hate to... something different. Plus, he's my boss, which is... I don't know. I just don't know. I'm confused." She dropped her head onto his chest.

"Hey, it's okay to be confused. Feelings are complicated, and sometimes they just need a little time to work themselves into something you can understand."

"Maybe I need a distraction. I wish I could focus on something else for a while," she sighed.

Carson held her away, and she immediately missed the safety of his arms. How often had he consoled her, counseled her, parented her since she was twelve? He was her rock.

"I've got something that could distract you. Fair warning, though, it's a pretty big distraction."

Summer sniffled but felt her interest pique. "What big distraction could you have that I haven't heard about?"

He walked to his room and back. "This." He handed her a thick envelope.

Summer pulled the folded papers out. "Limited Liability Partnership offer between Mise en Place Cuisine LLC and Carson Richardson," Summer read. Her eyes skimmed over the cover letter details, and then she flipped through the next few pages, her eyebrows rising as she absorbed the scope of what Carson was showing her. "You're being offered a partnership in a restaurant. In Thailand." She lowered the papers onto her lap and looked up at her brother's shining face. "You didn't underestimate the size of this distraction!"

"Now before you give me your hundred and one reasons why I can't do this, you need to know—I think I'm going to do this," Carson said firmly.

"Have you had someone look this over? And Thailand! That's so far away. Oh, you!" Summer whacked his arm with the papers as something became clear to her. "This is the real reason for all the heavenly food you've been cooking for me this week. You're a brat!"

He pretended to cower from her attack and then grabbed her and hugged her again. She let herself be swept up in his enthusiasm, hugging him back, papers and all.

"We are a pair. At least I was saved from joining the corporate world and owning a newspaper, but you're going to be a restaurateur! The ultimate snob."

"Before you imagine some white linen elegance, you should know this is a simple cookery near Chiang Mai serving locals. I've made sure I get to cook alongside the current owner for a while. I'd be partnering with the company buying it. They're out of France, believe it or not."

"Sounds complicated." She frowned, looking back at the paperwork. "Maybe..."

"Maybe... what?"

"Maybe you should ask Landis if he could have someone look this over. Just to make sure your best interests are protected," she finished, handing the papers back to him. "He knows a lot of people," she said grudgingly.

"You're not going to argue against this? I know having family around you is important."

"It is important. And I feel too overwhelmed right now to argue about it, so I'm reserving my right to do that later. But it's not fair to guilt you into staying here. We've been together for almost two years, and it's been heavenly. Mostly." She laughed as she fake-punched his arm. But her heart was heavy with thoughts of living in the loft on her own and her brother so far away.

"I agree with mostly," he replied with a tug on her hair. "Why don't you go for your swim and I'll get going on a quick dinner?" Summer nodded and watched Carson retreat to his bedroom. Before she overthought it, she got up and grabbed her sandals.

***

THE SAND BENEATH HER FEET FELT HEAVENLY AND THE BREEZE BLEW through her lace cover up, fluttering the edges against the skin just above her knees and pulling golden strands out of the messy bun she'd piled her hair into. Instead of swimming, she kicked through the surf's edge, sidestepping sticks and seaweed debris that washed up in the seawater. First, she walked toward the tall bluff north of the inn, and then turned around.

She was chagrined that Carson worried she wouldn't want him to pursue his career away from her. She loved this happy nest they'd created in Cranberry Hill, but she'd always known he was meant for bigger things.

Their shared space in the barn loft was a way station secreted away from the real world. It had given them time and privacy to heal and get acquainted with their new realities—him living with an artificial leg, and her with a permanent reminder of her crime reporting days back east.

She thought about all her planning last night and realized that running a company was not her destiny either. Immediately, in her mind popped an image of Landis.

Landis as he'd looked this morning, standing beside Gage, his gray pants hugging athletic legs, his open collar exposing his strong throat. She'd never noticed a man's throat before. Or those hands she'd become fixated on. Everything about him pulled at something deep and earthy within her, which was the exact opposite effect his photos on her tablet had the previous evening.

A hook-up, Katy had suggested. The idea was tantalizing and scary. She'd never hooked up before. She hadn't really had many relationships, for that matter. There was never time.

The men she'd been involved with had done the asking, the planning, really most of the work that went into a relationship. She'd ended them all, because there hadn't seemed to be a point to them. Her work and her family had always come first, and the men had been diversions for a time.

Summer walked farther into the surf, kicking at the water every once in a while and bending down to watch a tiny crab run around on the sand beneath. A hook-up by definition was short. Short and fiery and with no regrets. At least, that's the type of hook-up she'd want to have. He was leaving Sunday, so there would be no expectations about anything more serious, which was good.

She didn't want serious; she wanted passionate and sexy and fun. Summer hugged her arms around herself, feeling parts of her body come to life. How long had it been since she had a lover? Chicago and Nick, she remembered. Nick, who had been more dangerous in a literal sense than an emotional one.

She gently slipped her hand into the water to see if she could coax the crab onto it. He was too shy and scooted away.

She wondered how someone initiated a hook-up. How did you put the idea out there? She disregarded Katy's advice, as it just seemed silly that imagining it and looking into someone's eyes would make it happen. Maybe she should just say, *"Landis, I think we should hook up."* Simple. Straightforward.

Except... what if Landis didn't want to hook up? There was that redhead in the charity event photos. She should have done more Internet searching about her. She thought back over theer day together and swore she couldn't have been mistaken about the spark of awareness she felt from him, at least before she lashed out at him.

Something made her think he wouldn't hook up with anyone if he were emotionally connected with someone else. There had been a moment, near the painting, when she'd taken a half step back to get a photo, and he'd put his hand on her back briefly to steady her. She could close her eyes and feel the heat from where his hand had been, could imagine his hand on the bare skin of her back.

It was getting later, and her thoughts were making her restless. Maybe a full stomach would help. As she retraced her steps toward the stretch of beach where the path back to the loft was, she noticed a figure farther down the beach, jogging toward her. She stopped, her toes curling into the hard sand. Landis.

He ran across the same stretch of hard, wet sand where she stood, between the water and the soft, dry berm near the road. He was shirtless and wore red shorts, and it seemed as if his face was fixed on her. As he got closer, she had no doubt he was focused on her.

She could feel his dark eyes on her, even though they were hooded in the shadow of his brow. Her skin raised in goose bumps as she watched the purposefulness of his stride.

When he was several yards away, his jog slowed to a walk. His hair was wind-ruffled and the sharp angles of his face lifted her heartbeat by ten. She could see part of a tattoo—a dragon's head?—curling over one shoulder, which surprised her. But then he stopped in front of her, an arm's length away. She felt immobilized in some elemental trance.

"I went for a run to get you out of my head. And here you are." His voice sounded gritty, startled. His arms hung taut by his sides, and she could feel tension rolling off his body. Her eyes swept over his physique, and she couldn't shake the thought of those arms around her, pulling her body against his, feeling her legs against his own muscled ones.

Her eyes settled on his, and she watched as they moved over her face, her neck, memorizing it, or perhaps searching for a specific detail that he couldn't recall. He swayed slightly closer, and the breeze carried his rough, sweaty scent to her.

"I could say the same." Her skin was alive, his nearness raising goose bumps on her goose bumps. Her eyes stayed on his until they came back from their search. "I don't know what to do." The words fell helplessly from her mouth, surprising her with the aching shyness she heard in them.

"Tell me what you want to do and I'll help you." There was carefulness in how still he held himself.

"I want... to touch you," Summer whispered, her eyes sliding down to his neck and chest.

Landis reached for her hand and placed it on his chest, intentionally pulling her closer as he did it. "Like this?"

"Yes," she breathed, loving the dampness of his skin under her hand. She felt his fingers around her other wrist, lifting her hand to his neck.

"How about this?" he asked, letting her palm stay there for a moment before moving it from his neck to his cheek, closing his eyes and turning his mouth into her palm.

Summer watched helplessly, the electricity that jumped from his mouth to her hand making her heart shift gears. Some words slid past her lips, but she didn't know what they were. She watched as he nuzzled her hand, his eyes closed. His other hand curved around her back and pulled her against him.

He placed her hand back on his neck and stroked his way along her arm to her shoulder, then over her lace cover-up to her back.

His pupils dilated, turning the silver to black, and it seemed the most natural thing to rise up on her toes and press her lips against his.

His mouth was both hard but soft, and when her legs felt weak and she lowered from her tip-toes, his head bent to allow his mouth to stay pressed against hers.

Slowly, their broke apart, yet their lips stayed close. Their unsteady breathing bathed each other.

"You're leaving Sunday," Summer blurted, moving to put more space between them, but not leaving his embrace yet.

"Yes."

"And... you're technically going to be my boss now." Her hand drifted down from his neck and her fingers traced his collarbone. She felt him shudder underneath her light touch, as his own hand slid from her neck to the middle of her back. It held her firmly where she stood.

"That's true," he muttered, and she watched his chest lift slowly as he inhaled and then let the air go in a long stream that ruffled the hair on top of her head.

"So we should make the most of the time we have left." She sighed as he released his hold to look in her eyes.

"Yes, we should." He brushed a strand of hair from the dampness of her neck, and then slid his finger down to the hollow of her throat, lifting the fine silver chain she wore, his knuckle brushing her skin. It made it very difficult for her to speak.

"I... ahem, I have to play in a slow-pitch game tomorrow, but...."

"So do I." Landis smiled, and she lost all her words.

"Oh. Um. So. Uh, how is that?"

"Gage invited me this morning. Is that okay?" He slid his arm from her back to let his hand rest on her waist. With more space between them, her own hands dropped like dead weights. She quickly crossed them like a nervous teenager.

"Yeah. Actually, that's great. We need a heavy hitter." She watched as he pulled a gray T-shirt from the waistband of his shorts, gave his chest a swipe, and pulled it on. A little part of her died as his chest disappeared.

"What makes everyone think I'm a big hitter?" he laughed, sliding his hand down her arm to link his fingers with hers. Giving her hand a tug, he pulled her into a walk toward the path to the inn.

"Well, aren't you? You've got an athletic build."

"I played baseball when I was a teen. These days, I try to run every morning, or catch the guys for some pick-up basketball when I have time to go to the gym."

"Oh." The thought of a sweaty Landis playing basketball was hot. She'd always been into athletes, given the choice.

They crossed the street and followed the path that took them directly to the loft. Landis dropped her hand when Carson came into view up on the balcony by the smoking charcoal grill.

"Hey, you guys are just in time. Burgers are ready. There are enough for three...?" Carson questioned.

Landis waved his hand. "No, but thanks. I promised Katy I'd have dinner with them."

Carson saluted them both with his spatula and turned toward the loft with a plate of cooked burger patties in his hand.

With no one around, Landis turned to her, lifting his hands to her shoulders and squeezed them. Then he slid them down her arms to grasp her hands, bringing them up to his lips for a brief kiss. "You have me spellbound, Summer. I'm not quite used to that, but I'm going to enjoy it in the time we have."

She was disappointed when he gently lowered and released her hands, missing the skin-to-skin contact. He walked backward for a few steps, not breaking eye contact until he was at the head of the trail to the inn. He gave her a little salute and turned to head up the path.

Her body swirled with tingles and shivers. *Oh my God, the yaddah-yaddah is real,* she thought.

"Burgers are getting cold, kid!" Carson shouted from the loft, and she whirled around and ran to the stairs and dinner.

8

Later that evening, Landis sat on his bed. He stared out at the dim light that shone through the trees from the barn loft, and a light breeze lifted the curtain edge through the window screen. He'd felt good after returning to the inn for dinner, but since then, two things had unsettled him and now he was conflicted.

The first was the mild argument he somehow started between Katy and Mitch at dinner.

"Come and sit, Landis," Katy had invited, as she placed a bowl of steamed green beans on the table. He had just walked in from saying goodnight to Summer, and Mitch had just walked in from the BBQ on the opposite side of the house. Mitch put a platter of pork chops down and was eyeing Landis with a serious face.

"Thanks," Landis said as he slid onto the bench at the large table in the centrally located dining room. He was appreciating the layout of the inn—sitting room and lobby desk up front, family-style dining room in the middle, kitchen to the right, and guest rooms up the middle grand staircase—when he noticed the quietness in the room. "I love the layout here. Did you guys design this yourself, or did you use an architect?" he asked, looking from Katy to Mitch and back, wondering if he was imagining the tension.

DEADLINE ON LOVE

"Mitch did most of it, but Summer had some fabulous ideas about the layout. She's so creative, isn't she, Mitch?" Katy fairly sparkled, looking from him to Mitch, who was sending her a stern look. "You don't know that side of her yet, Landis, but you will. She told me about the editor position at the paper and your deal with Gage. That's fantastic!" she gushed.

Landis looked at her, wondering what was going on. He hadn't known her long, but Katy did not seem like a gusher. He got the pregnancy-crying, but not this over-the-top exuberance.

"Summer is very creative." Mitch slid into a chair opposite Landis and pulled out the chair beside him for Katy. "And therefore she's vulnerable. Plus, she's still getting back on her feet." He cocked his head at Landis, as if he asked him a question.

Katy grabbed a bowl of rolls from the counter before sitting down. "I don't think Summer is as vulnerable as you think. She's not a fragile butterfly that needs special care and attention." She snatched a roll and split it open, and then pointed one of the halves at Landis. "Although, I do think she needs some amount of care and attention. What do you think, Landis?"

He looked back and forth between the two, starting to puzzle out what might be going on. He squinted as he pointed between them. "Did you see Summer and me kiss?" He nodded when he saw their faces go blank, widened eyes staring back at him. "Okay, this makes sense now. First, she is creative, I agree. And vulnerable, but not fragile. And I agree she deserves care and attention. Did I cover everything for you guys?" He reached for a roll, and then spooned some green beans onto his plate.

"We didn't see you kiss, but I saw you holding hands when you came back from the beach," admitted Mitch, as he lifted a pork chop onto his plate.

"Me too, but I could tell by one look at Summer's face that she had been thoroughly kissed, and I say amen!" she gloated at her husband. "It's about time she took my advice."

"What advice?" both men asked, watching Katy select the smallest pork chop from the platter Mitch held for her.

"None of your business." But her broad grin gave them both an

273

idea.

"Before this gets any weirder, I want to say this. Whatever does or does not happen between Summer and me is between two consenting adults. I respect Summer, and, well…" He waved his fork at them as his words trailed to silence. "That's all I want to say about it."

He started to eat. He had to make it through Katy's secret smiles and Mitch's periodic glares, which started to make him feel off balance. He'd told Summer he was leaving Sunday. And she agreed to enjoy the time they had. But did Summer and Katy have some other plan? Maybe Katy just lived in that magical "in love" world and wanted everyone to live there too. He knew better, though.

The second unsettling thing waited upstairs. Melanie had forwarded Summer's contract, which Gage had emailed just that afternoon at Landis's request. The contract was fairly standard, but Melanie had drawn his attention to an important fact.

Summer had used a pseudonym in the past—Chase Richards—and the contract included parameters around the copyright to some of the IP written under that name. Melanie also included links to a few clips of some minor TV reporting Summer had done as Chase Richards, and one was still paused on his laptop on the desk behind him. Watching the clips had started turning the wheels in Landis's mind.

First, she was magnificent. She needed more practice to perfect her delivery, but her presence jumped off the screen, and that was something that couldn't be taught. Was her original career path to move up into broadcast news? It was an area Landis wanted to move into over the next few years but hadn't seriously started exploring yet.

So he worried on two counts. One, that he might be setting Summer up for failure by pushing her into the editorship at the Cranberry Chronicle, when she really wanted more. In his experience, all journalists dreamed of being a TV news anchor. And two, he worried he was burying talent in a tiny community newspaper, when he could be cultivating it for his other markets. That was just bad business.

The cogs in his mind started ticking over, grinding away at the problem. The thought of moving Summer into broadcast—to a station in New York—now, that had all kinds of potential. Blake Media had a small-market radio station that was seeing traction with web broadcasts of bigger news stories.

Putting a reporter of Summer's caliber there would be smart. He could easily find an experienced editor who would jump at a job on the west coast to keep Gage happy. The fact that it would put her less than forty minutes away from his office was just... coincidence. Wasn't it? For some reason, a normally easy decision had him uncertain.

He yanked himself away from the window and spent a few more hours on his laptop getting caught up on other business. When he couldn't keep his eyes open any longer, he called it a night. He was sure a solid sleep would give him some perspective.

He was wrong.

After a fitful night of whirling thoughts and strange half-dreams, he gave up on sleep. The dawn light was coloring the dark sky from a midnight blue to indigo, and he decided a run would put everything right.

But five miles later, he only felt more confused. Especially when his feet ran him back to the plot of sand where he had one of the most bewitching kisses he'd ever experienced.

His body still vibrated when he remembered how she stood on tiptoe to press her lips against his. *This is ridiculous,* he chided. He'd just been too long without female comfort. He marched back up to the still-sleeping inn and showered away the sweat of his run and the discomfort of his thoughts.

He was downstairs reading an industry magazine and sipping from an oversized mug of coffee, when Mitch joined him.

"Morning," he said, lifting his mug in greeting. It had a sassy pair of red lips painted on the side facing Mitch, and the words ***I'm a morning babe*** written in a playful script.

"Hey, that's *my* mug," Mitch joked, pouring himself some coffee in a generic mug and grabbing cream from the fridge. Sitting across from Landis in his regular chair, he said, "I'm sorry about the big brother stuff last night. After everything that Summer and Carson have been through, I guess we're a bit overprotective. I know you're a stand-up guy, and not the lady-killer you were in college." Mitch took a sip of coffee and then paused, lifting an eyebrow. "Right? You're not that guy anymore?"

He laughed, setting his mug down. "No. And I think I was a lady-killer for all of one semester. When it comes easy to you, it's just not fun anymore." He laughed and tapped his mug to the one Mitch held out to him.

"Man, you were bad back in the day. You were with a different woman every week!" He reminisced.

"You were worse! You had that whole jazz pianist shtick down, and ladies flowing through our room worse than I ever had."

"When you come from Have Nothing, Louisiana, you have to play every angle you can. I didn't have your fancy convertible, but I'm also glad I didn't have your nosy mom. Man, that was hard to watch."

"Yeah, thanks for reminding me." Landis grimaced, looking over the stacked basket of baked goods and selecting a blueberry muffin.

"She went *off* on you that day. You were the talk of campus for a long while. How long had she been yelling at you before I walked in?" Mitch asked.

"It felt like an hour, but it was probably only five minutes. She just walked in and went right into her speech."

"Why didn't you lock the door? I still feel bad for the girl you had with you."

"I thought I had," Landis groaned, remembering his own embarrassment, but not recalling many details about the woman he'd been in bed with.

"Speaking of girls." Mitch watched Landis break open the muffin and take a bite. "I didn't think blondes were your type."

"My type used to be somebody who didn't bore me. Now I don't even have time for that. Holy cow, man," Landis exclaimed in midchew. "This is amazing! Does Katy make these?"

"No, the guy in our barn does. Summer's brother."

"Are you kidding? He said he worked at a local restaurant, but I assumed he was a cook."

Mitch gave him a funny look. "He's more than a cook. He was a Michelin star chef."

DEADLINE ON LOVE

"What?" Landis leaned forward, looking at Mitch and then back at his muffin with more respect. "At the restaurant where he is now?"

"No, he was at a swank place in San Francisco for years. He dropped out of that whole scene when he broke his leg and they found cancer."

Landis whistled low. "Yeah, he told me about that yesterday. I'm looking forward to playing ball with him today. Are you on the team?"

"I was, but I'm on Team Baby with the due date so close. You got roped into playing?" Mitch asked.

"Gage asked me yesterday. I haven't played in years, but I think it'll be fun. Not to mention getting rid of some pent-up energy."

"Oh yeah? About a certain blonde, maybe?" Mitch hid his smile behind his coffee mug.

"No, and even if that was it, I'd be too gentlemanly to admit it. Actually, work is insane. It never ends. Buying a unionized plant has added layers of complexity that I didn't expect. I'm learning on the fly."

"And now you're expanding to the west coast," he added, pointing at Landis as he rubbed his neck. "There's your signature 'I'm stressed' move. You should stay here longer and unwind."

"I can't. There's too much to do, and no one else to do it. But buying the Chronicle was too good an opportunity to pass up, regardless of the additional workload." He drained his mug and got up to refill it from the carafe. "And on that topic, can I ask you a question?"

"Shoot."

"Does Summer ever talk about getting into broadcast news?"

"Hm, she did once, I think, before she moved out here. Everything changed later, when Carson moved in. She loves the paper and Cranberry Hill. I've heard her tell Katy she's never leaving, but you never know. Best laid plans, and all that." Mitch shrugged.

Landis paced to the edge of the dining room, looking through the kitchen and screen door to the trees that separated the inn and the barn. She was probably still asleep. He didn't like uncertainties, and this was gnawing at him.

"Why do you ask?" Mitch wondered.

"Oh, I was just curious. I guess I want to make sure the editor position would be a good fit for her, and I wanted some feedback from someone who knows her well."

"Are you kidding? I think it's perfect for her. She's practically doing the job already, from the stories I hear. But you should get Katy's two cents on it. She should be up in a couple hours."

Landis took a sip of the hot coffee and checked his watch. Eight fifteen. "Naw, I'll talk it over with Summer. I want her to know there are other options with Blake Media if that's where she wants her career to go."

Mitch shrugged again. "I doubt it. Like I said, she seems pretty happy here."

He glanced at Mitch and then away. His new, apparently capable editor was content at his newest paper. He should be relieved, and yet he wasn't.

He had conflicting thoughts about letting things lie and talking things over with her. He felt like he had a good connection with Summer, so speaking honestly about her career shouldn't be a problem. Should it?

⊙⊙

TWO HOURS LATER, LANDIS WAS SITTING IN THE MERCEDES WITH Summer beside him, following Carson to the ball park and wondering what the hell had just happened.

"Chase Richards is none of your business!" Her temper flashed at what Landis thought was a very simple question: *How would you feel about being Chase Richards for real?*

He thought he'd wait until the time felt right to ask, but in the end had just blurted out the question within seconds of her fastening her seat belt.

"I don't know why you're upset. It's a valid question." His seat belt suddenly felt uncomfortably tight.

"Chase Richards is dead. She's none of your business. End of discussion."

"It's just..." He could see the chasm in front of him, knew he should stop walking toward it, yet flung himself in with his next words. "She's exactly my business. She's mentioned in your damned contract. Now, from my perspective, you have a lot of talent and we could use you at one of our New York City based stations. Plus, every reporter dreams of moving into broadcast. Did you never think of that?"

"You could 'use' me?" She was incredulous. Her sarcasm ignited a spark of anger in him. She was twisting his words.

"You know I didn't mean—"

"Oh, now you know what I'm thinking? I know exactly what you meant. I also love how you presume to know what my dreams are. You live for stepping over all kinds of boundaries, don't you?"

❦

"Uh, don't worry." He threw some of his own sarcasm at her. "I don't presume to know the first *thing* about what goes on in your head most of the time." That fanned her temper even higher.

"Do they have job descriptions in New York? Is it a common for CEOs to do a reporter's job? Because you don't need me to be Chase Richards. I'm sure you could pull it off all by yourself!" she seethed.

"We're not going to get anywhere while you're angry. Maybe when you calm down." He could feel her rage rolling off her, and admittedly he knew using the word "calm" would trigger that. He was ashamed he took a small bit of satisfaction in that.

"I told you. Chase Richards is dead. In fact, she was never really born. There's my answer." Her voice was devoid of any emotion.

"Fine," he said, and reversed the car and drove down the driveway onto the road. Hopefully, Carson hadn't gotten too far ahead of them, because he was sure Summer would not even deign to give him directions.

He snuck a look at her, arms crossed and body rigid, pressed as close to the passenger door as she could get. From the way she was breathing, he could tell her anger was at boiling level. His own frustration drained away.

He wasn't ready to dissect why he'd felt the need to push the topic, but he knew he wanted to apologize. Even after that, he wasn't certain they'd ever get back to the intimacy they'd shared yesterday, and that made him a little sad.

He caught up to Carson's pick-up and followed it to the field, which was a few minutes past Main Street. He'd barely put it into park when she jumped out and slammed the door, striding out of sight toward the concession stand and dugouts. He sighed and got out of the car.

"Wanna help line the field?" Carson asked him, hauling big bags of gear from the back of his pick-up.

"Absolutely." Landis strode over to take one of the bags and followed him to the dugout where they dropped the bags in the dirt, and then to a small shed off the diamond by left field. Carson unlocked the door and pulled out the lime box, bases, and the assorted tools needed to set up the field. Once Carson had set home plate, they measured and marked the lengths for the bases, snapped the bags into the boxes that were embedded into the field, and went about marking the required areas.

Always in his peripherals, he was aware of what Summer was doing. She unpacked the team equipment from the canvas bags, hanging the bat bag on the chain link mesh near the dugout's opening, hung the catcher's gear on the back wall, and carried out an armful of game balls to the umpire who'd just shown up.

People were drifting in to both sets of bleachers behind each team's dugout. Everyone seemed to know Summer, calling out greetings or coming up for a hug. He watched her quiet manner switch from distant to warm and wondered if she'd talk to him once the game started.

"I don't know if you've played slow-pitch before, but we've got a few different rules in our league," Carson explained as they walked together to return the tools and lime box to the equipment shed.

"I've played baseball, but slow-pitch only once." Landis pushed the cart through the door and stood back while Carson dropped the tool bag inside and locked the door.

"The biggest difference is you can't steal a base until the pitch crosses the front of the plate. That means no lead offs. And we've all agreed on no stealing home, which is in deference to Pete—" Carson tapped his prosthetic "—and the fact that he helps me back-catch."

"Your leg is named Pete?" Landis smiled. He liked Carson more and more each time they spoke. "Does he count as a player on the field?"

Carson shouted a laugh. "Good one. No, we consider him an agreed-upon player assist." He put his arm around Landis's shoulders and gave him a shake. "You're all right, Landis."

The men headed to their dugout, where most of the team had assembled. Carson gathered everyone for introductions and tossed him a spare mitt from the equipment bag.

"This is Landis, everybody. He's staying at the inn this weekend and has agreed to help us finally beat the unbeatable Hurricanes." Everybody took turns shaking hands or waving a hello to Landis. Summer stayed at the end of the bench, watching her foot make circles in the dirt.

Carson pointed to each player one by one to assign warm-up, fielding, batting, or playing catch. He put his sister and Landis together to play catch until it was their turn for batting warm-up.

"Have you played slow-pitch before?" Summer asked stiltedly, throwing the yellow softball to him.

"Once. I used to play baseball." He threw the ball back to her. She caught it deftly, dropping it into her hand for a quick throw back.

"Baseball is fast-pitch. It has different rules," she said as her throw snapped into his mitt.

"Carson told me a few of them." He tried to match how quickly she'd thrown it, and the ball went a little wide. Her arm shot across herself to make a quick catch. "Sorry," he muttered, his face getting a little warm.

"No problem." She threw the ball back. "Did he tell you about no stealing home, or sliding into home?"

"Yes," he replied more sharply than he intended.

"Just checking," she responded with a defensive tone. That was the end of the conversation, and he mentally kicked himself for letting a bad throw affect him. Was his ego that fragile?

Everyone rotated through batting and fielding practice, and then the umpire called the captains to the plate. Summer sat at the end of the dugout on his right, and he sat four people over from her, between Hank, who he discovered was the compositor at the newspaper, and

Della, a curvy blonde who was part owner of the Speedy Mart on the main strip of town.

"The Hurricanes are almost all firefighters," Della explained, leaning against his right side and nodding to the opposing bench. "They're great all around, but they usually decimate us with their batting. They're all home run hitters."

"I heard." He attempted to lean a little away, but Della's body followed him.

"I've been working at getting more spin on my ball," Charles leaned forward to murmur. He sat two people on Landis's left and spoke in a low voice, as if to keep the strategy on the down-low. Although, there was no possible way even shouting could be heard above all the surrounding chatter. "I'm hoping they pop up more because of it."

Landis glanced down toward Summer, who was laughing as she chatted with a huge good-looking man in a Chutney Hurricanes T-shirt. He strained to hear what they were talking about, but Della was talking to him about the various players on the other team, and he swore her lips were almost on his ear.

"The bleach blonde guy is their best hitter. He can put the ball anywhere in the field he wants. Phil is their fastest runner. He's also the biggest guy I've ever seen. But I don't see him. Oh, that would be great if he didn't show up today." Della scanned the other bench then the bleachers and finally looked in the opposite direction. "Oh, darn, he's talking to Summer."

His neck tensed and he looked away to Carson, who was walking back from the umpire huddle. "Something tells me we're going to do well today," he told Della, who laughed loudly.

"That's the spirit!" She reached around his shoulders, squeezing his arm against her breast. He couldn't help looking at Della, who kept holding his shoulders, and saw Summer watching them. Her expression was blank, but she turned back to Phil with a broad smile and a few words he couldn't hear.

"Okay, everyone," Carson called as he entered the dugout. "We've agreed to allow bunting today. So for Landis's benefit, here are the signs." Carson went through the three signs they had—swing, don't swing, and now bunt.

"Play ball!" called the umpire, and all the players moved into action as the fans in both bleachers cheered.

Landis had expected the fun of playing would loosen him up and get him back into his easygoing state of mind, but somehow it had the opposite effect. At least, certain plays did. Like when the firefighters had caught Summer between second and third, throwing back and forth as they inched closer to her, and then instead of just tagging her out, the big man—Phil—had picked her up and swung her around, whacking her butt with the ball in his mitt and letting her slide down his body real slow.

She'd laughed joyfully, a sound no one could deny came from the depths of her heart, making a lot of others laugh along. But it made him scowl.

Then there was the third time Summer went up to bat. The first two times, she'd hit grounders and gotten on base. But this time, she knocked it over the left field fence. Right after that, Landis stepped up and popped up the first pitch, which was easily caught. And then there was every time anyone threw the ball to Summer at first base.

Nobody held back, their throws were bullets, each making his heart leap to his throat. But she caught every one with a quick snap of her mitt. The one time he'd thrown it from his position as rover in the field, he'd held back and the throw hadn't got there in time to get the runner out. She'd stood there with her hands on her hips, staring him down before tossing the ball back to Charles and shaking her head.

"Don't back down, man," Hank advised from shortstop. "She could probably catch throws in the majors." Landis nodded and smiled, but it did not come easily.

In the end, the Cranberry Belles lost by two runs. As they shook hands at the end, Phil told him, "Good game! You should come out again."

"I'm going back to New York tomorrow, but thanks," Landis replied stiffly.

"Ah, too bad," he said, moving on to shake a few more hands before getting to Summer, who was at the end of their line. Every one of the Chutney Hurricanes seemed to prefer hugging Summer to shaking her hand, which added to Landis's simmering mood.

He put on a friendly face as he said goodbye to everyone, agreeing to meet up with them at the pub. As he unlocked the car, he saw Summer jog over to him. He half expected her to say she was riding with Phil, but she rounded the car to stand outside the passenger door, her face radiating good cheer. "Two runs, arrrgh!" She rolled her eyes and held her hands out in agony, laughing.

"But we lost." Landis clicked his fob and they both slid into the car, buckling in.

"But that was the best loss we've ever had against them, thanks to you." She punched his arm good-naturedly.

A little of the tension in his stomach unwound. "I can't believe I flied out," he admitted, as he backed the Mercedes out and followed the stream of cars leaving the parking lot. He assumed most of them were heading to the pub that was midway between Cranberry Hill and Chutney.

"You advanced a runner and in the end got four game RBIs. That's phenomenal!"

"You're phenomenal. How did you get to be such a great player?"

"I played when I was a kid, and then I had one season with my college team. Whew." Summer rolled down her window and lifted the wisps of hair that had escaped her bun off her sweaty neck. "Is it okay to have the window down for a bit? I like how the lavender along this part of the road smells."

And just like that, the tension from the morning dissipated, and a tightness he hadn't realized had built in his chest melted to nothing.

Almost every car ahead of them drove directly to the Old Hemlock Pub, and he had to park very close to the road. He came around too late to help Summer out of the car, and as they walked to the pub's entrance, he noticed she was limping.

"Are you okay?" He took her arm and she let him.

"When I slid into second, I did it the old way." She turned to lift up her slider and show him her left thigh, but other than a jagged scar and some dirt, he didn't see anything.

"What old way?" he asked.

"I'm supposed to slide with my right leg leading instead of my left, but old habits die hard." She brushed off some of the dust and then looked up at him. "It's okay, really. But thanks for your concern." Her face was completely relaxed... and completely dusty. He reached up to give her cheek a light brush.

"I think you brought half the field with you," he joked, watching her wide mouth spread into a grin. "I'm sorry about bringing up your past. It seems like I'm always doing the wrong thing with you."

Now her mouth opened in a full smile and she linked her arm in his, the first real touch they'd shared so far today. "Let's start the day over." She tugged his arm a little to motion them both toward the pub. But Landis stopped walking and turned her to face him. "Great idea." He lifted his hands to her face and pulled her close for a deep kiss. After a few beats, his mouth released hers. He was pleased with the dazed look in her eyes. "There we go. A great start." He relinked her arm in his and led her into the pub.

"Summer!" came a chorus of voices from the back of the pub. They walked around the large center bar to where both teams and their fans had populated most of the tables. Summer slid her arm free and walked amongst her teammates and friends, waving and high-fiving and firing off a little good-natured ribbing in the other team's direction, which led to some outrageous insults being hurled in return. It all drew friendly laughter.

"Here's a welcome-to-the-team beer," Carson called out, walking over to stand beside Landis and hand him one of three beer bottles he held, all with limes sticking out the top.

"Thanks." Landis squeezed the lime against the inside of the bottle, pushed it all the way in, and took a long drink, feeling the liquid make a refreshing path down his throat and into his stomach. He continued to watch Summer make her way back to where he stood. At one point, he lurched toward her when her limp made her stumble but relaxed back when she caught herself by leaning on a chair back.

"Summer hurt her leg today," he explained to her brother, who'd turned to look at him questioningly when he jerked forward at Summer's stumble.

"Oh, that? That's just an old war wound." Carson lifted his beer for a drink.

"War wound?"

"Summer!" Carson invited loudly as she joined the two men, taking the extra beer he held in his hand. "Tell us about the time you were shot in the leg."

Groans went up from their friends in the surrounding tables. There were various shouts of "Oh, not that one again!" and "Anything to get a free beer!" as Summer exaggeratedly rolled her eyes at Carson and the group.

"You don't want to hear about that." She drank deeply. Everyone laughed again and turned back to their conversations. But he couldn't.

"I'd like to hear it," he said quietly, setting his beer on the nearest table and sitting down, looking steadily at her.

He knew the second she realized he wasn't going to back town, and she sighed and sat down. "Well, it sounds worse than it was."

"I can't think of when being shot would be less worse than talking about it, but try me." He pointed his bottle toward her and then took another sip from it.

"Well, when I worked at a paper just outside of Chicago, I sometimes freelanced. I'd buddied up with another woman who wanted to get into broadcast news as a cameraperson for a big-time station. I guess we both wanted a TV career of some sort. Anyway, my friend, Christine, had gotten a tip about an accountant who was set to testify and expose a small-time Chicago crime family during a trial.

"She and I were outside the courthouse, following this guy up the steps, trying to get him on record about what he was going to say, when suddenly I'm lying on the steps with a burning pain in my leg." She paused to take a sip of beer. He could tell by her slack face that she'd been transported back to that day.

"Are you okay?" he asked. She nodded, and some life came back into her eyes.

"Anyway, the next thing I knew, Christine was on top of me, Mr. Accountant was running away screaming, and my ears were ringing from a loud bang." Summer paused to take a long drink of her beer and stirred herself, as if from unwelcome memories.

"To make a long story short, it turned out that my then-boyfriend was involved with said crime family, and that became a thing I needed to get away from. Because of the way the bullet hit me, it took several surgeries and some long months of rehab to walk properly again. Christine's footage missed almost everything, but it gave the cops enough of a license plate to track down who did it. It also got her on staff at the number two station in Chicago, and I took a lateral move to live out here." Summer lifted her beer with a half smile that said "everything worked out."

Landis couldn't explain the stab of fear that he felt when she described being shot. It made no sense to him, as he had nothing to compare the feeling to. He'd never felt that level of concern for anyone before. But then, nobody he'd ever known had been in such a dangerous situation, either. He took another sip of beer to buy time to sort out his thoughts.

Summer looked at him curiously. "What are you thinking? You have a weird look."

"I'm thinking... well, I've never known anyone who was shot before. Mostly, I'm thinking I'm grateful the bullet only hit you in the leg." He wondered if she'd notice the tiny warble in his voice and was relieved when she just nodded.

"You could say it was my one and only 'shot' at being a network TV reporter. Badda-bing!" she said with a laugh.

He tried to laugh along but found it difficult. "What happened to the then-boyfriend?"

"The license plate led back to Nick's family. I was in California with Carson when the D.A. finally sent somebody to get a deposition from me. They asked particularly about a few dates and times, and thank goodness I keep track of my life through my calendar. That was about it. I'm pretty sure that family can buy their way out of anything legal, so I haven't really followed up on what the outcome was. I'm much more interested in Carson and the family I've made here. I want to stay present, and not try to fix things that happened in the past."

He touched her hand gently. "I like that. It's a good philosophy."

Summer turned her hand so their fingers linked in a C-shape. "It seems to work for me," she said.

"Hey, you two." Carson knocked on the table to get their attention. "I'm heading out. Believe it or not, I've got a business call in an hour and I want to prepare."

"Business call?" Landis asked, a familiar spike of interest pulling part of his attention away from stroking Summer's fingers.

"My big brother is going into a partnership with a restaurant in Thailand," she inserted.

Carson pursed his lips. "There are still a lot of steps before it actually happens, but yeah... that's the plan."

A dozen questions cascaded through Landis's mind, but he felt a gentle tug on his fingers. "Just jump straight to where you ask him if he's had someone look over the contract," Summer coaxed with a knowing smile.

"There's already a contract tabled? You should definitely have someone look it over before you make any serious plans on your phone call. I know someone. I could have them take a look as soon as tonight."

Landis slowed down when he saw the smug look on Summer's face.

"That is, if you'd like me to do that." He wasn't sure why it mattered to him what Summer thought, especially when it came to business. He'd always been rewarded by acting fast on his instincts, and slowing down in this instance to ask permission was uncomfortable territory for him. But it felt right.

"That would be great, Landis, thanks. I can email it to you, if I can get your address." Carson reached for his phone and entered the contact information Landis told him. "Appreciate it. Have fun, you two." Carson held up his hand in goodbye and headed out of the pub.

Landis turned to look back at Summer and saw a speculative look on her face. "What?"

"That's your thing, isn't it? Doing business, making deals?"

He shrugged cautiously. "I don't know any other way. What about you? Are you already composing 'Local Cook Cajoled by Off-Shore Cuisine Conglomerate'?"

"First of all—" Summer picked up her bottle and pointed it at him to make her point "—Carson is a chef, not a cook. Secondly, that was some very nice alliteration."

"You're right, but 'cook' was better for alliteration than 'chef'." Landis lifted a shoulder and smiled. Word sparring with her was fun. As he took another sip of his beer, though, he noticed Summer stretch and retract her left leg. "Is your leg bothering you?" he asked, concerned about her injury.

"A little," she admitted. "Sorry to be dull, but I should probably call it a night."

He stood immediately and stepped closer to assist her, whether she needed it or not. Something about her touch calmed something inside him he didn't realize had been racing. And not just racing today, but a frenetic energy that seemed to be a constant presence, in his body and in his mind. It made him wonder if he'd ever felt completely calm, ever.

"Bye, everyone!" Summer called to the crowd, who all turned and gave her a wave. He noticed happily that Phil looked at them a little longer than the others, possibly with some regret, but Landis couldn't tell for sure. *That's right, buddy. She's with me.* The instant the thought entered his head, he rolled his eyes. What was this, high school?

He walked her back to the car and helped her get in and belted. He pulled out of the parking lot and found he didn't want to rush back. Summer had rolled down her window and the sea salt air was making her hair flutter in a way that matched his heart rate.

He thought about not seeing her after Sunday, and something in him rebelled at that. He believed he knew why she had balked at the mention of Chase Richards. It didn't mean her ambition for broadcast news wasn't still there. The logical side of his brain cranked up, taking a small idea and building it up and up until it was something he could put words around.

"I want to spend the day with you tomorrow. Until I have to leave for my flight." He reached over and slid his hand over hers as it lay on her leg. "I just had an idea I want to propose."

She rolled her head toward him on the headrest, the dash lights making her silver-gray eyes glitter in her tanned face. "Oh yeah?" she asked, the long day giving her voice a husky sexiness. She turned her hand over to give his a little squeeze.

"Oh yeah," he said, squeezing back and feeling something in the pit of his stomach squeeze tighter as well. He mentally shook his head to get back on track. "I know you feel a connection here, to Cranberry

Hill. But you're a phenomenal talent, and something struck me. A slightly different path for you, if you will."

Summer sat up a little straighter, her head coming off the headrest to look more fully at him. "What kind of path?"

"Well..." He hesitated at her voice. He'd thought she was leaning toward him with interest, but her voice had lost all hints of huskiness and instead sounded cold and defensive. "It's just... in the clips I watched, you were very good. Incredibly good. Obviously, you have a face for television." He felt her hand slide away from his and her leg move from under his hand. He put his hand back on the steering wheel. "Am I wrong? Were you not at some point thinking about a future in front of the camera? Not in the field, but in a studio?"

"Are you rescinding the offer of the editor's job at the Chronicle?"

Landis grimaced. Her voice was shooting chips of ice at him. What happened? He hadn't mentioned Chase Richards. In fact, he wanted her as far away from Chase Richards as possible, since that alter ego had been shot.

"No, but I just thought... you're an amazingly talented woman, and we have this radio property in New York that's dipping its toe into web-based video reporting. And I see that being something that could take off. We could put in someone to take over the more mundane editorial work at the Chronicle, so you could.... I mean, you're practically doing the public a disservice by not getting in front of a camera."

He didn't know where to go from there. Every word seemed to inject more distance between them.

"A 'disservice' to the public? I think I've paid a steep enough price to choose where I want to work." She lifted her leg slightly to emphasize her point. *Oh boy,* he thought, *this is so not how I pictured this going.*

"No, of course. You paid a huge price. And you've created a nice family here in Cranberry Hill, with your brother and Katy and Mitch. But don't you think your skills are lying fallow here? Even as editor, don't you think you'll be bored?"

Summer folded her arms over her chest. "If you don't think I can do the editor's job, just say it. Don't try to butter it up with compliments about my skills. People like you always think flattery will get you everywhere." Instead of raging, her voice was quiet and stiff.

"'People like me?' What's that supposed to mean?" Landis gripped the steering wheel tightly, taking the curves in the road a little sharper than he intended. "I make hundreds of decisions every day that affect people's lives, yes, but I weigh them all against one guiding principle—how can everyone win in this situation? I definitely don't need to butter anybody up with false flattery." His voice came out more cutting than he intended, too, but he couldn't help that.

People who've never run a large company like he did could rarely comprehend all the minutiae he had to deal with every day. And if she couldn't see the huge compliment he was paying her, well... that was her problem. "But let's drop it. You prefer to sell ads and edit a bi-monthly small-town newspaper. Fine. Just keep the revenue growing, and you'll never have to listen to my false flattery again." He cringed inwardly at that last sentence. That was not the mature CEO of a media company talking.

"Fine," she responded. They drove the rest of the way to the inn in silence.

As he turned into the gravel driveway, he caught sight of a new car parked beside Carson's pick-up. He held back the groan that almost escaped him. He'd forgotten about Stella showing up.

As they both unbuckled, he got out quickly, wanting to help Summer, even though he was sure she would reject him. He was right. He stood helplessly beside her as she fumbled and grappled her way out of the car, stubbornly ignoring his outstretched hand.

Over the roof of the car, he saw Stella rise from the deck chair she was sitting on, wearing a short skirt and glamorous heels. Her fiery auburn hair sparkled in the muted glow of the porch light.

"Well, hello, handsome," she said throatily, making her way toward his car. Summer swung around, almost losing her balance as her sore leg came close to buckling beneath her. Her hands flew to the roof and doorframe to steady herself until she could shake and stretch her leg out.

"Hi, Stella. This is Summer Richardson. Summer, this is my friend, Stella Carmichael." He gestured toward the curvy redhead but still watched Summer in case she needed his help.

"Hi," Summer greeted shortly, shutting the car door and spinning to find herself in Landis's personal space. She jerked away. "Excuse me, I need to get home," she murmured, turning to walk-limp around the front of the car. He followed for a few steps. This wasn't how he wanted the night to end.

"Summer," he started, but he had no idea what to say. She stopped and half turned to face him just as Stella's hand grabbed his jaw and turned his head into her waiting lips for a long, deep kiss. When she let go, she wore a salacious smile. "Happy to see me?" she asked.

Landis turned back to Summer, seeing a blankness slide over her face. "It was nice to meet you, Stella," she said. "Goodnight." She turned and walked up the dimly lit path, her limp getting less pronounced and her back getting more rigid as she went.

Landis let out a sigh and looked up at the clear night sky. "That was not how I wanted that to go." He turned to look at Stella, one corner of his mouth quirked up tiredly.

"Did I get you out of a jam, or into one?" She let a husky laugh trail after her words.

"I'm not sure if your role playing will help me or hurt me this time, but I appreciate the thought behind it."

"I saw her body language when you pulled in, and it made me think you needed assistance. I'm no stranger to infatuated girls getting the Landis Speech. I *was* one of those girls years ago." She linked her arm through his and pulled him toward the porch. How she could walk so elegantly over driveway gravel on her towering heels was impressive.

"The Landis Speech? What's that?"

"The talk you have with women, either when you don't want to start dating them, or when you don't want to keep dating them. You gave it to me when we were in college, remember?"

"I don't remember. Anyway, that's not what I was talking to her about. It had to do with the newspaper I'm going to buy, and her role there. Or more accurately, the idea I had to change her role."

"I'm sorry if I created unnecessary trouble. It's probably not too late." She glanced toward the path Summer had taken. "I can go catch her and explain everything," Stella offered.

"No," Landis replied. "I'll sort things out later. If I can figure out how to sort them." He rubbed the back of his neck and turned to look back at the path to the barn.

Stella leaned back and looked at him with wide eyes, "Oh my," she said.

"Oh my what?"

"I've never known you to be uncertain about how to sort things out." She dragged him to sit down on the outdoor couch.

"Me neither, to be honest." His body sank into the cushions but remembered one thing from earlier in the night. "Oh, by the way, I told Summer's brother you'd look over a business proposal he's received. It's regarding a restaurant co-purchase in Thailand. Sorry, I meant to text you about it as a heads-up, but I got caught up in other things."

"Or caught up in other people," Stella laughed. "You must mean the grouchy guy I met earlier, who apparently lives in a... barn... with his sister?" She angled her head disbelievingly, and then shrugged when Landis nodded. "I'm not surprised they're brother and sister. They could be twins. Blond surfer twins. You know, I never thought blondes were your thing."

"Stop already. There's nothing romantic going on." He paused, his thoughts flying back to yesterday. "Not exactly, anyway. I mean, I thought about it, but... I don't think it makes sense to start anything. Especially now. Arrgh." He dropped his face into his hands and the last word was muffled.

"What happens between consenting adults is fair game. But personally speaking, the woman who got out of your car a few minutes ago doesn't seem to want anything to do with you. If you want my two cents on the issue."

"Thank you so much for your two cents." He looked sideways at her, resting his head on a hand. "I'll take it under advisement. I need to find Katy and ask her something. I assume you're all settled in and everything?" He got up and stretched his back. It had been a grueling day, not just physically but mentally. But he had one thing he wanted to clear up with Katy before he went to bed.

"Yes, Katy and Mitch are lovely. They got me all settled in, and I even got to put a pillow in a pillow case, just like regular folk." She winked and wiggled a designer-shoed foot at him. "Go inside and do what you need to do. I'm going to finish my lemonade. Oh, I left a copy of my proposal on your bed. I don't meet with my people for four days, so any thoughts you could share in an email is much appreciated."

"Great. I'll look it over on my flight to New York tomorrow." Landis gave her a small wave and a smile and entered the kitchen to talk to Katy. He found her in the front room, sipping tea in a huge plaid wing-backed chair.

"I heard you led the team to their best loss ever against Chutney, and I mean that in a good way." She raised her tea cup to him with a grin.

"Guilty. It was a fun game." He sat down in the chair beside her, a small table between them. He leaned toward her with his elbows on his knees. "So. Summer was shot?" He'd wanted to lead up to the question and startled himself when the words came out with as much emotion as they did.

"Did she tell you?" Katy asked.

"Yes. Everyone at the pub goaded her into it, but she didn't seem to mind telling the story. I feel like there's more to it than she's telling, though."

"You know I prefer not to tell other people's stories, but I've heard her play it down like it was no big thing. It was a very big thing for her. And Carson's diagnosis coming soon after threw a big wrench into her life plans. She likes to think her future is here and she's excited about moving forward, but really, she and Carson came here to heal in private and get a break from the big world they had been so ready to take on. Summer in particular wants nothing to do with her old plans and big ambitions."

A puzzle piece in Landis's head clicked into place. No wonder she'd reacted so strongly to his suggestion that she get in front of a camera again. It irritated him that he couldn't see that for himself. What was his problem when it came to Summer? He was constantly making all the wrong decisions when he was in her orbit.

"You look aggravated about something," Katy enquired, balancing her tea cup and saucer on her belly.

"About myself, for the most part. My assistant sent me some video

Summer did as Chase Richards, and it made me think what she really wanted was to pursue a broadcasting career. When I mentioned it, she acted like I was... raising a demon, for lack of a better explanation."

"Hm, interesting, isn't it?" She tapped a forefinger on her lips, staring at him intently.

"You're no help at all, are you?" he asked.

"Nope!" she replied happily. "If there's anything I learned from my relationship with Mitch, it's that no one can tell you how to read your heart. You have to figure that out all by yourself."

"Nobody's talking about hearts here. I'm talking about jobs and careers... well, maybe feelings. But that's as close as it gets to talking about hearts."

"Sure you are." Katy nodded. "Landis, you're in for a bigger fall than I think any of us realize." She smiled kindly at him. "But I'll tell you this—and I probably shouldn't say a thing, but your expression is tugging at my heartstrings. The best thing that could happen to Summer is to let Carson move to Thailand, and for her to move out of the barn and find her own place somewhere nearby.

"She needs to stand on her own feet again and realize she's strong enough to do that. I love her like a twin sister, and she'll always have a place with us whenever she needs it. But right now, she needs to see her that emotions are intact. And she can go back to deciding what's best for her, instead of pushing that away to do what's best for everyone else," Katy finished with a dainty sip of her tea.

Landis mulled her words over, something inside him aching like a bruise. But at the mention of Thailand, his eyebrows shot up. "I asked Stella to look over Carson's partnership agreement. She's a genius at international acquisitions, so you can be confident about him making a good decision there."

Katy's laughter tinkled out. "That's another situation I wish I could watch. They did not take to each other at all, in the little bit of conversation I tried to listen in on when Carson got home. It's too bad she's only in town overnight; that could've been fun. Oh well." Katy shrugged.

Landis looked down at his hands as they dangled between his knees. He felt muddled and tired and agitated, all at the same time, and not in the least interested about Stella and Carson. "I should go to bed." He rolled to his feet just as Mitch walked in.

"Everything's ready for tomorrow, which means we are off duty, wife." Mitch took Katy's almost-empty teacup and saucer from her hands and gave her his other arm so she could pull herself to her feet. "Come on, Mama. It's time to get you to bed."

"Okay, Papa," Katy said indulgently, as she pulled herself up in a rocking motion and slid her arm through Mitch's. "Have a good night's sleep." She winked at Landis.

"I definitely will," he asserted.

But two hours later, he was still lying in bed, listening to the ocean waves through his open window and trying to remember the last time something hadn't gone his way.

9

Summer held her back rigidly straight until she made it around the corner of the barn and out of sight of anyone—namely the super model redhead and her boyfriend—who might be watching her through the trees. Anger could be an amazing motivator, she realized. But as she headed up the stairs, every painful step reminded her the motivation came with a price.

Once in the loft, she headed to the bathroom to start a bath and find some Ibuprofen. She could hear Carson's voice murmuring from his bedroom, and she remembered his business call. She backed off the tap so the water cascading into the tub made less noise.

She filled the glass on the sink with some water and downed two small tablets. After a second, she opted to take a third. She hoped the over-the-counter pain-killer would work. She didn't like taking her more serious prescription pills if she could avoid it; they upset her stomach. And she wasn't sure if her stomach could take more upset right now.

It had been an emotional day. She'd literally been blinded when he said the name Chase Richards that morning. Something had popped in her mind, and her vision had flashed pure white for several heartbeats. She didn't remember if they talked or argued after that, but once they arrived at the park and she got out of the car and moved around, she let some of her emotions bubble up so she could examine them.

The biggest one was an old bit of anger she hadn't realized had been festering inside her. It was directed at herself for not seeing the truth about Nick. Not just the hints about his involvement in the shady dealings of his family, nor the misogynistic undertones she let slide in his treatment of her.

And it wasn't that she didn't see it. It was that she willfully ignored that she saw it. She hadn't wanted any of it to be real. She'd just wanted to focus on her career and use Nick and his family's social connections to build a useful network of people. She'd met the mayor and many big Chicago players, for crying out loud!

Her shoulders slumped as the pain of that realization hit her. Nick may have used her as arm candy and to gain respectability points, but she used him as well, and that was a hard truth for Summer to face.

She reached for the jar of Epsom salts and poured a generous amount into the tub. Sitting on the tub's edge, she reached into the hot water to swirl the sparkling crystals around and around, watching them dissolve. Breathing in deeply, she sat up straight and closed her eyes.

Carson was going to Thailand. Loneliness was another emotion that bubbled up. She'd put a brave face on her feelings for his benefit, but deep down it seemed too soon for him to leave.

She wanted to protect him the way he had protected her all these years, but when she thought about the excitement on his face when he mentioned the conference call, she had to admit he healed and moved on faster than she had. She thought they'd have another year or two here together in the comfy nest she'd made for them. Maybe three years, even.

As she rolled that around, something else bubbled up. Resentment? There was definitely a tender spot when she thought about all the work she put into their lives here, and the fact he was walking away from it.

She turned the tap off and started taking off her clothes, tossing them one at a time across the bathroom to the wicker clothes basket that sat in the corner. With each piece, she made a resolution. Shirt—

she would tell Carson she was happy for him and his new adventure in Thailand. Shorts—try to forgive herself for her past mistakes. Baseball slider and panties—talk to Landis. She hesitated before throwing them.

If she looked at his suggestion with unbiased eyes, from a business perspective as he probably intended it, it was a solid idea. He was right; many reporters wanted to make the leap to television reporting, because it was exciting, somewhat glamorous, and a huge jump in pay.

She'd even known a few writers who tried to make the switch to editing and knew from personal experience it was a totally different skillset. He was right to be playing out the entire situation with an eye for protecting his investment. And she'd let her bias get in the way of seeing his suggestion for what it was.

As she rolled her head to stretch her stiff neck, she caught sight of herself in the mirror, wearing a bra, with her slider and panties still clamped in her hand. She tossed them to the basket and changed her last resolution as they landed perfectly. "Apologize to Landis," she corrected. Something in her chest loosened, and she reached around to unhook and toss her bra, easing herself into the hot water of the tub.

An hour later, wrapped in her thick terry cloth robe, she padded out of the bathroom to see Carson on the deck. He was staring out into the dark trees that surrounded the barn, the moonlight giving his blond hair a blue tint.

"Hey, big brother, how did your call go?" She took the glass of iced tea out of his hand for a drink.

"Good, I guess. It was mostly a get-to-know-you call. I took Landis's advice and didn't make any commitments." He took the glass she passed back to him and tilted it for a drink.

"I'm really happy for you. I want you to know that." She wrapped her arms around his shoulders and leaned her head against his arm. "And I mean truly happy, not fake happy. This is what you are meant to do." She smiled as he put his hand on her arm and squeezed her back.

"Are you sure? I feel like you had an idea that I'd take over the Trestle Table someday, and we'd both just live here forever." He laughed.

"Well, maybe after you moved in here I thought that. I probably made some assumptions about how long it would take us to get over our... setbacks, I guess is one way you could look at them." She smiled up at him.

"*Probably* made assumptions?" he teased her, squeezing her arm. "I can't blame you for that. For me, getting back to playing sports went a long way in helping me come to terms with not having a leg. And I'll always live with the possibility that the cancer could come back, even though they say the chances of that are very slim. I knew when I left California I wanted to get out of hyper-competitive cuisine. I want to test myself in an entirely new situation—new country, new language, new cuisine, new people. I don't think there's any scarier way to grow than having to make your way through that."

Summer let him go and turned to lean back on the railing to look into the loft. When they'd moved in, it hadn't felt new at all; it had immediately felt like home. Moving had always felt like that to her—the excitement of moving into her college dorm, and then to Chicago with Katy. Maybe it was time to try something scary again. "I think you might be on to something."

"Yeah? You think you're ready to move on?" He half turned to face her, and she looked up at the stars.

"I was thinking while I was in the tub that I never really forgave myself for staying with Nick as long as I did. For telling myself it was okay to be with him if I held the things I knew about him at a distance. I'm going to work on that. And apologize to Landis."

She turned to him with a loud sigh.

"I was pretty rude to him this morning, and just now in the car. When he'd proposed what the old me would have considered an amazing opportunity, I lashed out at him." At Carson's questioning look, Summer gave him a short overview of Landis's suggestion she 'become' Chase Richards, and then that she consider doing some local web broadcasts.

Carson groaned when she described how she responded. "I know, I know," Summer said. "Not my proudest moment."

"Speaking of Landis, did you catch his hot girlfriend hanging out on the porch in her mini skirt?" Carson scoffed. "I thought only women under a certain age could get away with a skirt that short."

"Yeah, I met her. They were practically making out once we got out of the car." Summer's face flushed as she remembered her behavior had more of an audience than just Landis.

"She is one glossy, big-city gal, that's for sure. She flashed her legs at me like I was easy pickings."

"You are easy pickings when it comes to redheads, Car. Admit it."

"Not redheads who are that far out of my income bracket. And she is nosebleed-section high. I bet she would be lost if she couldn't get a manicure every other week."

"They are both out of our league," Summer commiserated, "and they'll be out of our lives tomorrow from the sounds of it. So we only have to hold on for one more day." She bumped him with her shoulder. "Can you do it?"

"I can if you can." He bumped her back.

"I can. I have to apologize to him first, but after that, I'll steer clear. I want to do some thinking and planning about this editor job, too."

"Now there's the sister I know. I bet you'll have five spreadsheets laid out by lunchtime," he chuckled.

"You're probably right," she agreed.

Carson drank down the last of his iced tea. "All right, I'm hitting the sack. Night, sis."

"Goodnight." Summer turned to watch him head into the darkened loft to his bedroom. Just as she thought she wouldn't be able to fall asleep right away, a jaw-cracking yawn changed her mind and she headed to her own room.

SUMMER'S EYES POPPED OPEN AT EXACTLY 6:04 A.M. SHE ROLLED OUT of bed to her feet and took a quick assessment of herself. Leg felt good, mind felt clear, spirit felt invigorated. She padded over to her open window and drew in a deep breath of the fresh Sunday morning air through the screen. A slow run felt like a good start to the day, she decided.

She pulled on her running shorts and her favorite purple racer back running bra. She grabbed a fresh pair of socks and her shoes from under her bed and headed past Carson's still-closed door to the outside. Sitting on the bottom step of the stairs, she put on her socks and shoes and couldn't help but smile.

A bubble of excitement from deep within percolated upward and made her shimmy her shoulders. She would have a run, set things straight with Landis right after, do a little research and brainstorming on her new role, and then find some time to visit with Katy and Mitch. Maybe make amends with Landis's girlfriend for her abrupt behavior last night. Slapping her hands on her thighs, she bounced to her feet and started her warm-up moves.

Ten minutes later, Summer was jogging down the path and turning onto the road that led toward town. She felt good after her first mile, which was marked by her passing the crooked sole Madrone tree in Bentley's field.

She decided to up her pace slightly for the next mile, which would get her to the farthest set of beach steps. She focused on breathing to the three-and-two rhythm she'd used for years. She listened to her running shoes hit the pavement and enjoyed the early morning mist that settled into the shallow dips in the field on her right. Looking to her left, she saw the wet beach in the distance. Seeing it reminded her of running into Landis the other day, and the deep kiss they'd shared.

He hadn't seemed like a man who was involved with someone when he held her and kissed her. But she had to admit, she didn't have a particularly strong radar for that sort of thing. It was possible he and Stella had an open relationship. And that was fine, although it was something she didn't believe in for herself.

Katy had made fun of her back in college about her inability to even casually date more than one person at a time. Her bestie firmly believed dating was one thing, and a committed relationship to one person was another—and all that mattered was all parties understood that. But Summer could not imagine keeping track of her feelings for multiple men. She hadn't felt dating was all that important, anyway. Not compared to her career.

As her mind drifted back to Landis and their time in the car together when they went to the estate sale, she couldn't ignore the butterflies she still felt in her belly. From the minute she'd seen him, she felt drawn to him. It wasn't a feeling she had with anybody else. The closest thing, she guessed, was how she felt drawn to her career, to telling peoples' stories. Ever since she'd handwritten her first neighborhood newspaper when she was nine years old, she'd known journalism was her calling. Could a man be a calling? Let alone an unavailable man?

She followed the rising curve in the road and saw the handle of the beach stairs far ahead come into view. She was glad. The more she thought about Landis, the more she wanted to put things right with him. He was going to be her boss, and she definitely wanted that to be on friendly terms.

She needed to detach herself from the physical attraction part and focus on the business relationship. And who knows? Maybe he was right and she'd get bored at the Chronicle and want to branch out. It would be foolish to assume it might never happen. And if it did, being on good terms with Blake Media would certainly give her options.

She glanced behind her to make sure there were no cars and ran across the road. By this point, the beach was a few levels of stairs and landings below. The road had sharply inclined as it approached the bluff covered in Madrone trees. She jogged lightly down the stairs and landings to the beach.

Once on the sand, she stopped to take off her shoes and socks. Tying her shoelaces together, she tucked the socks inside and draped them around her neck, holding them so they wouldn't bounce as she ran. She loved the feel of the sand between her toes as she went. She started off in a light jog toward the hard-packed sand where the tide was slowly moving in.

A movement caught her eye. Coming around the curve of beach jogged Landis. This time, he wore a short pair of black shorts and a red T-shirt, both of which clung and moved with each stride of his muscled body. Summer jolted to a stop, the sight of him causing her to suck in her breath with a ragged "*Hunh.*"

10

Landis loved the Pacific Ocean. The surf had a lighter feel to it, and the air rolling off the waves felt cooler on his skin. He wouldn't have thought there was any difference at all if anyone asked him about it before he came here. Looking out over the water, he knew his memories of this ocean would always include ones of Summer.

He was having an easier beach run today, weaving into the surf and then up to the sandy stretches. He was puzzling over how to apologize to Summer and reassure her that the editor's job was hers, and to ask her to ignore everything he suggested yesterday.

Despite his rationalizations on why he had every right to make those suggestions, he had to admit his emotions were just too involved in this situation. With the Chronicle being Blake Media's first west coast acquisition, he'd find a VP, create a new division, and put any personnel concerns into his or her hands. That still meant he had to find Summer and deal with his missteps of yesterday, though.

As if in answer to his thoughts, a figure in the distance caught his eye, and he knew in an instant it was Summer. Her body left an imprint on his mind, instantly recognizable. She wore some impossibly tiny purple running shorts, a purple bra top, and had her sneakers tied together and hanging around her neck. She stood still as he slowed his strides until he was walking. He stopped several yards away from her this time, wanting her to feel comfortable.

She moved her shoulders slightly, as if letting out a deep breath, and walked toward him. As she closed the gap, her gaze skittered over his face, away, and then back up.

Great, she can't even look me in the eye.

He focused on relaxing his face and letting his mouth turn up slightly at the corners—not a full smile, but approachable. He'd been told before that his idea of a relaxed expression could look pretty aggressive.

Then she smiled.

His feet took two steps before he could stop them. Her smile stayed and something in her posture seem to relax a bit, and his own body loosened up in response.

"I'm sorry about last night," she started, "and yesterday morning. Well, pretty much all of yesterday. Can we go back to being friends?" She held her slender hand out.

He looked down at it and shot his own out to grasp her in his palm. He gave it a brief shake. And then kept holding it. He glanced up and saw her eyes twinkling. Her hand moved slightly but didn't pull away.

"Agreed. Friends." He nodded solemnly. He gave her hand a slight squeeze, and then, reluctantly, let it slide away.

"I overreacted last night, and I don't entirely know why. First, when you mentioned Chase Richards and again when you suggested I do some web broadcasts. You might be right about the editor job. I might get bored or change my mind. But for now, it feels right. I'm ready to take on more at the Chronicle and move forward. So, I'm sorry for the overreaction, and thank you for the job offer... that is, if you haven't changed your mind because of my behavior."

Her voice sounded poised and professional. The words *move forward* floated in his mind, reminding him of what Katy thought the best path for her was. The least he could do was honor that.

"No, the job is yours. It will be up to you if you want to be contracted to Blake Media or work as an employee, but either way, it doesn't mean you can't move up through the organization. You're talented, and there's always a place up the ladder for talent." He smiled at how professional his words sounded. "And I should apologize for making suggestions when I'd just made you the job offer. That was, at the very least, probably very confusing."

She rolled her eyes and dug a toe into the sand. "That's kind of you, but I was being childish. This is business. You have a responsibility to put the right people in the right places. I respect that." Her words carried some embarrassment but finished forthrightly. Their dialogue seemed... almost too polite, he thought. "When I get back, I should probably apologize to Stella. I'm sure I came off as rude." Summer continued to walk down the beach toward the inn, half turning to Landis to signal him to walk alongside her.

"Don't worry about Stella. She's New York through and through, so the fact you even said hello probably shocked her." His long strides caught up and matched hers. Landis looked down to watch his calves moving in time with her slender muscled legs and found it difficult not to imagine both sets entwined in another scenario. Snapping out of it, he jerked his gaze up to the expansive beach and surf in front of them.

"So, are you and her... are you two together?" she asked.

"Ah, you're wondering about that kiss last night."

"That and all the photos online of the two of you at fancy events," she added. Her voice sounded casual, but he saw her hands start tapping the toes of the shoes around her neck together as she waited for his answer.

"Stella and I went on two dates in college, which was enough for us to realize we were meant to be good friends and nothing more. Although we did make a very serious pact that if we hadn't found someone to marry by the time we turned forty, we'd marry each other."

Landis brushed a fly away from his leg and noticed Summer's eyes following his movement, lingering on his legs for a few seconds. Something flickered in his chest when her eyes moved up to meet his for several heartbeats.

"She kissed me because she thought you were a local gold digger," he explained.

His laugh, when he saw her eyes widen and then narrow, must have echoed for miles.

"At least she's looking out for you," she muttered grudgingly. "So a marriage pact. That sounds like a good idea, actually. Although I don't have a lot of luck with men, so I might have to settle for being a fantastic auntie."

"I have a hard time believing you couldn't find a man." He shook his head in disbelief. "Phil from the fire department seems pretty interested in you."

Summer laughed.

"Phil's just a friend. That's my curse—I'm every guy's best buddy. Unless you're the wrong guy for me, then it's all systems go," she said derisively.

She came to an abrupt halt, turning to look at him.

"Wow. Until I just said that, I didn't realize I really believed it. I made a vow last night that I would work to forgive myself for bad relationship choices, and here I am breaking that vow. Well, no more."

She turned away from him and took a few steps toward the surf and ocean beyond. "I forgive myself!" she shouted up to the sky, arms out and eyes closed. He watched her inhale the salty air, watched the breeze twist and twirl the wisps of her hair that had escaped her ponytail. Her arms stayed outstretched for moments longer and then slowly dropped to her sides.

She turned back to Landis and her face was radiant, beaming a light that rivaled the sparkles that danced on the waves.

"That felt good. I need to do that every day," she said, her eyes dazzling. It drove right into him, squeezing something in his chest so tight he couldn't breathe.

Her smile faded slightly. "What?" she asked.

"I'm trying so hard not to kiss you right now." The words came out of nowhere, his voice a gritty whisper. Every nerve in his body tingled, every muscle taut. He could almost feel her eyes as they moved over him, from his face down his chest to his legs, and then back up again.

The air between them felt thick, like a lazy electrical current was caught in a loop. She seemed closer, although he would swear neither of them had moved. "I'm sorry. I shouldn't—"

"Why are you trying not to?" her voice rasped over his, a few octaves lower than he'd ever heard it.

"Because you've got a life here. Friends and a family you don't want to give up. And I'm going home tonight." He stepped closer, and the sea breeze surrounded them, bringing a mix of saltiness and the unique smell that was her directly into his bloodstream. His hand cupped her forearm then slid down, lightly grasping her wrist and feeling the fine bones there.

"But... that's tonight. We have hours until tonight." He heard the invitation in her words and watched as she leaned in, her eyes almost black, her blonde brows curved elegantly over them.

"Hours," he agreed, and when he felt her lips on his, he gathered her close so he could feel her softness against him.

※

HE LOVED THE AT FIRST COOL THEN WARMTH OF HER MOUTH'S TOUCH, but then he had to taste her cheek and her jaw and then the length of her neck. He inhaled the scent of her hair deeply, and again had the sensation of something squeezing deep inside him. Something alien that scared him and created a bubble of emotion he wasn't sure what to do with.

And then he felt her arms go from lightly embracing him to pulling him against her as strongly as he held her. He felt her slim body move restlessly against his, and his reacted on its own.

He groaned as her hands moved over the muscles of his back and shoulders. He wanted to strip off his shirt, but there was no way his arms were ready to let her go yet. When she followed the curve of his spine down to his lower back and pressed him even closer, he groaned again and moved his mouth back to hers.

This time, his lips were urgent, seeking. His hands came up to cup her neck and jaw. Her lips moved and her tongue darted and swirled, both of them glorying in the intensity that cascaded between them. He pulled her closer, fitting her body into the curves and planes of his.

Their lips parted, and he felt her hands on his shoulders, levering herself away a little to look directly into his eyes. It took a few seconds for his vision to sharpen and his breathing to even out. His hands were in her hair, gently cupping her head, and he couldn't resist dragging a thumb over her lips. When she responded by pressing them around it in a soft kiss, he groaned.

"I think I need to pause before we go further," she whispered roughly, closing her eyes and slowing her breath.

"Okay. But don't make me move away yet," he answered, pressing their dampened foreheads together and trying to calm his own breathing as well.

After what he felt was too short a time, Summer slid her hands down his chest and applied just enough pressure to break them apart. "I also vowed last night that I would focus on having a good working relationship in the future. I don't know if... this—" she waved her hand in the narrow space between their bodies "—is the right direction for that."

Landis's mouth tightened as he acknowledged the sense in her words. His hands moved from her face, down along her arms, until he was holding the hands she'd spread on his chest. He brought them to his lips and lingeringly kissed each one. He'd meant to step back and let them go, but he found them on his chest, covered by his. "You're probably right."

"But then another part of me says 'It's only one day. What harm could come of two adults agreeing to... a hook-up?' And then going back to the real world." She looked up at Landis, her face completely blank but her eyes glowing.

He'd been trying to figure out how to reason with his body to let her hands go, since his hands seemed to have gone renegade, when her words stopped him flat.

"Wait. You're suggesting we have a one-day affair, and then return to our working relationship?"

"Well, 'affair' seems to imply more than a day, but yes." She moved her fingers restlessly against his chest, but he flattened them to keep them still.

"No distractions, I need to focus," he admonished. "A passionate one-day affair, and then we go back to our lives like nothing happened?"

"Definitely passionate, good clarification." She nodded approvingly.

"And then it's over. We go back to our media tycoon and hipster reporter roles."

"And you don't want anything more?"

"No."

"No future dates, no flirty texting, no long-distance relationship?" It sounded perfect, and yet... some of his excitement was dulled.

"None of that. I only want today. Right now. These hours," she insisted, and her words carried an urgent note, as if this was something integral to her being. And despite the strength he heard in her voice, her eyes looked naked. "Can you do that?" she asked.

11

His pause made her nervous. For the first time in a long time, Summer was asking for something for herself, something that was a deep need, and it made her palms sweaty and gave her voice a steely tone.

He can say no and I'll be okay. I'll be okay.

She straightened her posture and saw a flame rekindle in his eyes. "I can do that. I can give you these hours. I can give you me." He squeezed her hands and tugged her body against his. "If you promise to give me you."

"I can do that. We share all of each other until it's time to go back to our separate worlds."

"Agreed." The word came out of him in a growl, filling her with nervous energy, and she expected his lips to slam down onto hers, but they didn't. Instead, there was a touching, a lingering and a sliding of his mouth over hers in a series of caresses and nibbles. She leaned into him, matching his kiss for long seconds. Then he pulled away and tapped a finger against her mouth.

"Ah, ah, ah," he whispered the reprimand, "I'm not rushing this."

His playfulness pulled a smile out of her, and she focused on logistics. "Are you game for an adventure?" she asked, stepping away but taking his hand. She started in the opposite direction toward the tall, rocky bluff, tugging him to follow.

"More adventurous than a hook-up? Is that possible?" he teased.

"Sooo much more adventurous." She nodded, lacing her fingers through his as he quick-stepped up to walk alongside her. She headed up the beach to where the sand turned into a rocky, slick, and seaweed-strewn intertidal area. This unfriendly stretch of beach butted up to a sheer rock bluff that towered hundreds of feet high and reached farther out into the surf.

They walked in a companionable silence. Every once in a while, one of them tugged at the other's arm to pull one body against the other, sometimes stealing a slow kiss. Always, she would break away to pull him along the slippery stones, continuing to make a straight line toward the water that was licking at the bottom of the rock.

The smell of the decaying seaweed was pungent, and Landis swatted his calves from time to time as the sand fleas swarmed in miniature clouds. As they got closer to the vertical rock face, she felt his eyes dart to her questioningly and then back to the wall in front of them. Finally, he couldn't take it.

"Will a door magically open, or is this a swimming adventure?" he asked.

"We will be getting wet, probably up to our thighs, but we won't need to swim," she explained, pointing to his shoes. "Do you want to take them off?" She let go of his hand to grab the shoes around her neck and thump them together. "You'll probably want dry shoes for the climb."

"Wading and climbing. Sounds... passionate." He undid his laces and pulled off his shoes, tying them and slinging them around his neck like she had done. She walked very close to the rock wall and then headed into the water. "It looks like it gets pretty deep out there." He sounded unsure.

"It looks like it, but it doesn't. There's a natural rock ledge that extends about six feet around the cliff. Farther out are some rock formations that keep the waves from breaking hard. It's easiest at low tide, but not bad as long as it's not at full high tide. Only a few locals know about the cabin, and nobody comes very far this way, because no one wants to hang out on slimy rocks."

Summer started wading out at a good pace, using one hand as a guide along the wall.

"Some of the rock has a sharp edge, so feel with your foot before putting any real weight down," she called back, just as she heard Landis shout and make a splash. She turned around to see him a ways back, gingerly scoping the water before stepping. She carried on, enjoying seeing him out of his element just a little bit.

"I'm clinging to your mention of a cabin," he called to her, just as she heard him splash and shout out again. She looked back again, this time with a giggle.

"But will you be able to make it to the cabin—that's the question!" she joked.

"Keep going," he responded, waving his free but dripping hand at her in a carry-on motion. She laughed joyfully and plunged ahead.

They slowly rounded the edge of the bluff and followed along a straight edge for ten minutes, their path taking them out of the early morning sunlight and into the cool shade of the rock. Finally, their path curved in and she saw the tall pocket of the crevasse where the stone had split centuries ago. A few minutes later, instead of continuing past the three-foot wide black crevasse, she plunged into the darkness of the rock and continued groping her way along the wall.

"Seriously?" she heard Landis's echoing question as he followed behind her.

"Getting cold feet?" she asked, continuing on.

"I'm getting cold everything, but not the cold feet you're referring to."

Slowly, the view ahead of her lightened, until the crack in the rock they'd been following opened into a wide funnel over their heads. She shouted "Hellooooo!" and listened to the deep, grand echo of her voice spiraling up and out of the natural horn of the opening.

"Wow," Landis said reverently, "unbelievable!" His deep voice echoed lowly, swirling around her before going up and up, the deep timbre of his voice raising bumps all over her body.

"Isn't it? Hang on, it gets even better." She followed the wall as it curved gently inward and upward, and the water trailed to just below their knees. The layers of the stone wall had worn away and she followed it until she got to the place where someone long ago had created natural-looking hand and footholds.

"Up we go!" she said, reaching up and tucking her hands into the worn grooves and her feet into similar ones at knee height. She pulled and stepped in an alternating rhythm, stopping about eight feet up to look down.

"Don't stop or I'll climb right over you," he called, his voice full of enthusiasm and energy. Even though she could feel her thigh starting to ache, she laughed and quickened her pace.

It was only a few minutes of climbing until the wall angled from a vertical ascent to an orientation where it was more crawling than climbing. To her left and right, the wall of the rock curved up into a slight protective cocoon around her. Then the climb ended on a mossy, flat plateau.

She turned to look at him as he pulled himself up, and they both looked out at the ocean. The plateau they stood on was higher than the rock edge of the cliff below, allowing them a spectacular lookout at the wild rolling ocean in the distance. Summer lifted her face to the salty breeze, loving the feel of the moist air moving over her cheeks and hair and the wind pushing through her clothes.

"You love this, don't you?" he asked, looking at her, his expression shuttered.

She shrugged and turned toward a big rock near the back of the plateau against the rock wall.

"It's all right," she said with feigned indifference, and Landis huffed out a disbelieving laugh.

The truth was she loved this spot. If the barn loft was her and her brother's shelter from the vagaries the world had inflicted on them, then this place was the salve to her battered spirit. She didn't truly know if she'd ever be able to leave this behind.

She looked at the rock wall and saw the worn but still strong rigging lines that snaked up to the next ledge. Summer walked to the base of the sheer wall where the rope disappeared behind a large rock. Both ends looked as if they fed into the ground, but she knew where to pull, and up popped a flattish piece of driftwood. Underneath, folded neatly into a natural hole, was a rope ladder.

"It's a little wet. Unfortunately, this hole doesn't drain. But the ladder is strong, so don't worry."

"Who did all this?"

"Locals. Or I should probably say parents of parents of locals." Summer pulled on one of the ropes, which ran up to a pulley at the top of the rock face and then ran back down to connect to the rope ladder. As she pulled, the ladder rose, unfurling from the hole in the ground. In no time at all, the ladder was fully extended. Summer slipped her end of the rope through a hidden anchor pin that had been nailed deep into the rock in the hole and tightened the ladder.

"Here, let me help," Landis offered, his hand out.

"Don't worry. I've got this," she said, expertly tying a knot at the end. "Mitch taught me how to tie a decent anchor hitch, which is something a good boater should know." She smiled up at him as he dropped his hand. "Not that I'm any kind of a boater. Are you?"

"I've done a bit of boating. Not a lot, though." He tugged on the ladder, which was snug and firm. She walked over and patted his upper arm.

"Don't worry. I promise to find lots of heavy things up top for you to lift and carry for me, so you don't feel left out." She grinned at him and jumped on the ladder to start her ascent. She yelped when he jumped onto the ladder and reached up to give her butt a smack.

"Maybe I'll start by lifting one smart-mouthed woman I know," he teased, and she laughed down at him.

Up and up they both climbed, Summer conscious of not causing too much movement on the ladder despite how firmly it was tethered. Soon, she was near the top of the last plateau. This one was more expansive than the last. She knew the land ahead of her stretched out halfway to the road before another impassible crevasse separated it from the mainland, effectively stopping any wandering hikers from getting to the cabin.

Grasping the natural stone plinths on either side of the rope ladder at the top, she pulled herself up onto the soft mossy ground. Madrone trees surrounded them, their bark a reddish umber and the outer skin peeling in gray strips. She turned to watch Landis hop up from the last rung and then freeze in wonder at the magical surroundings.

"Amazing, right?" she asked, looking over his shoulder to stare at the ocean's horizon, smudged in tangerines and misty grays as the sun climbed higher on the opposite side of the world, out of sight from where they stood.

"Is this national park land?" he asked, turning completely around until he stood arm-to-arm beside her. His hand brushed hers and then interlaced with her long fingers.

"The story is it was owned by four local families almost a hundred years ago. That's when the cabin was built. The family basically died off, and the last heir couldn't afford the costs, so it was deeded to the county in a trust. It's sort of been in a limbo ever since. The county parks department maintain the fencing back toward the road, but that's about it."

"How did you find it?"

She turned, tugging Landis toward the grove of trees behind them.

"Mitch took me here shortly after I moved into the loft." She hesitated, thinking back to that time. Nobody knew about it—not Katy nor Carson.

In that moment, feeling Landis's big hand in hers and a supportive strength in his presence, something inside her unclogged and poured out.

"I was messed up emotionally for a while after I moved here." Her voice shook, and she took a second to steady it. "Carson had just been diagnosed, and I was determined to come here and help Mitch and Katy with the final renovations to the barn. They'd always intended to renovate it as a private rental, but they sped up their plans for me. I was running around like mad, shopping, looking for work, painting. One day, I just lost it." Summer felt Landis's hand squeeze hers, and she squeezed back.

The surrounding Madrone trees closed in on them as they walked, along with fir and cedar trees, making the near-invisible path a winding obstacle course. Summer forged their way through the tall grasses, skirting nettles and fallen branches, and even though they had to change to single file walking, she wouldn't let go of his hand. Couldn't let go of it.

"I think Mitch saw the frantic look in my eyes and he took me here. He'd heard about it from one of his workers when he first moved here. When things between him and Katy got sticky—" Summer glanced back at Landis with a crooked smile "—his word, not mine," she explained, "the man told him the basics of how to find it, and he trekked up and found it."

"A hideaway," he mused, and just as the words left his lips, the path opened up into a small clearing, and in front of them stood a moss-covered log cabin.

The sides were dark brown with age, and the logs crisscrossed at the corners. Thick moss and stubby yellow grass covered its low-pitched roof, which was constructed from squared-off timbers. A front peak stretched a few feet out over the front door, creating a small area protected from rain.

"A hideaway," Summer agreed. She led the way through the doorless entrance. Inside, the cabin was a single room with a square-cut window centrally spaced in each wall, letting enough light in to see the bare surroundings. A rustic table and two chairs stood in one corner. On top of the table was a black plastic bag anchored with a rock, which Summer opened to pull out two blankets.

"Ta-da!" she sang, although her thoughts tempered her tone. Landis walked over, tested the table's strength, and then half-sat on the edge of it. He pulled her around to stand between his legs.

"Tell me more about Mitch bringing you here," he invited softly, linking their hands together.

"Mitch was... a savior," Summer started on a shaky sigh. "He saw me unraveling, and it reminded him of his own confusion back when he and Katy were working things out. I think I talked and cried his ear off, honestly. And he let me. It was exactly what I needed. I guess you could say I have a tendency to bottle things up, and I don't always know it until I'm about to teeter off the rails." Summer huffed a short laugh, as she realized her words spoke a truth she didn't realize before.

"Well." Landis unlaced and relaced their fingers, his face caring and his gaze steady with hers. "I'm humbled that you brought me here. Thank you."

Summer tipped her head slightly, not looking away from the intensity in his eyes. "You're welcome," she said. It was a moment she wanted to catalog in her mind, so she gave it space. But something in his eyes drew her in and her feet shuffled her closer to him of their own accord, bringing their bodies a whisper apart. "I have to confess, though... to having ulterior motives. This is the closest place where I thought we could be alone."

"I appreciate that, too. I can't remember the last time I was really alone. Even when I run, I can't seem to turn off my brain."

"That's what comes with being a big-time CEO, I guess."

"Don't you mean 'playboy media tycoon'?" he laughed softly, and she laughed along.

"In my defense, most of my online investigating showed you at glitzy galas with Stella hanging all over you. It screamed 'playboy millionaire.'" She raised her hand and stroked a finger over the chiseled line of his cheekbone and down to the smile line that framed his mouth.

"In *my* defense, the only thing I do outside of run the business is go to charity events. I'm on so many boards I've lost count." His voice trailed off, one hand reaching up to glide over her raised arm, his other lightly resting on her hip. "So, truly... thank you for sharing this. It's got me thinking I need to put some things into perspective as well."

She pressed even closer to him, their legs touching. The hand that cupped her arm slipped up to caress her neck.

Holding her lower back against him with one hand, he walked her backward on her toes, only letting her fully onto her feet when he turned to shake out and drop the blankets behind them. She kept her eyes fastened on his, wondering at the narrow fringe of gray iris that framed his pupils.

She brushed a stray strand of hair off his forehead when she was swept up and down in a quick movement, feeling the blankets rough on her back. He leaned on an arm, one of his hands cradling her head as the other skimmed over her body.

"I've fantasized about this spot... right here." He slid his fingers from her neck to the hollow of her throat, tracing small circles where her silver chain lay. He leaned down and kissed the same spot. Her eyes closed and they lost themselves in each other.

※

Her head on his shoulder and his fingers playing with her hand as it lay on his chest.

"That was... amazing." Landis's chest rumbled with his quietly spoken words. "It's been a while for me."

"Seriously?" she asked, watching her fingers play with his. "I find that hard to believe."

"That it was amazing?" his voice teased.

She swatted his chest and then continued playing with his fingers. "You know what I mean."

"Why is it hard to believe that it's been a while?" he asked.

"Well... you don't seem like the kind of guy who would be hard up for female companionship."

He was quiet for a few seconds, and she leaned back to look at him. His brows were pulled together in thought. "Sex has always been easy for me to find; you're right about that. I'm trying to remember when sex for its own sake got boring."

Summer put her head back on his shoulder, her thoughts scanning back to her own sexual history. She'd never been into sex for sex's sake. It had always been pretty far down on her list of priorities. For so long, her career had been number one, and then for the last few years, family had been number one. She hadn't realized she'd been missing the physical side until…. Now she felt her own brow crinkle. Not since Landis had shown up.

"What about you? I bet you could have no shortage of men's attention if you wanted it." Landis lifted his shoulder to nudge her.

"It's been a while for me, too. Since Nick, I guess. Which really soured me on relationships." She shifted a little, lifting and then resettling herself against him more comfortably. "Which I guess I still am, but you've reminded me how much fun sex should be, so thank you for that." She smiled.

She felt his face move against her forehead in what she guessed was a smile. "You're welcome," he said.

She pushed against his chest to lift herself onto her elbow, giving her a good view of his upper body. "Tell me about this." She skated her finger over the tattoo she had glimpsed earlier. It seemed to curve over his right shoulder to his back. What she could see was a head and arm with intricate black and green scales. "I never would have figured you for an inked guy."

"I got it after I graduated college. I went to Cambodia for a few months and met a talented tattoo artist." Summer tugged at his shoulder to get him to sit up so she could peer at the rest of the tattoo on his back. It was a gorgeous serpent-style dragon. The scales were shadowed expertly, seeming to shine, and the underbelly of the dragon where the body twisted was a gradient of orange to red. The eyes were purple with golden flecks, matching the spines and horns. She traced the lines on his back where the dragon's body curled into the upper and middle of Landis's back, each claw clutching a glass orb.

"It's really beautiful. The color is so vibrant." She traced a finger around one of the glass orbs. The tattooist had an amazing skill of making everything look so lifelike.

"Evelyn was shocked when she saw it." Landis laughed, making his skin vibrate under her finger.

"Who's Evelyn?" she asked.

"My mother."

She leaned around his shoulder to look him in the eye. "You call your mother Evelyn?"

"Well, it is her name." He laughed at her eye roll.

"You know what I mean." She moved her hand from his back to his shoulder, leaning in to plant a light kiss on it.

"I've always had a formal relationship with my parents. I guess because they always referred to each other by their names, so I did too."

"They didn't use endearments for each other? Like 'sweetheart' or 'honey' or anything?"

"No."

"And they never said 'Take this to your mom' or 'Ask your dad what he wants for dinner'?"

Landis hesitated and grimaced, as he answered, "Actually, we had a cook, and Evelyn just gave him a list every week for the meals. They lived such separate lives, really. Drew, my father, was always traveling. And my mother was in her home office a lot, but when I spent time with her, she never referred to my father." He looked at her expectantly.

"What?" she asked.

"I'm waiting for you to call me privileged about having a cook and a tutor and distant parents." He smiled, but his eyes looked cautious.

"Well, a few days ago, I might have said something like that, but now I just think it's sad."

"What about your parents?" He reached for the hand that was caressing his shoulder and brought it to his mouth to drift light kisses across her knuckles.

"My mom was 'sweetie' and my dad was 'baby' or 'handsome.' It blew my mind when I found out they had real names just like regular people," she laughed. "I was twelve when they died in a car accident. Seeing their full names when we had the funeral was surreal. As if it were two people I didn't know being buried."

Landis crossed his legs and lifted her into the nest they made, nuzzling her hair. "That must have been very hard," he murmured.

"It was, for the longest time. But our aunt and uncle were wonderful—are wonderful. They made sure we had comfortable lives and made sure we knew everything about our parents that we hadn't learned yet. I'm so grateful for them." She snuggled into the arms he'd wrapped around her. "What about you?" she asked, turning her face into his chest and breathing in his distinct smell.

"My father died of a heart attack when I was seventeen. He was a workaholic, rarely home, and when he was home, he wasn't very talkative. I was big into sports in high school, and I was convinced my parents would buy my way into a sports scholarship. Everything changed when he died. Evelyn made it clear that the family company was my future."

"Did you want it, though? That future?" she asked, leaning back to watch his face. His eyes stared off toward the doorless entrance, and he didn't answer for several seconds.

"I think I thought... I could do both. Have my glory years of football, and then work in the company. I never thought I'd be running it so young, though. I finished my business degree and felt the pressure of what Evelyn had laid out for me—an intensive year of being mentored and apprenticing at a family friend's corporation. I was only supposed to go to Cambodia for two weeks, but I stayed six months. It was my rebellion. But when I got back home, I realized I was ready to step into it. I ended up getting my MBA part-time over the next six years, and here I am—the media mogul you see before you." He laughed and tightened his arms around her, leaning back and pulling her with him.

"I could stay here forever," he said into her hair as he rubbed his lips against it, "as long as the cabin doesn't fall down on us." He ran his hands up her back and down her sides in slow circles, shifting his legs to nestle hers and keep them warm.

"But you can't, because you have a flight tonight," she said, her mouth pulling down momentarily at the corners, "and I have a new job to get ready for."

Landis's breathing stayed steady under her, giving no indication how he felt about her small mention of reality. "That's right. And I have a possible strike to worry about. It's been nice to be out of cell phone range here."

"You brought your phone?"

"I'm never without my phone," he muttered. "It's in the pocket of my shorts."

"Well, you should check it. The bottom of the cliff is out of cell range, but this cabin isn't."

She felt him tense under her, and then rolled with her to the side so he could grab his shorts. After some tussling, he pulled his phone out of a buttoned pocket.

"It was off," he groaned, powering it back up. Seconds later, it sounded the persistent dings of text messages arriving. His brow furrowed as his finger moved over the glass, tapping and sliding. "I've got to go."

She rolled off him and watched as he gathered his clothes and pulled them on. When his eyes met hers, he gave her a brief smile. "I'm sorry. I'd stay all day if I could, but there are some urgent calls I have to make." He gathered her two scraps of clothing and brought them over, kneeling down in front of her.

She smiled sadly, knowing this moment would come. He held her sports bra and she slid her arms through the straps. He kneeled back as she tucked her feet into her shorts and pulled them over her knees, pausing to swing her legs around so she could kneel and pull them the rest of the way up.

"I think I'm going to stay up here for a while longer," she said, putting her hand into the outstretched one he held out to help her up. Her words seemed to startle him.

"Why?"

"I love it up here. And I guess I'm not quite ready to go back to reality." She shrugged, and he nodded somberly before tugging on her hand and leading her out of the cabin.

"I don't blame you," he murmured, retracing their steps through the treed path to where the rope ladder waited. "You'll be okay getting back down on your own?" He turned toward her, linking their hands.

"Absolutely. I've done it a few times."

"And you won't stay too long? You'll give yourself plenty of time to get home before dark?" he persisted.

"I promise." She bounced their hands to emphasize each of her words, and he pulled her closer, chest-to-chest and hands beside their legs so they were hip-to-hip.

"So... no texts, no calls... just today. That's what you said, right?" He looked deep into her eyes, and she stared back, trying to determine if he was promising or asking. She couldn't tell.

"Yup, just today. This moment." At her last word, their smiles faded and they leaned in for a lingering kiss, mouths pressed together solemnly, reverently.

"Promise just one text, so I know you got home okay." His lips moved against her lips as they formed the words. Then he let her go to pull out his phone. After several taps, he handed it to her. "I probably have your phone number somewhere in my paperwork, but I'd rather have it here."

She entered her phone number and handed it back to him. "One text, I promise."

Landis took her hands and gave them a lingering kiss, his eyes looking steadily into hers. And then he was gone.

12

Landis watched the bank of clouds below the plane and shifted in the roomy first-class seat. He checked his phone for the hundredth time. Yes, it was already Tuesday, 10:27 a.m. New York was about an hour away, and he should be using the time to sleep. He was someone who could and did sleep anywhere, but not today. Not for the last two days.

It had been a marathon forty-eight hours. Things had been ugly at the plant when he arrived late Sunday. His "lock 'em out" order had been executed, and the employees had shown up in big numbers to picket the front gate. When his car arrived, the picketers broke their rotating line and swarmed around his car.

"What do you want me to do?" his driver had asked, nervous as the picketers marched around his vehicle, and chanted, "No lock out! Back to the table!"

"Sorry about this. Dammit." He'd gotten out of the car, and the picketers had backed up, quieting as he held his hands up. Behind the gate, he could see the security guards come forward to unlock the gate. "You're right!" he called to everyone. "Let's get back to the table."

The crowd cheered, and while some dispersed through the gate, two men had come up to him. "Thank you," said one in a worn baseball cap. "We just want a fair deal," said the other, holding out his hand. Landis shook it.

"We can figure this out," he said to the men.

And they did. It had taken four meal breaks, countless reviews of documents and financials, two concessions from the union, and four concessions from Blake Media, but after thirty-six hours, they'd brokered a three-year deal that worked for everyone.

Landis looked at his phone again. 10:31 a.m. He ordered a Mimosa, but the glass was on his tray, untouched. He picked up his phone and opened his text messages. He smiled again as he read how Summer had entered her name: "Summer—Elitist Journalist." He opened their conversation to read their exchange from two days ago.

Did you get home ok? he texted once he landed in Atlanta.

Yes, she replied.

Thank you, he typed, after agonizing over his word choice for a good seven minutes. There'd been no reply to that.

And now, around fifty-two minutes away from New York, he wondered what she was doing. How long did she stay at the cabin? What had she thought about? Was she sorting out her new role as editor, or was she waiting for all the paperwork to be finalized?

He shifted again in his seat and put his fingers on the foot of his Mimosa glass, swirling the liquid and watching it give up its last remaining bubbles. Evelyn had liked the idea of a lock out but had seemed disappointed that he settled things personally. He wondered what Summer would think of the outcome. He toyed with texting her about it but recalled their ground rules. No texts, no calls. Which meant no chats, no conversations, no sharing, no nothing.

He straightened his shoulders and glanced out at the clouds below. They were on a different footing now, a business relationship. There was no reason they couldn't be friends, but he'd have to let some time go by so the adjustment would be natural. When they next met, maybe at a staff Christmas party, they could shake hands and their time at the cabin would be a distant memory. He wouldn't be the guy mooning over a text message.

He slid his Mimosa glass to the corner of his tray as the attendant walked by. "I'm sorry, I guess I didn't want this after all." He handed the glass to the smiling attendant and picked up his phone again—10:37 a.m.

<hr />

THE RIDE TO HIS MANHATTAN OFFICE WAS LONG, SO HE ROLLED down his window to hear the traffic noise. He always loved the hustle of this city. It seemed like everything was happening at every moment, as if everywhere you looked there was excitement and potential. And the blue-glass buildings that soared overhead seemed like mountains that were meant to be climbed. Today, in the gray of late morning, they looked steely and appeared to choke out the sky.

"I am a free soul in a free world!" he heard a male voice shout above the honks and rumble of the city. He strained to see a large man in a ragged yellow T-shirt and green knit cap, facing away from him with his arms outstretched. "I am *free!* My *world* is *free!*" he shouted.

Landis's mind flashed to Summer, facing the ocean with her arms thrown open, shouting to the surf. And the glow of her face when she'd turned around. Pure joy had beamed from her.

It had reached down into him like nothing he'd ever experienced before. It had unlocked something in him that he still couldn't explain. It let him open up to her when they made love, in a way he didn't know was possible. It was something he turned over in his mind since he'd gotten in his rental car to head to Atlanta, and he could still feel the vibration of it echo through him, mysterious and unresolved.

Have you landed? chimed Evelyn's text.

Yes. Be there in 5 mins, he typed.

Blake Media Inc. took up the top three floors of the Century Tower on 10th Avenue and West 30th. It was an elegant but emotionless glass building. Landis's office was on the middle of the floors, facing west toward the High Line, a defunct elevated rail line that was converted into a walking park. He often ran along it when he could free up more than twenty minutes.

"Hey, boss," greeted Melanie as he approached her wide desk. She wore her usual uniform of white T-shirt under black blazer and black dress pants, underneath which her black Converse sneakers stood out. She described it as "casual sass."

"Good morning. Are things *fully* insane or just *mostly* insane today?" he asked.

"I'd have to say not that insane at all. Your messages are on your computer, and only one seems urgent. Oh, and Evelyn is in your office." She raised an eyebrow at him. "I think she's on her third espresso, so you've been warned."

"Thanks for the heads-up." He nodded and headed around the white wall behind her desk to his own office door.

"You're out of espresso," Evelyn informed him from her ladylike perch on the end of his couch. She wore her familiar steel-blue Gucci pantsuit with the high collar, her short hair slicked back, and it reminded him of the relentless facades of the office buildings he'd just driven through.

"Maybe you should pace yourself with those," he suggested with a quirk of his mouth.

"Why do you use that instant machine? Why don't you have a proper espresso maker?"

"I like my Keurig." He shrugged out of his jacket and set his briefcase down. "What do you need? I updated you on everything this morning."

"Not on everything. There's something going on with you, and I want to know what it is." She untucked her long legs from the couch and walked over to the credenza to put her small cup and saucer on it.

"There's nothing going on, other than I need to find a west coast V.P. I think we should look at other properties over there." He hit his spacebar to activate his computer screen and looked up at Evelyn, who was watching him with folded arms and a dissatisfied expression. "I thought that would make your day. You've been bugging me about expansion for the past year."

Evelyn tapped her fingers on her arm and took several slow steps closer to Landis's desk. "Nice try. What's going on?"

"Why do you think there's something going on?"

"You could have sent our lawyer to negotiate a settlement and signed everything digitally. Why did you go personally?"

"On the phone, you said—"

"—to get back to deal with the strike issue. Not to fly to Georgia to deal with it. You did that on your own."

He swiveled away from his monitor to face her. Her eyes examined every inch of his face. There was nothing he didn't share with her. Practically every decision or event in his life, he ran by her. But this... whatever his meeting Summer was... it felt dangerous to share something so personal.

"Oh my God," she said, dropping her arms and walking briskly to his desk. She leaned her hands on it, staring him in the eye. "Is something wrong? Why did you really go to Seattle?"

Her voice cracked and he saw fear on her face. He reached out to put his hand on hers. "Nothing's wrong, Evelyn. I... met someone in Seattle. In Cranberry Hill, actually, and it's got me confused. That's all."

Evelyn gripped his hand and leaned closer with surprise. "You met someone. In that tiny town where we bought the newspaper?" He nodded, and she stood up, moving to roll a chair behind the desk to face him. She delicately sat in it, crossing her ankles and brushing invisible specks from her silk-panted leg. "This must be someone important or disgraceful, because your face looked terminal."

He laughed and leaned back to rub his chin, grimacing at the stubble he felt there. "It's someone I think I like, but I don't think she feels the same way. Actually, I'm pretty sure she doesn't."

"Well, give yourself time and your confusion will disappear."

"Time. That's your best advice?"

Evelyn looked at him critically and then patted his knee. "Time and a shave. You look like a pirate."

Landis sighed and leaned back in his chair, the last few days flashing through his mind—Summer's last words to him, and him kissing her hands on the cliff. "Have you ever done something your head said was right, but every fiber of your being knew was wrong?"

"I've rarely thought that hard about decisions. I've just charged ahead. Either they're right and they work out, or they're wrong and you move on to either fix it, or implement Plan B." Evelyn folded her hands on her knees, examining her son. "This thing that you've done. Does it have to do with this person you met?"

"It's not exactly something I've done, more like something I agreed to not do."

"But the thing you've agreed not to do... it has to do with this woman?"

"Summer is her name. And yes, it has to do with something she and I promised not to do."

"Well, that's easy. Trust your gut, Landis. If you think the right thing is different now, then do it. There are no wrong moves, just complex recoveries."

Landis smiled at her words. "You make it sound easy."

Evelyn gave an elegant shrug. "Everything is easy. It's emotion that makes things confusing. And you definitely look emotional, my dear." She unlaced and re-laced her manicured fingers. "Tell me about this woman. This... Summer." She made a small face. "I've never known you to date anyone more than twice, let alone allow some woman to make you emotional."

Landis looked through his floor-to-ceiling office windows, out beyond the western city skyline. "Summer Richardson. She's nothing like Stella or you. She's a sassy blonde hipster reporter, more than likely a socialist, and you'd probably drive each other nuts. But you're right—she's become important. She's fiercely loyal and loves her family, and is honest with everybody, especially herself."

Evelyn rolled her eyes and flicked her own silvery-brunette hair. "A blonde hipster reporter sounds like my worst nightmare. But I can respect someone who's honest with themselves. What did you agree not to do?"

"We agreed not to contact each other, and I want to respect that, because I'm her employer. She has a full life out there, and my life is here. And I have a weird feeling she's categorized me and somehow I come up short for her."

Evelyn hissed a disparaging *pfft* of air through her lips. "That's ridiculous. Now I question this woman's judgment if she can't see the kind of man you are." She stood up and rolled her chair to the other side of his desk where she'd found it. "But remember my number one rule."

He swiveled from his view of the window to the slim woman standing in front of him. "Never make assumptions?"

"Never, ever make assumptions." She nodded. "Until this woman tells you in her own words that you are not what she wants, do whatever you need to get that tragic look off your face." She clapped her hands together and headed for the door. "Now, I have the west coast to conquer."

Landis turned back to look at the horizon and think over Evelyn's words, when Melanie entered.

"I just had another call from Gage Harcourt. He sounds pretty anxious to talk to you, but I didn't want to interrupt your time with Evelyn."

Landis frowned and tapped his keyboard, seeing Melanie's phone call message window pop up. "Did he say what he wanted?"

"Despite my FBI-level interrogation skills, I couldn't crack him. You'll just have to call him and find out the old-fashioned way." She smirked, drawing a smile from Landis.

He reached for his phone and stole a quick look at the time. It was still morning on the west coast. His heart took an extra beat as he dialed Gage's number.

13

Summer leaned on her desk, folding yesterday's Quote-a-Day calendar page into a tiny paper airplane. It hadn't been a particularly inspiring quote, in her opinion. Something about planting a tree and waiting years for the shade. However, Sunday's quote... well, that had been worth saving.

"If fear is the great enemy of intimacy, love is its true friend." —Henri Nouwen

She'd memorized it. And put it in her pocket. She'd been thinking about her time with Landis at the cabin a lot over the past couple days. Katy had seen it in her face when she returned from the cabin Sunday afternoon.

"You...." Katy said, pointing a finger and drawing a circle around Summer's face. Summer plopped down on a stool in the kitchen and plucked up one of her brother's bran muffins.

"You missed Landis this morning," Mitch said as he moved around the kitchen, putting away clean dishes.

"Oh, I don't know if she missed him. Maybe you ran into him jogging on the beach?" Katy reached over to steal a piece of her bran muffin.

Summer just beamed at her.

"You missed Stella, too. She left after Landis," Mitch added, looking from one woman to the other as he dropped some clean forks into the utensil basket. "What?"

"I had a wonderful morning, Mitch. I did exactly what I wanted, and now... I'm going to carry on with my life." Summer tossed a piece of muffin in her mouth and grinned widely.

"That's... great?" Mitch gave a questioning look to Katy, who squeezed his arm and gave her head a tiny shake.

"That's awesome! Exactly how I hoped your Sunday would go." She reached for Summer's forearm and gave it a firm shake.

And Summer had picked up the muffin and gone back to the loft. Carson wasn't there, but there had been a text from Landis waiting on her phone.

Did you get home okay? he asked.

Okay? she wondered. She was more than okay. She was phenomenal! She'd done something purely for herself, and it was incredible on so many levels. First, the sex itself had been glorious. She had never felt so fulfilled. But the best part was it had been on her terms, and that made her feel invincible. Something inside her felt unstuck, and that in turn made her feel lighter than air.

Yes, she responded to his text.

A few hours later, he replied, **Thank you.** She'd smiled at the text and put her phone face down. That was that. They had a remarkable interlude and now were moving on.

Monday was work as usual, except for the fact that Gage had spent the day at home getting June settled in after her release from the hospital. It meant they had to postpone their chat about her editor role.

On Tuesday, she fine-tuned the last of the articles for the next edition and had finished her work just after lunch. That's when she noticed she hadn't caught up on her calendar pages and had found the Nouwen quote.

Intimacy. That word reached inside her and tweaked something. She looked it up: closeness, togetherness, affinity, attachment. The words stirred her when she looked at Landis's text and thought about their time together. And they jarred when she thought of meeting up with him at a future event as an employee on a professional footing.

There could be no closeness, togetherness, or attachment. She had set those rules, had explicitly agreed to no texting, no dating. They had a professional relationship now, and though her common-sense brain stood proudly in those words, her heart took a different view.

"That plane is definitely not going to fly," Hank judged as he looked down at the tiny airplane she'd made. She pressed a button to put her phone—and Landis's text—to sleep and watched Hank pick up her plane and inspect it. "The body is too short." He turned and tossed it toward his desk, and they both watched as it flew directly into a nosedive to the ground.

"It was a display model." She glared at him and walked over to the mini kitchen to refill her water bottle. "What...?" She fished a small plastic Keurig cup out of the garbage. "Hank, we talked about this! Peel these open and dump the grounds into the compost. *Then* you can recycle the cup and throw out the foil."

"I'm sorry, Summer." His face scrunched up in apology. "I can never think straight when I'm past due on my afternoon coffee."

She tore off the foil and emptied the grounds in sharp movements, tossing the empty cup into the blue recycle bin with some force.

"Geez, Summer. I said I was sorry!" She caught his startled expression and pushed the hair off her face with a big sigh.

"I'm sorry, Hank. I've been out of sorts all day." Before she could say anything else, the newspaper's door burst open and Gage hurried in.

"Hey, you two! I've got some great news! Thrilling news!" Gage swung his arms wide, the briefcase in one hand almost knocking over a desk lamp.

"Great," Hank said, shifting a look at Summer and back. "Summer's been compost-shaming me again, and it's freaking me out." He smirked when she stuck her tongue out at him.

"Hank, I have a mission for you." Gage reached into his pocket and pulled out a few dollars. "Run down to the Oasis and bring back whatever looks good. We're celebrating!"

"You got it, boss!" Hank happily left on his errand.

"Summer, come and sit down." Gage waved her excitedly over to his desk, and then pointed to the chair opposite. She sat. He placed his briefcase on his desk and opened it to take out a bundle of papers. She peered around his briefcase and recognized the crumpled sheets of her proposal. On the top sheet, he'd made handwritten notes in red.

"If you tell me you proofread my proposal for typos, I might kill you."

Gage clapped his hands together and held them against his mouth. "I'm not selling the paper!" he almost shouted.

All the breath left Summer's lungs and her mouth moved, trying to make words.

"I'm not selling the paper!" he said again, slamming his hands on his desk and her proposal to punctuate his words. "At least, I'm not selling to Blake Media."

"What?" she managed to get out. She leaned back in her chair and forced her entire body to be still. She wasn't sure what just happened, but she wanted to understand whatever explanation Gage was about to make. "Then... who?" She gave up and just waited for Gage to explain.

"Your proposal was—*is* brilliant. I looked it over after you left, and it got me thinking. Why couldn't I put together a group of buyers myself? That way control stays right here. News gets reported the way we want it to."

Summer was nodding and arranged her mouth in a smile, but it was a mile away from what she was feeling. Which was lost and empty.

"No, no, no," Gage said, catching her expression. He jogged around his desk to lean on it in front of her. "You'll still be the editor. Everything that was in Landis's proposal stays the same. The only difference is I'm going to create a shell company of investors, and that's who will buy the paper. And I have you to thank!"

He gave her arms a squeeze and returned to his chair, moving his briefcase out of the way and sorting through more papers.

"I have to call Gordon and see if he or Rally can put the legal agreement together. Then I'm having a meeting at my place with the investors. You know all of them!" Gage started making notes on random pieces of paper.

"Did, um... did Landis try to talk you out of it?" Summer asked, still feeling numb as the weight of everything sank in.

"Well, I was wondering if that would happen. But it didn't. In fact, he congratulated me and said he thought it was a great idea. Said to let him know if there was anything he could do to help set everything up. Super guy, that Landis."

"Yeah, he's super, all right. When did all this happen?"

"Well, the idea took off when I took your proposal home. But I talked to Landis this morning." He paused to put his pen down and reach out his hand. "Congratulations, Editor-in-Chief!" She took his hand and tried to match his firm handshake.

"Hey, what'd I miss?" Hank asked as he entered the room, carrying two baker's boxes.

"Everything!" Gage laughed, moving to pull another chair to his desk. "Sit down and we'll tell you all about it."

※

LATER THAT AFTERNOON, SUMMER LISTENED TO HER BIKE TIRES HUM on the hot pavement. There was very little wind, and the air as she rode moved over her in a humid thickness. Even the surf was lazy and dull.

She straightened the backpack over her shoulders and tried to put all her thoughts about intimacy and Landis Blake aside. There would be no future meetings. No chance encounters. It was done. She could focus on her new position and make the Cranberry Chronicle the exact kind of paper she always wanted—not that it wasn't pretty close already.

And yet, a part of her was crushed. That same part of her chose to take the long way home so she wouldn't have to see the Madrone grove where the cabin hid on the other side of the impassable crevasse. It didn't want to see the beach where she'd kissed Landis.

I just need a few days of separation from the memories, that's all. A month, tops.

Her bike clattered off the road and into the familiar dry dip of the ditch then through the space in the fence. The dusty trail wound through a small field of dry yellow grass and then the evergreens at the back of the inn's property, ending at the barn. She pushed open the big barn door and stored her bike, and as she closed the door, she heard an unusual sound. She waited, thinking it was a bird. This time, the sound rolled out low and guttural, and she knew in an instant what it was.

"I'm coming!" Summer shouted, running flat out down the flagstones to the inn.

On the porch, she could see Katy sitting on the edge of the wicker couch, her hands on the railing and her head dropped down, as if she was trying to push the railing off.

"How far apart are they?" She reached Katy's side, putting a hand on her lower back in a firm, massaging motion.

"Fast, fast," Katy panted.

"I've got the bag!" said Mitch a little shakily, coming out of the kitchen and closing the door. Summer took the bag and stepped aside so he could assist Katy to the car.

"Okay. Bag's going in the front, and I'll sit in the back with her." Summer stood on the passenger side while Mitch helped Katy into the back of Goose the Subaru on the driver side. Katy was halfway in the car when she stopped, one hand on the roof and the other on the doorframe, and started panting heavily.

"Good job, baby. Let the contraction work. I'm so proud of you." Mitch's voice broke on the last word, and Summer felt tears nip at her eyes.

"Okay," Katy said after about a minute, her panting subsiding. She eased into the car and leaned against the seat. Summer slid in and closed the door. She reached into the bag in the front seat and pulled out the dampened cloth in the ziplock bag.

"Here, this will help," she said, as she pushed the hair off Katy's forehead and dabbed the cool cloth on her sweaty brow and cheeks. She tweaked Katy's yellow sunflower dress with a grin. "Leave it to you to look utterly awesome on your daughter's birthday!"

"You keep saying it will be a girl, but you don't know." She tried to smile, and then her eyes closed in concentration.

"Oh, I *know*. Keep breathing, Mama, and she'll be here soon."

"Soon" turned out to be eighteen hours later. Katy's labor had mysteriously stopped as soon as they got her into her hospital gown. But after some starts and stops, lots of floor walking, and a few showers, things clicked into place and Katy delivered beautiful Grace Elizabeth Howard. Summer held all seven pounds four ounces of baby Grace, and could barely take her eyes off her, wrapped in a blanket and sleeping with one hand tucked beside her cheek.

Beside her chair, curled up in the hospital bed together, lay Mama Katy and Papa Mitch, watching her sing to Grace. Summer looked up from time to time, addicted to the love shining from their eyes as they watched her with the baby. A bleeping sound came from the bed, and Mitch pulled his phone out of his back pocket. He smiled and showed his phone to Katy.

"Landis says congratulations." He kissed her cheek. Katy smiled and looked over at Summer.

Her face felt odd. Her eyebrows started to twitch and her chin began to wobble, and she felt a little panicked about that until the first sob hitched out of her chest.

"Oh dear," Katy said, trying to reach out to her. Summer looked down at beautiful Grace, trying to at least quiet her sobs so she didn't wake the baby.

Mitch eased out of the bed and walked over to Summer. "Okay, Gracie, let's let Mama and Auntie Summer have a chat." She held the bundle out so Mitch could scoop her up and exit the room.

"C'mere, kiddo." Katy scooted backward into the space Mitch had vacated and patted the mattress in front of her. Summer climbed up and turned her face into the pillow, her body hitching sobs from the deepest part of her. Katy's hand felt good on her back, patient as she expelled a wealth of pent up emotion. Finally, she could speak.

"Landis isn't buying the paper, and Carson is moving to Thailand, and I don't know how to be an editor, and… and…." The words were interrupted by strange gasps, and Summer was helpless to stop another spate of sobs. Katy stroked her hair until she'd cried it all out.

"Let me understand this," Katy started, when she'd finally rubbed her eyes dry on the pillow. "Gage is selling the paper to local buyers, Carson is starting an amazing business venture in a beautiful country, and you're getting a dream job you can probably do in your sleep for a lot more money, and... I think you had one more 'terrible' thing that was happening in your world?" Katy coaxed.

"I think I love Landis," she whispered.

"Ahhh, I was wondering if it was something like that." Katy snuggled in closer so Summer could put her head on her shoulder. "Tell me about it."

"We had that hook-up and it was great. It was amazing! And I was all ready for him to go back home and to not see him again except at work gatherings. I was okay with that. But now, with him not buying the paper, I'm never going to see him. And even before that, I was... kind of... missing him. And I felt dumb about that, because it was just supposed to be a hook-up, with no commitments or promises. And now I'm acting like one of those women on TV who cry because they think they love some guy after two dates."

"Hmmm, I see. You're right; nobody wants to be that woman. Except, I was kind of that woman, and it worked out pretty good for me."

"You found Mitch, your soul mate," she huffed. "It's not the same."

"The guy who was squatting in my house and called the police on me?" Katy laughed. "It took a while for us to figure out the soul mate part, but not that long, to be honest."

"I just feel so empty, like something's missing."

"Have you ever felt like that before?" her bestie asked.

Summer mulled that over, going back in her memory to past relationships. She tried to remember the first meetings and the breakups, and honestly couldn't land on anything that had felt so emotionally charged as these last few days.

"No, I haven't."

"So do you think it's important enough to you to find out if this is important to him too? To find out if he's feeling the same things?"

"I guess so." She groaned and covered her face. "How do I do that? Do I just come right out and say it? Or ask him? I feel like I should draft something on paper." She frowned when Katy rolled her eyes. "Don't laugh at me. I do my best thinking on paper."

"Hey, kiddo, you're the woman who, when faced with a corporate bully taking over her newspaper, was going to form a consortium to buy it out from underneath him. You can do anything!" Katy hugged her and kissed her head.

"How am I supposed to win over the same bully?"

"Just say what's in your heart. Don't write anything out; just get in touch with your feelings and let your heart speak for you." Katy pulled Summer's hands away from her face. "Trust me, it works."

"What if he doesn't feel the same?" she asked.

"He might not, sweetie. But then again, he might. Just remember what you told me when I had the same fear about Mitch—either way, you're going to be okay."

Summer reached around Katy to give her a big hug. "I will be, won't I?"

"Plus, you're Gracie's role model. You have to show her how it's done."

That got her to lean back suddenly. "Holy cow, you're right! I need to book a flight."

14

Landis slowed his pace to a walk, feeling a line of sweat trickle from his scalp down the back of his neck. Even at 7:00 a.m., it was muggy and shaping up to be a scorcher of a day. His foot had that weird cramp it got when he didn't pay attention to his running form. And that meant he hadn't been successful at clearing his mind and getting back into the groove of work.

The High Line was fairly quiet this morning, and he was able to lean on an empty bench to stretch. He pulled out his phone as he sank into a long calf stretch, telling himself he was only going to turn off his running app. Which he did. And then he held it for a moment, looking at the screen. *This is ridiculous,* came the admonishment he'd told himself many times over the last two days. He jammed the phone into his back pocket.

He'd reached out to her and she wasn't interested. At all. Period. Although, admittedly, he'd reached out with a chatty **Congratulations, Auntie!** a short while after Mitch had texted him about baby Grace. Maybe he should have sent an honest **How are you? Because I'm not great.** But he'd opted to go with a safe conversation starter. And nothing. Not even a thank you, which rankled him as well.

He hadn't been able to text her after his discussion with Gage. He must have typed and deleted over twenty messages, but he couldn't seem to find the right words. Despite the encouragement Evelyn had given him, he was nervous. Almost from the moment they met, every time he'd said something to her, it had the opposite effect. And now the stakes were even higher to say the right thing, because she had specifically not wanted further communication. And if a simple congratulations wasn't the right thing, then what the hell was?

He switched legs and leaned deeper into his stretch, then stood back to stretch the sole of his sore foot. His runs usually invigorated him for the day, but looking up at the office building, there was an emptiness in him. His normal kick of excitement just wasn't there.

Suddenly, jarringly, his phone chimed and vibrated in his pocket. He grabbed it and saw her text.

Thanks!

His heart jumped into his throat. He kept watching the screen, willing the three dots to appear, indicating she was typing. It didn't happen. He sat down, his thumbs hovering in a circle over the keyboard, and then he started to type.

Believe it or not, I was happy Gage took you up on your idea. Nice work! he sent.

He looked up and across at the city looming in front of him. The restlessness left him, and something in his chest surged. Something more than his usual motivation. The sounds and colors of the city seemed to flow through him, charging him up. He was going to open his heart and share it. If she didn't want to have anything to do with him, so be it. But he wasn't going to let this go without exploring whatever *this* was, fully. He saw now it was the only way he'd be able to move on.

The conviction of his decision swept through him, leaving a path of goose bumps in its wake despite the humidity. He wanted to stand up and shout his vow to the city, the same way she'd faced the ocean a few days ago.

His phone chimed. **Can I talk to you?** she asked. The words yanked him to his feet.

Of course. I'm free to chat right now. Should I call you? He quickly tapped his screen, not quick enough to match his heart rate though.

Actually, I'm in NYC.

The words sent a jolt through his body. **Great! Where are you right now?**

I'm downstairs in your office building. You have really good timing! I can't come upstairs without an appointment.

I'm out on the High Line. Stay there. I'm coming to you.

Sore foot be damned, his walk turned into a jog and then a run, until he was down two flights of stairs and at street level. Within seconds, he covered the two blocks to his building's plaza, and then he saw her.

Her gold-spun hair was down past her shoulders, and wisps floated around her face. Her cloth backpack hung from one hand, limp, almost dragging on the ground. Her yellow sundress lifted in a lazy draft of air, and her other hand tugged briefly at the edge of her faded, short cotton jacket. Her eyes looked red and her cheeks looked damp. She was adorable.

He prided himself on having clever replies for every situation but seeing her there in front of him left him speechless. He was so damn happy to see her that he had no words at all. He walked up to her and pulled her into his arms, pressing her head against his sweaty T-shirt.

"First, you should know I hardly ever cry," she murmured into his shoulder. He felt her arms close around him, tight.

His heart leaped and he felt twin tears bubble up in his own eyes. "Oh yeah?"

"But I've been doing nothing but cry for the past twenty-four hours."

"What's the second thing?"

"The second thing is, I've had a horrible empty feeling since you left, and I think it means I love you. And I'm putting that out there, even though it scares the crap out of me, because I'm somebody's auntie and I'm showing her how it's done."

Landis leaned back to look at her, letting her see his own tears, smiling when it prompted more from her. "I'll second your second. I've been a wreck since I left, thinking you wanted nothing to do with me. Which was soul-splitting, because I want everything to do with you."

He pulled her close again, burying his face in her hair and breathing in ocean and seagulls and everything he never knew he wanted in a woman. "I'm pretty sure Evelyn was on the brink of calling in a psychiatrist."

"Hmm, Evelyn," she murmured, snuggling into him. "I don't know if I'm ready to meet her yet."

"No one's ever ready to meet Evelyn. But I think she's impressed by you. She never thought a blonde hipster would be able to turn my heart inside out."

She peered up at him, her breath fluttering the strands of hair around her face and her hands sliding around his back. "Is that what I did?"

He hugged her as close as possible, right off her feet. "Completely."

EPILOGUE
FIVE MONTHS LATER

The island of Manhattan twinkled through the tall windows of their Hell's Kitchen apartment. A thick curtain of snowflakes fluttered by, having not let up since the morning. Their twelve-foot Christmas tree twinkled in the corner, and Summer was sprawled on her stomach underneath it, staring into the glow of her laptop screen. After the normal *beep-boops*, a video window opened and she was staring at three faces on the screen.

"Gracie, sweetie, Merry Christmas!" she called, smiling at the chubby baby face on the screen.

"Merry Christmas!" sang Katy and Mitch. Grace sat on Mitch's lap, who sat on a chair, and Katy was leaning over his shoulder so all three could be seen by the camera. Grace greeted Summer by shoving her fist in her mouth.

"Holy cow!" said Landis, sitting down beside Summer on the floor and handing her a glass of wine. "Look how good she is at sitting up! Hi, Gracie. Are you having a glass of hand?" He laughed, leaning closer to the screen. Grace popped her fist out and stared at him, spellbound.

"Man, what is it about you? Every time you speak, she's mesmerized," Mitch commented, looking from the baby sitting on his lap and back to Landis.

"I'm magic with kids. What can I say?" Landis smiled smugly, rubbing Summer's back.

"I know. I'm miffed. I had it all planned that I would be the favorite," she groused, but leaned over to kiss his knee.

"So what's this important favor you have to ask us?" Katy asked, leaning around to wipe some drool off Grace's chin.

"Well, we were wondering if you had anything much happening at the inn in March?"

"Not really, why?" Katy asked.

"Summer thinks it's cliché to get married in summer, so we were thinking of tying the knot in March... at the inn."

"What?" Katy's question turned into a squeal, startling Gracie. Summer joined in, and both men smiled.

"I thought Evelyn would make sure you'd have a big fancy wedding out there," Katy prompted after the squealing ended.

"I told her she could throw a big fancy reception out here. We—" Summer looked up at Landis, reaching up to touch his cheek gently "—want to have something very intimate and very special at the place we met."

All four joined in to talk about the details, from decorations to food, and planning how long Landis and Summer would visit.

The foursome was startled by Landis's phone. He picked it up and looked at the screen then showed it to Summer. *I thought she was in China,* she mouthed, and he shrugged.

"Hey, Red, Merry Christmas!" he said with a big smile, and then paused. Summer could hear an excited voice on the other end and lifted her eyebrows at Landis. "Whoa, hold on. Calm down. Summer's right here. Let me put you on speaker phone."

She sat up, concerned. She could still hear Stella talking right over Landis's words. He tapped the phone and her voice flooded out.

"...going to keep me as a sex slave or something!" she shouted and stopped talking in order to catch her breath.

All of them were speechless, except for Grace, who said "Gooooggghhh" in a wet coo.

Summer's phone on the floor suddenly rang. She held it up and showed Landis that Carson was video calling. She answered, and the glow from the phone lit up her face. "Carson, what's going.... What on earth are you wearing?"

༺❦༻

THANK YOU FOR READING! I HOPE YOU loved meeting Summer and Landis. Are you curious about what is happening in that phone call between Carson and Stella? Read **RECIPE FOR LOVE** to find out!

Can you fall in love someone you hate?

Stella only knows a life of privilege, comfort and getting her way—especially when it comes to her career in corporate acquisitions. So she's shocked when Carson, a gorgeous, successful restaurant owner, isn't afraid to label her a spoiled socialite with a pretend career.

Not only does he refuse to hear Stella's deal, he leaves the city. Convinced he's being bull-headed, she braves heavy rain to follow him to a remote Thai village.

When the rain becomes a monsoon, they're stranded in the village. Spending days together, the socialite and the chef realize there's more to the other than they expected.

When old insecurities creep back in, will they be able to trust the love they're discovering?

"A hilarious opposites attract with a heart-felt happily ever after!"
—*Cheryl S., Amazon Reader*

ALSO BY NALA

Maple Cove Dog Lover's Society

Small Town Shepherd (Sam & Brody's story)

Beauty and the Bulldog (Vi & Noah's story)

Foxhound Foes (Rylee & Matt's story)

Billionaire Beagle (Olive & Xavier's story)

Westie Besties (Quinn & Levi's story)

Second Chance Corgi (Eliza & Phil's story)

Cranberry Hill Inn Series—Paperback Books 4–6

Everything for Love (Rally, Cassie & Garret's stories)

For contests, prizes & free reading, join my Reader's Group by visiting https://www.subscribepage.com/l4m3s1

COPYRIGHT

All the characters in this book are fictitious, and any resemblance to actual persons living or dead is purely coincidental.

Copyright © 2018 by Nala Henkel-Aislinn

All rights reserved.

No part of this book may be reproduced, or stored in a retrieval system, or transmitted in any form or by any means, electronic, mechanical, photocopying, recording, or otherwise, without express written permission of the publisher.

Published by Nala Henkel-Aislinn

Edited by Hot Tree Editing

A CRANBERRY HILL *Clean* ROMANCE

Recipe for Love

NALA HENKEL-AISLINN

DEDICATION

To my husband, partner, love of my life, and Alpha Reader (naturally), Eric.

To Taylor, Dara, Keegan, Piper, Al, and Dave.

To my wonderful friend and Alpha Readers, Eric, Regina and Wendy.

PROLOGUE

Stella twitched the knee of her Michael Kors crepe pantsuit as she sat outside on the rustic couch on the rustic porch of the oh-so-rustic Cranberry Hill Inn. Even though it was summer, the morning air blowing in from the Pacific was cool. Other than sleeping in her bed, this porch and couch were the only places she'd been since she arrived last night. And a night of sleep hadn't taken the edge off what had been a miserable day of travel.

When she'd finally arrived at this off-the-beaten-track inn, she'd been attacked by mosquitos, almost hobbled when her heel caught between the boards of the porch, and then, worst of all, forced to witness her sometimes-friend-with-benefits Landis chasing after some surfer girl reporter. Not to mention meeting the surfer girl's crabby brother.

Mr. Crabby had been in a hurry when he'd driven up and parked. Although the very pregnant innkeeper, Katy and her husband were tolerable, their constant cheerful chatter had driven her outside to wait for Landis. Apparently, he'd been at a baseball game; God only knows why. When the brother showed up instead of Landis, she'd almost gone inside to avoid small talk with a stranger. But as she watched him get out of his truck and fuss with a large bag in the back, she changed her mind.

He wore sweats and a T-shirt, but she could still make out his athletic body. His hair was a little on the long side, blond with lighter streaks and a slight curl to it. His forearms though... they were lean and muscled and tan. Strong arms were her weakness. And large hands. Thinking about them now made her uncross and recross her legs. She must have done something similar last night, because he'd turned suddenly to look at her.

Even across the driveway, she could see his pale eyes widen against his tanned face. When she sat up straighter, his eyes had gone right to her legs, mostly bare thanks to the short skirt she'd been wearing. Her legs were her second-best feature. He had walked slowly across the driveway, adjusting the thick strap of the bag over his shoulder.

Finally, she'd thought, *some fun, flirtatious chat to break up the boredom.* But then he spoke.

"Well, well, well, the glam girl is here," he sneered, which confused her. It was not the first reaction she usually got from a man, especially after the man in question had been checking out her legs. She examined his face and saw mockery. She'd tugged on the short hem of her skirt before she could stop herself. From her seated position, it wouldn't matter anyway.

"I don't believe we've met. Or have we?" she asked as condescendingly as she could, and waited for him to wither. He didn't.

"No. I've just seen photos of you in the newspapers. Why are you here?" His voice rang like a hammer on granite.

She could almost see the anger rolling off him, and it muddled her thoughts. Why was this asshole angry with her if he didn't know her?

"I'm a guest." She held up her glass of lemonade as evidence. "I assume you work here?" She meant it as an insult, but it flew right over his head.

"Hm." He smirked at her, not moving. Her anger built, but he spoke before she could think of a good putdown. "I get that women like you need to defend their territory or whatever, but leave Landis and Summer to sort things out between themselves."

She stood so suddenly some of the lemonade swirled over the edge of her glass. "Women like me?" The words shot out like bullets and she tried to calm her voice. "You don't even know me, or why I'm here. Why don't you run along to the staff quarters and stop insulting guests?"

He looked her up and down, gave another derogatory "Hm," and turned to walk away, following a dimly lit path at the end of the driveway. Her heart was racing. In her world, the only confrontations she had were in the boardroom. And even there, harsh words were veiled in chilly professionalism. She stared down the path, unable to look away. Faint lights turned on through the trees, and a few seconds later, she heard a door slam.

"Is everything okay?" Katy had asked from the other side of the screen door.

"Who was that?"

"That's Carson, Summer's brother. They live in the renovated barn loft out back."

Just remembering it cranked her residual anger up to a low boil. She'd let a barn-dwelling asshole question her integrity. But when Landis and Summer had shown up a half-hour later, she'd questioned her reason for coming here. Especially when she'd seen how Landis had acted. He was uncertain and indecisive—about a woman! She'd almost fallen over at the sight of it. It made her wonder if her plan to restart a casual hook-up with him stood a chance.

"Oh, Stella," said the object of her thoughts as Landis walked out of the inn, his briefcase and overnight bag in his hands.

She stood up, careful to avoid the porch gaps with her heels, and pushed the memories of yesterday aside. "Are you leaving?"

"Yeah. I've got a strike meeting to get to in Atlanta." He was distracted and jittery. His eyes had a strange look. Like he had a migraine, was the only thing she could compare it to.

"Are you okay?" Her plan had been to flirt and suggest they get together when she returned from China. She hadn't really believed this Summer woman to be a problem, but now she wasn't sure. Nothing was going according to her plan.

"To be honest," he said, walking down the porch stairs and forcing her to follow across the gravel in her heels. Her stumbling steps were not creating the sexy picture she aimed for. "I don't know. I'm confused and I feel... off. And I don't know why, but I have this anxious feeling." He put his bags in the backseat and turned to look at her. She saw something in his eyes that almost made her step backward, a look so raw and real she wanted to push it away with her hands.

"I.... Does this have to do with Summer? The woman you met, what... yesterday?" It was hard to keep the scorn out of her voice, but something was crashing apart in her and she couldn't control it. She was woozy, as if she'd been standing near a cliff and in a blink found herself hanging from it by her fingertips.

"A few days ago, yeah." He rubbed a hand over his eyes and forehead, and then rested it on his hip. "It's something I didn't really believe in. If anyone had said something like this could happen so fast...." His voice faded away and his eyes shifted from hers to a distant stare. This time, she did take a step back.

"Wow, that's... what, love? You're saying you love this woman?" As she stated the words, she heard the scorn in her voice. This was a Landis she'd never seen before. A Landis she didn't think she liked.

"I don't know; that's the problem. I only know it's something I don't recognize." He gave a laugh that had no humor in it, and reached for her hand. "I'm sorry. We haven't had a chance to talk or anything. And I didn't have any time to look over your contract, but I can do that on the plane. I promise."

She squeezed his hand back and then dropped it, stepping away. "No hurry. My meeting is a couple days away." The words came out in a mechanical rush, as if she were operating her body from far away. "Have a good flight, and good luck with the union." She turned and walked as elegantly as she could back to the porch. She heard him say "Goodbye," and she waved a hand behind her to acknowledge it. She was relieved she was packed and ready to go. If she were lucky, she'd avoid seeing anybody before she left. Her goal was to focus on this trip to China and put this feeling of... whatever it was, behind her.

FOUR MONTHS LATER

"This is pretty cool," Dex said to Carson as they stood in the line on the jet way, waiting to board the plane. "I've never been on an international flight, believe it or not. I've also never traveled this close to Christmas."

Carson smiled, tapping his old friend and fellow chef on the shoulder with his boarding pass. "If I'd known a trip to Thailand would win you away from the restaurant, I would have done this a month or two ago."

"I wish you would have used Pete to get us on board first." Dex elbowed him.

"I only use Pete for good, not evil," he said, knocking on the carbon fiber socket of his prosthetic right leg through his pants. He'd nicknamed it Pete shortly after he'd gotten it.

"How is getting seated earlier evil?"

"I'm able bodied. I prefer other people that need more help than me to get seated first." He tried not to sound frustrated, but almost all his friends said this to him whenever they wanted to park in a handicap spot or get other privileges. While he knew they meant it in jest and didn't really see him as handicapped, he just wished everyone would get over it. It had been well over a year since he'd lost the leg to cancer. He wanted it to not be a thing any more.

The line inched forward and then started to move smoothly onto the plane.

"Ah, the privileged class," Dex murmured and then gasped. "Fifth row left, window seat," Dex whispered to him quickly, and then walked down the aisle.

Carson saw her immediately, and almost groaned out loud. Stella Carmichael. He was sure everybody would notice the stunning redhead regardless of where she sat. She was nodding as she held her cell phone to her ear, staring out her window. As he approached her row, her head swung around and she made eye contact with him. He held her glance for a moment then shifted his eyes away as if she was a stranger. He continued shuffling with the others down to the back of the plane where he and Dex sat.

"She looks like she should be famous. Do you think she's a model? She must be a model. Although she looked sort of business-y to be a model."

"Whoever she is, she's way out of our league." He did his best not to roll his eyes. The league Stella was in wasn't worth wanting to be a part of, in his opinion.

"I wonder if they let economy passengers buy first class passengers drinks."

"I'm pretty sure everything in first class is free. Plus, I don't think she's the kind of woman who's impressed with guys who buy them drinks. Maybe guys who buy them diamonds, though. Do you have any diamonds on you?" He wanted to forget she was on this flight, but the words tumbled out before he could stop them.

"Wow, someone's bitter," Dex said. "I know you have a thing for redheads, so something else must be bugging you. Is it that she completely ignored your rugged good looks, or that she's sitting in first class?"

Carson closed his eyes and rolled his shoulders as he thought about whether he could answer in a way that would put the topic to rest. "I met her this summer when I still lived in Cranberry Hill. Her childhood friend is my sister's fiancé. I haven't seen her since then, and I'm glad. With her, beauty *is* skin deep—and something she uses like currency."

"Whaaat?" Dex's voice was high-pitched and amazed, and ignored most of what he'd just said. "You're practically family. Why are you not using *that* to your advantage? You could be sitting up in first class right now!"

"First class isn't my style. Also, snotty society girls with fake roles in daddy's company are also not my style. I wouldn't be able to last two minutes sitting beside her. And I don't really want to talk about her. We should be talking about your role at the restaurant." Although right at that moment, Carson didn't want to talk at all.

The sight of Stella brought back memories of a challenging time. The night he'd met her had also been the night he'd decided to go into a business partnership in a foreign country, started the ball rolling on his move to Chiang Mai, and then had to deal with his giddily-in-love little sister every other day.

Before Dex could reply, the announcements started and the two men didn't say anything until they were climbing to altitude.

◊

"... so I'll be managing a couple people?" Dex asked, deep into their conversation. Carson paged through papers on his fold-down table.

"Yeah, but more likely we'll add a few more. We've got our eye on a second location in the south of the city, and I'd like to train up a few more people before that goes through."

"How experienced are they?"

"It's a mix, actually. Two came from the community organization that places homeless people in the city. But we've also brought in a few graduates from the local cooking school...." He trailed off when he noticed Dex was no longer listening but leaning into the aisle and looking at something ahead. Craning his neck over the seat in front of him, he saw the distraction. An aloof redhead was walking down the aisle, a champagne flute in one hand while the other one touched a head rest every now and again for balance. He thought Dex's eyes would pop out.

"Show some dignity, man," he grumbled to Dex, who waved him off.

"Excuse me," she said to Dex, her voice purring, "could I ask you a favor?"

"Of course!" Dex smiled.

"Could I bribe you with this champagne to switch seats with me for just a few minutes? I cleared it with the attendant in first class," she said with a semi-pout and tilt of her head.

Carson hid his grin when Dex's excited smile faded. She didn't give him a chance to reply, just put the glass in his hand and walked a little past his seat, giving him room to stand up. "Thanks so much," she added in her syrupy voice. As Dex unbuckled his seat belt with one hand and got up, he glanced back over his shoulder. His disappointment was clear, but all Carson could do was shrug.

"You can say no, Dex," he offered, but before Dex could answer, Stella was sliding into his seat.

"You're really doing me a big favor." She reached up to give Dex's arm a squeeze. "I promise I won't be long, and feel free to order more champagne if you need it."

Carson was sure she beamed her best smile at him, and he saw the few shreds of disappointment in Dex's eyes melt away as he sipped the champagne and turned to go to first class.

"Impressive," Carson murmured, as he leaned away from her while trying not to barge into the personal space of the older man in the window seat to his right, "and alarming at the same time."

"I alarm you? I guess that's better than disgusting you, although not by much."

He frowned. "When did you disgust me?"

"When we met. Your attitude was less than kind, but then I guess you were warning me off your sister's 'man,' so I can't blame you. I'll admit I was there with an ulterior motive." She shrugged a slim shoulder, and it was hard not to notice how the silk fabric of her dress moved over her chest. He stared down at the papers and shuffled them around.

"What was your ulterior motive?" he asked.

"Landis and I had always been an on-again, off-again thing. I wanted us to be on-again. Until your sister changed my plans. Landis and I even had a pact that we'd marry each other if we never found love."

"I hope you didn't come back here to run my sister down, because—"

"Oh, stop. I'm not here to do that. For a crusading hippy reporter, she's tolerable. I've talked to her a few times, and it's obvious she and Landis are hopelessly, pathetically in love—God help them." She crossed her legs and tugged lightly at the skirt hem that barely covered one knee.

"So... are you scouting for a new marriage pact guy then? Because Dex might be up for that." He thought it was a clever joke, but when she stayed silent, he glanced at her. Something in her eyes made him shift in his seat. "What do you want to talk about?"

"Your restaurant, Malee," she said in a hard tone. "Summer mentioned you were going to be opening a second location. Is that true?"

"Yes," he replied, silently cursing his blabbermouth sister. "Why?"

"I have a client in New York who wants to invest in a small restaurant chain in Asia. Four locations at least. I'm going to visit one in Chiang Mai on his behalf, but I'm pretty sure it's not what he wants." She spoke in a brisk tone, and he turned to face her.

"Why do you think that?"

"I don't think it will live up to the quality he's looking for. They definitely don't have a Michelin star chef in their kitchen." She looked at him with a tight smile.

"To be accurate, I was chef at a Michelin star restaurant."

"And I find it interesting that word on the street says Charisma is going to lose that star next year. I think losing a certain chef a few months ago has everything to do with it," she said. He watched her hand smooth her skirt over her leg, and dragged his eyes back to the seat in front of him.

"Lots of things go into winning and losing those stars. It's subjective, and an elitist thing to chase, which is perhaps why some people care about it." He could feel the air between them drop ten degrees.

"Good food is good food. Restaurants should be ranked on how busy they are."

"I happen to agree with that last part," Stella told him, "and from the research I've done on Malee, you're very busy, very popular, and very delicious. Uh, the food is delicious, I mean." He looked over just as she looked away, but he could still see a pink flush rise on her cheek.

"Why Malee?"

She looked around as if the answer was somewhere in the overhead bins. "Well, I have a client looking for a multiple-location Asian restaurant to invest in. Malee almost perfectly fits the bill. And when I saw you were on my flight, it seemed serendipitous.

"You're proposing an investment opportunity," he stated more than asked.

"I'm testing the water, yes. Is it something you would ever consider?"

"No," he said without a pause.

"Can I ask why?"

"The second restaurant has a more humanitarian cause behind it than profit motive, which your investor wouldn't be interested in. And our third project—"

"There's a third location in the works?" she asked, her eyes widening to large circles.

"No, it's a *project*," he emphasized. *Sheesh, she's a piece of work.* "And it's going to take my full attention to get it off the ground. I'm barely going to be able to get away for Summer's wedding."

That made Stella sit up straight, and he watched a wall crash down, blanking any expression from her face. "Did they set a date?" she asked, her voice sounding strained.

"Sometime in spring, but no date yet. Is that a touchy subject for you?"

"No," she answered, but he thought her smile looked forced. "I shouldn't have given your friend my champagne. We could have toasted to the happy couple."

"Let's toast without the champagne. To two people finding love," he said, curious to watch her response.

"To two people forming a successful partnership," she amended with a raised eyebrow. "I'll leave the love to you." She rose elegantly from the seat and turned to look at him. "I'll send your friend back to you." And before he could say anything else, she was gone.

A few minutes later, Dex returned, handing him one of two champagne flutes he held. "She said to congratulate you on your business, and that you're gaining an incredible brother-in-law," he said as he settled into his seat. "First class is amazing, by the way. You should get over your elitist pride." Dex tapped his glass against Carson's and sipped. After examining the tiny bubbles for a moment, Carson sipped as well.

I

Two things woke Stella up. The first was the drone of the intercom voice announcing they were twenty minutes away from landing. The other was her phone buzzing against her knee. On the second leg of her trip to Chiang Mai, she had both seats in her side of the aisle. After reviewing the agenda for tomorrow's meeting, she'd curled up with a blanket and pillows and slept for the rest of the flight. She fumbled for her phone and saw it was Jason.

"Yes?" Her voice was raspy.

"Did you land yet, babe?" he said in a cozy tone.

"Don't call me babe. And no."

"How long until you land?"

"Soon. What do you want?"

"I'm just checking in, that's all. Can't a guy do that?" His whiny tone was one of her least favorite things about him.

"We're not a couple any more. We're friends, and you're on the edge of that."

"Fine, I'm checking in as a *friend* then," he said testily.

"As you can hear, I'm alive, but tired. Next time, can you check in by e-mailing, and not by phoning and waking me up?" She held the phone away to find the red disconnect button.

"I just wanted to run an idea—" His voice was cut off by her thumb.

"Coffee, Ms. Carmichael?" asked the attendant. Stella closed her eyes and let out a dramatic sigh.

"Yes, good Lord, please... yes!" The attendant held out the prefilled cup of black coffee—exactly how Stella needed it. She inhaled the steam of the rich roast and sighed again. *Heaven*, and she took a sip.

She reached down to the side compartment of her purse and pulled out her ear buds. She plugged them in and called her wonder woman assistant, Freddie. She put her phone on the seat and snuggled back into her blanket, one hand holding her coffee against her chest.

"Tell me again why I shouldn't block Jason's number?" she asked when Freddie answered.

"Because he's a friend. Unless he's harassing you, then I'll get him blocked. Is he?"

Stella weighed the idea of lying, but she knew Freddie would see through it. Freddie could always tell. "No," she groused. "He's not. But he's getting close."

"Here's an idea. How about you don't answer his calls? 'Wow, Freddie, thanks for such simple advice.' 'Oh, you're welcome, Stella. How about a raise?'"

Stella couldn't stop her laugh. "Wow, Freddie, thanks for such great advice. I'd offer you a raise, but you almost make as much as me."

"Funny. And you say you don't have a sense of humor." They both laughed. "Everything here is under control. Where are you?"

"Twenty minutes or so out of Chiang Mai. And you'll never guess who followed me all the way from San Francisco."

"Ryan Gosling!"

"No."

"Someone who looks exactly like Harrison Ford from *Indiana Jones and the Temple of Doom*?"

"No... what? Why that movie?"

"He's the perfect amount of scruffy in it."

"You're crazy, but no. No famous people. Landis's future brother-in-law has been on both flights. Carson."

"Carson, Carson... the Carson you met at that bed and breakfast in Seattle?"

"Yeah, well, close to Seattle. But yes, the same guy."

"Didn't you get into an argument or something with him when you were there?"

"No, he acted like a jerk and I didn't put up with it."

"So you *did* get into an argument. You didn't pick a fight with him on the plane too, did you?" Freddie asked.

"Did I... what...? I *do not* pick fights with people," she argued.

"I didn't mean fight, fight. I meant a more psychological flinging of words." She could hear the laughter in Freddie's voice.

"Anyway..." She dragged out the word loudly. "My point is that I found out his restaurant Malee might be opening a third location, which is exactly what Monticello is looking for," Stella explained.

"Monticello wants to invest in something with at least *four* locations, and you can't jump ship in the middle of your due diligence. The Monticello people really like the company you're meeting with. They're ready to sign."

"You're right," Stella sighed. Freddie was always right. "He didn't sound interested anyway."

"There you go. Focus on the sure thing. If it makes you feel better, you can think of the... what was the restaurant called?"

"Malee."

"You can think of Malee as a contingency plan if Central Group decides not to follow through with the deal."

"Okay," Stella agreed, rubbing her eyes. "As usual, you're right again. I don't know what's wrong with me."

"I do, but you don't believe me," Freddie muttered.

"You think I'm burnt out, but I've never been burnt out. My whole life has been at this pace and I've never had a burnout."

"See? You don't believe me. Even Evelyn thinks you're burnt out," Freddie mumbled the last part under her breath, and it made Stella frown.

"When did you speak to Ev?" she asked. She hadn't spoken with Landis's mother in... wow. When she thought about it, she realized it had been a long time. Three months maybe?

"After you and Jason... didn't have a big fight at the Plate By Plate benefit a couple months ago," Freddie said carefully.

Stella tapped her fist against her forehead. She knew that would come back to haunt her. She should have slept with Jason and moved on. Why she ever believed him when he said they would make a great power couple, she didn't know.

"I'll call her," she said to Freddie, but she knew she wouldn't make the call yet.

"Good. I think she misses you. Now let me get back to work," Freddie complained jokingly.

Stella laughed and they disconnected. After a sip of coffee, Stella opened her contacts and scrolled to Ev Blake.

Ev and Freddie had started throwing around the idea of 'burnt out' after she'd returned from China. Which had been after her side visit to the inn to fire things up with Landis. Where she'd met the prickly and self-righteous Carson, who was still some kind of reverse snob. It was also right after that trip that she'd let her guard down and jumped into a relationship with Jason.

She took another sip of coffee and put her phone down. She could feel her heart trip-tripping in her chest, and decided to put her coffee back in the cup holder as well. She admitted that she'd been having sporadic moments of anxiety. Maybe this is what Freddie and Ev saw as a burnout? Anyway, it wouldn't hurt to cut down on the caffeine.

Stella waited under the covered airport entrance for the hotel limo, watching the pouring rain. Customs had been quick, and even with her quick stop in the VIP lounge for a martini, she was fifteen minutes early for her ride.

Glancing to her right, through the crowd of people trying to find transportation, she noticed Carson and his friend. They were walking from a door farther away, toward her and out in the rain.

His friend held his jacket over his head, but Carson stood tall and patient, as if there was no rain at all. He'd been wearing a sleeved shirt on the plane, but now he wore a T-shirt. He raised an arm to a vehicle, and even from the distance, she could see the lean muscles in it. She scanned the road in front of her and saw a man in a pick-up truck waving. Sure enough, the truck pulled quickly into a small space closer to where she stood than the two men.

It must have been the martini hitting her blood stream, because she grabbed the handle of her large wheeled suitcase and marched into the rain. She was determined to get to where the truck waited before they could pile in and drive away.

"Just throw your bags in the back," she heard Carson say, as he threw his own large backpack into the truck bed. A short, black-haired man got out of the truck and greeted Carson with the traditional *wai*, palms together near his nose with a quick bow and a "*Sa-wa-dee kruh.*" The man wore a white cotton short-sleeved shirt and brown cotton pants that somehow wrapped around his waist and tucked through his legs into his waistband.

Those look so comfortable, she thought as she pulled at her wet, clinging skirt and she walked.

"Carson!" she called, the rain soaking through her hair and dress. Her suitcase skittering beside her, the wheels catching on the cracks that separated the slabs of sidewalk. All three men stopped and looked at her. "In case you change your mind about an investor, or want to expand your restaurant...." She reached into a pocket of her Gucci shoulder bag, pulled out a business card, and held it out to him. He looked down at it and back at her, as if the card was an alien thing.

"Thank you, thank you." The sandaled man took the business card and pressed his hands together, bowing slightly. She let go of her suitcase handle to echo the traditional greeting, also replying in Thai, "Thank you." For good measure, she pulled out two more business cards and held them out to Carson and his plane friend as well.

"This is Somchai Buyung," Carson said to her, probably because she just stood there staring. She greeted the man again. "He's my partner in Malee. You already know Dex."

She smiled at Dex. Stella didn't quite know how to reply. Carson was being polite, and she wasn't sure some putdown wasn't about to smack her in the face.

"You should come visit the restaurant," Somchai invited. "Carson says you are in the restaurant business. That you..." He squinted and looked up as he searched for the words. "That you make partnerships between restaurant owners and investors."

Stella almost fell over. *Carson told him about me?* "That's correct. I work in the restaurant division of my family's business. I look after acquisitions." She pushed her sopping hair behind her ear. "It was nice to meet you. And thank you for the invitation to your restaurant." She looked back at Carson, whose expression had gone from polite to sullen. As she took hold of her suitcase again, Somchai pulled out his own business card.

"I hope to see you!" he said.

"*Khau khun ka,*" Stella thanked him, and took the card. Looking back, she saw the hotel's limo parked in the covered curb area and a driver looking nervously through the crowd. She tucked Somchai's business card into her shoulder bag, and wondered if the morning meeting she'd scheduled would end before she could sneak away for lunch.

2

Carson sat a little sideways in the small truck cab, jammed against the passenger door—on the left, as Thailand was a left-side driving country—with Dex in the middle and Somchai driving. The rain and muggy air combined with the warmth of their bodies, and he shifted once in a while to unstick himself from Dex.

He noticed Dex kept pulling at his collar and shifting in his seat, and Carson smiled. He wondered how long it would take his friend to get used to the constant humidity, and now the constant rain, since the rainy season had started early.

He'd loved everything about Chiang Mai when he'd arrived, from the unrelenting heat and humidity to the crowds. He loved the history and the people, and the philosophy of Buddhism that was so different from back home. But his trip to San Francisco, even though it had only lasted four days, had ignited something in him. The cool, crisp air of the west coast and the towering silver buildings still owned part of his heart.

"This is very good, Carson," Somchai said. He pulled out Stella's business card and held it out to make a point. "This is our way to go to America with Malee!"

"I don't know," Carson hedged. He regretted saying anything about Stella when he'd called Somchai to let him know they'd landed. He wasn't even sure why he'd mentioned her at all, except he thought Dex might go on and on about her, and he'd have to explain eventually.

"*I* know," Somchai insisted. "She's a restaurant investor. In America. We are a restaurant wanting to go to America." He leaned forward to look past Dex and raise his eyebrows at him.

"You guys want to expand in the U.S.?" Dex whistled. "San Francisco's a hard market if you want to go there."

"Exactly—" Carson looked over to Somchai. "—but Somchai and I agreed we'd get established here first and look at expansion to the U.S. next year." That was the wording in the partnership agreement. Carson knew, though, expansion to the U.S. had played a big part in why Somchai had asked him to form the partnership.

"Yes, but it doesn't have to be San Francisco," Somchai argued.

"I'm not saying no, I'm just saying—"

"You're not saying no, because you *can't* say no!" Somchai agreed happily.

"True, but let's stick to our strategy. We have a really good plan to get Malee to where it needs to be in Chiang Mai, plus a second location in the works. We need all of that to go well before we can look at launching it in the U.S. *Successfully* launching it."

"Why can't you say no?" Dex asked him.

"Because," Somchai jumped in to explain, "Thailand businesses must be fifty-one percent owned by Thai people, unless you want to do the paperwork for the Foreign Ownership Agreement. It's a good law," he said, chuckling.

"How are things going at the restaurant?" Carson changed the subject.

"Very good. Ekapol found a cooking job near Pae Gate," Somchai announced.

"Excellent! Does he start right away?"

"Next week."

"Good. Ekapol is a great cook," he said to Dex. "He's really looking forward to meeting you and learning more about American cuisine."

"Man, I'm hoping to learn all I can about Thai cuisine." Dex laughed.

They talked about a few other business details, when Dex commented on the scenery they were passing. Carson listened as Somchai gave expert commentary on the history and architecture of the seven-centuries-old city.

Malee was in the northeast corner of the Old City, an area that in its early days had been surrounded by a moat and a wall. The ancient brick wall still existed in some places, but was long gone in others. The quickest route to get to the restaurant was by crossing one of the gates where only the moat existed. Even though Chiang Mai was less hectic than Bangkok, its streets were still full of cars, motorbikes, and tuk-tuks—small, three-wheeled motorcycle taxis. Power poles and wires were so heavy in the city that they sometimes blocked the signs on the buildings.

When Carson first arrived, he thrived on the pace of the city. He could disappear into the mass of people that moved on the streets and sidewalks. He hadn't realized at the time that it was an invisibility he needed. When he wasn't at the restaurant, he roamed the city, picking up cultural customs and helpful phrases—hello, thank you, where is— very quickly.

The street food vendors had been a marvel to him. There were three streets they populated, heavily filling the air with spices and fired-meat aromas. He watched in awe as the vendors prepped, cooked, and served. They were always gracious in responding to all his questions, and he had endless questions. One time, an older woman waved him behind her grill and showed him with hand motions how to make an amazing version of Thai fried chicken.

As the truck turned onto a narrow street, Carson's thoughts were pulled to their surroundings. Ahead were two of the most luxurious hotels in Chiang Mai, and he wondered if Stella was staying in one of them.

"Are you thinking about a certain redhead?" Dex teased, elbowing him.

"Trying to forget is more like it," he lied. "Besides, women aren't a priority for me right now." When he'd worked with Dex in San Francisco, he didn't remember him being this fixated on women. He hoped it wasn't going to be a problem. It was easy for foreigners to get into trouble with women here, and hard to get out of it. He'd seen it a few times. "They won't be for you either, because you're going to be busier than you've ever been."

"Pfff," Dex derided.

"Don't worry," Somchai inserted confidently. "We will see her for lunch tomorrow."

"How do you know that?" Carson frowned. He thought she'd been carefully non-committal.

"I just know." Somchai shrugged.

※

MALEE WAS NOT A FANCY RESTAURANT BY ANY MEANS. LAST MONTH, they'd received permission to take over part of the sidewalk for seating, and built a raised platform with a bamboo awning. As the rain hit the thatched grass roof, it made a loud, sustained hiss. Somchai stopped in front of the entrance to let Carson and Dex grab their bags and go inside.

Carson knew Somchai would have to park the truck down the block and in the back alley, wherever there was a spot. He hoped he'd be in his room and able to avoid him and anymore talk about Stella or expanding the business.

"Modest," Dex said as he looked around. He'd gambled that Dex wouldn't be underwhelmed, that he would value the complexity of the Thai/Burmese blend of flavors Carson was trying to achieve. The furnishings were simple—wooden tables and chairs, plaid plastic table coverings, and plain cushions on the seats. The art on the wall were authentic silk pictures, some donated by staff and some bought in the night market.

"Hmmm," Dex said suddenly, his nose pulling his body to the kitchen in the back, and Carson relaxed with a big grin. He was glad his instinct about Dex was right.

They spent the next hour talking with the kitchen and wait staff. The night market closed at midnight, and he and Somchai agreed to keep the restaurant open until one in the morning to take advantage of the late-night shoppers, most of them tourists. A few trickled in now, and after a scan of the customers, he decided they didn't seem rowdy and gestured for Dex to follow him up the back stairs.

"Our rooms are over the restaurant. It's pretty simple accommodation, but the mattress is comfortable and the rent is good. Meaning it's free." He smiled at Dex, who was finally showing some fatigue from the flight.

"Thank God," he said. Their feet trudged up the wooden steps in the very narrow stairway to their rooms. Carson walked to the end of the hallway and stood by an open window.

"Your room's there. Sleep in tomorrow. Somchai marked up a map and left it on your dresser in case you want to wander around tomorrow. If you go right when you walk out of the restaurant, walk to the next street and turn left." He pointed out the window at the glow of lights they could see over the next building. "That's basically street food alley. Walk until you see the farmer's market. There should be a big X on your map. Ask for Lin. She'll give you an awesome rundown on the hyperlocal spices and vegetables."

"Sounds gooo—" Dex's words faded into a huge yawn.

"When you're feeling up to it, we can get into everything in the kitchen."

."Thanks, man." Again, Dex yawned the last word.

"Goodnight." He nudged Dex into his room and went to his own, one door down.

He threw his backpack on the floor, undid his pants, and let them fall to the floor. Sitting on the edge of the bed, he looked down at Pete. He'd named it after he'd "made peace" with it, which for him meant he stopped seeing it as a reminder and started seeing it as his leg. It had taken about a week.

He pressed the silver button on the inside of the carbon fiber socket that covered the stump of his thigh. He heard the light sigh as the suction released. He gave the charcoal-colored socket a tug and it popped off. He rolled down the silicone cuff and sealing ring and sighed as the damp but refreshing air hit his skin. He examined the skin and treated a bit of redness with the cream he kept beside his bed.

After his leg-care routine was over, he grabbed a bottle of beer from the tiny fridge he'd asked the guys to haul up here a couple weeks ago. Twisting off the cap and taking a long pull, he slid open his window and perched his butt on the ledge to look out at what he could see of the city through the heavy rain.

In the distance, he could see the ultra-bright glow of the two hotels they'd driven by, and his thoughts drifted to Stella again. The memory of the first time they'd met, seeing her bare legs crossed as she sat on the porch of the inn, was vivid. He could imagine her looking at his stump and being horrified.

Maybe that was unfair, but the only other woman he'd shown it to had been horrified. Not his sister. Summer's first question had been "What do you weigh now?" No, it had been Patricia who was horrified. When he'd shown it to her, she couldn't hide the flash of disgust that crossed her face. He'd shrugged it off, but it had added to the list of resentments that had been building in his mind.

"I never did like Patricia," Summer said when he'd told her he'd broken things off with her. He hadn't been able to tell her about Patricia's reaction for some reason, but regardless, Summer had never liked her. "Nothing matters to her but her restaurant. You're better off without her."

He tipped his beer up to his lips for another drink, and saw that he'd downed it in two gulps. *Just as well*, he thought as he set the bottle beside the fridge. The morning would come soon enough.

3

Stella gathered the linen napkin from her lap and placed it to the side of her coffee cup. The gentlemen across from her sipped their coffee, and from their expressions, they didn't seem to be enjoying it. She couldn't blame them. When she'd come down for an early breakfast on her own, the meal had been uninspiring. This mid-morning social meeting with coffee and pastries had been abysmal, as far as the food went. She should really stay to evaluate lunch, but she was determined to take Somchai up on his offer. She'd still be able to have dinner here tonight and get some more work done later.

"Pranyi," Stella addressed the petite dark-haired interpreter beside her. "Can you ask *Khun* Thanyoi if he would kindly arrange for a tour of the kitchens at his convenience?"

Pranyi relayed the message, and Mr. Thanyoi smiled and nodded graciously, his voice and gestures conveying agreement. "*Çhan yindi thî ca sædng hxng khraw.*"

"He would be honored to show you the kitchen," Pranyi said to her. Mr. Thanyoi spoke again, and Pranyi nodded. "He asks if tomorrow afternoon would be accommodating for you."

"That would be excellent, thank you." She tipped her head and pressed her hands together as Pranyi translated her response. "*Khau khun ka,*" she thanked them.

"Could you be available after lunch for the full afternoon? I'm not sure how long the tour will take, so I'd like to book you... I guess until after dinner tomorrow?" she asked Pranyi.

"Yes, Ms. Carmichael," Pranyi said, nodding politely. "I will meet you the same as today, in the lobby?"

"That would be perfect, thank you, Pranyi," she replied, and dipped her head in the traditional farewell. After Pranyi left the restaurant, she headed out in the opposite direction. She pondered whether she should change out of her blue silk dress. The long sleeves and high neck were fine for this air-conditioned restaurant, but she wasn't sure how comfortable it would be outside in the humidity. *And rain,* she thought as she looked through the window at the sheets cascading off everything in sight.

Screw it, she thought. There was an excitement in her that didn't want to take the slow elevator up to her room to change.

"Can you arrange a car to take me here?" she asked the lobby manager, holding out Somchai's business card. He nodded and led her to the curb. He waved up one of the waiting taxis, told the driver her destination, and returned the business card to her. "*Khau khun ka,*" she thanked him.

As the taxi made its way through the congested traffic to the main street, Stella searched through her bag for a hair elastic. In the sixty seconds since she'd gotten into the car, her hair was sticking to the back of her neck.

Motorcycles and tuk-tuks wove and darted through gaps in traffic, and all the drivers seemed to respect that smaller vehicles were free to move at will, as long as they didn't slow the flow. There were very few honks and no yelling. In fact, many of the drivers seemed to know each other and waved.

The rain continued to pour down and she could see ripples starting to spray around the tires of oncoming vehicles, the splashing sound of ground water adding to the hiss of the rain. With the rain, the humidity, and the water, she was thoroughly soggy by the end of the ten-minute ride.

"Thank you, *"Khau khun ka,"* she said to the driver. He waved her off when she tried to pay, saying *"Khun* Thanyoi." She took that to mean the ride was compliments of the men she'd just met.

Stella wove through the milling people on the sidewalk to the shelter of a straw-covered awning. A few men were installing a bamboo railing on the edge of a raised platform outside a very simple-looking restaurant. A glass door was propped open with customers trickling in and out. She assumed this was the right place, although she couldn't see a sign saying Malee or an address posted anywhere.

A delicious aroma enveloped her before she even entered the doorway. One thing she considered to be her secret power was her sense of smell. She couldn't cook worth a damn, but she knew when magic was happening in a kitchen. And she could tell at a glance—as she was doing now, looking at customers who were focused on eating plates of fabulous-looking food—when a chef with a vision was cooking.

"Ms. Stella Carmichael!" Somchai called from the back of the house. He hurried over and bowed to her, gesturing to a table against the wall of the narrow restaurant. "I knew you would be here for lunch."

"Hello, Somchai. I'm glad I could make it." She sat on the wooden chair at a small square table. On its top was an oval plaid plastic table covering, with a woven basket holding utensils in the center. Somchai pulled a simple two-sided menu out of his apron.

"Everything is good, but today the shrimp are very fresh, so I would suggest Tom Yum Soup."

"Then that's what I'll have. And green tea?" she asked, setting her shoulder bag on the chair beside her. When Somchai returned to the kitchen, she looked around and noted the large number of Thai customers. That was another good indicator of authenticity in the food offering.

At the back of the room, she saw a narrow window into the kitchen. From time to time, she could see Dex's head as he moved around. He was smiling and laughing with someone else. She assumed it was Carson, although she couldn't see him. Suddenly, Dex's head appeared and he was looking purposefully out into the restaurant. When his eyes found her, he smiled and waved. He turned to say something to someone and then disappeared. She waited to see if Carson would look out, but he didn't.

She swiveled in her seat so her back was against the wall. She could see both the restaurant and the outside, since the wall at the front of the restaurant was actually tall windows that folded open like shutters. Half of the windows were open, with customers seated in that section. The other half where men were working was blocked off. That's when she noticed almost all the customers were couples. Some sat with heads close, hands almost touching, engaged in shy but attentive conversation. Others were eating, but making constant eye contact.

She smoothed her skirt over her knees and swung back around, away from the customers. She pulled out her phone and got caught up on her e-mail. Jason had been hounding her by text to help him review a marketing strategy for his health food store chain. Despite it being Jason, it was satisfying to focus on something that took her attention from the couples around her.

"Here is your soup," Somchai said moments later, sliding a white plate with a white bowl of steaming beauty in front of her. The fragrant aroma floated up and she couldn't stop herself from closing her eyes and sighing loudly.

Five plump shrimp glistened on a bed of coiled noodles, surrounded by coconut milk and tomato broth. The scent of garlic and lemongrass spiraled up when she turned the bowl forty-five degrees. The kaffir lime leaves and sliced shiitake mushrooms added wonderful color to the savory soup.

"Heavenly," she said, smiling at Somchai. He nodded knowingly, as if to say "I told you so."

"You eat. Do you have time to see the kitchen after?" he asked.

"Absolutely!" She was thrilled that she didn't have to ask—she definitely wanted to see Carson at work. *Well, the Malee chefs at work,* she corrected herself.

Her first taste of the soup was simply beyond anything she'd experienced before. The scent primed her senses for the flavor explosion of the shrimp, which were plump and bursting with the perfect hint of what she guessed to be a lime and cilantro marinade. The broth was exquisite, and the chili heat was a perfect finish on her palate. *This is pure love*, she thought.

She knew without a doubt that Carson had made this. He didn't like her, and showing his skill was one way to put her in her place. But this... there was no denying his culinary expertise, or the passion he put into his cooking. Sure, he was rude and arrogant to her, but she would have questioned a *lack* of arrogance in someone with this level of skill.

"You liked the soup," Somchai stated when he returned. She looked at her empty bowl and saw that she had scraped every possible bit of sauce out of it. Normally, she didn't finish her meals. It was a habit her mother had encouraged, because to show appreciation was to show weakness. And to eat all of something showed a lack of restraint that bordered on gluttony. And above all, Marie Carmichael's daughter was *not* a glutton.

"Like is not the right word. I'm... in awe of the soup. It's spectacular!" she added, in case "in awe" didn't convey how completely she enjoyed it. In awe was exactly how she felt. She was a little nervous to go into the kitchen now and face Carson. She closed her eyes and pictured the look on his face when he'd asked her if she was looking for a marriage pact replacement. *Like I was slime*, she thought. Her fists clenched.

"Yes, spectacular," Somchai agreed, bringing her back to the present. "Come to the kitchen." He beckoned and walked to the back of the restaurant.

She grabbed her purse and followed Somchai to the back. A narrow doorway was blocked by a curtain of wooden beads. It turned out to be a hallway that led to the back of the narrow building. On the right was the service counter, and beyond that was the small kitchen.

"Carson and Dex." Somchai gestured with an open hand to the two men near the hot cooktop. Dex looked back to nod while he was moving a pile of greens back and forth with two flat spatulas. Carson stood adjacent to him, dipping a metal basket in and out of a tall pot that was separated into three sections. His strong hand moved confidently. His head flicked briefly back to her, but he didn't give any other acknowledgement. To his left was a longer gas cooktop, each element covered by woks in various sizes.

"What is Carson cooking?" she asked Somchai quietly, not wanting to disturb the men.

"Thai hot pot. Three different kinds of broth for different noodles and vegetables," he explained. "Right now, he's cooking Radna noodles in spicy broth."

She watched as Carson bobbed the basket up and down, and then pulled it out to shake it and check the consistency of the noodle. Then he lowered gently into the broth to repeat the process. His sleeves were rolled up, and the muscles in his tanned arms flexed and stretched as he worked. It did funny things to her stomach.

"That is Ekapol and Chaiya preparing vegetables." The young men at the back looked over with big smiles and nods. "Daw cleans. I serve," Somchai finished.

"Very nice," she admired. The tools were old and well used, but the kitchen itself was tidy and organized. She'd expected no less from someone of Carson's caliber.

"Would you sit in my office for a moment?" Somchai asked. When she nodded, Somchai said something in Thai to Carson. He looked at both of them with narrowed eyes, but he nodded.

They walked past the kitchen and a narrow flight of stairs to an office that was only big enough to hold an old desk and two chairs. A brown articulated screen served as a door. It was tied open by a piece of twine that looped around the screen and fastened to a hook on the right side of the wall. Somchai indicated that she sit down, and she did.

"Your family has a big hotel and resort company," he stated.

"Yes. Most of its properties are in the U.S., but there are a few in Asia. In China," she clarified.

"And you work on the restaurant side."

"Yes. I'm not involved with the property division at all. I work directly with investors that want to put money into restaurants. I evaluate the restaurants and draft the contracts."

"Do you think there is a market in the U.S. for Thai and Burmese fusion cuisine?" he asked, leaning forward with interest.

RECIPE FOR LOVE

"I think there's always a market for quality food, as long as there's good management to back it up. If you can bring something unusual on top of that, there's an excellent market for it," she said. Thai-Burmese fusion cooking sounded amazing to her. She was sure she could find investors back home for that. She was about to ask more, when Carson's large frame stepped into the doorway. The look on his face wasn't promising.

"Lunch rush is almost done. I'm going to head out to the school to make sure they're ready for their first class."

"Ms. Stella says there's a market for our style of cooking, because it's new," Somchai said. There was an "Ah-ha!" quality in his tone, which deepened Carson's frown.

"You know how I feel about expansion in the U.S. right now," he said, then pinned Stella with an angry look, "not interested."

"Discussion is just the start." Somchai got up to follow Carson when he turned and walked away. Somchai's voice faded but didn't stop, and she heard their footsteps go up the stairs.

Alone in the office, she wasn't sure of what to do. *Should I wait? For how long?* She got up and peeked out the doorway, and then banged her arm against the wall when her phone startled her.

"Christ, you startled me, Freddie," she accused, embarrassment at her reaction making her voice sharp.

"I'm not in control of whether or not your phone rings. It's what phones do," said Freddie, her tone dry.

"What do you want?" She decided to leave, since she had no idea when or if Somchai would come back down soon. She also didn't want to be there if Carson came back down even angrier than he'd gone upstairs. As she walked through the kitchen, she caught Dex's eye. "The food was delicious! Tell Carson and Somchai thank you," she whispered to him.

"You bet! See you later," he replied.

"I want to applaud you for ignoring Jason's calls," Freddie started, "but now he's calling me. He says you promised to review a marketing strategy for him. Is this true? Because I don't see anything about it on your schedule."

Stella groaned in annoyance. "I told him I would help him, but then I was hoping he'd forget. So I didn't add anything to the schedule."

"Let's add it to your schedule. That way I can manage him and you don't have to give in to him and his requests."

"Good idea. I think I have time tomorrow."

"How much time do you need? And what do you need from him?"

"Half an hour, and I need his business plan along with whatever his marketing strategy is. Hopefully, he's written it out instead of some thought he had after too many beers."

"It might be the latter, because he just called me and it's two in the morning here," she said the last few words very loudly.

"Ugh, I'm sorry, Freddie. I had no idea breaking things off with Jason would drag on like this."

"Let's just get him what he needs and then file a restraining order if he doesn't lighten up."

"Sounds good. Now go back to sleep. Everything here is under control."

Freddie disconnected, and Stella speed dialed the hotel to request a ride back. She thought about her jumpy stomach when she'd seen Carson in the kitchen. It must be the thrill of discovery. Finding high-caliber talent had only happened to her once before, and she always dreamed of it happening again. After tasting that soup, an excitement sizzled through her at the thought of bringing Malee to the U.S. It was a wild, scary, and wonderfully out of control prospect.

As she waited under the awning for her hotel taxi, she composed an e-mail to Freddie to find out who in their roster of investors had ever expressed an interest in neo-Asian cuisine.

4

Carson sat in the back of the truck taxi, his arms on his knees as he watched the city disappear behind him. They were zigzagging out of Chiang Mai on their way to Mae On and the homestay school. Instead of staying overnight, he decided he would stay a few extra days. He had to get rid of the anger that boiled in him, first when he saw Stella at the restaurant, and then when he argued with Somchai—yet again—about expansion.

Three other people were in the taxi with him. Two young men and an older woman. The two young men were examining Pete, his leg, with expressions of wonder. He'd opted to change into his favorite cargo shorts for the ride to Mae On and the school. The round metal of his knee joint was exposed, as was the calf-shaped pylon that attached to his foot, which fit into the right shoe of the Teva sandals he was wearing.

"That's cool," said one of the men, pointing.

"Thanks." He smiled.

Pete wasn't state of the art, but it worked perfectly for him. It might have only taken him a week to get used to the idea that Pete was a part of him, but it had taken a lot longer to learn how to put it on, take it off, and move and live with it. To really *see* it as a part of him.

He'd even been able to play slo-pitch with it back home in Cranberry Hill. Catcher, no less. His doctor had told him there would be certain things he'd find difficult, so when he joined the slo-pitch team, he'd chosen to play that position as a "screw you" to the world. With a couple accommodations in stance, he'd been able to pull it off.

Back in San Francisco, right before he'd left for Thailand the first time, a tattoo buddy offered to engrave the metal with intricate patterns. It's what the man across from him was pointing at.

"Cooking!" the man said, as he looked more closely at the design.

"That's right. I cook," Carson replied, turning his leg when the man tried to glimpse more of the art. His buddy had drawn a whisk, bowls, chopsticks, a sauté pan, and a lotus flower, all connected by curving wisps of steam in a dotted pattern. It wasn't unusual to meet other amputees in Chiang Mai, surprisingly, and most people only commented on his leg when they noticed the artwork. Being close to Myanmar, he'd learned there were still people who would accidentally step on long-forgotten landmines from past conflicts. Chiang Mai had a top-notch clinic sponsored by the Thai Royal Family that provided prosthetics free of charge to anyone in need. He'd visited the clinic a few times for adjustments.

As the truck continued to leave more of the city behind, his thoughts went back to Stella. It seemed she'd been in his thoughts on and off ever since he'd first seen her photo. That had been when Summer was researching Landis and his media company. She'd shown him photos on the Internet, and they'd all been glam shots of Landis and Stella at gala charity events, wearing tuxedos and glittery gowns.

He'd imagined Stella's days and nights full of do-nothing meetings and black-tie dinners, so when he'd found out she actually worked, he'd been surprised. He still doubted she did anything of value for her family's company. Probably matched up rich friends who thought it would be fun to own a restaurant.

But there'd been no denying that she was hot. Dex was right; he had a thing for redheads, and her shade of dark burnished auburn was his absolute Achilles' heel. Throw in pale, flawless skin that wouldn't do well in the hot Thai sun, and curves that all her tailored clothing accentuated.... Damn, another good reason not to think about her. But he knew better than to get involved with her, even for a one-time hook-up. He'd been down that road before with Patricia.

Patricia was a lot like Stella—a trust-fund baby with copper hair. She owned Charisma, a popular San Francisco restaurant her parents had bought her. It had been lust at first sight during his job interview, and they'd gotten together later that night, which probably broke a few employee/employer ethics boundaries. It had been a fun year, working and playing together, although the attraction had started to fade once they'd gotten their Michelin star. She'd gotten pretty bitchy with the staff, and once she started ordering him around, he knew it was just a matter of time before he'd want to break things off.

Then had come his baseball injury. First, the x-rays, and then the tests. And then the cancer diagnosis. It had been a scary time, and though Patricia tried to be supportive, he saw her pulling away. Then he'd shown her his stump for the first time. He couldn't ignore the look that came over her face. He didn't think he'd been very kind when he'd broken things off, either. In fact, he might have accused her of being a selfish bitch, if he recalled correctly.

Thank God for Summer. She'd ordered him to move north to Cranberry Hill and live with her in the barn loft that Katie and Mitch had renovated.

"*Hyud*," said the older woman, banging on the glass window of the cab and startling him out of his thoughts. He noticed they were well out of the city now, with rice fields across from him, and a treed landscape behind him. The truck slowed down and pulled over to the side of the road very close to a house. The older woman made her way toward where he sat, and he got out to help her down. "*Khau khun kah*," she thanked him in the singsong tone. He returned the greeting and climbed back into the truck.

They pulled back out onto the highway, the rain still coming down. Rivulets ran across the road, and the tires sent up a big spray, some of which floated into the back and got them wet. After another fifteen minutes, the two other men got up and left at their stop, smiling and saying goodbye to Carson. He was in the truck alone for the last twenty minutes of the ride.

The truck let him out at the outskirts of Mae On. He threw on his pack and started walking into the village to the school. He pulled out his phone and gave Dex a call.

"Hey, Dex" he said. "I'm going to be spending a couple more days here. Are you okay with that?"

"No problem. I've got everything I need, and the guys are awesome."

Carson hesitated, and then asked, "Is Somchai okay, or is he pissed?" He'd never known Somchai to be so frustratingly stuck on something the way he kept on about Stella helping them expand the business. He wondered if there was more to it. Maybe he'd call him later and talk it out.

"Nah, he's fine. Take all the time you need. Ekapol and I have everything locked down here."

Carson disconnected and put his phone in his pocket. The road into the village was narrow and paved, barely able to hold two compact cars passing each other. Usually one had to slow and pull over so they could both pass. He walked near the middle of the road, since water covered the thin dirt sidewalks. The rain had lightened, but he didn't care. The smells of dust and grass and warmth were rejuvenating. Sometimes in the city, the car fumes overwhelmed him. When he reached the Buddhist temple, he turned left and the school was two lots down on his right.

"Carson!" called Arjan. She was twenty-one years old and the daughter of Somchai's younger sister, Rosie. Meeting Somchai's family had been a vital part of them partnering on the restaurant. If the whole family didn't approve, it would have been a no-go.

"Hi!" he called, bracing himself when the young woman ran to him and jumped into a warm hug. They'd connected since the day they met, when Arjan told Somchai about her idea to add cooking to the English classes they taught. It had instantly become a project closer to his heart than the restaurant.

"I didn't think you would come. It's raining so much we might not have classes tomorrow," Arjan said excitedly, linking her arm in his and pulling him into the covered area of the property. Carson and Arjan walked into the outdoor living area. Wide banners were draped over rough timbers above, with strategic collection points and drains taking most of the water away. A few drips made it through, but both of them knew where to walk to avoid the puddles.

There were two buildings on the property. Ahead of them as they walked through the wood and cushioned couches was the largest one, the bunk building, and the only one that had two floors. On the bottom floor was an open space where guests would sit and listen as the family played traditional Thai instruments. Rosie had her bedroom near the front, and Taja—her mother and Arjan's grandmother—had a smaller bedroom at the back. Taja was visiting family in the next village, so he wouldn't get to visit with her. The top floor was the guest sleeping area. It was a rustic sleeping room with many thin mattresses and mosquito netting, but not much else.

To the left of the bunk building was the open-air kitchen, which was actually tucked under the high roof that extended from the bunk building. The second building was to the left of the open living room. Rosie called it the shed, although it was much larger than the name implied. It housed dry food goods, emergency water, and costumes and other musical instruments when they had outdoor performances. Beyond that were fuchsia plants, bamboo, and a few rubber trees, tapped long ago of all their rubber sap.

"Tell me about this man you brought from San Francisco," Arjan requested. "Is he funny, or is he serious like you?"

"He's funny... like me. Don't you think I'm funny? I think I'm pretty funny."

"Well... *that* is funny."

"What?"

"That you think you're funny." She covered her mouth as she giggled. He gave her a stern look but ended up laughing with her. He didn't have that much of a sense of humor, he decided. Although he used to.

He pulled open the screen door that led to the sleeping quarters and threw his backpack onto the stairs. He let the door slam shut.

"Let's go check out what you've done in the kitchen," he said. He pulled a bandana out of his cargo pants pocket and tied it around his head to hold his hair back. "And while we work, tell me the latest man your mom has picked out for you. And why you don't think he's perfect," he teased.

Arjan was so much like his sister. Summer was independent, funny, loved his cooking even if it was plain rice, and was easy to tease. Arjan was the third of five siblings. She had two older sisters and two young brothers. With her sisters married with children, and her brothers younger by several years, she'd adopted Carson as an older brother. He thought it was because he never bullshitted her. He always gave her the truth, and she seemed to appreciate it.

"Oh my goodness, Carson." Arjan rolled her eyes as she pulled boxes of cooking pans and utensils from under the work stations that were set up in a square. "She's picked out Jai. He lives near the mushroom farm. He's going to start college next year to get a teaching certificate."

"What's wrong with that?" he asked. As Arjan continued to pull out boxes, he circled the cooking area to check the propane level for each small stove. "You have a teaching certificate. And your name is Thai for teacher. Maybe you're destined for each other." He prepared for the jab in the ribs she gave him.

"I don't like him like that. I don't like any boys like that. I'm never getting married. My sisters got married, and all they do is cook and clean and run errands and look after children.... That is not for me." She stacked all the like items on one counter, and then turned the taps on in a large basin beside it, which was set up against the wall of the bunk building.

"Why don't you explain it that way to Rosie? Maybe she'll leave you alone," he suggested.

"I tried that. She doesn't listen. Hey!" She spun around to look at him, her eyes wide. "Maybe you could talk to her? She listens to you about everything."

"Huh," he grunted. "Nobody seems to be listening to me lately."

"Who's not listening to you?"

"Well, your uncle for one. A woman from the United States wants him—us—to open a restaurant there. I know he wants to do it, but we agreed not to consider anything like that until next year." He went to the back of the kitchen, where the aprons and linens were hanging, and started splitting them up into piles.

"Ooo, a woman!" she said. "Tell me about her. Is she pretty? Is she smart? I should call my uncle and find out what he thinks about her."

"No!" he replied abruptly. "I shouldn't have said anything. She's annoying. In fact, I'm going to stay here a few extra days so I can avoid her. Maybe she'll have left the country by the time I get back."

Arjan clapped her hands excitedly. "I'm glad you're staying. But what makes her annoying? Explain to me."

"She's rich, she's conceited, and she doesn't listen when people tell her they don't want to do something. I have more, but that's enough."

"Being conceited and not listening are bad. Being rich is not necessarily bad. But you didn't say if she was pretty or smart. Is she?" She added soap to the sink and filled the basin with the pots and pans and utensils.

"Sometimes a person's traits make them unattractive," he started, but couldn't deny the truth. "She's actually quite beautiful. She has long red hair, although I don't know if it's real or not. I don't know if she's smart. I mean, she works for her family's business, so I guess she's not entirely an idiot." He shrugged.

"Now that's funny," she said. "It sounds like you like her but don't *want* to like her. Do you want to have sex with her?" Arjan asked.

He was shocked. They'd never talked about sex before, either specifically or generally. He almost didn't answer, not sure if this kind of discussion would be culturally acceptable. But then he decided not to hold back. "I guess part of me does, but another part of me knows it's just opening a can of worms. Do you know the expression 'opening a can of worms'?"

"Gross. Who would want to open a can with worms in it?" She grimaced as she washed a pot and then placed it in the rinse basin.

"Yeah, that's pretty close to what it means." He laughed.

"Having sex with her would be gross?" she asked.

"Well..." A vision of Stella at the airport flashed through his mind, when a few strands of her hair had been curled damply against her cheek, her blouse had been wet, and her skirt clung to her legs. He shook his head to clear the visual away. "I think the headaches that come afterward would be gross. The way you feel about being married."

"Why would there have to be an afterward? Couldn't you just do the sex and then leave? You could tell her 'it's just for the sex,' and if she agreed, then there wouldn't be an afterward." She looked at him and shrugged, as if to say it wasn't rocket science.

"I suppose so," he said. "I just think sometimes it's better to not even start."

After he laid the last bundle of linens at a cooking station, he looked over to see her smiling. "What?" he asked.

"I think you're afraid of this pretty woman. This fire-haired woman. I never thought a woman would scare you."

"I'm not scared," he denied as he walked over to the pantry to the left of the wash station where Arjan stood. Although he had to admit, a few years ago he would have totally been trying to pick her up—rich, snobby socialite or not. He'd never been afraid of a challenge. Not that he was afraid now. He frowned.

"I can tell what you're thinking, Carson," she said in a teasing voice. "You're thinking 'Oh my goodness, I *am* afraid!' I am going to call my uncle and tell him to bring this Fire Woman out here." She laughed out loud. Carson turned and shook a stalk of lemongrass at her.

"You call your uncle and I'm going to tell your mom that you're secretly excited to get to know Jai." He smiled when he saw the laughter fade out of her face.

"Never mind," she relented, turning back to wash the utensils.

"Never mind what?" Rosie called from the living area. They heard the click-click of her bicycle, and then the clank as she leaned it against the other bikes by the storage shed.

"Nothing!" Arjan called, firing a warning look at him.

"Nothing!" he chimed in, winking at Arjan.

"The highway is blocked," Rosie said as she walked into the kitchen and gave first Arjan and then Carson a welcoming hug. "It washed out."

"That's good. Maybe Carson will have to stay longer," Arjan replied. She pulled the plug on the sink to drain the water and then started drying the pots and utensils.

"It might mean we don't have a class tomorrow," Rosie added, disappointed. "And it's our first one!"

"It might just be a smaller class," he supposed, and then his phone rang with a sound he didn't recognize. He pulled it from his back pocket and the screen said Unknown Caller.

"Hello?" he answered.

"You need to come and get me." Stella's voice came through shrilly, even though static flooded the line. He was speechless. How did she have his number? "Are you there? Carson? Carson! Can you hear me?"

"Um… come and get you? I'm not in Chiang Mai any more. If you need a ride, call a cab."

"I took a cab. I'm stuck on the highway. I mean the cab is literally stuck on the highway. It might even be washed away by the time you get here."

Again, he was speechless. *What the hell?* "Where exactly are you?" he finally asked. Both Arjan and Rosie were staring at him with questioning eyes.

"I told you, on the highway. To Mae On to see you."

"What? Why? What's going on, Stella?" He was angry now, even more so when he saw Arjan cross her arms and grin at him.

"Somchai said you wanted to talk to me and gave me your address."

"I don't want to talk to you. Or see you," he insisted, covering his eyes with his free hand.

"What?" Now she sounded confused, and he realized this was some game Somchai was playing. "Look, can we figure this out later? Right now, I'm in a car that has water swirling in the door. It's like we drove into a river."

"Where on the highway are you? What's nearby?" he asked. Moving the phone away, he looked at Rosie. "Can I borrow Lao's truck?"

"I'm sure you can," she said, frowning and nudging Arjan when she giggled. "Is everything okay?"

He held up a finger, but nodded when Stella started talking again. "There's a rice field on one side, and on the other is a big house with flags and a whole bunch of poles with models of houses or temples on them." She sounded confused and annoyed and a little scared.

"Okay, I know where you are. Are you safe in the car?"

"I think so. The driver keeps making phone calls and says we're okay, but I don't really know what's going on."

"All right, I'll be there in about fifteen minutes."

"Okay," she said and disconnected.

"What's going on?" Rosie asked. "Who was that on the phone?"

"It was the Fire Woman Carson doesn't want to only have sex with." Arjan laughed, her voice getting louder when Carson scowled.

5

Stella sat in the back seat of the car and watched her phone. She'd started a timer to countdown from fifteen minutes, and it now had only three minutes left to go. She'd explained to the driver that help was coming, and he'd smiled and nodded. He'd continued to make calls, but she couldn't really tell what he was saying.

They'd been driving along the highway making good time, but occasionally streams of water crossing the highway would make them slow down. When the driver didn't, huge fans of water shot out either side of the car.

"Can you go a little bit faster? I have a meeting," she'd asked the driver. When Somchai had called her to say Carson wanted to talk to her at the school, she'd assumed the school would be in town and it would be a quick trip. She hadn't taken the time to change clothes, because she didn't want Carson to change his mind about talking. The next thing she knew, they were heading out of the city. She'd double-checked the written address with the driver, but he'd only nodded and smiled, pointing down the highway.

And then he'd driven right into a washout. To give him credit, he had been making excellent time after she'd told him to go faster. And most of the water streaming across the highway had only been a couple inches deep. As she looked out her window at the churning stream that was still seeping in the bottom of her door, she realized he'd guessed wrong about this one.

He'd sped right into it and the car had bounced as if going over rocky terrain, given a loud *clunk*, and then the back end had sunk down, stopping the car entirely. Something bad had happened, because when he tried to accelerate, the engine revved but the car didn't move at all. Then the driver said the one thing she understood.

"Uh oh."

Just as her phone was fifteen seconds from zero, the driver said "*Du!*" and pointed out the windshield. A beat-up white pickup truck approached the far side of the washout and stopped. She reached down for her bag and pushed her door open against the swirling water. It rolled over the opening and splashed her feet, but only filled a few inches of the floor before the flow slowed down.

"*Kheau kalang ma!*" the driver said, and Stella looked up to see Carson about twenty feet away, carefully making his way across the washout. He wore a white T-shirt and had a red bandana tied around his head. He was being very deliberate with each step, which was frustrating, but since her view blocked him from the waist down, she couldn't tell how deep the water was. Maybe he was being smart, especially if the ground was broken bits of asphalt, but she still thought he could be a bit quicker.

"He's taking his time," she muttered under her breath. Looking at her heels, she realized he'd have to carry her. If he was on uneven ground, it would be worse for her. Suddenly, she wondered if she should have called Somchai instead.

"All right, princess," he said as he walked around her open door. "Let's figure out how to get you out of here." She looked up at him, then to the hand he held out, then to a glint of silver. She didn't know what she was looking at for a second, and then the reality of his prosthetic leg sank in. She looked back at his face, to see his expression had hardened. She put a hand on her chest, not sure what to say. She was shocked and confused, and surprisingly speechless. Her eyes dropped back to his leg as she struggled to say something.

"Here, have a better look," he said, and planted his foot squarely on the door opening, and she scooted backward. An arc of water came with it, spraying her legs.

"Hey, watch it!" she shouted, unable to temper her reaction. Weirdly, this seemed to satisfy him. She glanced down and saw a crude, pal foot strapped into a sandal.

"C'mon." He waved at her small purse and she handed it to him. He draped the thin strap over his head so it lay across his chest and stepped his leg back into the water. "Let's go." He waved again at her hand, and she put it in his. The warmth of it closed over hers, engulfing it, and again she was without words. "Scoot, scoot, c'mon." He sounded impatient as she hopped her butt closer to the door.

"You can't carry me," she stated, as he maneuvered farther away to give her some room to get out.

"You can't walk," he replied, looking disdainfully at her heels. "Not in those things. But if you want to try, you can. It would make my life easier."

She hesitated, not knowing what to do. She didn't like that, because she always knew what to do.

"*Chan chuy khun dai mi?*" Carson leaned down to ask the driver. The driver answered and Carson nodded, pointing to his truck. She watched as the driver got out and also carefully walked through the water and over the uneven ground of the washout.

She looked back at Carson, who was leaning on the car door, waiting with a raised eyebrow and a bored look. "You could always camp out here. The rain will eventually stop and they'll repair the road. Although the water could be up to the windows by then," he smirked.

"You're insufferable," she muttered, reaching out her hand and waiting for him to take it before she moved. She looked down at the swirling water and back to him. "How do we do this?" she clipped out.

"Duck your head," he said, and suddenly she was scooped up and in his arms. Her arms automatically wrapped around his shoulders, and her cheeks burned as his hands adjusted against her thigh and waist.

He paused to check his footing and then slowly stepped one foot at a time, first backing away from the car, and then heading to his truck. He sometimes felt ahead with one foot before stepping, and she tensed, holding tighter.

"Don't be a baby," he scolded when his foot slipped a little and she made a tiny gasp.

"I'm not being a baby. Just pay attention to what you're doing."

"That's what I'm trying to do. Why don't you try to stay silent while I rescue you? Or is that even possible?"

She felt a little hysteria rising up and tried to breathe through it. It didn't work. "You know, you're a jackass!"

"How am I the jackass here? Who drove out to the country in torrential rain wearing heels?"

"I didn't know the highway would be washed out! I thought Mr. Asshole Chef wanted to talk about business, so I thought I would be accommodating!" Her knees jerked on the last word, and his feet slipped.

"Don't!" he gritted, finding his balance again. "Can you be still for two minutes? Just two minutes! Can you do that, for the love of God?" he muttered.

She complied, stubbornly holding her body away from his as much as she could. The rain had become a fine mist, and she could feel it coating her navy silk dress. By the time they were across the washout, her dress would be soaked. Other than her business earlier today, this whole trip was feeling like a washout. It made her want to throw something.

"Don't worry. We're almost there," he said, making her scowl.

"I'm not worried," she said stubbornly.

"I get it. A one-legged guy is carrying your rich ass across a torrential stream and could drop you at any minute. Absolutely nothing to worry about."

"Is this a ploy to get me to feel sorry for you? Because I don't. Wait, I *do* feel sorry that you're a jerk."

"Why am I the jerk? I'm out here saving you."

"You're a jerk, because for some reason that I had nothing to do with, you hate me. If I did something to hurt you, fine. But I've done nothing to you."

He was silent, which made her think she'd finally silenced him. *Good*, she thought. After three more careful steps, she felt one leg lift a bit higher to the other side of the washout. Just as his second foot stepped up, she squirmed out of his arms and landed on the pavement. Her arm and hip and thigh felt suddenly cold from where they had touched him. He looked down at her with his cool gray eyes, his face expressionless.

"I don't hate you. Get in the car." And without waiting for a response, he gave her the small purse, walked past her, and got into the truck. She did as he asked, wordlessly getting in on the left-hand side and squishing against the taxi driver, who sat smiling in the middle.

※

THEY DROPPED BAHN, THE DRIVER, OFF AT THE OTHER SIDE OF THE small village. Then Carson circled back, past a gilt Buddhist temple that had wrought iron fencing on top of a beige stucco wall, and dropped her off at a covered driveway.

"This is the school. Go through there. Arjan and her mom Rosie are inside. They'll get you settled," he said, leaning over to point out her window. "I have to return the truck."

"What do you mean, 'settled in'? I'm not staying."

"Uh, yeah. You're staying. Did you see the washout back there?"

"Yes, I saw the washout." She rolled her eyes. "Doesn't someone around here have a bigger truck that can drive through it?"

He stared at her, his forehead creasing as if she'd posed the most difficult question in the world. "Go," he said, and leaned across her to pull the latch on her door and shove it open.

With a frustrated grunt, she swung her legs out and slammed the door. He was already driving away before it closed completely. "What an asshole," she grumbled. She walked down the driveway and came to a covered outdoor living room. There were low shelves and two couches that faced each other over a wooden coffee table. To the right was a long table with benches that looked like it could seat ten or more. Straight ahead was a large wooden building, and to the left of it was a big kitchen area.

"*Sa wat dee ka,*" two women called to her, waving her over. "I am Arjan," said the younger one with glossy long black hair in a braid. She wore a faded blue cotton tunic with frog-loop closures. "This is my

403

mother, Rosie." She gestured to an older woman who could have been her twin. The only difference was she had short black hair and a few more lines around her eyes. She wore a similar tunic, only in dark brown.

"*Sa wat dee ka*," she returned the greeting and gave the traditional *wai*. "My name is Stella Carmichael."

"I'm sorry you got stranded by the rain. We have no guests staying, so you can stay here until you have a way to get back to Chiang Mai."

"I appreciate that. But is there nobody with a big truck?"

"There's only that one truck in the village, the one you came here in."

Stella felt a twinge of anxiety. She was supposed to meet with the people from Central Group tomorrow and tour their kitchen. And then visit their other location. She had to arrange a final meeting and conference call the Monticello people in, and set the preliminary terms, and then fly home. She also had to review Jason's marketing strategy and talk to him. She pulled at the silk fabric at her throat and tried to keep her breathing from turning into a panicked pant.

"I'm back!" Carson announced, walking into the kitchen from a path in the back. He opened a cupboard beside a sink and started stacking some ingredients on one of the workstations.

Normally, she'd be intrigued by the school and the teaching kitchen, but despite her efforts, a pressure built in her chest.

"Is there a restroom?" she asked, trying to keep her face still. It felt jittery and her eyes were darting all around but not seeing anything.

"Yeah, this way," Carson said, and she blindly followed him back through the living room to the other side of the big building. It was a short walk to the bathroom at the end. He pointed and stepped back for her to enter. It had a mirror and sink, and a squat toilet against the far wall. Beside it was a tub of water and a scoop. She turned to look at him and saw his smug expression. She watched as it changed to a frown. "Are you okay? You look sick."

"I'm fine," she replied sharply, and closed the door on him. She turned on a tap and held her hands under the cool water. She felt waterlogged from the rain, but her hands were hot and her head was swimming, and she hoped this might help.

And it did. Once her hands were cool, she pressed them on her neck and the dizziness faded away. She looked at the squat toilet and decided to take advantage of that while she was in here. She knew Carson thought a 'rich girl' like her would be horrified, but she'd been in China enough times to get used to them.

When she was done, she stepped down and scooped some water from the bucket into the toilet, letting gravity do its work. She washed her hands and went outside where Carson was waiting for her. He held a stack of clothing out to her.

"You can change out of your wet clothes here, or go around the corner and up to the second floor. That's where we'll sleep." He turned to walk away and then paused to look back. "Nobody stays for free, so when you're dressed, report to the kitchen." He gave her a smug smile, and it was all she could do not to flip him off.

6

Carson expected Stella to pout and delay and eventually show up just in time to eat dinner, but after only a few minutes, she walked into the kitchen. Of course she totally ignored him and went over to Arjan.

"I'm ready to work for my supper," she said, sounding cheerful.

Arjan pointed to a cutting board and a bowl of small green eggplants. She explained about cutting them into slices, and Stella picked up the knife and got to work.

He tried to focus on his own task of grinding cloves of garlic and shallots in a mortar and pestle, but he couldn't stop glancing at Stella. The clothing matched what Arjan was wearing, although the frog loops strained over her chest, and the pants, which hung loose on the younger woman, seemed to hug Stella's curvy hips.

"No." Arjan laughed, picking up a knife and choosing a round eggplant from the bowl. "Watch." Stella stopped to watch Arjan swiftly slide the knife through and then turn each piece to quickly quarter them. She pushed a strand of her auburn hair behind her ear, and he could see a fairly large looking diamond sparkle. "One long slice. Don't push; glide the knife. Right, Carson?" Arjan looked over to him with a twinkle in her eye, smug that she'd caught him staring at Stella.

"That's how the pros do it," he said, looking back to the mash of garlic and onion in front of him, willing his expression to be blank. He emptied the paste into a glass bowl and added more to the mortar, continuing to pound the vegetables while he listened to the women talk.

"Your fingernails are beautiful," Arjan said longingly, as she watched Stella pick another eggplant and try to slice it as she'd been told. "They're so thick and shiny. Is it hard to do?"

"It doesn't seem to be," Stella said absently, slicing away. She picked another eggplant and sliced it more quickly. "I'm getting the hang of this!" she chirped happily. She smiled at Arjan, who was looking at her questioningly. "Oh, I meant I don't do my own nails. I get them done, so it's very easy for me."

"I would like to get mine done like that someday."

"If you want my advice—" Stella continued slicing. "—don't do it. These are gel nails, and they basically suffocate your real nail. My nails are in such bad shape I have no choice but to get them done regularly."

"Suffocate them?"

Stella put her knife down and held out her hand. "Give me your hand." Arjan immediately held it out. "See how strong your nails are?" Carson could hear her flick Arjan's nails, making a clicking sound. "If I didn't have gel nails, mine would bend right over like paper. And look." Stella held out her hand palm up, and pointed to the underside of her fingernails. "See how discolored they are? They've been painted so many times I'd have to let them grow out for months and months to get them back to normal."

"But mine are so plain," Arjan said, holding her own hands out.

"No, yours are beautiful. Don't let my nails fool you." Stella's smile looked kind as she went back to slicing.

"Are those eggplants sliced yet?" he asked. Arjan was getting too friendly with the enemy, in his opinion.

"Yes, chef!" Stella called out, finishing the last one with two expert slices. Arjan giggled when Stella made a big show of bringing the bowl of slices over to him. "That was fun. What else can I do?" she asked.

"For someone whose business is the restaurant industry, you're not that skilled in the kitchen." Watching her chatting easily with Arjan made him feel testy, and for some reason, he wanted to make her feel the same way. But it didn't work.

"I'm terrible in the kitchen," she agreed, putting her hands on her cheeks and grimacing. "It's quiet embarrassing actually. But I know the business side of things. And I know what quality food is."

"So you're ready for your next task?" he asked. He scraped the garlic and onion paste into the glass bowl, and watched as she looked at it with excitement. "See that bin over there?" He pointed to a red tub on the other side of the kitchen. Various stalks and stems hung over the side.

"Yes," she replied, walking around and picking it up. She looked back at him with confusion in her eyes.

"Go to the back and feed that to the chickens," he said. He laughed out loud at her grumpy expression. Arjan laughed too.

"That's right; chickens have to be fed," Arjan told her with a smile and pointed to the path that led out back.

Stella narrowed her eyes at him, but trudged out as ordered. He caught the corners of her mouth turn up slightly. He prepped the rest of the ingredients for their meal and was ready when she returned.

"Put this back over here?" she asked as she walked over to where the tub had been.

"Yes," he said, wiping his hands on a towel. "Are you ready to learn?"

She kept her face blank, but he definitely saw her eyes light up. "Yes."

Arjan left to do some laundry, and he led Stella through a simple lesson to make *Nam prik ong*. She was very careful, almost fearful, and he saw a lot of himself when he was first learning. Something about her felt softer and more approachable. And he felt something in himself soften too.

The four of them sat on pillows on the main floor of the bunkhouse and ate. They all shared about their days—Rosie worked at the purse factory on the other side of the village and Arjan had cleaned and prepped most of the day, which looked like it might be for nothing if the cooking students cancelled. Most of them lived outside Mae On. Stella was surprisingly quiet.

"I had a work meeting and then came here," was all she said. He'd expected her to go on about a busy day full of busy things and then ending with nearly being swept away in a 'flood.'

"Are you missing much by having to stay here?" he asked. He saw a look cross her face that he couldn't identify.

"A bit. Which reminds me, I should check in on e-mail. I'm glad there's good cell reception here." He watched her get up with her bowl and leave the room. He could hear water run in the kitchen and the ceramic bowl being placed on the counter.

"I like the Fire Woman," Arjan whispered. Rosie nodded too.

"She's a nice woman," Rosie agreed. "Too fancy, maybe too... bound up, but nice."

He grunted and finished up the food in his bowl. Both women were looking at him.

"What?" he said, maybe a little defensively. "So she's nice. But you just met her. Don't complain to me when she freaks out about having to sleep on the floor upstairs," he muttered.

"I bet she won't," Arjan said.

Rosie smiled at her daughter and then looked over at Carson and gave a slight shrug. "She might," she whispered, making Carson chuckle.

The three of them returned to the kitchen to clean their dinner things. Stella was in the living room, her phone giving her face a bluish glow as she alternately read and typed. After fifteen minutes, she quietly joined them, taking the rinsed items and drying them with the thin towels hanging near the sink.

"Goodnight, Stella," Arjan said, and gave her a hug. Stella looked uncertain and then uncomfortable, but she returned her hug with pink cheeks. Rosie bowed in the traditional way and wished them a good night. The two women entered the door to the ground floor of the bunk building.

"We're up there," he told her, leading the way upstairs with her slowly following with tired steps.

The top floor was a huge open room with support posts at regular intervals. Seven large but thin mattresses were spread out in equal distances on the wood-plank floor, each with its own mosquito netting and piled linens, pillows, and blankets. Glassless windows with wooden shutters looked down to the kitchen on one side and the open living room at the front.

He went to the far wall where he normally slept, and noticed Arjan had made up the mattress right next to his for Stella. "If you prefer to sleep on one of the other mattresses, you won't hurt my feelings."

"I'm too tired to care," she said, lifting the mosquito netting and flopping on the mattress. "I'm too tired to even care about brushing my teeth. If I had a toothbrush that is," she groaned.

"You can borrow mine if you want." He picked up his small case of toiletries and looked over at her. She lay on her back, eyes closed, and her hair spilled all around her head on the white pillow. She looked like a painting.

She lifted a hand and murmured, "It's okay." It was hard to look away from her, but he finally turned and went downstairs to the bathroom to clean up.

He expected her to be asleep, but as he got to the top of the stairs, he saw the glow of her phone lighting her profile as she lay on her side. He lifted his netting and crawled over his mattress to set his case down.

"I have a whole process to do with Pete, so if he makes you uncomfortable, you should roll over," he warned her, stretching his legs out on the mattress and getting ready to start the process of removing the prosthetic. She didn't say anything, and when he glanced over, he saw a puzzled look on her face. "Pete is my leg," he explained.

"You named your leg?"

"Yeah. It seemed like the right thing to do, since we were going to be living together."

"I had a client who had a tumor on his ear, and he named it Glen," she said, and then slapped a hand over her eyes and rolled onto her back. He couldn't hold back a startled laugh, and then he really laughed while she peeked at him from under her hand. "Thank goodness you laughed! I really didn't mean to compare your... Pete to a cancerous tumor." She laughed as well and rolled back to look at him with a shy smile.

"It's close. I hurt my knee playing baseball, and the x-rays showed something odd, and that's when they found the cancer. The cancer part is kind of similar."

"I don't feel uncomfortable about Pete," she said, putting her phone to sleep and laying it on her mattress. "But I admit it caught me by surprise at the taxi." She watched him steadily and he shifted self-consciously on his mattress. "Can I ask you a question?"

"Yes, but I get to ask you one too."

"Okay." She smiled, and his breath hitched suddenly. Her smile—her real smile—was stunning, even in the dim light. "What was it like, to lose a part of your body?"

He pressed the valve on his leg to release the vacuum and thought about her question. He didn't mind questions; the irritating part was usually how people dealt with his answers.

"Hearing you have cancer is upsetting. Just hearing the word caused this panicky feeling. I remember wanting to know why I got it, and why no one else in my family did. As if that would have made anything better." He remembered his anger that *he* was afflicted with this, even though his sister had just been in the hospital herself, dealing with a leg wound of a different kind.

"And then they tell you they have to operate, which I expected. But then they say they have to take your leg. I guess I thought they could somehow remove the cancer and put a pin in my leg. But the cancer had been through my knee joint and down the tibia. Amputation was the least complicated and most recoverable surgery."

"So you were okay with it?" Her eyes were wide.

"Oh, no. Not at all. It took a week of constant conversations with my oncologist, a lot of yelling from my sister, and finally a second opinion to help me face reality."

He pulled the socket off and rolled the sheath down and off. He was self-conscious again, but the air on his exposed skin felt too good, and he lay back with a long sigh. "That is the most amazing feeling." When she remained silent, he continued talking, keeping his eyes closed. "I finally saw that amputating my leg was the best course of action. But it really hit me was post-surgery, looking down at the bed and only seeing one leg. It was hard. It was really hard," he finished.

He wondered what she would say. Most people expressed some

level of remorse or sadness, and he ended up having to console them. Which was aggravating, because they had both their legs. But Stella didn't say anything. When he finally rolled his head to see if she'd fallen asleep, she was looking at him with a tiny compression of her lips.

"What's your question for me?" was all she asked.

He thought back to something he'd noticed on the flight over here. "When I mentioned Landis's and my sister's wedding, you seemed to... tense up. And you said something about them being... how did you put it? "Pathetically in love." What's up with that?"

Now it was Stella's turn to roll to her back and let out a long sigh. "I guess because, basically, I don't believe in love. My mother and father married because they were a good match. Both families had money and they were raised from an early age that marrying in their social circle is what you did. The only marriages I've seen that work are partnerships. And when I've known people who "fell in love," it ended with cheating or incompatibility or drinking issues."

"So you don't believe Landis and Summer are in love?" he asked, leaning on his elbow. He wished he could see her expression better.

She let out another long sigh, rubbing her temples with her fingers. "No, I can't deny that they're in love."

"Are you upset that your marriage pact is broken?" he pushed. He felt like he had to know and he didn't know why he cared about it.

"Hey, what happened to just getting one question?" she asked, and he heard something in her voice. Nervousness. *Is she hiding something?* he wondered.

"You're right, my bad. But let me give you an extra answer to be fair. My parents were in love. They married for love, and stayed in love until the day they died." He saw her stretch her arm up and roll over to face him, her head cradled on her arm.

"Landis said they died when you and Summer were teenagers."

"I was sixteen. I remember being glad they died together. They were so in sync that sometimes Summer and I felt like we were a third wheel. But they also loved us unconditionally, so it wasn't anything you could be resentful about. I tell you, I've never seen a love like that. Maybe Landis and Summer have it. I don't know."

"Yeah, maybe," she said, but he could tell she was being polite. "That's why I think finding a good partner and friend... well, it seems more achievable than true love."

"Or a soul mate. My last girlfriend told me I was hers." His voice trailed off. He'd seen actual soul mates up close. That was a once in a lifetime thing, or once in a few lifetimes. "Anyway, we have a lot to do tomorrow, so you should get some sleep."

"When will the road be fixed?"

"Things can move pretty slow, but if the rain lets up..." He paused when a rumble of thunder echoed in the distance. "They might be able to patch it by tomorrow night, maybe the next morning."

She rolled to her back, and he could see the shine of her eyes as she stared up at the wood-paneled ceiling. "Another day. The world won't fall apart in a day, right?" She said it so quietly he had to strain to hear the words.

"It shouldn't," he replied, and rolled onto his back as well. He marveled that just this morning he'd been hoping she'd finish her business and leave the country so he wouldn't have to see her again. He heard her moving around and turned to look at her. She arched her back as if she was stretching, and then moved into what looked like a self-hug. She gave a soft grunt and then pulled something out from one sleeve and then another. Lifting her netting, she dropped a purple lace bra onto the floor.

"Ahhh," she sighed, tugging her blanket up. "Probably not as close to your feeling, but getting there." She laughed quietly.

His eyes were fixed on the lace. He could detect her faint fragrance in the air that her movements stirred. When he closed his eyes, he imagined molecules of warmth from her body heat touching his face. *Getting there*, he thought to himself, and willed himself to fall asleep.

7

She sat on the vinyl backseat of the taxi, the water at window level. It was caramel-brown and sluggish, and as it inched higher, the interior of the cab darkened. Then she heard a rush of bubbles, and walking slow motion through the water was Carson. He was sharply visible despite the murky water. He raised his hand and pounded on the window, and the sound moved as slowly as a recording played on the wrong speed—*thuummp, thuummp.*

She was scared. Instead of opening the door, she rolled down the window. Somehow, she was sucked through the opening and torpedoed through muddy-tasting water, hands extended above and being pulled by an invisible source. When she surfaced, the water was only calf-deep. She wore a sheer tiny slip, surrounded by gray sky, gray water, and gray mist. Her feet sunk into silty muck, and a wind whipped goose bumps up on her body. The wind picked up, and the cold mud swallowed more of her legs—up to her calves now. She moaned, waiting for the mud to suck her down.

Arms reached around from behind her and she spun, wanting the warmth of the broad chest she felt. It was Carson. His eyes gleamed silver, pinning her, demanding that she understand words he wasn't speaking. Suddenly, his hands were tugging her hair and he was saying "Oyster mushrooms."

"Stella, wake up," Carson whispered, and her eyes opened to see the silver eyes in her dream fade to a light gray. His face seemed only inches from her, but when she moved her arms so she could put her hands on his cheeks, she had to fully extend them.

"You got me out," she said, moving her feet under the covers, relieved there was no mud. His face was getting bigger, and she realized she was pulling him closer to her.

His eyes flashed back to silver and widened. His hands had been in her hair and now clenched, tightening every strand against her scalp. She focused on his lips. They were parted, soft, and pink. She expected to feel his breath puffing lightly against her own lips, but she didn't think he was breathing. Then she realized she wasn't breathing either. And then their lips were touching. She felt a small quiver and couldn't tell if it was her lips shaking or his. A loud noise from the kitchen broke them apart.

"Oh," she gasped, shooting up straight as he pushed back to crouch awkwardly at the end of her mattress. His body was tense, as if he was on the verge of diving to safety. His eyes were riveted on her, and she realized whatever she said next would set the tone for everything that came after this moment. And then, without thinking anything through, said, "That was the best-ever ending to a nightmare I've ever had." And then she laughed.

Carson's body relaxed and a smile crept over his face. "You weren't moaning like it was a nightmare," he said.

"I was moaning?" She covered her mouth with a hand as she thought back to her dream. "I was in the taxi again, except it was under water. You came to help me. Somehow, I got out, and then we were.... Oh, right." She felt her cheeks get warm.

"What?" he asked, smiling even wider when she covered her mouth again and shook her head. "What!" He pushed at her blanket-covered legs. "Were you having wicked dreams about me?" He gasped theatrically.

She couldn't help but smile back at him. She liked this laughing and smiling Carson. She'd never believed he existed. "*And*... you even talked dirty to me," she teased, making his eyebrows shoot up.

"What did I say?"

She pushed the covers back slowly, sliding her legs under her and leaning forward, putting on her best sexy expression. From the way his pupils blackened, it seemed to be working. "You said... 'oyster mushrooms,'" she whispered breathily, and then giggled when he immediately frowned. "Worst dirty talk ever. Tell your dream self to work on that!" She choked the words out through her laughter.

He nudged her shoulder and pushed her sideways onto the mattress. She partially turned toward him, expecting him to flop down beside her, but instead he leaned away and lifted the netting so he could stand up. "We've got a full day, you bad girl, and I've got breakfast to whip up." He looked down at her, his hands on his hips, looking like a superhero. "You haven't lived until you've had Eggs Carson."

She wasn't sure which was stronger—the emptiness in her growling stomach, or the emptiness that bloomed in her chest. "Do your eggs have oyster mushrooms in them?" She rolled to her side, realizing how much she wished he would lay beside her and talk the day away. As soon as the thought entered her mind, she pushed it away.

"At least I'm already dressed," she said, jumping up to her feet.

Carson turned abruptly and walked away. "See you downstairs," he said.

※

SHE BORROWED CARSON'S TOOTHBRUSH AND FRESHENED UP IN THE bathroom. He'd offered it last night, so she didn't think he'd mind her using it this morning. Or a little of his toothpaste. Back upstairs, she quickly slipped off her top, put on her bra, and pulled the soft shirt back on. She checked her e-mail, fired off a few messages, and then hurried downstairs.

Everyone was in the kitchen already, moving around efficiently. She stood awkwardly on the edge of the activity, momentarily unsure of how to fit into their flow. *Stella Carmichael, unsure of how to play to a room. Unheard of!* she thought.

"Stella!" Arjan called out when she saw her. Her hands were deep in a bowl, kneading dough, so she bowed her head in Stella's direction and gave her a big smile. Just like that, her reticence melted away.

"Good morning, *sa-wa-dee kah*," she greeted everyone, and then walked over to Carson. "So what's all this talk about Eggs Carson?" she asked. She loved watching chefs work their craft. In her role, she didn't get to do it a lot. Usually, she saw glimpses when she was evaluating a restaurant, and then typically spent the rest of her time buried in financials and contracts. But here she was, with a whole day to spend with a world-class chef, and all she could do was watch his hands.

She'd never told anybody about her strange fascination with strong hands and muscled forearms, because even she thought it was weird. And Carson's were the sexiest she'd ever seen. His hands were smooth, but she detected the telltale white scars of knife nicks, mostly when his palms were up. His fingers were long and tapered. They moved with confidence and speed, which made the muscles in his forearms move and stretch like a sensual ballet. They were strong hands that could each juice a lime in one quick squeeze—as he was doing now. She swallowed.

His hands had stopped moving, and she looked up to see he was staring at her. "What?" she asked.

"I was telling you all about Eggs Carson," he said. His eyes roamed over her face, and she realized it was too late to hide whatever expression was on it. *Maybe he'll just think I was daydreaming*, she hoped. But something in his wide grin said otherwise. "Let me begin again. Eggs Carson are eggs poached in ghee and a hint of rice vinegar, topped with roasted spring onions and strips of fermented galanga, which is a form of Thai ginger and possibly the greatest love of my life."

"Ah," she responded, doing her best to maintain eye contact.

"I'm doing this in your honor, you know. Thai breakfast is usually recooked dinner from the night before, or early cooked lunch. Most of the U.S. tourists, though, expect some kind of eggs for breakfast."

"Ugh," she joked along, "how provincial." She was pleased when he chuckled.

When they sat down to eat, she had a completely different mindset. Jason always made fun of how she ate. She had a system, and she never deviated from it. First, she examined every item on her plate, mentally describing the shape, color, and texture of each food. Then she breathed in the aromas of the food, turning the plate as necessary, to let each food item have its moment in the spotlight. And then she tasted, letting her mouth note all the same things for itself. She preferred if nobody talked while she did this, and once she even snapped at Jason to "can it" when he babbled on about something inconsequential, but most of the time she could zone people out.

In this moment, as Carson slid the plate in front of her, something in her opened to more than just the food. The patter of rain that hit the roof high above them, the murmurs of appreciation from Arjan and Rosie, the cool air that brushed against her bare ankles under the table, and even the hard dirt floor that seemed to vibrate through the bottom of her borrowed sandals—it all swirled through her and registered in her heart. She went through her familiar ritual, but now it felt like it had a hundred miles of depth to it. And as she savored the first bite she put into her mouth, held it, and then chewed, a connection was made in her to something bigger and she was overwhelmed.

When she opened her eyes, she saw everyone was watching her. She had to wait until she was sure she could speak.

"You look like you ate a bug," Arjan teased with a knowing smile.

Carson looked at her with steady eyes, and she knew he was divining exactly what was going on in her.

"No bug," she said, her voice sounding a little shaky and her eyes blinking away a sheen of moisture that sprang up. "It's just... simply amazing," she told Carson.

He didn't say anything, but he reached over to her hand and squeezed it hard and long. Then he released it, and everyone went back to enjoying breakfast and chatting about the day to come.

A HALF HOUR LATER, SHE FOUND HERSELF IN THE WEIRDEST situation yet—riding a bicycle in the rain, wearing decades-old Converse sneakers, and feeling a scratchy helmet transform her hair into one big rat's nest with every turn of her head. Ahead of her rode Carson, of course sexy and athletic, even though his bike had red plastic streamers coming out of the handlebars.

"How are you doing?" he called over his shoulder.

"Sixty-six percent," she called back.

"What does that mean?" he asked, slowing down on the narrow road until they rode side by side.

"It means I'm sixty-six percent doing okay and thirty-four percent wondering what the hell I'm doing on a bike." If her memory was accurate, she'd ridden a bike for one summer, which was the summer she learned how, probably before she started first grade. And she hadn't touched one since.

"You look great. If it makes you feel better, statistically, if you were going to fall off, you would have wiped out by now." When she darted a look at him, he had a big grin on his face. It was hard not to smile back, especially when he started ringing the bell on his handlebars repeatedly. "Attention! Stella Carmichael, big-time executive, is riding a bike in Thailand."

She laughed out loud. "Take a picture, because this might never happen again," she told him.

And then he actually did it. He pulled out his phone and snapped a pic. Her front tire bumped over a rock and her handlebars trembled as she steadied herself. And she kept hearing the shutter sound of his camera. "You're about to make Stella Carmichael wipe out on her bike in Thailand," she said nervously, part of herself bracing for the moment her bike slid out from under her. But it didn't happen. "How far are we going?"

Carson, goddamn him, pulled ahead of her then slowed down so he rode on her other side, weaving exaggeratedly as he spoke. "First, we're stopping at an oyster mushroom farm so you can harvest what we need for lunch."

"What? The oyster mushrooms of my dream are real?"

"Absolutely. After that, we're stopping at the rice farm so you can mill our rice. Then we'll get some vegetables, and maybe say hi to Rosie if there's time. She works near the vegetable stand," he enumerated.

She pedaled steadily, trying to focus on a point on the horizon so she could keep her bike in a straight line. She was completely out of her element, but she had to admit his company was fun.

They spent a half hour at the oyster mushroom farm, which was a tiny house on a small plot of land with a shed barely as tall as she was.

It was stacked with sawdust-stuffed plastic bags out of which a metal tube protruded. In some of the tubes grew gray, velvety oyster mushrooms. A narrow walkway ran down the middle of the long, skinny building, and the bags were stacked on either side from the ground to her eye level. Carson followed behind her as she harvested enough of the soft mushrooms for their lunch.

At the rice farm, a tiny Thai woman name Mai Le indicated that Stella foot-stomp a long board, the other end of which had a rounded hammer that dropped into a reservoir that held a handful of raw rice. She stomped for several minutes, switching legs when one got tired, until the woman told her to stop.

"Rice is vital in this village," Carson explained. "In all villages. Everyone helps plant, harvest, and mill. It's year-round work."

"*Kin khaw*," Mai Le said, pointing to the rice in the reservoir then to a round woven tray she held. Stella scooped the rice onto the tray and Mai Le shook the tray in a circular motion. She did three circles and then bounced the end up, letting the chaff blow away in the slight breeze. She did this three more times and then handed the tray to Stella. She was terrible, but enjoyed trying. Mai Le seemed to have fun too, laughing and saying "*Mi di*" to Carson, which she could tell meant she wasn't the best rice thrower she'd ever seen.

"You'd better get better. We need to take home a few pounds of rice," he said. Her heart dropped, but she carried on. He watched her for a little longer before he reached behind a counter and lifted up a sack of milled rice. "Luckily, I had this ready for us."

"You brat!" She laughed, throwing a handful or rice at him.

They rode another ten minutes to the vegetable stand, where Carson gave her an education on the various kinds of eggplants and local spices. They also said hello to Rosie, who was a seamstress in the purse factory next door. Three women sat at tables just large enough to hold a sewing machine, colorful cloth purses stacked all around them.

When they returned to the school, Stella was surprised at her disappointment.

"Think you'll buy a bike when you get back to New York?" Carson asked as he took off his helmet. She couldn't get her buckle undone, and he came over to help her. He used both hands and his cool fingers slid against her skin as he squeezed and released the clasp. It was hard not to turn her head into his touch.

"Um, yeah. Because the insanity of New York city streets is not much different from what we did today," she joked.

"Maybe with practice...." he started and then laughed. "Nope, you're right. I don't think I'd want you commuting in the city." He smiled. Her heart skipped a little at the idea that buried in his sentence were the words 'I want you.'

They carried their purchases into the kitchen, where Arjan was gathering the linens Carson had laid out at the workstations the day before.

"The last person cancelled for class today," Arjan said. "I'm going to help Jai with planting."

"That's too bad, but I'm not surprised," Carson replied. "Look, don't worry about this. We'll put everything away." He looked over at her, and she nodded.

"Yeah, you go ahead," she said to Arjan, who looked relieved. Stella had a good idea after today of how hard the people in this village worked. She took over gathering the linens as Carson walked around and put each station's supplies away.

"Do you mind if I go check my phone? I want to keep on top of what I can," she asked Carson.

"You left the house without your phone? And you didn't melt?"

"Funny guy." She smirked at him and went upstairs.

She flopped down on her mattress and turned on her phone. She waited for it to stop making sounds before she reviewed the latest onslaught. Besides a flood of e-mail, there was a voice-mail from Freddie, three from Jason, and three from the head of the Monticello acquisition group. Instead of listening to any of them, she scrolled through her contacts and chose a number.

"Yeah, boss," answered a groggy voice.

"Sorry, Freddie. I know it's a really bad time to call you."

"No kidding," she mumbled, and then groaned loudly, which Stella assumed accompanied a long stretch. "I'm used to you calling me at all hours. Did you get my message?"

"Yes, but I didn't listen to it." She appreciated that Freddie didn't grouse, she just got on with business.

"Everything is fine with the Central Group boys. They know about the flooding. Apparently, there are a lot of washouts all over the region. But the Monticello guys are panicking. They're used to getting regular updates, like, multiple times a day. What should I tell them?"

"Of course the Central Group guys are fine. This would be a big cash infusion. But honestly, the service and food and management are not up to Monticello's standards. Maybe Monticello won't care, because it's their first Asian investment and the property is turning a profit. It's one of those situations where nothing's exactly broken, but it would definitely stand out alongside Monticello's other properties if they were compared side by side. And not stand out in a good way."

Her shoulders slumped as her brain clicked back to the work dilemma that had been picking at her for a few days. She wasn't sure why she cared. Her job was to review, recommend, and then facilitate the business transaction. Monticello's top line requirement was profitability, and this deal achieved that.

"What do you need me to do, boss?" Freddie asked patiently.

"Leave this with me for today. I want to think on it some more. Carson thinks I'll be able to get back by tomorrow. Let Monticello know I'm being a little extra thorough, since this is their first Asian acquisition. That should buy me a day."

"You got it. Want to hear about Jason?"

"No, let's do this instead." She got up and paced over to a window that looked down to the kitchen. She opened one of the shutters and saw Carson below, peeling an apple. "I'm going to block his number. Ask Alex if he'll do me a favor and look over his strategy. I'm sure he'll do it. Tell Jason that Alex will look after him, and that Stella strongly suggests he take advantage of it and move on." As the words rolled up and out of her, a tension left her shoulders, letting them relax. She walked to the middle of the room, hearing the floorboards creak under her feet. "And I don't want to hear his name again. I should have done this right after I ended things."

"Hear! Hear!" Freddie said. "That's the Stella I remember. Welcome back."

"I didn't realize I was gone, but thanks." They hung up. She knew what Freddie meant. She just wasn't sure she felt entirely back. It reminded her of Freddie's comment about burnout. A day without her phone had given her some space to just breathe. Maybe there was something to that comment.

"Didn't realize you were gone where?" Carson asked as he came up the stairs.

"My assistant thinks I'm suffering from burnout. So does Landis's mom," she added.

"Evelyn? The Dragon Lady?" Carson asked. He held a plate of apple slices out to her and she took two.

"Ah, you know her."

"Summer told me all about her. And I've heard part of a conversation Landis had with her when Summer was moving to New York. Yikes, is all I can say. Actually, you remind me of her. Sort of." He looked at her analytically. "Maybe less so, now that I've seen you on a bicycle."

"I'm going to take most of that as a compliment." She strolled over to perch on one of the windowsills overlooking the living room. He followed. "Ev was my role model growing up. She valued me for my brain and drive—two things my mother told me I spent too much time cultivating. If Ev hadn't encouraged me to follow my instincts, I would never have pushed my father to start a restaurant acquisitions division, or changed my major, now that I think about it."

"You started the restaurant division?" Carson looked surprised.

She popped her last apple piece into her mouth and then smiled. "Uh oh, are perceptions crumbling?" He held his plate out to her and she took two more slices.

"Maybe. I don't know if I'm ready to admit that yet. Say something a conceited society girl would say," he challenged, backing up and leaning against the wall.

"How about, I hope the road is fixed soon so I can get all the village dust washed out of my hair," she said, and couldn't resist a toss of her head to swing her long hair around.

"Don't do that," he warned gravely, the amused light leaving his eye. His eyes were magnetic, and her feet moved of their own will, taking her within a foot of him.

8

"Why not?" she asked, and he didn't trust himself to answer. He didn't even know what he would say if he could form words. Instead, he looked at her hair, and the next thing he realized was the apple plate dropped on the mattress and his hands were in the gleaming red mass of it. They slid through its weight, letting the strands slip through his fingers to fall back on her shoulders. Then he laced his fingers through it again, pulling it toward his face so he could inhale.

Her eyes drifted shut, and he slid his hands deeper into her hair, cupping her head. She inched closer and he could smell her. Her forehead came up to his nose, and he inhaled slowly. *Purple*, he thought. *She smells like purple. How is that possible?*

He felt her hands rest on his hips and his breath hitched. She stepped closer until only inches separated them, and the sway of her body when she breathed meant her hips grazed him. He could feel his breath entering and leaving in short bursts. The air stirred her hair, and as he dropped his head to press his lips against the fiery mass, she took one more step closer and he felt her. And didn't feel her. One leg pressed against his left, and nothing pressed against his right. He froze. A cold curtain crashed down, and he backed away.

"Let's... not...." He saw the dazed look on her face, and he had to turn away from it. "I'm going to start lunch."

He did his best not to bang pots and utensils around, although that's what he wanted to do. He was angry, but only at himself. Well, and Stella a little bit. He wasn't sure if she was playing a game with him, or really was attracted to him. And there were little intricacies for him when it came to sex, as far as what he was comfortable and not comfortable doing. It was too complicated to go through for a casual hookup.

He had some broth ready to simmer and greens ready for stir-frying by the time she came down.

"Can I help with anything?" she asked, her voice a few degrees cooler than a few minutes ago.

"You could grab a couple bowls from the cupboard." He gestured behind him with his spatula, not taking his eyes off the vegetables in the wok. She found two bowls and forks and walked out of sight to the group table on the other side of the living room. When she came back, she filled the tin kettle with water and set it on one of the workstations' gas element to heat. She found two mugs and a tin of green tea and disappeared again.

He finished cooking the rice in the broth and found a large bowl to use as a serving dish for their meal, rice on the bottom, and the stir-fried vegetables on top. He walked it over to the table and sat opposite her, where she'd set his bowl. She'd put a tea bag in each of the mugs, and steam rose as they steeped.

"Go ahead," he said, turning the bowl of food so the serving spoon was pointing at her from the dish. When she stared at him without moving to dish up, he shrugged, took the spoon, and served himself a large helping.

"I know what didn't happen, but... what *did* happen?" she asked.

"What do you mean?" he stalled, keeping his eyes on his bowl as he ate.

"Do you not want to have sex, because of something I said? Or did? Or because you don't like me?"

He had to look at her then, because something in her voice cracked the tiniest bit. He sighed. "I want to have sex, because I like you.

What I know about you, anyway. We've only really gotten to know each other today. The reason I backed away has more to do with me." He shrugged. He didn't think he could explain it any better than that.

Her eyebrows came down in a line as she thought that over. She served herself a small portion of the rice and vegetables and they continued to eat in silence.

She moved slowly as they cleared the dishes. He watched her plug and fill the sink with soapy water. He was in a strange position of wanting to start a conversation, but not knowing how. She was reflective—a state he'd never imagined her in before he'd gotten to know her—and he knew when he was in that kind of mood he didn't like intrusions. Then his phone sounded.

We are staying overnight at Jai's family home, Rosie texted.

Sounds good, he typed.

"Rosie and Arjan are staying with Jai's family tonight," he said.

"Hm?" She looked up from the dish she was washing. "Oh, okay."

As she put the soapy dishes in the rinse basin, he took them out and dried them. Because it was just them, their work was done quickly. Just when he thought he knew how to broach a neutral topic, she turned to face him.

"Look," she started, drying her hands and then hanging the tea towel on the small hook on the wall behind the sink. "I want to have sex with you. And if I'm being honest, a part of me worries that you'll go back to that mean guy I met at the inn." She shrugged at him, and her face was tinged with worry to back up her words. "But I..." Her hands lifted, palms up, and then she folded them tight against her waist. "I just want to. And that's the feeling I want to go with right now." She hunched her shoulders in a self-conscious shrug and her smile was small and unsteady.

He was defenseless against that smile, and stepped close enough to wrap her in his arms. He rubbed his cheek against the top of her head and let the smell of her seduce him all the way to acceptance. Then he scooped her up in his arms, as he did from the taxi, and took her upstairs.

9

She guessed, from what he said earlier, that the issue was his leg. It could be that he disliked himself for being attracted to a spoiled, rich socialite, but she was ninety-three percent sure it was his leg. She didn't always have the best instincts when it came to compassion for other people, but in this case, she decided the best thing she could do was keep quiet and let him take the lead.

She forced herself not to worry when he carried her up the stairs, or tell him he didn't have to bend down to lie her on the mattress instead of set her on her feet. And when he winced as he removed his leg, she worked hard to keep her face blank, even though that time she truly felt bad.

"What's that?" she casually asked, when he rolled down the silicone sleeve and she saw a red line on his stump.

"Chafing. It happens a lot in this climate, but it's not a big deal." He shrugged it off, so she did too. She leaned on an elbow and watched with interest as he massaged his upper thigh and then applied moisturizer. He looked down at her with a half smile. "You must be asking yourself 'How good could this guy possibly be in the sack?' And I will tell you, I'm pretty good."

She laughed at his boyish grin. "I never doubted it," she said honestly.

"There are a few positions that are problematic for me, but great sex is more about partners being open, responsive, and communicative."

"Responsive and communicative? You're already proving better in bed than most of the men I've ever been with," she told him, grinning.

"Should I quit while I'm ahead?" he asked, moving to lie beside her. He shimmied until their faces were close. He rested his forefinger on her bottom lip.

"Not on your life," she replied, placing a small kiss on his finger.

THEY SAT ON A BENCH NEAR THE OUTDOOR SHOWER, WRAPPED IN towels. He held her hair aside while he used a dry cloth to blot water off her upper back where the towel drooped.

"Your back is gorgeous," he murmured. "I've never thought of a woman's back being so sexy, but yours is."

"Thank you. I think my back is my best feature, although some people don't agree."

"What do they think is your best feature?"

"My legs. Sometimes my hair, although I think a lot of people don't go for redheads, because of the whole angry stereotype that comes with it."

"Before I saw your back, I would have said your hair. It's incredible." He tapped her shoulder to get her to turn, so he could dab water droplets off her neck and shoulders.

"Do you know what I think your best feature is?" she asked, enjoying his gentle care. Nobody had ever done this small thing for her, and she loved it.

"Hm," he murmured, intent on his task.

"Your hands and forearms."

"My forearms? I've never heard that before."

"Oh yeah, when you're working in the kitchen and the muscles are tensing and flexing when you're slicing. Very hot."

He draped the cloth over his shoulder and swept a strand of her hair over her shoulder. He trailed his fingers down her arm to her hand, lifting it to press a kiss against it.

"I'll make sure I do extra flexing next time I'm chopping onions," he said with a sexy smile.

He stood, helping her stand, and then hopped a half turn to grab his crutches, since Pete was upstairs. They walked down the stone path, palm leaves making a natural canopy over their heads. He held the screen door and she climbed the stairs to the top floor of the bunk building, Carson following behind her.

Dropping onto her mattress, he waved her down beside him and snuggled her under his chin.

"The rain stopped," she said, lifting her head to listen and then settling back down. *Dammit.* She would have been okay staying here another day.

"Yeah, it has, hasn't it?" He sounded less than excited as well. "Tell me about your work. It must pay well to keep you in all those colorful panties."

"Actually, the job doesn't pay all that much. My trust fund lets me buy all the panties I need."

"Ah," he said, lightly trailing his fingers up and down her back.

"Don't say 'ah' like that."

"Like what?"

"Like that explains everything."

"Well, it doesn't explain why you work. Why do you, if you don't have to?"

She shrugged, running her own fingertips over his chest. "I like the work. I love the creative environment, and I love eating."

"Me too. Cooking is like... creative chemistry."

"Exactly! The more I taste incredible Thai food—food everyone can afford—the more I wish the average person could afford high-end cuisine back in the U.S.," she said.

"You could finance a chain of poor people cuisine, if you feel like you have enough panties," he joked. She poked him. "Ow!"

"It's not funny. I'd love to see your level of skill at local restaurants. And I'd love the challenge of making the economics work. Decent salaries for a great chef and staff, the best ingredients, and a menu with a price that people could afford. And I mean afford at least once a month instead of once a year."

"Let me get this straight. You don't need to work, but you do. Plus, you want to bring haute cuisine to the common people."

She leaned back to examine his face, certain he was poking fun at her, when she was being serious. But there was no hint of joking in his eyes. "Yes," she said simply. He didn't reply, he just pulled her back against him, smoothing her hair and kissing her on the head.

10

Carson hummed as he prepared ingredients for their dinner—garlic, palm sugar, shrimp, lime, long beans, fish sauce, and a green papaya.

"Ooo," Stella said as she walked into the kitchen, her hands on her hips. "What are you making?"

He liked her like this—no makeup, hair damp, the simple cotton of her tunic skimming her body. Somehow her body made the rough garment take on a feminine shape.

"Papaya salad, but with a twist—fermented tea leaves from Burma. They're called lephet," he replied, holding up a small unmarked jar of chopped greens in a liquid. "Want to help?"

"Absolutely!" She stood beside him, her arm brushing against his. "This Thai-Burmese fusion cuisine with a North American twist you're working on... I've never heard of anything like it. It's exciting to witness a new way of cooking being born."

"It does feel pretty cool." He grinned, responding to the naked enthusiasm in her voice. He knew her work gave her broad exposure to a high level of cuisine, and her respect for what he did made him stand a little taller. "I've always loved Thai food, but Somchai has family farther up north, and I realized a ton of possibilities when I watched them cook. I could see this being big in the U.S. some day." He knew it was definitely what Somchai wanted. Maybe he was wrong to want to slow him down.

She smiled up at him, no trace of anything but admiration on her face. "I agree, and that means a lot because, if you didn't already know, I'm a pretty big deal in the restaurant game," she teased, bumping him with her hip. "So, what can I do to help?" She looked down at what he'd arrayed on his cutting board.

"Well, the most important thing to remember when preparing this is to thoroughly kiss your assistant before you start," he said. She glanced up at him, momentarily confused, and then smiled when he pulled her against him.

"Have I told you I like the way you chef?"

"You mean the way I use my hands? You kind of told me in the shower," he murmured, remembering. Heat flowed through every artery in his body at the memory, and he touched his lips to hers to start a long, slow kiss. He gathered her close so he could feel every warm part of her against him. She didn't hold back, and he loved it.

"All right, enough!" he said as commandingly as his breathiness would let him. "Back to work. Here—" He held out a peeler grip-first so she wouldn't get nicked by the blade. "—you get to peel the papayas."

She took it from him and picked up one of the oblong, green-skinned fruit. He watched her examine the peeler and then pull it over the thick skin. A long strip easily fell away from the fruit. "Wow, this is the best peeler ever," she said.

"Just wait until you use this." He held out the julienne tool to her.

She dragged it over the flesh of the papaya and made perfect, long papaya threads. "Incredible!" she exclaimed, her eyes big.

"There's no glory in knife work when there are better tools to do the job."

"I know a chef in Paris who would tear you apart for using a gadget."

"And I'll show you a chef who's never worked without four assistants slaving to prep all his food. The only pride that should be in a kitchen should be pride of food."

He couldn't believe how quickly and efficiently they worked, even though he paused now and then to answer a question or show her a technique. Sometimes she would giggle over nothing, and sometimes he couldn't resist the urge to kiss her. Or touch her. One time, he heard some strains of music in the distance—the plucking of a stringed *grajabpi*, a Thai guitar—and he couldn't stop himself from pulling her into his arms for a spontaneous slow dance. She was stiff at first, but then softened against him as they moved in a slow circle. He wondered if she ever did anything spontaneous.

They ate sitting on pillows on the floor of the bunk building. Then he brought out two slim stringed instruments from a cupboard and showed her how to form notes on the slender neck, and strum and pluck the strings with her other hand.

"This is the instrument we heard earlier," he said, looking down at his own hands, and then over to her. He saw she was studying his hands and copying his movements on her instrument.

She wasn't very good, yet she refused to quit trying. The Stella he thought he knew wouldn't have picked up the instrument in the first place, let alone kept working at something she wasn't good at.

"You're not perfect," he observed analytically, looking her over as she sat cross-legged on a pillow in front of him. Her hair was loosely tied back with a strip of cloth, a reddish strand curving down beside her face. Although her face was without any mark, he knew her chest and arms were coated with faint auburn freckles. Her left big toe was crooked, and she had an oval scar on her left ring finger. He'd asked about that, and she'd explained that's where a lawn chair had pinched her when she was five.

"Perfect? God, no," she said, pulling him out of his reveries. She frowned over the strings as she looked from her left hand on the neck of the instrument to her right hand strumming the strings gingerly. "Perfection is overrated. I think the best things come from mistakes."

She was so different from how he'd imagined the sequined model he'd first seen on the Internet. He didn't move in her glitzy world, but he was starting to think she might come home to her fancy apartment in her ball gown and still be excited to julienne a carrot.

"You're not perfect, either," she accused smugly. He froze, glancing down at Pete and then back to her. "Your hair is shaggy. You look like a beach bum." She then glanced up through her lashes at him, a giant grin on her face.

"You... are a liar. You kept grabbing this beach bum's hair yelling 'More! More!'" He laughed out loud at the fake outrage that blossomed on her face.

"I did not! And if I was thinking it, it's not gentlemanly of you to point it out."

"Whoever said I was a gentleman? I think you dig my ungentlemanly behavior. And possibly my rough, peasant ways, although I haven't shown you all of *those* yet." He said it jokingly, but there was something in him that wondered how she did see him. He knew he was nothing like what she was used to. He shocked a lot of people in the restaurant world when they first saw him, and her world of the ultra-rich was levels above that.

"I *do* dig your peasant ways." She sighed with resignation. Then she looked directly into his eyes. "We're a good team," she said, sounding surprised. He watched her cheeks turn pink and her eyes flicker away.

"Hey," he prompted, lifting her chin back up. "We are a good team. The peasant and the trust fund socialite joining forces."

She reached for his hand and pressed it against her cheek, then turned into it with a kiss. His chest tightened and all he could see was her face, and the warmth that sparked to life in her eyes.

She set her *grajabpi* aside then lifted his out of his hands and placed it beside hers. "Speaking of peasants, I think you should have your peasant way with me again." She moved like a cat, crawling to him then over him as he lay back. She reached behind and beside him and pulled more pillows around to make a colorful bed.

"Oh my," he said. He gripped her hips as she straddled him, sliding her against his hardness. He watched her eyes flare and he knew she'd figured out that he liked her idea.

11

It was amazing what a morning clear of rain clouds could reveal. Stella looked out the passenger window of the truck at the sun-dappled green hillsides, the trees, and then the hatted men working in the fields, harvesting rice in one section and planting new stalks in another.

"That is my cousin's farm," Jai said, glancing to where she looked and then looking back to the road.

"Is it helpful that the rain has stopped?" she asked.

He shrugged. "It's almost the rainy season. We are used to it."

The sunny morning matched her sunny mood. She didn't normally go all teenager over a guy, but she definitely had a giddy feeling in her stomach this morning. It was the exact thing she made fun of in other women, not that she had a lot of women friends.

When Freddie had come to work beaming after Tony had proposed, Stella had turned them into 'Frony' and called her that for a week. The weird thing was Frony loved it, no matter how sarcastic Stella had gotten. And Freddie never put up with any of her crap. Now she had an inkling of what that felt like. She would be Starson, which was sort of badass.

"Do you go back to work?" Jai asked.

"Yes," she sighed, "unfortunately." *But not yet*, she thought. She had an hour before Jai got to her hotel.

She pulled out her phone and scrolled through her contact list. She wanted to talk with someone, but all she could find were colleagues, clients, and vendors. "Oh!" she said out loud as she remembered. She scrolled to Ev's number and tapped it.

"This is Evelyn Blake. Please contact me through my assistant," came the bored voice. She waited through the phone number until there was a beep.

"Ev, it's Stella. I'm sorry it's been a while since we talked. Here's a shocker—I actually took a day off. Call me if you get the chance. I should be back in New York by the end of the week." She paused as she thought ahead to the Monticello deal she still had to sort out. And possibly spending more time with Carson. "Maybe," she amended, and disconnected the call.

It felt good to connect with Ev, even though it was by voice-mail. She really should have talked to her sooner, whether she felt like it or not. She scrolled through her contacts again and tapped another number.

"Hey, red! Long time no talk!" He sounded genuinely pleased to hear from her.

"Hi, Landis. Yeah, it's been a while."

"Is everything okay? I touched base with Freddie and she said you were unreachable because of weather."

"Yeah, I had a meeting in the country, and the highway was washed out."

"Where are you now?"

"Heading back to Chiang Mai."

"How's the reconnaissance going?"

"Pretty disappointing, but it ticks most of their boxes."

"Huh. You don't sound excited about that."

"I'm not. I have one more idea though. I might see if Malee would be a good alternative, since they'll have two locations in another year."

"Malee? Carson's Malee?" Landis laughed, and her forehead wrinkled in a way her mother would have reprimanded her about. "Why not just sell your client a restaurant on the moon."

"Why do you say that?"

"You and Carson, putting a business deal together? First of all, I thought you hated the guy."

"Hate is a strong word." She shifted in her seat.

"And second of all, he can't stand you. Something along the lines of 'she worships the ground she walks on' is what he told Summer." He chuckled at that, and it sparked Stella's temper.

"For your information, he was on my flight over here, and we had a chance to get to know each other. And now we are... on friendly terms." She rolled her eyes at her description. "Landis?" He was silent for so long she checked to see if the call had dropped.

"Yeah, I'm here. I'm just... you're on friendly terms with Carson? Carson Richardson, my future brother-in-law. *That* Carson?"

"Ha ha ha," she drawled sarcastically. "Yes, Carson Richardson. We both realized we'd made assumptions about the other and found common ground." She should have known better than to try to have any normal kind of chitchat with Landis. "I'm bored talking about this. Tell me about you. Is there a date for the wedding yet?"

"You want to talk about the wedding?" He sounded even more amazed.

"What's so odd about that?"

"Nothing, for a normal person. You never want to talk about the wedding. You've never even wanted to *hear* about it," he argued.

"I resent that you think I'm not normal." What she resented was that he was crashing her phenomenal mood. "Do you want to tell me about the big day or not?" she asked coldly. He gave in.

"It's going to be at the inn. Probably in March, but we haven't confirmed with Mitch and Katy yet. Summer talked to someone at the restaurant Carson used to work at for the catering, but there's talk it may be going up for sale. They tell us they'll still handle the wedding, but it's got Summer a little stressed out."

"There's a restaurant near the inn that has Ev's stamp of approval?" She found it hard to believe Ev wouldn't insist on flying out chefs from New York to cater it.

"Evelyn is so busy with the White Ball Gala and her after-wedding grand party in New York that she doesn't seem to care about getting too involved with the plans."

"That sounds like Ev," she admitted.

Landis told her a few more details about the guests and Summer's dress, and Stella was surprised at her level of interest. Landis was right; she normally changed the subject whenever he'd mentioned the wedding. She wondered if she did that because her feelings for Landis had gone deeper. Now she knew it had more to do with rejecting love in general, something her mother had given her a thorough training in.

They ended their call a few minutes later, and she tried not to think about anything for the rest of the drive to the city.

Her luxurious hotel room was just how she'd left it—tidy, sterile, clean. Her clothes were neatly hung up in the closet, her bras and panties color coordinated and laid precisely in a drawer. She took off her rumpled dress and heels. The nude-colored pumps were scuffed beyond repair.

The hot shower and the smell of her favorite shampoo brought her mind back around to business. Wrapped in a towel, she texted her Central Group contact and asked if she could tour the kitchen before dinner service.

Yes. You are free to ask for Chef Ayung any time, and he will show you around, read the text.

She pulled on her plum raw silk dress suit and black patent heels and headed to the kitchen. As she headed down the hall to the elevator, her phone blinged with a text from Carson. It was a selfie of him in the bottom corner and a group of smiling faces behind him wearing white aprons.

Class is in session! he wrote.

They look great! she texted back. Then she took a selfie of herself next to a painting in the hallway and sent it to him, saying, **Back to work for me too**.

An hour later, she was back in her room, getting ready to have an impromptu call with the Monticello group. The kitchen, as she'd expected, was disorganized, unprofessional, and—in her opinion, worse—led by an uninspired chef.

She brushed a strand of hair back into its twist and then adjusted her laptop screen so she was centered in the camera's frame. She pressed the group Skype button to initiate the call.

"Good afternoon, Mr. Tennelly," she greeted the man that sat at the head of a long table. Three other men sat near him, also facing the camera.

"Good evening, Ms. Carmichael. Thank you for going above and beyond for this acquisition."

She smiled coolly, acknowledging his words with a tilt of her head. "Certainly," she answered. She went on to explain her overall findings, presenting both sides of the opportunity—that the acquisition will be profitable for them, but that it wouldn't add any value to their brand.

"In fact, if you want crossover business from your customer base, the experience could hurt your brand. Now—" She held out her hands as she gathered her thoughts about how to frame her idea. "—if you're not in a hurry to acquire a property in Thailand this year, I think I might have a spectacular opportunity for you."

The men's looks pinballed off each other as they weighed her words. "What kind of opportunity?" Mr. Tennelly asked.

Yes! she exulted. If anyone else had asked, it would have been out of business politeness only. With Tennelly asking, it meant it would get serious consideration.

"There's a Michelin-caliber chef here in Chiang Mai who's pioneering a new cuisine." The men looked at each other again, this time with excitement. A great sign. "Like all genius chefs, he's not big on working with suits, but his partner is a Thai native, and majority owner in the restaurant they're currently running. With your permission, I'd like to at least sound them out about the possibility of going bigger than the two locations they currently have, since you were looking for a four-door chain at the low end." She looked to the side, making a few random doodles on her notepad out of range of the camera. She'd learned that the more bored and unconcerned she seemed, the more men interpreted her to be good at her job.

She sensed the men leaning forward to confer with each other quietly. In less than ten seconds, Tennelly was facing the camera.

"Talk to them," he said shortly. "We're interested." Those two little words had millions of dollars behind them.

"Give me four days. The chef is determined to stay small and local, so I'll need to structure something I think will be amenable to both partners. I'll have Freddie send a draft to you in the next few hours, and with your approval I'll start our discovery meeting with that in my back pocket."

"Agreed. Thank you, Ms. Carmichael." He ended the video before he heard her "Thank you, Mr. Tennelly."

She closed her laptop and then did a little happy dance in place. Carson had said he thought his cuisine could be big in the U.S. Maybe he was thawing a little when it came to Malee. She hoped so. But she decided to play it safe. Picking up her phone, she scrolled until she found what she was looking for.

Would you be free tomorrow for a meeting? she texted. After a moment, the little typing bubbles appeared.

Yes. Please come to the restaurant. Any time, Somchai replied.

12

Carson threw his bag to the curb, gripped the handle on the back of the truck, and swung down, hopping on one leg until he could get his crutches positioned.

"*Khau khun kruh*," he thanked the driver, who gave a short wave and drove away in the morning light. He swung his bag over his shoulder, its shape awkward since he'd had to shove Pete in it, and tried the door of Malee. Locked. First, the chafing on his leg, which looked worse this morning, and now he was locked out of the restaurant, because he forgot his key.

He took a few steps until he could see over the awning to the upstairs bedrooms. "Dex!" he shout-whispered, willing his voice to travel directly to his window and not wake up anybody else. "Dex! Dex!" His voice got louder each time until he saw the curtain move. Then a tired face appeared. "Come down," Carson hissed, waving his arm widely to get him to come downstairs. A few minutes later, Dex appeared at the door and unlocked it.

"It's early, man," he complained, shuffling back the way he came as soon as Carson entered and relocked the door. "How was the school?"

"Good. How are things here?" Carson followed him to the back.

"I heard that red-headed chick followed you up there. She doesn't give up, does she?"

"That was Somchai's idea." He waited for Dex to get partway up the stairs before grabbing the railing and navigating his way up with his cane.

"What gives with the crutches?" he finally noticed, probably when he heard the cane thumping on each step.

"Chafing. It hurts too much to wear Pete."

"Hm," he mumbled. Dex turned the corner, went to his room, and closed his door. When Carson got to the top, he heard the rumpled sound of his buddy falling into his bed.

He did the same when he got to his room, although he wasn't all that tired. He pulled out his phone and opened his text app. He pressed Stella's name and saw the message he'd sent, letting her know he was heading back. There was no response. He scrolled up to the selfie she'd sent. Her face looked fresh and sassy, and her hair was soft, pulled away from her face with a headband. It looked like she was wearing a very shiny and very expensive top.

Behind her was the brocade wallpaper of her hotel and a gorgeous piece of art. She looked happy to be back in her business world, but he also remembered how happy she'd seemed at Mae On, hearing her free-spirited laughter in his mind. Even riding the bike, she'd been able to laugh at herself. And then he remembered her face when he'd been inside her, or kissing her, or showering with her. She had a thousand different smiles, it seemed.

He dropped the phone on his chest and looked up at the ceiling. There were two holes where he'd tried to pushpin a mobile he'd bought in the market. When he needed to puzzle something through, he always lay here and found them with his eyes like a calming touchstone. He found them now, but since he couldn't name what was making his brain fidget, they weren't much help.

He leaned over and grabbed his medicated cream from his drawer. Pulling up the leg of his cargo shorts, he sat up and applied the ointment to the angry chafing mark. It looked like it wanted to blister, and he hoped a day or two without Pete would settle things back down. He threw the tube of cream back in the drawer and flopped on his pillow again.

"What is it?" he asked the two spots on the ceiling. Sometimes they looked like eyes staring back at him. *You tell me, Carson. What is it?* they asked. He picked up his phone from where it had slid off his chest and looked at her picture again. He tapped it and saved it to his photo app and dropped his phone on his chest again. *I met someone*, he said telepathically to the eyes on the ceiling.

He imagined calling his sister and telling her about meeting Stella on the plane, about having sex with her. He half-chuckled out loud. After all the scathing things he'd ever said to Summer about Stella, he imagined she'd fall out of her chair if he told her they were a thing.

Are we a "thing"? he wondered. They hadn't really talked about anything in the future when she'd left yesterday. He'd walked her out to the road, and when he thought nobody was looking, he'd hauled her against him for a deep kiss before she got into the truck. She'd played it low key when Rosie and Arjan got home that morning too, so he wasn't the only one uncertain. He'd never been a big PDA guy, and maybe she wasn't either. Truth was, he didn't know.

<hr />

HE WOKE UP WITH A START, SCRAMBLING FOR HIS PHONE. HE WAS confused not to find any notifications on his screen. He rubbed a hand over his face and checked the time—in the blink of an eye he lost three hours. What had woken him up? He sat up on the bed, listening. Then he heard it—Stella's voice from downstairs. Low murmurs and then a high laugh. He scrambled for his cane, which had fallen to the floor, and rolled his stiff body out of bed.

"Hey, sleepy head," Dex greeted him from the kitchen, but his eyes were laser focused on Stella, who was standing in the hall, looking over the service counter at the men. At Dex's words, her gaze swung to him and her eyes sparkled. He almost didn't recognize her.

Her auburn hair was slicked back and up, her lips were a shiny, deep red, and her dress was a gray silk that shimmered like water over her curves. As she turned toward him, her lips parting to say something, the corners of her mouth curving, he turned away and into the kitchen.

"Good morning, Carson," Somchai said, his demeanor kind but muted. Carson twisted the handle of his cane, glancing at Stella, who had a polite smile on her face. "How was the class?" Somchai asked.

"Good, really good. Great." He cleared his throat. Somchai's eyebrows rose, but he didn't comment. He knew what his partner was thinking though. Months ago, once Malee's kitchen and menu had been set, he'd thrown himself into the school. He'd talked Somchai's ear off about it every night. And now, after the first class, he'd left early and said it was "good." As he looked at the cool businesswoman opposite him, he couldn't recall what had him in such a hurry to come back to the city.

"What's that?" he asked, nodding to a glossy black folder Stella's fingernails were lightly tapping on.

"Stella has a client who is interested in investing in Malee," Somchai said.

Stella lifted her crimson-tipped fingers—*those have been updated*, he thought they'd been a different color yesterday—to include the three men facing her from the kitchen. "It's just a bare bones plan, and I worked in a lot of flexibility on terms, which we can look at in the second or third draft. But I think it meets all of your goals."

"You talked to your client about that?" he asked, again nodding at the black folder.

"Yes."

"You figured this all out before even speaking to us?" His heart thundered in his ears, and he glanced at the faces around him, wondering if everyone could hear it.

"Well, not exactly. I did speak to—"

"How do you even know what our goals are? Oh, wait—" He turned to Somchai, who was leaning against the stove, his face calm. "—you sent her to the school to do a little reconnaissance, didn't you? I forgot about that." He knew his voice could get loud when he was making a point to sous chefs in frantic moments during dinner service, but right now, his voice had a high pitch that sounded on the verge of losing control. In fact, his whole body thrummed with an anxious energy.

"He did, but that wasn't...." Stella's reasoning tone notched up his anger.

"Dude, calm down." Dex's rational tone literally propelled him back out the door.

"This is bullshit. I'm outta here." He took the biggest steps he could to get away from the kitchen. Turning into the stairway, he reached as far as he could to grab the handrail and hauled himself up multiple steps at a time, not caring that his crutches clattered and scraped against the railing and wall.

He slammed his door and went to the window. All he could hear was his own breathing and his heart thumping in his chest. He couldn't breathe properly. Were they downstairs talking about him? He walked over to the door to listen, but he couldn't hear anything. He groaned, thinking about how he'd clambered up the stairs. Like an idiot.

He heard footsteps and turned to sit down on his bed. After a tap on his door, Somchai opened it.

"Are you okay?" he asked.

"Yeah. Sorry about that," he said. He exhaled and felt a hundred pounds of tension drain out of his shoulders. "Something about her just...." He didn't know how to finish that. Twenty-four hours ago, something about her made him feel the opposite.

Somchai closed the door behind him and crossed the room to sit beside him on the bed. He rested a hand on his shoulder and gave him a kind smile. "You are my partner. In such a short time, you have become my brother. My family. I know what I want to do, and I know I have the power to do it. But I have to respect what you want too."

Carson didn't know what to say, and he struggled to keep a flood of emotions under control.

"You have done nothing but work on this business. I think you work harder than I do, and I am the hardest worker I know." Somchai laughed, and it was hard not to laugh as well. "I think you need a real rest. A vacation, with no thought of business."

Carson's mind flashed to the barn loft at the inn. It's the place where he'd literally healed after his surgery. But when he thought about that time, it had been filled with work at the local restaurant, playing softball, baking for the inn, and then working on this restaurant partnership. He hadn't had a moment of rest.

"I don't know where to go," he said, his gaze dropping to his lap. His voice sounded like a lost boy.

"Ekapol's family has a meditation house at Wat Suan Doi. You will go there."

"But—" he started, but Somchai interrupted him.

"You will go there." He put his hand on Carson's leg and gave it a reassuring shake. "Everything here is okay. *Okay*," he emphasized with another shake.

Carson nodded, breathing in and out and grimacing when his breath was shaky. Nothing felt okay right now.

13

Stella watched Dex as he moved around the kitchen, preparing for lunch. When she checked her watch, she saw they had about forty minutes before they opened. They'd run out of small talk, and Stella picked up the folder and wandered into the dining area, her heels loud on the floorboards with every step.

"Stella," Somchai said, and she turned to the man. "Please, sit." He pointed to the table she'd sat at for lunch. It was only days ago, but it felt like a lifetime. "I'm sorry for how the meeting went."

"I don't understand. You said he would be open to this. And I thought he would be too." *Especially after their time together at Mae On,* she thought to herself.

"I have to confess to you. I knew when I sent you to Mae On that Carson would not be happy to see you."

"So why did you send me?" she practically sputtered. She'd thought something was off about that, but she'd wanted it to be true. Deep inside, she wanted to be part of a culinary coup, introducing a new cuisine to the U.S. Freddie had tamped the idea down on the plane, but after eating Carson's tom yum soup and finding out there were a few other clients on their roster interested in Asian food opportunities, well, that's when anything had justified the means.

"In my family, I am good at matching people. When Carson called me and told me about meeting you on the plane, I thought, 'maybe there is something here.' And when I met you at the airport, I knew for sure. That's why I invited you to the restaurant."

Stella closed her mouth, because it had fallen open. "I thought you were interested in a restaurant in the U.S. You said so." She frowned at him.

"Oh, that?" He waved a hand at her. "Carson is right. We agreed to look at that next year. But *you*, you and Carson is something I wanted to see."

"Are you saying you're a matchmaker?" She wanted to look around and see if there were hidden cameras in the corner of the room. It felt like an elaborate joke Freddie might set up.

"Sometimes." He shrugged with a tiny smile. "I can see when people love. I can't explain how, but I'm always right."

"I don't believe in that kind of love," she said, the words so automatic they came out of her without a thought.

"I know," he told her, and spread his hands toward her, palms up. "Which is your problem."

"I beg your pardon? You don't even know me." Her mind was churning. She'd thought Somchai was an ally, but now he seemed like a complete stranger. An unstable stranger.

"You're right; I don't know you. I only know love. It's my gift and sometimes a curse." He gave a slight shrug and grimace.

She picked up the folder in front of her and pushed her chair back. "Has this just been a game to you? I have serious investors that want to negotiate a deal with Malee. Did I go out on a limb for nothing?" She was trying to keep her outrage tamed. She still wasn't sure what was happening, but her heart was telling her it wasn't good.

"Not a game. I checked into your company, and this Monticello group. I like what I learned, and I am sure we can come to an arrangement. But not without Carson."

She stared at Somchai. She had no idea what to make of that. *What the hell is going on?* she wondered.

"In two days, you will go and talk to him. I will keep this." He held out his hand for the folder, which she held out to him automatically as if his words were magic that she couldn't disobey. "I know you don't believe in love, but it exists. Everyone learns that, but sometimes they learn it too late."

She watched him get up and walk away, tapping the black folder against his leg. A full minute went by before she stood up and called to Dex to unlock the door and let her out.

※

SHE'D INTENDED TO PACK HER SUITCASE AND HAVE FREDDIE arrange for an immediate flight home, but somehow that hadn't happened. Instead, she'd arranged a meeting with Central Group to tell them the deal had fallen through. She'd expected them to either try to bargain with her to resuscitate the deal, or leave in an angry huff, but they did neither.

Instead, they asked her why. When she told them, they eagerly asked her how they could improve. She'd spent two hours going through the restaurant with them, explaining what amenities mattered to her U.S. investors. Then they told her about their goals, and she realized she might have a better investor for them.

She threw herself into her work, keeping at it late so she could video Skype with Freddie during Eastern Time work hours. This was what she was good at. This was her calling, what mattered. Not love. In fact, whenever her thoughts strayed to Carson, her concentration faded away. So whenever he popped up in her mind's eye, she focused on the business aspect—bringing Malee to the U.S. Even though Somchai implied that was a distant future, she thought at the very least she'd be prepared for when it happened.

As she typed an e-mail, her phone alerted her to a text. She picked it up, expecting it to be an investor. It was Somchai.

Ekapol will pick you up tomorrow morning at 7. It will take an hour to get to Carson, he texted.

Okay, she replied.

She closed her laptop without finishing the e-mail, and walked to the window. *Carson is ready to talk*, she thought. Despite her flurry of work the last day, and her surging conviction about her purpose, her legs felt like jelly. Why was she even going there, other than Somchai said no deal would happen without Carson?

Did Somchai really believe they would fall in love? She turned and looked at the work she'd been doing—the flip chart she'd ordered management to bring her, and the notes she'd taken. She was on the verge of making a new deal between Central Group and a consortium in Belgium. This was who she was. Meeting with Carson would be a step toward a future business deal, nothing more.

She walked back to her laptop on stronger legs. *Business and nothing more*, she thought.

14

It was no good. Carson could hear the birds, and the music of the small mountain stream nearby. He listened to the wind as it rustled through the leaves of the fig trees outside the compound, lifting his head and breathing in that air, positive the thick smell came from the leaves. But the answers he wanted weren't appearing.

When he'd arrived two days ago, he didn't know he was looking for answers. He thought he just needed a break from work and from thinking. Wat Suan Doi felt like the perfect place when he first saw it. An hour north of Chiang Mai, most of the drive to the temple was up a mountain on a narrow, paved road. It ended at stone stairs—416 of them, surpassing the 306 of nearby Wat Phra That Doi Suthep—that led to the compound.

The temple was in the middle of the mountaintop clearing, surrounded by four buildings, and then surrounded again by a waist-high fence of plaster and bamboo. The buildings were made of aged logs, but the temple itself sat three tiers up on white steps and was gilt in bright gold. Hanging from a brass bar on either side of the temple were cast iron bells. Ringing them, or hearing their sound, was meant to herald the teachings of the Buddha.

Loh Chanin, Ekapol's cousin, had greeted him down at the road when he'd arrived in the late afternoon. He spoke fluent English, and as they climbed the steps to the temple—Pete aggravating the almost-healed chafing—Loh Chanin explained the rules of their community.

"As a guest, you are not bound by the rules, but it shows great respect if you follow them. We all waken at first light. You will hear the bells at four in the morning. We have breakfast together. Then we meditate. We have lunch at ten-thirty and then clean the compound, followed by more meditation. We go to sleep at ten o'clock. You can keep your phone with you, but it must be off while you're in the inner compound. Also, there is no talking at all in the temple. In the courtyard, you can whisper, just stand very close. When you want to leave, find me and I'll arrange for Ekapol to come and get you."

Loh Chanin gave him a white cotton top, loose pants, and sandals. Each monk and guest had a small room in one of the outer buildings. It was big enough for a plank bed and a one-foot space surrounding it. A mattress about two inches thick and a thin pillow lay on the bed.

That first afternoon, he'd fallen easily into the minimal routine, joining the monks as they swept the courtyard. The only sound had been the rustling of leaves and brooms, the odd bell tone from the breeze, and birds. Afterward, meditation began in the central temple.

His goal had been to empty his mind, but he couldn't. So he decided to think about this anxiousness inside him, to just connect with that feeling. It kept pulling him to images and thoughts about Stella. He kept trying to push them away, but they kept bobbing back up like balloons in water. From months ago, when they'd first met on the porch on the inn, to their conversation on the airplane, to how they'd been at the school in Mae On, they appeared like visions in his head. When he fell asleep that night, he'd dreamt about her the way she'd been at the school, carefree and relaxed, but then she transformed into a floating demon. Her hair had ignited in red flames and her face crystallized into a porcelain mask.

He'd awoken lethargic and at odds with the peaceful surroundings. No matter how hard he tried, he couldn't find peace. Not in the sunrise, or breakfast. And not now, hours later, listening to the birds, the stream, and the damn leaves that rattled over his head.

"You look unhappy," Loh Chanin said quietly from behind him.

He looked back and invited Loh Chanin to sit beside him on the low wall of the compound. "I feel at odds with everything," he admitted.

Loh Chanin tapped his arm. "Come with me."

He followed him into a room off one of the outer buildings. He pulled down an orange bundle and passed it to him, indicating that he should strip down and put it on. He did, with Loh Chanin helping him adjust the wrapping of the orange sheet. He found some string on a table and passed it to him, indicating he should tie back his hair. Then he reached into a drawer for something Carson couldn't see. Loh Chanin turned to him and pushed his finger low on his forehead over the bridge of his nose.

"This is urna," Loh Chanin whispered, standing back. "It allows you vision into the divine world, the ability to see past your suffering. Go meditate, and only think of this eye," he advised him.

He walked back to the low wall and sat. He could feel the thick mark Loh Chanin had smudged on his forehead. When he closed his eyes and tried to visualize the mark, he heard a voice in his head. *I like that fire woman,* Arjan had said. The image of Stella, as she'd been in his dream, appeared behind his closed eyes. He sighed. This time, instead of fighting to push the vision away, he tried to sit with whatever would come into his mind.

15

Stella looked at the stone steps ahead of her. When she'd gotten dressed that morning, she went full business right down to the shoes. She knew she'd be going to a retreat where there would be a temple, and most of them had a few steps going up into them. She'd just thought there'd be a reasonable number of steps, not over four hundred. She looked down at her black Valentino slingbacks and then to the top of the stairs. Tension had been fluttering in her stomach since Somchai had texted her, and it kicked up a notch now.

She looked back at Ekapol, who had turned his truck around and parked on the side of the road. "I don't know how long I'll be. Maybe an hour?"

"It's okay," he called. "I'll wait as long as you need. I have my phone and you have my number, in case something happens and you need me." He held up his phone, and she held up hers as well, although she wondered what could happen to her at a Buddhist retreat that she'd need to call him. It added to the butterflies in her belly.

"Okay," she said, and turned back to the stairs. *One step at a time*, she thought. She tried to keep a slow pace, because with the humidity she was already starting to sweat. But her nerves kept making her feet speed up. The soles of her shoes tapped on the stones. She counted seven steps, landing, and then seven steps again. The top didn't seem to be getting any closer.

She wondered what she would say to Carson when she saw him. A large part of her wanted to skip this meeting. He'd made his views on a business deal clear, and if there'd been any feelings for her in him, he wouldn't have dissed her at the restaurant. But a small part of her, the part that made her stomach dance, chose clothes and shoes and walked her downstairs from her hotel and into Ekapol's truck. She didn't print off the draft agreement, thinking it would set him off. She had it memorized anyway, if they actually talked about it. She'd told herself she'd keep this about business, but that small part of her kept thinking about Somchai's words. *I know you don't believe in love, but it exists.*

She laughed out loud, and the sound had a frantic tone. She should turn back, and yet her feet kept walking up the stairs.

When she got to the top of the steps, she paused to catch her breath. Her calves ached, but her feet weren't too bad. Several monks in orange robes strolled around the compound, while others were working. Some men wore all white, also walking or working. She couldn't see Carson though.

Wood buildings surrounded a stunning gold temple. It shone so bright it seemed to have a glow of its own. She took a breath and headed farther into the compound, wondering if she should knock on doors, or just wander until she found him. Other than taking off her shoes before entering temples, she didn't know any of the rules about these places. She also didn't see any women, which added to her stress. Everyone seemed to be watching her, but gave no acknowledgement and said nothing.

"I'm looking for Carson Richardson?" she asked one of men wearing white. She guessed him to be American, but he shrugged and said nothing. She asked two more men until finally someone pointed to the back of the compound. She picked up her pace, her heels clicking on the stones.

She saw him sitting on a low wall behind the last wood structure. He was facing away from her, but she recognized the way he held himself, the shape of his body, and his sun-streaked hair, even though it was tied back with a string. The anxiety that had been a low murmur inside her grew stronger. He wore the orange robes of the monks, and nervousness crept out of her in a manic giggle.

"You're a monk?" she asked, her voice sounding alien to her. "Of course you are." He turned, shock in his eyes. "This seems extreme, even for you." His mouth opened, but no words came out. "Nothing to say? Huh." She turned on her heel, to see two very large monks striding toward her. "What...?" she said as they each held her by an upper arm. "There's no need. I'm leaving." But they continued to hold her arms tight, tight enough to hurt. "Ow, hey," she cried, but they continued to march her out.

"Stella." She heard Carson's voice, and instantly tears sprang to her eyes and spilled over. He was right behind her and yet a million miles away. "Wait," he called, but if he was talking to her, it was a mistake. She didn't have much of a choice.

She looked through blurry eyes to her phone, trying to scroll to Ekapol's number and tapping it. She saw Landis's face appear and she realized she'd somehow tapped the wrong number. When he answered, his deep voice reminded her of home, and she lost it.

"Hey, red," he said, which unleashed more tears.

"I'm being taken away by monks." Her voice hitched as her breaths came and went awkwardly with each sob. "I don't know what's going to happen. I mean... it's not like they're going to keep me as a sex slave, or something," she finished on a hysterical laugh. *I'm losing it*, she thought, shuffling along. In the next instant, she was released, and the stone steps to the road were in front of her.

"Never mind that," she heard Carson's voice. She turned and saw him behind her, holding his phone up to his face. "I'm with Stella. Tell Landis she's fine. I'll call you later." He dropped his arm and looked at her, his face blank and his eyes empty. She wiped her eyes, not caring about her appearance. She knew she was a horrible crier.

"This was a mistake," she said, and instead of hysterical her voice sounded dead. She walked down the steps without looking back.

The first few minutes of the ride back to her hotel was spent convincing Ekapol that she was okay, just sad. The truth was she felt nothing. Not sadness or anger or even confusion. Just... nothing. She gave herself another fifteen minutes to think through what her next move would be. She knew she wanted to fly out immediately, but she didn't want to go to New York. She wanted to go to a place similar to what Carson had found, without having to surrender herself to some religion. When the solution popped into her mind, she called Freddie.

"I need a flight out of Chiang Mai immediately," she said, not bothering with "how are yous" or any of Freddie's jokes.

"Chiang Mai to JFK, got it."

"No," she interrupted. "Chiang Mai to Seattle. And clear my calendar for at least a week."

"Thank God!" Freddie replied. "I mean, absolutely, boss. I'll email your boarding pass right away."

She disconnected the call and dropped her hand and phone to her lap. The only thing she had the energy to do was look out her window.

16

He literally couldn't move. Some invisible force kept him frozen to the spot, watching Stella quickly and regally walk down the 416 steps he'd walked up just a couple days ago. All the noises around him—the birds, the wind through the trees—were muffled. The only thing that fluttered up to him clearly was the sound of her crying.

Something in him drained away with every step she took. At the very bottom, her figure didn't hesitate, just walked around the truck and climbed in without looking back. He wasn't sure if he hoped she would or not. The truck immediately left, and deep inside he knew she was gone for good. He wouldn't be surprised if she went straight to the airport.

He'd been shocked when he'd heard her voice. He'd been surrounded by memories and images of her, and for a moment, he thought what he was seeing was a projection of that. And then her voice, he couldn't remember what she'd said, but he remembered the high ache in it, like her throat was closing up in pain. He puzzled over that for the next few hours, bouncing back and forth between wanting to understand it and thinking it didn't matter, because she was gone.

Along with envisioning her on a plane out of Chiang Mai, he

pictured her returning to her own world. An insulated and affluent world of Armani suits, glitzy galas, and small talk that said nothing. It was over. Well, whatever attraction they'd had was over. It was fun, and maybe he felt sad about it. But he'd be over it in a day or so. *She's better off*, he thought, and then corrected himself. *I'm better off.*

He tried to get back to meditating, but everything was wrong. The robes scratched, his forehead was itchy, and his nerves were raw. By late afternoon, he was down on the road waiting for Ekapol to pick him up.

※

HE FILLED THAT AFTERNOON AND NIGHT WITH WORK, NOT PAUSING for a moment for any casual conversation. The next morning he headed out early to the local markets for the day's fresh produce and fruit. He got the prep going unusually early and afterward found Somchai waiting in his room.

"What's up?" he asked Somchai, who sat on his bed. His plan was to get a couple hours sleep before they opened for lunch, but it looked like that was going to be delayed.

"You have been very busy since you got back from the retreat," the older man said. Carson walked over and propped himself on the windowsill.

"Yes," he agreed, not going into any detail. Somchai just stared back. "What? I took a couple days off and now I'm back to work."

"Stella has left," he told him.

He guessed as much, since he hadn't heard from or seen her. Even so, a lump formed in his throat. "What did you expect? She didn't get what she wanted, so she left. It's what I knew would happen."

"And what do you think she wanted?"

"You know what she wanted. A deal. Our restaurant with one of her investors." He almost spat the words and willed himself to calm down.

"I don't think so," he said.

Carson sighed, rubbing his eyes. "Somchai, I'm exhausted. Can we talk about this later?"

"I'm worried about you."

"I'm fine. Everything is fine." He paused, but Somchai just stared. Finally, he blurted, "I'm glad she's gone. She was a distraction."

"Why can you not love yourself?" Somchai asked, his eyes caring.

"What? I do."

"You don't. You are more than your leg or your cooking or your drive. I will tell you what I told Stella. I know love when I see it. And I see it in you and her, for each other. But only you can act on it."

Carson wanted to say something in response, something about how love wasn't real, but he was oddly without words. Somchai got up and patted his shoulder. He left his room, closing the door behind him.

Carson sat on the windowsill until the sun poked in through the buildings across the street. He'd been pushing thoughts of Stella away since the day he came back from Mae On. And despite that, he'd still been dreaming about her. Not her fiery hair and a brittle face, but her soft skin and sultry voice. In other bits of dreams, she had a warm touch and intoxicating laughter.

Sure, he was sexually attracted to her. Their time in Mae On was proof of that. And if she could stay the woman she was there, he would have pursued her. He would have made her stay while he ran the cooking class with Arjan, or he might have left when she did. Arjan could have handled the first class on her own.

But she wasn't that woman. She was slick and obsessed with perfection and conceited and *rich*. The opposite of him in almost every way. Well, except she could laugh at herself, the way she did when she was riding the bike. And she wasn't above jumping in to help with whatever chore needed to be done. Other than one eye roll, she hadn't complained very much. Or acted in that way where you don't say something is beneath you, but you make everyone understand that's exactly how you feel.

He got up and flopped onto his bed, looking up at those dots on the ceiling. Okay, they had some similarities. But she was obsessed with perfection, from her clothes and hair to her nails and whatever she did to keep her skin looking like alabaster. And he... well, he wasn't perfect, was he? *You are more than your leg or your cooking or your drive*, Somchai had said.

RECIPE FOR LOVE

His mind scanned back over past relationships, none of which lasted past a few weeks. The longest, actually, had been Patricia. And he'd had good reason to break things off with her last year. She treated the staff terribly, and was only concerned with Charisma being successful so she could see her name in magazines and win awards. When he'd seen how different their values were, it had been an obvious choice. Sad, for sure, but the right decision to break it off.

Stella had pages of Internet photos of her at glitzy charity events. But none of her accepting awards or announcing personal accomplishments. Was he judging her too harshly? She had a passion for food more than success, she was good at her job, and she was kind to everyone he saw her with. And a giving, adventurous lover. Looking at it from her perspective, he honestly didn't know what she saw in him. He sat up suddenly. *Whoa, where did that come from?* He wasn't a self-pitying kind of guy. He never felt self-conscious about his leg or his abilities with anybody, just her. Why? Why did he care what she thought of him? He'd never cared what anybody thought about him until now.

He lay back and grabbed his phone, scrolling to the last series of photos he'd taken. He saw a cautious but excited Stella riding a bike. He swiped over to her text thread and looked at her selfie for a long time before he finally dozed off.

❦

Lunch was busy. He'd have to ask Somchai about the numbers, but it seemed like they were turning over more customers and seeing higher take-away orders than ever. He couldn't figure out why he wasn't thrilled about that.

When business tapered to only a few customers, he found Somchai in his office. He was going to ask him about the revenue numbers, when he pulled a black folder out and slapped it on the desk, gesturing him to pick it up.

"What's that?" he asked, but he knew. It was confirmed by the Carmichael Industries logo on the front.

"It's a deal. A very generous deal Stella is trying to put together for us with an investor."

"And you want to do this, I suppose?" he asked, folding his arms instead of picking up the folder.

"I want you to read it." He pushed the folder closer, and Carson grudgingly picked it up.

Retreating upstairs to his room, he sat on his bed and pulled out three papers. He read them over twice. It wasn't a huge sum of money, but the terms were very generous. It allowed a U.S. location to open in two years, giving them a more than satisfactory cushion of time to get firmly established in Chiang Mai.

It was flexible on whether Monticello would advance expansion funds as a low-interest loan, or buy-in for a partnership stake to be determined by Carson and Somchai. It allowed for the Mae On school to continue without any involvement of Monticello, but noted the company would be willing to stake future schools either in Thailand or the U.S.

He put the papers back and closed the folder, setting it beside him on the bed. He stared out the window while he thought over what he'd just read. She'd proposed a deal that would give them everything they wanted, according to their timeline, and with more flexibility that most investors would allow.

"What the hell?" he asked himself out loud, pushing his hair back. He opened the folder again and paged through the deal one more time. There had to be some catch. A clause or something he'd missed. It was too good to be true. He picked up the folder and went downstairs to Somchai's office.

"What is this?" he asked, hearing the raw tone in his voice. He threw the folder down on Somchai's desk. Somchai turned away from his computer monitor and smiled up at him.

"It's a very fair deal that will allow us to expand."

"It is. It's very fair. I don't understand." The words were tight and hard as he said them. It was the truth—it was an incredible deal, and it had him baffled. And angry. His brain was searching for the cause of this sense of betrayal he felt. It didn't make sense, but the harder he tried to figure it out, the closer his anger felt to igniting into rage. And that added to the confusion.

"You don't understand, because you were expecting something else. Something that wasn't fair and wasn't in our best interest, because you've decided that Stella is a bad person. And that's confusing, because part of you knows that's not who she is."

The honesty in Somchai's words snapped against him like a cold bucket of water, sending a chill through his bloodstream and diffusing his anger. As the tension left him, he fell into the chair across from Somchai.

"You're right. I've been hanging on to thinking of her like that, because... because... it's easier to push her away if she's the kind of person I can't stand. And if I keep her at a distance, I don't have to risk her rejecting me." The words were rough and sharp, and he had to push them out, because they wanted to cling to his throat like thorns. But once they were said, it was like a poison had been drained from his body. He was lightheaded, and a bitterness that had been tightening in his chest slipped fully away.

"I'm proud of you, my friend. That is not an easy thing to say, and you've had a life full of challenges making it even more difficult."

Carson saw it all so clearly now. Her constant presence in his thoughts. The intimacy and playfulness he'd felt with her at Mae On. And the way he'd kept trying to find the bad in her. A fresh energy flowed through him, and he almost jumped out of the chair.

"I need this," he said, reaching for the folder from the desk and going back to his room. Somchai said something from the bottom of the stairs, but he was beyond listening.

In his room he pulled his laptop out of its case and booted it up. While he waited, he flipped through the papers in the folder and then turned it over to look at the back. "Ah-ha!" he said with a smile, reading the address of Carmichael Industries' head office. He opened his browser and searched for flights to New York.

IT WAS EVENING BEFORE CARSON CALCULATED THE TIME DIFFERENCE and called his sister, Summer.

"Hey, big brother, how's it going?"

"Good. How are things on your end?"

"Quit the chitchat and spill the beans, Car," she said in a knowing voice. "I was going to grill you about this curious sex slave thing, but I can tell there's something else going on."

And spill the beans he did. From the conversation on the airplane to the moment in Somchai's office when he realized he was in love with Stella Carmichael. *To hell with what she thinks,* he thought.

"Summer?" he questioned when she'd been silent for a full minute. "You still there, or did I just say all of that to a dead line?"

"I'm here, I'm here." He could hear shock in her voice, which he fully expected. What she might say next wouldn't change anything, but it would be nice if he didn't have one more thing to deal with. "I'm just... so happy for you, big brother! I can hear it in your voice and...." Her last word ended shakily, on the verge of a sob.

A big sigh drained out of him. "I'm so glad you're not going to remind me of all the terrible things I said about Stella before I really knew her."

"Oh, I'm going to say them some day—trust me. I'm just not going to now. Now is the time to celebrate love. I'm so, so happy; I can't believe it."

"I can't either, almost. Now that it's happened, I can say I don't think I ever truly believed love was a thing that would happen for me. Having seen Katy and Mitch and then you and Landis, I don't know.... I think part of me thought lightning wouldn't strike three times." He realized how true his words were. He'd written off love entirely.

"And now it has. And almost in the exact same spot, come to think of it. The Cranberry Hill Inn must be a magical place. So what are you going to do now?"

"I'm going to New York to talk to her." He smiled when Summer squealed. "Settle down. We didn't part on good terms, so I'm expecting our first meeting to be messy. I don't even know if she feels the same as I do."

"That's ridiculous; you're a catch if I ever saw one. But I admit I'm horribly biased, and I know firsthand you can be an ass."

"I'm in a good mood, so I'll let that slide," he muttered.

"So," she said loudly over his laughter, "even though Stella can be a snob, I've never seen her be unkind. Landis raves about her, and he doesn't sugarcoat it when he talks about people he doesn't respect. I think she'll be fair and listen to what you have to say."

"I hope you're right."

"Call her right now. I'll hang up, and then you can call me back and tell me how it went," she ordered eagerly.

"No. I want to meet her face-to-face without warning. I don't want to ambush her. I just don't want her to have a chance to get her guard up."

"Hm, I guess that makes sense. How are you going to do that?"

"I saw her assistant's name in the folder she left. Fredericka Ashton. I'm calling her next, to see what I can find out. If nothing else, I'll let her know we're going to proceed with the investor."

"That's great, Carson, really. I hope everything works out. Just be patient. Sometimes it gets rockier before things smooth out. I should know."

They chatted for a few minutes longer before ending their call. He picked up the folder and flipped it over to call the number on the back.

"I'd like to speak to Fredericka Ashton, please," he stated after a cool voice answered.

"May I ask who's calling?" asked the sterile voice.

"Carson Richardson. It's regarding the Malee/Monticello deal, if that helps."

"One moment."

He listened to classical music for about ten seconds before a strong voice came on the line.

"Freddie Ashton speaking," she greeted.

"Hi," he replied, "this is Carson Richardson, and I'm calling about two things, really. We've been reviewing a deal Stella Carmichael proposed. But she—" He realized he didn't know how to frame her leaving Thailand, and didn't want to accidentally get her in trouble, if that was even possible. "—I haven't been able to reach her." His lie sounded so obvious, but it seemed to work.

"Yes, Mr. Richardson. I'm aware of the deal. Ms. Carmichael is traveling, so that may be why you can't reach her."

"I have some changes to the agreement, and a draft of a contract for our new general manager that she might want to review. Should I fax them?" he asked. Interesting. Either she wasn't in New York, or Freddie Ashton was covering for her. *Probably the last one*, he thought.

"Absolutely, fax them to me. Ms. Carmichael will be unreachable for several days, but Walter Burten will be acting as her backup and can work through the details with you. Shall I arrange a conference call for an initial meeting?"

"Uh, actually I'm planning to be in New York by tomorrow. Perhaps I could meet him in person, if that's possible?"

"Let me check with his assistant and get back to you. What number can I reach you at?" He gave her his cell number, she gave him her direct fax number, and she ended the call, promising to call back once she could confirm a meeting time.

17

She didn't even mind the rain. She could hear it trickling through the eaves on the edge of the porch as it flowed to the downspout at the corner of the inn.

"London Fog," Mitch said, handing her the enormous mug. "Or as I call it, a Cranberry Hill Mist." She snuck an arm out from under the thick plaid blanket and 'oohed' as she accepted the tea.

"Thanks, Mitch." She inhaled the steam and her eyebrow shot up at him. "I think I get why it has a different name. Did you spike this?"

Mitch couldn't hold back the grin, and the baby girl with adorable dark curls that was snuggled against his chest in a carrier burbled. "You looked like you could use it. Want some company?" He pointed to the railing.

"Oh, you can sit here." Stella scooted to the end of the couch.

"Thanks, but Princess Gracie likes me to be mobile." He leaned against the railing, bobbing the cute bundle from time to time when she thrust out a fist and yelled.

"Thanks again for letting me stay on such short notice."

"I'm just glad the barn loft was free. It lets you have more privacy. We don't have any bookings in it until New Year's."

"If I'm still here at New Year's, you have my permission to shoot me and drag me to the curb." She smiled at him and sipped the heavenly brew. "Seriously, I'm only here until the weekend. Then it's back to New York."

"You can stay as long as you need. But if you have to go, I'm sorry you'll miss Katy. She'll be back from her marketing conference late Sunday night."

"I'm sorry too. But you've been amazing to let me unburden all my crap on you. I did not expect my first night here to be crying on your shoulder, literally." Thinking about how she'd burst into tears at Mitch's simple question about what brought her to Seattle still made her wince.

She'd spilled the whole story, from her airplane conversation with Carson, to leaving after realizing no deal involving Malee would happen. She left out the bit about driving him to become a Buddhist monk. It seemed that should be something she owned up to directly with Summer, assuming their paths would cross before the wedding.

"Don't worry about it. Although Katy would have been more comfort I'm sure. She's very intuitive when it comes to emotions. In fact, she predicted there might be something between you and Carson. She's been right so many times I'm looking forward to telling her she was wrong for once." His expression froze. "Oh, I didn't mean…. Sorry, that was a dumb thing to say."

"You're fine," she said, but she felt her own expression tighten. "You're right; she was wrong about Carson and me." Her heart twinged a little as she said it. "I thought maybe we had something, and it turned out… we didn't. Story as old as time, right?"

"I guess," he said. She told herself he was looking at her with kindness and not pity. She bet Mitch scoffed at Katy's idea that she and Carson could be a match. The thought made her throat close up.

"If you're okay for a bit, I'm going to throw on our daddy and daughter poncho and take a little walk in the rain," he told her, standing away from the railing but looking uncertain about leaving her.

She worked to muster up a small smile. "More than okay. I'm loving sitting out here listening to the rain."

Mitch walked to the door and reached inside to pull out a plaid cape-like rain poncho. He found the opening and pulled it quickly over himself and Grace. Her head poked out of an expandable front section, and Mitch pulled a tiny green rain hat with earflaps over her head. "We'll be back soon," he said.

She waved them off and looked out at the view. The porch was on the side of the house near the driveway, and across that she saw a ranch-rail fence, then an empty field with tall dead grass, and then the bit of winding road that went into Cranberry Hill. The rain fell in a mist that obscured the Pacific Ocean beyond.

She'd been at the inn, in the loft more specifically, for two nights already. Flying back had taken most of a day, and she'd been wiped when she'd arrived. She'd planned to spend all her time in the loft, thinking and doing nothing, eating from the freshly-stocked refrigerator Mitch had kindly looked after for her.

But each morning, she found herself wandering to the main house to sit on the porch. Something drew her there every day. Maybe it was the couch and its large comfortable cushions that she could sink into. Or the thick blanket that easily covered her head-to-toe while she watched the rain. But she also wondered if it was the martyr in her, because more often than not, she stared at the spot where Caron's truck had been parked all that time ago and recalled their first angry conversation from that day.

Mitch was always kind enough to chat to pass the time. He'd had a young couple for the weekend, but they'd already left. She'd been huddled inside the thick blanket on the porch couch when they'd toted their suitcases to their rental car.

"This was fabulous, Mitch. We'll definitely be back next year!" said the woman. Her husband had smiled and nodded, both of them including her in their farewells. Stella had waved and then quickly looked away. The old Stella would have had some veiled but sarcastic response to their cheery happiness and obvious love for each other. But now they just reminded her of what she didn't have.

She sipped her spiked Fog, wondering if a pre-noon buzz was a bad thing, when her phone buzzed. She groped under the thick blanket and found it half tucked between the cushions. She smiled when she saw who it was.

"Ev! My God, I thought you'd never call me back!"

"Darling, I've been so busy I'll need an extra Christmas break to recover." The familiarity of Ev's voice made tears prick at the corners of her eyes. "Why aren't you back in New York? Freddie wouldn't tell me where you are, like it's some big secret."

"I'm in Seattle. I'm at the inn, actually. Where Landis met Summer."

"Good Lord, why?"

"I needed a break."

"Your voice-mail said you'd already taken a break. What happened that you need another one?"

"I met someone and it ended badly. So I'm taking a real break, not a two-day one where I still work."

"That must mean you got Jason out of your system, and praise be for that. He was an idiot and unworthy of your time."

"You could have told me that," she said, although her memory of Jason had faded to invisibility, as if he'd never happened.

"Darling, I tried to tell you right away. You didn't want to listen. However, being obstinate is a trait I respect, so I didn't push it. I knew you'd see sense sooner or later. It's in your DNA. Now, tell me how you can meet someone and have it end in, what... the span of a week?"

"I don't know. It's what I'm trying to puzzle out."

"There's nothing to puzzle. Just write it off as a fling and move on. When you get back, I'll have you meet Randall Humphrey. He would be the perfect complement to your ambition, and his family has several hotel chains in Europe. I don't know why I didn't think of this last year, after his divorce."

"It's just... it didn't feel like a fling. It felt like it could have been more."

"More what?"

"I don't know, more serious than a fling, anyway. And he's an amazing chef. A little arrogant, but I expected that."

"A chef. In Thailand?"

"Yes." She cringed, because she was debating not telling her who it was. But her indecision drew the word out, and it had the effect she was afraid it would.

"What aren't you telling me? Stella! Who was this chef." It was a demand, not a request.

She braced herself before she said "Carson Richardson, Summer's brother." She covered her mouth, getting ready for Ev to blow up.

"Summer's brother? *That* chef?"

"Yes." She uncovered her mouth to say the word and then covered it again. She realized what Ev thought mattered more to her than what her mother might have told her. In fact, all this time, she hadn't even emailed or called her mother.

"That's... surprising."

Stella couldn't read anything in her monotone. "Why?"

"Darling, come on. You're in the highest social circle before royalty. And he's the brother of a known hippy." She gave a little laugh.

"Your soon-to-be hippy daughter-in-law," she accused.

"I know. Thank Gucci that I love her, or Landis would never let me see my future grandbabies."

"So why is it a problem for me to be with a hippy if your son can?"

"Landis has a humanitarian streak in him. It's why he loves getting involved in union negotiations and company picnics. But you, darling... you get weekly manicures, buy Dior, and fly first class. Carson probably votes Green—" She paused and made a shuddering sound. "—rides a bike to work, and drinks Fare Trade coffee. You're opposites. How could it ever work long term? Honestly, Stella, you deserve so much more."

Stella switched the conversation to work, and eventually they said their goodbyes. But an hour later, she was still fidgeting over Ev's opinion of her and those words *you deserve so much more*.

What, exactly, did she deserve? What did anyone deserve, when it came to love?

"Whoa, what?" She said it out loud, jumped to her feet from the couch, and pulled the blanket more tightly around her. *You said love,* whispered a voice inside her. *I don't believe in love,* she told herself. But even though her mind had responded automatically, she realized she wasn't sure about that any more.

"Hey," Mitch said as he walked into view from around the house. Gracie was sound asleep under the poncho. "Can you do me a favor?

Katy just called to remind me I have to check out the local caterer, and I could use someone who knows food. Want to do dinner with us?"

"Yes!" she exclaimed. She was so ready to stop thinking about relationships or love or anything that Ev had said.

"What time?"

"How about... around four?"

"Sounds great. I'll meet you back here at four."

As she headed back to the loft to figure out how to occupy her thoughts until four, she turned her phone off. She'd been ignoring the multitude of notifications that still came through, but maybe not hearing them at all would give her brain a chance to de-stress.

⁂

She ended up spending the bulk of that time walking along the beach. The rain had let up, and she'd enjoyed feeling the thick sand under her boots and exploring the remnant tide pools for hermit crabs.

The drive to the Trestle Table restaurant had taken them a half hour. Grace had been snuggled in her car seat in the front beside Mitch, and Stella sat in the back. She'd been maintaining an awkward staring contest with the baby for most of the ride.

"I don't think Grace likes me."

"Nah, she's that way with everyone. For reasons I can't understand, she only truly loves Landis. It's a puzzle for the ages, I guess." They both laughed, and even Grace giggled before slipping back into her solemn stare.

The server at the Trestle Table set the plate in front of her. She'd ordered cedar-plank steamed Pacific Salmon, truffled mashed potatoes, and asparagus with almonds. Mitch had ordered broasted squab with black currant stuffing and braised Brussels sprouts topped with crisped onion strings. He'd also asked for a small bowl of plain mashed potatoes on the side.

"Thanks for helping with this. They're going to be catering Summer's wedding, and she doesn't have time to come out to test drive them. Rumor is—" He lowered his voice dramatically. "—they're selling the restaurant, and Summer's worried it's something to do with the quality of the food."

"Ah. Interesting. And helping out is no problem. I love doing this." She started her usual routine, examining and smelling each item on her plate.

"What is squab again?" he whispered.

"It's a young domestic pigeon," she answered. He looked down at his plate with raised eyebrows.

"Ah, I see it now. Sounds like the veal of game birds. I can't imagine Summer would want to serve that, but what do I know?" He gingerly cut into the tiny bird in front of him.

Stella dug into her dinner as well, flaking some of the salmon with her fork, examining it up close, and then sliding it into her mouth. She followed her normal ritual, smiling at a staring Mitch when she opened her eyes. "Not bad. I would give the salmon a six-and-a-half out of ten. How many people will be at the wedding?"

"Somewhere around fifty."

"They might do all right, if you decide to go with fish. It depends if the chef caters often. Cooking for a dinner service and cooking for a group of people that need to be served simultaneously is a real skill."

"Is food tasting part of what you do for your job?" Mitch asked. He put a spoonful of the plain mashed potatoes on a small plastic plate he'd taken from the diaper bag, and put it in front of Grace. She looked from the plate and over at Stella, let out a gurgling "Gggoooohh," and then planted a fist in the potatoes.

"She won't... throw it, will she?" Stella wasn't sure if she should be ready to duck, or just politely admire her food-smashing skills. She'd never been as close to a baby as she'd been these past few days. Her nerves thrummed with a constant low-level anxiety that at any moment Mitch was going to thrust Gracie at her and say "Watch her for a while, will you?"

"Surprisingly, she's not a food thrower." He sounded disappointed.

Stella watched her squish some more of the mashed potatoes in her hand and then put some of it in her mouth. She must have had a stricken look on her face, because Mitch laughed.

"Sorry if it grosses you out. Now that she's sitting up and drooling less, we're experimenting with soft foods. I love letting her get her hands into it and have fun, but it drives Katy crazy." He leaned over to Gracie, who looked up at him with a big smile. "Isn't that right, Gracie? We like to put our hands in our food."

"Gah!" she yelled in agreement.

"To answer your question, yes, tasting food is part of what I do. I conduct due diligence checks of restaurants for my clients as part of the acquisition process. It's not a normal thing that most companies do; I just really like doing it. And touring the kitchen to get a feel for how the chef runs things. Less exciting is all the financial due diligence that has to happen. But you get a much more rounded idea of how the restaurant has been run by one person looking at all aspects."

"Are you in between clients right now?"

"Sort of. Freddie tells me she's got everything under control back at the office. Before we left the inn, she texted that she had things more in control than even I could imagine, which makes me a little nervous."

"Are you anxious to get back to New York?"

"Yes and no. I've enjoyed taking this emotional break from the constant go-go-go of home life. But I also don't want to be out of the loop for too long. I get antsy when I don't know what's going on."

"Home life? Sounds like your home is on the road."

"Yeah, I guess it has been." She couldn't remember the last time she'd been home for more than two weeks.

"It seems like you're feeling better about things. If I could give you any advice about moving forward, it would be to get some perspective on the heartache, but stay friends with Carson. He's good people, and he and Summer have been a tiny family for so long they deserve as many friends as they can get."

She thought about being at a place where she could be friendly with Carson. She knew right at that moment she wanted more, so much more with Carson than to just be friends. She even thought she would have wanted a potato-smashing baby. But all that was over. She covered the sheen that covered her eyes by lifting her wine glass.

"Here's to friends," she said, and touched her glass to his raised water glass.

18

Carson slid the bandana off his head and wiped his sweaty neck with it.

"What's the big deal with all the clanging so early?" complained Dex as he walked into the kitchen.

Carson gave him an apologetic smile. He was about to answer, when his cell phone buzzed. He pulled it from his back pocket and saw Summer's photo smiling at him.

"One sec, it's my sister," he said to Dex, and answered the phone.

"Hey, sis, what's up?"

"I need a huge favor. I wouldn't ask, except you're flying in anyway."

"What's going on?" he asked. Summer sounded amped up, and it got his heart pumping a little bit faster.

"I'm having the Trestle Table cater the wedding, but Katy says there's some kind of rumor about the chef being a problem, and I thought you could touch base with the owners just to make sure everything's okay."

"James took over when I left, and he didn't seem like a flakey guy at all." He frowned. He'd hired James himself and he was rock-solid.

"James won't be doing it; they have someone else doing the meal."

"Let me call the owner and find out—"

"No!" she shouted down the phone line. "Please, Carson, I want to make sure the food is perfect, and you're the only person I trust to do it. It's only an extra day or two, and then you can fly on to New York."

She sounded pathetic, which wasn't like her. But then maybe she was one of those women who became a Bridezilla.

"Please, please, please, please, plea—"

"Stop. Okay, I'll change my flight. Stella won't be in New York for a week apparently, so that works out. Can I stay with you and Landis when I get there?"

"Of course, silly. I'll let Mitch know you're coming to the inn. You should at least stay a night there and say hi."

"That would be great, thanks. Maybe book me a few nights there."

"I will. Okay, I've got to run. Have a good flight, and call me after and let me know how it all goes. Love you!"

He echoed her goodbye and hung up, making a face at Dex, who started clanging pots into place to get ready for the day.

"Sisters, huh?" he asked Carson.

"Man, you have no idea. Now I have to change my flight. Sorry about all the noise, by the way. I woke up at five and couldn't get back to sleep. I decided giving the kitchen a deep clean before I left was a good idea."

"I noticed," Dex said, nodding. "I guess getting woken up early by clanging woks is better than me having to spend a couple hours cleaning, so thanks, buddy." Dex put his hand out and Carson clasped it, thumb around thumb. "I hope you can still get a flight out today."

"Probably, it's just going to cost me a lot," he murmured. He pulled off his apron and balled it up to throw it in the dirty linen basket.

"So how's the business deal? Is everything still a go?" Dex asked.

"Yup. How does it feel to be a general manager?" he asked with a big smile, already knowing what Dex's answer would be.

"Dude, seriously, I'm honored." The look on Dex's face was more serious than Carson expected, and he got serious as well.

"I can't think of anyone better to take over my role here. Your contract is one of the things we're finalizing before I leave."

"What's going to happen with the school?"

"Rosie and Arjan are more than capable of keeping things going there. But feel free to check in on what they're doing. There could be some great flavor discoveries students bring in from their own home experiences." Carson headed toward the doorway, thinking he would check his e-mail before Somchai got up.

"Uh, where do you think you're going?" Dex asked, making him look back. "As general manager, I suggest you grab a fresh apron and get on food prep."

Carson checked his watch and then raised an eyebrow at Dex. "You've got me for ten minutes, but then I have to make some flight arrangements." He grabbed a new apron and tied it on. "You're bossy for a new GM," he grumbled.

Dex gave him a sassy smile. "You bet your ass I am."

※

CARSON PUT A PITCHER OF WATER AND TWO GLASSES ON THE TABLE an hour later as he sat down across from Somchai. They had about another hour before they opened for lunch.

"You know, you look pretty pleased with yourself," he commented on Somchai's broad grin as the older man leaned back in his chair with his arms folded over his chest. "It's not very humble of you."

"Who said I was humble?" Somchai asked, grinning even more widely. "Did you get your flight changed?"

"Yeah, for an extra three hundred dollars. But believe it or not, I got a direct flight to Vancouver instead of Seattle. So I leave later, but I'll get to Cranberry Hill around the same time."

"That is opportune! A sign of things to come, I think," Somchai said happily.

"Could be," Carson replied. He slid the folder from in front of Somchai over to him and opened it. The folder was worn at the corners now, and held three times the number of papers it had when Somchai showed it to him. Had that been only a day or two ago?

"Do you have any issue with Dex's contract?" he asked. He flipped through the stapled document on the top of the pile of paper to look for notes. There weren't any.

"Did you find out where Stella is yet?" Somchai questioned.

"No, not yet," he said absently, flipping through the contract a second time. "Are you sure you didn't have a problem with the additional commission structure I suggested?"

"Why didn't this Freddie person tell you? I thought she was Stella's personal assistant."

Carson sighed and looked at Somchai like he was a five-year-old. "You won't let me get through this until we talk about Stella, will you?"

Somchai just smiled then gave a shrug and shook his head.

"Freddie said Stella's taking some time off and won't be back in the office for at least a week. But thanks to this—" He turned the folder over and pointed to the address printed on the back in gold. "—I know where to be when I'm ready to track her down."

"What do you mean, 'when you're ready'?" The smug smile left Somchai's face, and Carson enjoyed his bewildered look for a few seconds. "I thought you had that all figured out."

"I do. I just want to have all this—" He hovered his palm over the folder in a circle. "—figured out first."

"I don't know why you didn't just fly out there right away. We could have sorted this out any time. There's no rush."

"There was some kind of rush when you sent Stella after me in Mae On."

"I sent her on a journey of love, not business. And you almost figured that out." He smiled at him, making Carson roll his eyes. Somchai had no idea how much they'd figured out at Mae On, and he wasn't going to enlighten him.

"I was pretty frustrated with you over that. You're lucky I'm a laid back guy."

"Stop changing the subject and tell me what you mean by 'when you're ready.'"

"I'm not going to hang around an office in New York City for a week like a stalker, waiting for her to show up. Summer is having some kind of issue with the caterer for her wedding. So I'm going to Cranberry Hill first, and then New York. Besides, I wanted to put this together while we can talk about it face-to-face. I'm not entirely sure when I'll be back here."

"I predict you will be back here with Stella in a month."

Carson took a sip from his water and gave Somchai a grim smile. "I hope I'm anywhere with Stella in a month. I might not be with her at all if she doesn't feel the way I do."

"Of course she feels the way you do. That's why she left so soon! You know nothing about love. It really is squandered on the young," he mourned.

"I'm taking nothing for granted with her. I'm definitely not going to make any assumptions about how she feels, either. I already had preconceived ideas about what she was like and what mattered to her, and I was wrong."

"So what will you do when you see her?"

"Well," he started, leaning back and tapping his pen against his lip, "I have a few thoughts about that."

That was an exaggeration. He'd been thinking about it continuously since it dawned on him that he cared what Stella thought about him because he cared about her, period. He'd fallen in love with her back in the kitchen in Mae On. Once he'd been able to see her and not what his assumptions had made her, it had been obvious that he was in love. Now he only had to fight his fear of being rejected by her. Somchai seemed sure she loved him, but as he'd just said, he didn't want to take anything for granted.

"I was thinking I would tell her about when I fell for her. And when I *realized* I was in love with her. I'll tell her it wasn't until she left Thailand and I had this emptiness in my chest that got bigger everyday until it took me over body and soul, that I really looked inside to see what was causing it. And the emptiness was a hole, because she'd taken my heart with her. I'm less of a person without her, and I hope she feels even a little bit of what I feel. Love is what makes a good partnership great." He was staring at the corner of the room, feeling the words flow from a place deep within. He brought his attention back to Somchai, who just stared at him. "At least, the plan is to say something like that."

"I would tell you to memorize that so you can say those exact words to her, but it wouldn't be from your heart. If you can remember the pain of her leaving once you realized you loved her, those words should come back to you. Very good," Somchai said with a pleased nod, as if he were a student who'd completed an assignment.

Carson toyed with the folder in front of him. "I shouldn't have a problem remembering. Remembering her is almost all I've been doing, aside from this." He lifted a corner of the folder. "I'm more worried about freezing up the moment I see her. Or that I won't get a chance to speak to her at all. She probably has a whole staff of people who can keep me away from her."

"I'm telling you, she loves you too. It won't be a problem; I'm sure of it." Somchai sounded almost giddy, and he clapped his hands together like a toddler getting ready for a bowl of ice cream. "Now let's get all this paperwork reviewed and back to Freddie so I can take you to the airport."

19

Stella rolled over, half her face buried in the fluffy pillow and the other half facing the open door of the bedroom. Beyond the doorway was the open kitchen of the barn loft. She hadn't expected it, but the mattress was heavenly. They'd shelled out some dough for this. It was on par with a W Hotel.

She'd felt pretty good after the tasting dinner the other evening. But the following day had been hard. She couldn't even rouse herself to walk the short distance to the porch for tea.

She let out a big sigh and rolled onto her back. Murky light glowed through the curtains, and she guessed it was still early morning. She had two more nights before she flew back to New York, and everything seemed to be going backward. The knots and marks on the cedar ceiling had no answers for her, so she rolled back over to the edge of the bed and put all her effort into sitting up. Her legs dangled from the thick mattress, not touching the floor.

Her oversized flannels were incredibly soft and cozy. They'd been neatly folded and in the dresser with a sachet that smelled of pine and something else. She tucked her face into her shoulder to inhale deeply, but she couldn't discern what the scent was. Sandalwood maybe?

She slid off the high bed and padded over the large coiled rug to the bathroom, which connected to the other bedroom. The small bathroom had a retro pedestal sink and luxurious claw foot tub. She put in the plug and ran the water. In a wood crate on the floor was a selection of green, white, or red bath salts. She picked up the red jar and smelled it. Cranberry. Of course.

"Mmmm," she murmured as she poured a generous amount into the running water and leaned into the mist. Deep down, a spark of delight jumped to life. She opened the side door, which led out to the main room. It was a sharp angle, but she'd be able to look out the floor-to-ceiling windows as she lay in the tub, and that was a delicious idea.

She took off her flannel PJs and slid down into the water. Leaning back, she admired the room. The walls were bleached timbers, and flowing white linen curtains bracketed the two narrow windows on either side of the tub. The flooring throughout the loft was a few tones darker and dotted with more of the coiled rugs.

Pulled off to the end of the tub was a shower curtain on an oval rod that was suspended from the ceiling. The ceiling in the bath continued at an angle beyond the bathroom, peaking over the kitchen and then angling down to the far side of the room. It really was a gorgeous place to stay.

When the water cooled, she pulled the drain plug and slid the two shower curtain panels around the tub. Hanging on the edge of the tub was a caddy holding a selection of shampoos and conditioners. They smelled wonderful. She started the shower and lathered up her hair, standing a long while in the hot stream and letting the heat bring her a little closer to her old self.

After wrapping her hair in a thick towel and climbing into a matching thick terry cloth robe, she slid her feet into the slippers under the sink and walked out to the living room. She pressed a button and the gas fireplace jumped to life. She sank onto the couch and stared with shock into the corner.

"A Christmas tree," she said out loud. "How long have you been there?" How out of it was she that she only noticed it now. And there was no way Mitch snuck this in while she'd been here. She laughed out loud that she could have overlooked the monster tree. The star on the top touched the ceiling, which was at least ten feet tall in the corner.

Underneath was an assortment of wrapped gifts, which she guessed were part of the decoration.

She realized she hadn't brought anything back for Freddie for Christmas. They'd already arranged client gifts and gifts for her family back in October. And Freddie always received a healthy bonus from Stella personally, as well as something smaller from the company. But she'd especially wanted to get Freddie a silk sarong.

She sighed and looked back outside. The glint of her phone case on the coffee table caught her eye, and she picked it up. The black screen looked odd to her. She never had her phone turned off for more than a half hour, and even then that was only in a meeting. The last two days had been peaceful. But she admitted she'd also been wallowing. The bath had energized her; maybe she was ready to turn the phone back on.

She pressed the buttons on the side and watched as it went through all the systems as it started up. Then the dinging started. And kept on going, as e-mail, voice-mail messages, and other notifications flooded in. After all the noises stopped, she hovered her thumb over the text icon. The red number indicated she had eighteen new text messages. She looked at the Christmas tree then back to her phone.

Putting her phone on the coffee table, she got up and walked over to the tree, looking behind it for the power cord. She found it and plugged it in, watching the lights come to life and then start to twinkle on and off. It was a gorgeous smelling Noble Fir, and simply decorated. It had a mass of lights and retro-style reflector ornaments and nothing more. Katy must have scoured stores to put this collection together. Stella touched one of the fragile faded ornaments.

She was more concerned she hadn't noticed the tree before now that she was overwhelmed with its scent. She must have really been out of it to not see or smell it. She stood up straighter, and then turned back to grab her phone. She wasn't going to let some guy screw her up. *I can do that all on my own*, she thought with a smile.

She pressed the text icon and scrolled through the messages. None were from Carson.

"Okay," she said to the room. She waited for the sadness to come over her, and it did. But not as strong as it had yesterday. *Every day will get better*, she told herself. She saw a number of texts from Freddie, and as was her habit, she speed-dialed her.

"Hey, boss," Freddie greeted. "How are you doing?"

"Feeling pretty rested, actually. How are things at the office?" She sank back onto the couch and watched the twinkling lights.

"Fantastic, actually. The Central Group deal is all but done. Go ahead and find some champagne for a toast, 'cause we put that puppy to bed."

"Great work, Freddie. I should give you a day off. Maybe sometime next year." She laughed half-heartedly, thinking her favorite joke had gotten old.

"Har har. Do you want to hear the real exciting news now?"

"Sure."

"You don't want to guess?"

"Hm, okay, I guess that Jason has been harassing you and you finally got the chance to press charges."

"Oh, that *would* have been exciting. Why'd you have to spoil my news?" She laughed.

"Sorry. What's the big news?"

"Monticello has come to terms with Malee Inc."

Her body reacted before her mind could make sense of the words, making her sit straight up from the comfortable cushions.

"Boss? Did I lose you?"

"Uh, no. I'm here. You said Monticello and Malee have come to terms?"

"Yeah. Carson Richardson called me earlier this week with notes on the draft proposal you left with him. I put Walt Burten on it, and we're just waiting for final signatures. Congratulations!"

Her jaw was moving, but nothing was coming out. The robe that had felt so cozy felt on the hot side now.

"Congratulations should go to Walt," Stella said, the words sounding strained. She cleared her throat to inject some lightheartedness into the next sentence. "I wasn't able to get anywhere with them when I was there."

"You had the idea and roughed out the proposal. If you hadn't guided Monticello to rethinking their investment strategy, nothing would have panned out. Take the congratulations and celebrate, boss."

"Yeah, okay. Can you send me the final paperwork?" She jumped off the couch and strode to the bedroom.

"Of course. It's already in your e-mail. Are you okay?"

"I'm fine. I'm going to have some tea and get caught up on e-mail." She started flinging off her robe, hair towel, and slippers and rummaged through her open suitcase for underwear.

"You don't sound fine. This is the voice you use right before shinola hits the fan."

"Don't be silly. I'm going to read my e-mail, relax with tea, and enjoy my last two nights here. I'll e-mail you if anything urgent comes up." She didn't wait for Freddie's reply, just disconnected the call.

The nerve, she thought, going through the winter clothes Mitch had put in the dresser for her to use. *I serve him up a sweetheart of a deal, everything he said he wanted, and it's still not good enough that he has to make revisions?* She threw the cable-knit sweater and thick woolen leggings on the floor in frustration, and then with a loud sigh picked them up and pulled them on.

"He is a selfish, thoughtless, all-around greedy asshole," she said to the Christmas tree as she boiled a kettle of water and dropped a teabag into a huge pottery mug. While it steeped, she went back to the bedroom to grab her laptop. After another two minutes, she slipped on borrowed boots and an oversized corduroy jacket and headed to the main house and her favorite spot on the porch.

"You can come inside, you know," Mitch said after she'd settled herself on the couch and pulled the blanket over her legs. Everything was shrouded in a mist, but she loved the feel of the cool air on her face. For once, the rain had stopped. She took a tiny sip of her hot tea and put the mug down on the table beside the couch.

"I know, but I love it out here." She watched as Mitch reached inside to grab something and tuck it into the pocket of his quilted vest. He stepped outside and gently closed the kitchen door behind him, a steaming mug in his other hand.

"I love it out here too. Especially when it's misty like this. I promise not to interrupt your work." He sipped his coffee and moved to the other side of the porch, sitting on the railing and looking in the same direction she had been. She looked back and closed her eyes. She could hear the waves in the distance, a lot more muted than usual because of the mist.

"It's okay. I'm just catching up on e-mail. Where's Grace?" she asked.

"Sleeping in. I've got the monitor in case she wakes up." He patted his pocket. "I talked to Katy last night, and she says I'm supposed to tell you she would love it if you could stay an extra day so she could get to see you." His eyebrows lowered into a straight line as he watched her. He took a sip of coffee and continued his stare.

"And does that... annoy you?" she asked, wondering about his expression.

"What? Oh, sorry, no. It's just... odd."

"Why?"

He sighed heavily. "It's just..." He rubbed his beard as he pondered. "She sounded strange, I guess. And you guys don't really know each other that well."

"That's true," she agreed. She hadn't interacted with Katy at all since the last time she was here.

"Yeah. Weird, right? Don't take that the wrong way, it's just... weird."

"I... kind of agree. Why would she want to 'get to see me'? No offense from me either, but I don't really know her."

"Exactly!" Mitch pointed his mug at her, his eyebrows flying upward. "I *know* something's going on."

"How do you know?" she asked, sipping from her mug.

"She tells me everything unless it needs to be a secret. I'm terrible at keeping secrets. And when I asked her why she wanted to get to see you, she said 'Do I need a reason?' which is the kind of thing she says when she *has* a reason but won't tell me. So there's some kind of secret being kept, and it must involve you."

"Fascinating. You two could do a *TED Talk* about relationship dynamics," she joked, smiling over her mug.

"You have no idea," he agreed solemnly.

"I should get back home, but there's nothing urgent. Aside from this asshole—" She flicked her eyes from Mitch to her laptop screen. "—who is making changes to a pretty amazing business proposal that's totally in his favor. But I can handle all of that through e-mail." She shook her head, putting her mug back down. "Sorry, I digress. What I'm trying to say is that an extra day won't kill me."

"Okay, I'll let her know." He stood up from the railing and went into the house, coming back with his phone. After several taps, she heard the *boop* sound of a message sending.

"Ha!" He shook his phone at Stella triumphantly. "Let's see what she says to that."

Stella opened her laptop and her e-mail program. She scrolled through and found Freddie's e-mail with the agreement attached. She opened the original she'd done and put them side by side. The only change that she could see was the management list. Both Carson and Somchai were listed as co-owners, but Dexter Chambers was shown as General Manager of all restaurant business in Thailand. Carson Richardson was listed as General Manager of restaurant business in the U.S.

"Huh," she said out loud.

Just then, Mitch's phone made a *boop* sound, and he looked at the screen. "Huh," he said, echoing her.

"What?"

"She said 'Great.'"

"What does it mean when she says 'Great'?" she asked.

"Nothing, usually great means great." He pointed his phone at her emphatically. "But I'm going to get to the bottom of this."

"Okay. Let me know when you do."

"I'm going to the other side of the house to pull a few potatoes for soup for lunch, if you want to join me and Gracie."

"I'll see. There is some work I should catch up on."

"Oh, and one of Katy's friends is coming tonight, but she'll stay in a room in the house. Just in case you see someone else around."

"Okay, thanks," she said, and turned back to her laptop. She opened an e-mail for Freddie and started typing.

Hi, Freddie,

> *Thanks for sending the agreement. Am I blind, or are the only changes in the agreement to the management structure?*
> *Thanks,*
> *Stella*

A few seconds later she received Freddie's reply:

> *Management structure, they shortened the open date in the U.S. by a week, and they changed the cooking school arrangement to be a 50/50 agreement between Malee Inc. and Monticello instead of 100% for Malee Inc.*

"Huh," Stella said out loud yet again, closing her laptop. *So not an asshole*, she thought. Just the thought of Burten finalizing the deal made her weepy. She tossed the blanket aside and took her laptop and tea back to the loft.

She rinsed her mug and put it on the drain board. Noticing a bookshelf on the other side of the room past the kitchen—what else had she missed seeing?—she saw a range of business books, books about blues music, and a few thrillers. She'd read all the business books, so she chose a book called *I Am the Blues: The Willie Dixon Story*. She turned on the fireplace and snuggled under a throw on the couch.

※

SHE WOKE UP STARTLED, THE BOOK SLIDING OFF HER CHEST WHEN she sat up. *What's happening?* she wondered. The light was charcoal gray, and she checked the time on her phone. It was almost five o'clock! She kicked off the blanket and stood up into a stretch. Her stomach grumbled. She'd slept past lunch.

She opened a missed text from Mitch.

There's leftover soup if you feel like it, he'd texted a few hours ago.

Sorry, I fell asleep. Is soup still on? she texted, grabbing the jacket and sliding on the boots again.

You bet, he replied.

Just as she was approaching the porch steps, a car turned into the driveway. *Must be Katy's guest*, she thought. She stepped up on the porch as the car parked near her rental, not quite across from the porch. She had her hand on the screen door handle, ready to pull, when she heard the car door open and slam. Something made her pause and glance back.

The porch light overhead made it hard to see any features, but she could tell by the outline that it wasn't a woman. And the instant she realized that, she realized exactly who it was.

"Carson," she whispered. She turned away, staring at the screen of the door. She wanted to go into the kitchen, to get away, but she couldn't move.

"Stella?" he called out, and something in his voice turned her back, loosening her grip on the door. She took a few steps to the railing in front of the couch. "What the hell...?" He trailed off, slowly walking over to the porch. When he entered the light cast by the porch, she saw he was wearing a business suit with an open-collared white shirt underneath. He looked tired and shocked.

"Hi," she said, and her voice caught in the middle of the short word. She cleared her throat and tried again. "Hi, Carson."

"This...." He ran a hand through his hair, and she could see he was trying to make sense out of what he was seeing. "Why are you here?"

"Why are *you* here?" She thought she would wait for him to answer. Play it cool like she usually did with guys. But suddenly, a thousand questions pressed at her lips and she couldn't hold them in. "Why aren't you at the Buddhist retreat? I thought you became a monk. And why are you wearing a suit?" The questions tumbled out in a flood, and she had to bite her bottom lip before it got out of control.

He walked up the steps and stood in front of her. Very close in front of her. She could feel his body heat through her coat and sweater, and she had to work hard not to collapse backward onto the couch, pulling him with her. *Damn, he smells good.*

"I get it now," he said, a glint in his eye.

"What?"

"Summer asked me to stop here on my way to New York to meet

with the caterer who's handling the wedding. But now I am wise to her Jedi ways."

"What Jedi ways?"

"She wanted to get us together," he answered.

"Why would your sister want to do that?" She was so confused, but his expression and smile were making her insides melt. Her pulse sped up every second she looked at him.

"Because I told her how I feel about you. I told Somchai. I would have told Freddie, but Freddie's all business."

"Oh nice," she groused, but her heart was thumping. "You tell everyone but me."

He just smiled. "Well, I wanted to tell you face-to-face." He reached down for her hands, which he had to unbury from the long sleeves of her coat. He brought them both to his mouth, closing his eyes as he kissed them.

Nothing in the world mattered except what this incredible man was about to say to her next.

"Don't you want—" Mitch opened the door and started speaking until he saw Carson. "Ohhhh." He drawled out the word and then comically tiptoed back inside, closing the door behind him. They could both hear him say "I knew it!" as he walked away.

"This is not how I pictured doing this, but to be honest, I thought this conversation would start with you throwing things and me ducking."

That startled a laugh out of her. "Why? Do you think I'm that bitchy?"

"No, I think I hurt you and that I'd have to do a lot of apologizing before getting to the good stuff." His boyish smile raised her blood pressure right along with her pulse, and she leaned into him for a deep kiss. He was breathing heavy when their lips parted.

"Sorry, I just thought we should skip to the good stuff first," she murmured.

"I want to tell you something." He let go of her hands so he could cross his hands and lace his fingers through hers, pulling her even closer. "But I don't want you to freak out."

"When people say that, it almost always guarantees someone will freak out."

"I love you. I know you don't believe in love, you believe in—"

She broke off his words with another kiss, soft at first and then harder. His hands unclasped from hers and slid around her back, gathering her as close as their clothes would let him.

"I believe in one thing," she said when they came up for air several seconds later. "That I love you too. Now if you don't pick me up and carry me to the loft so you can make love to me all night, I'm going to throw things at you."

Without a pause, he scooped her up and gave her a cocky grin. "I don't know; I had a long day of flying. Plus, I don't know if being threatened is high on my list of 'things I find hot.'"

"That's too bad, because I slept all day and I'm full of energy." She laughed at the big smile on his face. She knew it matched her own.

EPILOGUE
THREE MONTHS LATER

Carson adjusted his tie and looked at himself critically in the dresser mirror in the loft's bedroom. "How're you doing, babe?"

"Unnnhhhh," Stella groaned from the bathroom. He went to the door to see her standing in front of the toilet. She was exquisite with her hair up and her deep green dress, but she had a hand on her stomach and a face much paler than normal. She alternated between standing but slumped, to reaching over and putting a hand on the toilet seat. "I can't decide if I'm going to be sick or not."

He grabbed a washcloth from the sink and dampened it. "Here, let's put this on the back of your neck." He pressed the cool cloth against her neck and her hand came up to cover his.

"Why did you have to get me pregnant?" she moaned.

"Why did you have to wear that purple lingerie when I told you we were out of condoms?"

She bent down again, hesitated, and then stood back up. She straightened her shoulders and squeezed his hand. "Okay, I'm definitely not going to be sick."

And then she bent over and threw up.

RECIPE FOR LOVE

EVERYONE HAD PLANNED FOR RAIN, BUT THE WEDDING OF HIS little sister and the man she'd once compared to a conceited pirate took place on a March day that was downright balmy.

Stella gave him three-to-one odds that he would cry, and he was relieved he hadn't put any money on it. His gorgeous sister walked beside him in a champagne lace-covered chiffon dress, a clutch of pale pink tulips in her hands. At the flower-covered arch on the side of the yard, backed by the vibrant garden he'd tended last year, stood an emotional Landis in a charcoal gray morning suit, and a beaming Katy and Mitch. Snuggled into a front-facing carrier was Gracie, dressed in an over-the-top pink and green frilly dress. Though he faced forward, Landis's arm was raised to let her shake his hand with the tenacious grip she had on his fingers.

"I love you, sis," he whispered at the end of the aisle, as he took her hand and Landis's free hand and joined them together. "I love you too, brother," he said to Landis, who could only nod in reply. He wiped the corner of his eye as he watched the two look at each other.

"I love you, babe," Summer said to her groom, but his face crumpled even more at her words. "I know," she whispered in a wavering voice as he struggled to get words out.

"Time to let go, Gracie," Mitch whispered, prying his fingers between hers and Landis's. She howled, making the guests laugh.

Carson stepped back and found his empty seat beside Stella. Both Stella and Ev, who sat on her other side, had tears welling and trickling down their cheeks. "Oh boy," he said, and pulled two linen handkerchiefs out of his pocket and handed them to the ladies.

Ev looked at the white material, reaching out and rubbing it between her fingers. She looked at him and tapped his knee. "Good man," she said quietly.

Stella wound her fingers through his and squeezed, dabbing at her eyes with her other hand. Suddenly, Stella sniffled, which drew Gracie's attention, who then proceeded to howl. Mitch went into his bouncing shuffle and after a minute she settled down.

The foursome turned to the Justice of the Peace and the ceremony got underway.

It was brief, but the words of the Justice of the Peace were elegant and soulful. Carson hoped someone was recording it, because they echoed what was in his heart. And in the blink of an eye, they were husband and wife.

※

THE INTIMATE CEREMONY WAS WELL ATTENDED. CARSON SAW several of his teammates from the Cranberry Belles, as well as Phil from the rival slo-pitch team in Chutney.

"Hey, buddy, how's it going?" he asked, shaking the tall fireman's hand firmly. "How's the team?"

"Kicking your old team's ass worse than ever, now that you're not catching."

"Phil, this is my... girlfriend, Stella."

"Nice to meet you, Stella," Phil said, extending his hand, which engulfed Stella's.

"Nice to meet you too," she replied. Both men looked at her strangled tone.

"Are you okay?" Phil asked, leaning down to look into her face. "She looks like she might pass out."

"No, I'm...." Stella trailed off, and Carson put his arm around her and guided her to a chair. "I just feel gross."

"Sit," he insisted.

"I'll go grab some water," Phil offered, disappearing toward the food tables.

"Sip some water and then when you feel a bit stronger I'm taking you back to your room."

"No, everyone will think I'm being weird."

"You're pregnant," he insisted. "Everyone will understand."

"You can't tell anyone I'm pregnant. This is Summer and Landis's day."

Carson rolled his eyes at that, but he wasn't going to argue.

"I almost spilled the beans to Phil about our marriage when I introduced you." He smiled at her, smoothing her hair back from her damp temple.

"I know. That was a good save." Stella smiled weakly.

"Here you go." Phil approached them and handed her a glass of water.

"Thanks, Phil," she said.

They were all distracted by sudden loud voices coming from the other side of the inn. Most of the guests were milling between them and the food tables, but Carson could see Mitch handing Gracie to Katy.

"Mitch!" he called, standing. "What's going on?"

"Rally's ex is here," he called to them. "Phil, can you come with me?"

"You should go too," Stella said, urging him forward. "Just in case they need help."

"No. My place is with you, sweet. Between Phil and Mitch and Marshall, they'll sort this guy out."

He moved a folding chair from the ceremony around to face his sweaty, pale, beautiful wife. He picked up her right hand with his, looking at the simple wooden bands they both wore. Their marriage in Thailand had come as Somchai predicted—one month after he'd left.

"Today, we are the mismatched couple, Stella the socialite and Carson the peasant. But tomorrow—" He tapped both of their rings with his forefinger. "Tomorrow, we switch these rings to the right fingers and step out as Mr. and Mrs. Richardson."

Stella leaned her forehead against his with a soft smile. "That's a deal I can get behind."

✦

THANK YOU FOR READING **RECIPE FOR LOVE**! I HOPE YOU enjoyed watching enemies find love. But the Cranberry Hill magic doesn't end there...

What was the commotion at the wedding? And what's the story behind the dashing EMT, Phil? (He first showed up in DEADLINE ON LOVE with a crush on Summer!)

As an EMT, Phil's not supposed to feel this way about a patient.

As a woman with a past, Rally's learned what can happen when you let your heart make decisions for you.

When a man from Rally's past threatens her, normally calm Phil responds fists first. Now, living at his place until the danger passes, will this love-shy couple find their way to a happily ever after?

Keep turn the page to dig into Rally and Phil's story.

"What a sensational book! HIGHLY recommend!"
— *Gina B.*

BONUS RECIPE!

Hey awesome reader!

When I was writing the second book in this series, *Deadline on Love*, the character of Carson popped out fully formed as a Michelin-star chef. Since I'd recently taken a trip to Chiang Mai, Thailand, I used that location for the restaurant he wanted to buy a partnership in. I fell in love with Chiang Mai when my husband and I visited in late 2017. We travelled all over the country, but this city holds my fondest memories. We took a cooking class there, saw a Muay Thai boxing match, visited Wat Phra That Doi Suthep, rode bikes around the city, visited an oyster mushroom and rice farm, and stayed in the homestay described in this book.

Nam Prik Ong is the first delicious Thai dish I ever made. There's a popular saying in Thaliand when describing restaurants—"Simple food, but good food." It is 100% true. Nam prik ong is a simple and simply delicious dish. Everyone should make it and eat it once in their life. To help you, I've added the recipe:

Nam Prik Ong (serving for 1—multiply as needed)
    For the chili paste:
    2–3 dry chilis

BONUS RECIPE!

    1–2 cloves of garlic
    1–2 cloves of shallots
    1 tsp. coriander root
    ½ tsp. shrimp paste
    1/3 tsp. salt

For the dish:
    3–4 large grape tomatoes
    ½ cup minced chicken
    1 tsp. fish sauce
    1 tsp. sugar
    1 cucumber or other sliced veggies

Directions:

- Grind all chili paste ingredients with a mortar and pestle; set aside
- Grind tomatoes in mortar; add to hot wok with 1 tbsp. oil; stir until heated
- Add minced chicken to wok; stir until just cooked
- Add chili paste to wok; stir and cook until tomatoes are cooked thoroughly
- Put contents of wok into a serving dish; slice cucumber and other vegetables to use as scoops—enjoy!

Thai cultural customs

The head is the most revered part of the body, the feet the least. Never sit with your feet pointing at a statue of a Buddha, and never step over someone who's sitting on the floor. Never touch or pat someone on the head for this same reason.

The wai is a traditional Thai greeting where you press your palms together and hold them to your mouth as you give a slight bow. If you're greeting a monk, you hold your hands to your forehead.

Monks only eat until noon during the day. They fast the rest of the day until very early in the morning. It is the custom in villages to bring a food offering to the local temple in the morning in exchange for a blessing.

Temples

Temples are called Wats. Wat Phra That Doi Suthep is a real temple in the mountains near Chiang Mai. It is said to house a bone of the Buddha, obtained from a monk who traveled from Sukhothai in ancient times. Wat Suan Doi in the book doesn't exist, but is an amalgamation of several temples I visited throughout northern Thailand.

ALSO BY NALA

Maple Cove Dog Lover's Society
Small Town Shepherd (Sam & Brody's story)
Beauty and the Bulldog (Vi & Noah's story)
Foxhound Foes (Rylee & Matt's story)
Billionaire Beagle (Olive & Xavier's story)
Westie Besties (Quinn & Levi's story)
Second Chance Corgi (Eliza & Phil's story)

Cranberry Hill Inn Series—Paperback Books 4–6
Everything for Love (Rally, Cassie & Garret's stories)

For contests, prizes & free reading, join my Reader's Group by visiting https://www.subscribepage.com/l4m3s1

COPYRIGHT

All the characters in this book are fictitious, and any resemblance to actual persons living or dead is purely coincidental.

Copyright © 2018 by Nala Henkel-Aislinn

All rights reserved.

No part of this book may be reproduced, or stored in a retrieval system, or transmitted in any form or by any means, electronic, mechanical, photocopying, recording, or otherwise, without express written permission of the publisher.

Published by Nala Henkel-Aislinn

Edited by Hot Tree Editing

Made in United States
North Haven, CT
28 October 2022